Book 4 of the Parallel Ops series

I0654181

THE
TEACHERS

R.J. ARCHER

NWIDI Press ~ San Ysidro, CA, USA

This book is a work of fiction.
All names, characters and incidents are either
the product of the author's imagination or are used fictitiously
and any resemblance to any persons, living or dead,
is entirely coincidental.

For more information on the Parallel Ops series, visit:
www.ParallelOps.com.

Library of Congress Control Number: 2013911110

823.0876

"The Teachers" by R.J. Archer

p. cm.
ISBN-10: 0-9884236-2-6 (softcover)
ISBN-13: 978-0-9884236-2-6
Science Fiction, general
ISBN-13: 978-0-9884236-3-3 (digital)

Published 2013 by NWIDI Press, San Ysidro, CA, 92143
©2013 by R.J. Archer.

Cover design by Diseño International, La Paz, BCS, Mexico.

Manufactured in the United States of America.

"After the Seeds of Civilization series (some serious treasure hunting on steroids) and the first three books of the Parallel Ops series, hang on for the exciting conclusion. *The Teachers* reunites the entire NWIDI team for an epic battle between good and evil—one which could very well decide the fate of mankind!"

Tommy Vawter
Explorer, Adventurer and International Treasure Hunter
www.TreasureWorks.com

"I have been a fan of mysterious archaeological fiction even as a child. New technologies are helping reveal unknown secrets from our past via satellite imagery and R.J. Archer takes a fictional look at some amazing discoveries and puts his own spin on them. In *The Teachers*, his grand finale, he finally answers the 'Who?' and 'Why' questions his readers have been asking since his first book."

Angela Micol
President, Satellite Archaeology Foundation, Inc.

About the Series

In my first series, *Seeds of Civilization*, I introduced you to Frank, Tony, Linda and Jim—accidental adventurers who joined forces to investigate several of archaeology's many unsolved mysteries. In the *Parallel Ops* series, we catch up with each of the Seeds characters five years into the future. Join Jim (*The Scientists*), Linda (*The Informants*) and Tony (*The Guardians*) as they independently search for that which was lost in the closing pages of the Seeds series. And don't miss *The Teachers*, the exciting conclusion to this series and the entire seven-book adventure.

Acknowledgements

Once again I would like to thank my wife, Marty, for her invaluable contributions. She reads (and corrects) every chapter the minute it's finished, she gets invested in the story and she helps with plot development. Even more, she keeps me going when I would rather throw in the towel and quit.

I would also like to thank friend and fellow expat Maureen Ryan, of La Paz, Mexico, digital artist/actor Jon Hudson, of Savannah, Georgia, and explorer/adventurer Tommy Vawter, of Guatemala City, Guatemala, for their critical eyes during the final stages of revision. Their comments and suggestions were greatly appreciated and have been incorporated into the book you are about to read.

In this, the final novel of a twelve-year, seven-book adventure, I absolutely must thank *everyone* who has encouraged, coached or otherwise helped me arrive at this point. When I wrote the first chapters of *Tractrix* I was really just experimenting with fiction. Three novels later, when I completed the *Seeds of Civilization* series, I thought I had finally finished the project. But then I was convinced to begin the four-book follow-up series, *Parallel Ops*. And now, at last, I'm at the end—or am I? Some interesting ideas are already kicking around for a follow-up to the follow-up—something completely different from what I've done so far. Stay tuned!

Prologue
(Tuesday, May 13, 2008)

"How did this happen?" screamed Buzz Edwards as he paced back and forth across the front of the room. "Will somebody *please* tell me how this happened?"

Not a muscle moved on any of the twelve faces around the long table in the makeshift conference room. Unofficially known as the Committee, Edwards and the others in the room represented an elite group of individuals who directed the global operations of the largest, most dangerous super-cartel in the world, known simply as "the Six." And the members of the Committee had lived openly and freely, their true role in world events unknown to all except each other—*until today.*

Edwards scanned the room, his face red with anger.

"How did a second rate college professor and a few associates unravel years of careful work and learn the names of many of us in this room?"

Edwards was referring to Jim Barnes, former anthropology professor at the University of Washington and, more recently, member of a small team of amateur investigators interested in ancient civilizations. Over the course of a couple of years, Barnes and his NWIDI teammates had discovered evidence suggesting that an alien influence had played a role in the advancement of several early cultures. These discoveries remained highly classified, of course, due in large part to the man at the front of the room.

Edwards made eye contact with Hans Schröder, the interim representative from Germany.

"Whatever tip Barnes got probably came while he was in your country, Schröder, and it probably came from that crazy old man..."

Edwards' voice trailed off as he searched for the name.

"Professor Karl Schmidt," offered the German representative.

"Yes, that's it—Schmidt. But the question you need to answer is how much did Schmidt actually know and where did he get *his* information? I'm putting you personally in charge of this, do you understand? I want answers and I want them soon!"

"Yes, sir!" replied the newest member of the group.

"The rest of you know how we do things, so I expect you to give Schröder a hand until he gets up to speed. As you are aware, we had to eliminate his predecessor recently so help him out for a while. And I expect you all to keep tight reins on your own operations, too. Unfortunately, you will have to do that from here for the foreseeable future, but I expect you to adjust quickly. No one outside this group must ever know where you really are and no one inside your organizations must ever doubt that you are still in charge. If we lose control now, everything we have built will be lost. Be ruthless and maintain control at all cost! I want you all back in this room at 9:00 am tomorrow and I want operational status reports from everyone. That is all!"

The other twelve fled the windowless room instantly, leaving Edwards standing at the head of the table alone. He was still coming to grips with the events of the past two days, but he was thankful that his predecessors had secretly built the underground facility that now housed the de-facto command center of the Six. One hundred feet below the surface and hardened against any known type of attack, the facility was identical to others that existed around the globe to protect world leaders in case of catastrophic events or military conflicts. However, this site wouldn't be found in any country's registry of government installations. This site was known only to the Six and this was the first time it had ever been pressed into use.

Edwards slammed his fist down hard on the table.

"I'm going to get you!" he shouted to no one. "I'm going to get all of you for this!"

Chapter 1
(Wednesday, May 14, 2008)

Just a few days earlier the NWIDI team had been reunited in a windowless room beneath the main administration building at the Naval Research Laboratory in Washington, D.C. where they had reluctantly accepted an ultra-secret mission from the President of the United States. The Navy had immediately moved them to their current location and, after taking a few days to get reacquainted and familiarize themselves with their new surroundings, they were about to settle down to business for the first time.

Jim Barnes, Linda McBride-Reyes and Tony Nicoletti had been members of the original NWIDI group organized by retired aerospace engineer Frank Morton. Together they had investigated archaeological mysteries on Mexico's Yucatan Peninsula, on Japan's tiny Yonaguni Island and deep beneath the Caribbean, from Cuba to the Bahamas. But it was now more than five years since Frank had gone missing in the Bahamas while making a deep, difficult dive. Although he had been officially pronounced dead by both the U.S. Navy and the Bahamian government after the incident, his team members had never really accepted the official version of what had happened.

Several months after Frank's disappearance, the remaining members of the team, along with the husband-and-wife flight crew that piloted the team's Learjet, had reunited in Cancun to celebrate Linda's wedding to Javier Reyes. But soon after the wedding Tony had disappeared and, at Jim's urging, Linda and Javier had fled to Mexico's Baja Peninsula and taken assumed names.

For the next five years, only Jim remained publicly visible, albeit under the watchful eyes of the U.S. Government. He had lived and worked at AUTEC, the Navy's research facility on Andros Island, The Bahamas, and in rare cases when he was allowed to travel he was closely shadowed by FBI or CIA agents. Jim accepted his life under a microscope as a fair trade for use of the state-of-the-art facilities at AUTEC, where he continued to investigate the ancient—and alien—artifacts he and his teammates had discovered off the coast of Cuba. During a speaking engagement in Munich, Germany, Jim had been handed a dossier that connected the artifacts to a group called the Six. The dossier also suggested that the Six were intent on destroying the artifacts and their original owners, another mysterious group known as *the Teachers*. When he returned to AUTEC he had been immediately whisked away to the Naval Research Laboratory in Washington D.C. and put in charge of a project to determine the true nature of the artifacts and to learn the identity of those who sought to destroy them.

During that same five-year period, Linda and Javier had settled in La Paz, on Mexico's Baja Peninsula, assumed the surname of Moreno and had a daughter named Mariana who was now four. Their peaceful and intentionally low-profile lives had been interrupted when Javier stumbled onto encrypted radio transmissions being beamed out into the Pacific. The pair's natural curiosity and Linda's background as a newspaper researcher soon had them in the crosshairs of international terrorists and the Mexican Secret Police.

Tony's five-year hiatus had been much less pleasant. The day after Linda's wedding, he had paid a visit to Buzz Edwards, a Department of Defense staffer who had served as liaison between the U.S. Government and the NWIDI team since its first mission. Edwards had pressed Tony for details about Frank Morton's disappearance and, in typical Tony style, he had pushed back. Fearing that Tony knew more about the incident than he was letting on, Edwards had Tony detained in a secret underground facility called MX-2, located deep beneath the Cancun airport. After more than five years under house arrest at MX-2, Tony had managed to slip away one rainy Sunday night just two months earlier. He fled to Belize City where, with the help of some new friends, he had mounted a mission to stop Edwards and the Six from destroying a group Tony knew only as *the Guardians*.

Jim sat at the head of the conference table and gazed around the room. To his right sat Fitz and Susan Fitzgerald, the former NWIDI flight crew and to his left were Linda and Javier Reyes. At the far end of the table, Tony Nicoletti swigged coffee from a travel mug and chatted with Linda. The Fitzgerald's dog, Sandstrom, and the Reyes' daughter, Mariana, were in the care of staffers being provided by the Government.

"Could I have your attention?" began Jim, waiting for the buzz in the room to die down. "I feel very uncomfortable chairing this meeting, but that's the way the boss wants it, so I guess that's the way it will be. I have a short, informal survey they've asked me to conduct and then we can get down to the business that brought us all here.

"The first question is regarding your living quarters. Is there anything any of you need in your suites? Linda, do you guys have enough room for the two of you and Mariana?"

"We're very comfortable, thank you," replied Linda, glancing at her husband for confirmation. "And Mariana just loves her new nanny!"

"Does anybody have any housing issues?" asked Jim, as he scanned the room. When no one spoke up, he glanced down at his notes and continued.

"Okay, next question. Are there any special dietary needs that the staff should know about—religious considerations, allergies or other health issues?"

At the end of the table, Tony waved his hand like a school boy.

"Tony?

"Ah, yes, my doctor has me on a special red meat and beer diet so I need thick steaks every day—just like those we had last night."

Nods and murmurs around the room echoed Tony's reference to the previous evening's meal.

"And could you get a draft beer tap installed in my room?"

Jim grinned, expecting nothing less from Tony.

"I'll see what I can do. If there aren't any *other* dietary issues, I'll move on to the last question—the catch-all. Are there any other questions, concerns or complaints that need to be addressed by our hosts?"

Again, Tony's hand flashed up and this time Jim frowned, but nodded.

"Tony?"

"I haven't been able to get any cell reception since we arrived. At first I thought it was just my cell provider and this remote location, but I've talked to Fitz and Javier and they're both having the same problem. What's up with that?"

Jim scratched something on his notes and then replied.

"I'll look into that, Tony, but I suspect this facility is in a communications black-out zone. We'll probably have to use a secure land-line to make any outbound calls."

"So are we being censored?" asked Linda, a bit put out.

"No, I don't think so, Linda. I worked with these security types at AUTEC and they're very touchy about outside contact. It actually has more to do with someone tracing your call back to this location than any concern about what you might say. If they didn't trust you to keep our secret, you wouldn't be here in the first place. But I'll ask the question and let you all know."

"And where exactly is here?" asked Fitz Fitzgerald, the husband half of the flight crew. "Judging by the length of time we were in the helicopter the other night, we can't be more than forty or fifty miles from Washington D.C."

"I'm a little curious about that myself," interjected Javier. "It's obvious from the incredible view that we're in rural *somewhere*, but what's the name of this place?"

Jim frowned and stared down at the table for a few seconds before replying.

"I was told not to discuss this unless specifically asked, but you've just done that so here's what I was told when we arrived the other night. The name of this place is Meriwether Mountain Operations Center and it's a 450-acre FEMA training facility located in the Blue Ridge Mountains of rural Virginia. Fitz, your sense of distance is very good because we're only forty-seven miles from Washington D.C. Each year FEMA trains more than ten thousand students in emergency planning and management at this facility."

"And?" queried Tony, when Jim paused.

"And what?" scowled Jim.

"That's up there!" declared Tony, pointing to the ceiling of the meeting room. "What about down here? There's a whole city down here in these tunnels! This building alone is three stories tall and it's *underground*. Come on Jim, spill it!"

"The below-ground facilities serve several purposes and I'm sure I wasn't told about all of them. However, the National Command Center for FEMA is down here, along with some space that's been set aside for the emergency evacuation of the National Art Gallery. There's also a large computer complex in one of the side tunnels that has something to do with the Continuity of Government programs."

"Jim, the doors we passed through to get from up there to down here are five feet thick! That's a bit excessive to protect a few government workers, don't you think?"

"Okay, it's also a Presidential Emergency Facility— one of the places that the President and other high-ranking government types could come if there were an attack on the country."

"You mean like the MX-2 facility in Cancun?"

"Yes…and no. This facility was built in the late fifties and was part of a ring of such facilities that encircle the Capitol. Most have been converted to civilian use but they all could be used for their original purpose, if necessary. The MX-type complexes were strictly black ops projects and, as we now know from Tony, at least one of them somehow fell into the hands of the Six for a period of time. Fortunately, that situation has been rectified."

"Wow!" exclaimed Susan Fitzgerald, the wife half of the flight crew. "Let's hope the President doesn't need to use this place while we're down here."

"Exactly," replied Jim. "Now if there isn't anything else, let's get started with our real business, shall we? We all heard the mission statement from the President a few days ago and we've all had time to think about it individually. The task is both incredibly awesome and unbelievably daunting. It may also be impossible. Does anyone have any general thoughts on how we approach this?"

"Very carefully," said Tony, without waiting to be acknowledged.

There were a few condescending chuckles.

"No, I'm serious! If we make the wrong move or even the wrong gesture we could end this effort before it gets started. There's a saying about only getting one chance to make a first impression and that's certainly going to be true here. I suggest that we agree right now that no one in the group will attempt to make unilateral contact. Any communications must first be run past at least one other member of the group and preferably more than one. And in my case, it should probably be filtered through the *entire* group. In case you haven't noticed, I have a tendency to talk first and think later."

This time the response was laughter, rather than chuckles, and even Jim smiled.

"I'm not sure you need to be quite that stifled, Tony, but your recommendation is an excellent one and I think we should adopt it, effective immediately. Are there any dissenting votes?"

With all heads shaking no, Jim continued.

"Good! So we've decided that we must approach the mission 'very carefully' and we've even agreed on what that means. Does anyone have any idea what our first words to these alien beings might be?"

***

The rest of the Committee was seated and waiting when Edwards entered the conference room at precisely 9:00 a.m.

"Good!" he smiled stiffly. "You're all here. I hope that means you're also prepared to brief the group about the status of the organizations under your immediate control. Let's begin, shall we?"

The Committee consisted of six senior delegates, one from each member nation, and seven minor delegates who represented nations being considered for full membership. Edwards, the Chairman of the group, represented the United States. Other senior members included representatives from the United Kingdom, Russia, Mexico, China, and South Africa. Also at the table were junior delegates from Germany, Iran, North Korea, Indonesia, Pakistan, Venezuela and Libya.

Over the course of the next thirty minutes, each painted a similar situation back in their home countries, best expressed by the delegate from South Africa:

"Day-to-day operations are still functioning more or less normally, but I sense a great deal of concern in the upper ranks. They have heard—or at least they sense—that something significant has happened. So far, this news has not filtered down to street level, but I fear it's just a matter of time before it does."

"And that's exactly why you must exert your influence quickly!" replied Edwards. "In some cases, we'll just have to cut our losses and move on. In my own situation, for example, federal agents stormed my office and detained my entire staff. Most of them were completely unaware of what was going on there, but a few were good soldiers of the cause. Unfortunately, I've had to write them off and move on. But things weren't that serious for most of you. Together, we control the world's largest industry and we must make sure the gears keep turning until this crisis passes. Fortunately, there will always be a demand for our product and it's our job to see that the product is always available. And, in general, it sounds like things are functioning as well as can be expected. That will be all for today, but I'll see you all back here tomorrow morning at the same time. Mr. Schröder, please stay a few minutes. The rest of you are excused."

When the room had cleared, Edwards sat down across the large table from Hans Schröder and studied the man's face.

"Schröder, I didn't want to concern the rest, but I'm very curious how things are going in Germany. Your organization was probably hit almost as hard as mine, so what's happening over there?"

"Well, Mr. Edwards, things are a bit strained, as you can imagine, but so far the German press is so obsessed with the story of a BKA bureau chief going rogue that they haven't had time to do any real digging. It helps, of course, that Kruger is dead and not able to defend himself."

"You're welcome!" smiled Edwards.

Schröder was talking about General Wilhelm Kruger, the recently assassinated director of the Munich division of the BKA—Germany's version of the FBI. Kruger had also been a junior delegate of the Committee and—in his effort to impress Edwards and the other member—he had attempted a botched kidnapping operation in the United States. That operation had exposed Edwards and the Committee and had forced them to all flee underground—literally.

"Do you think you can keep a lid on this?" asked Edwards, staring directly into the other man's eyes.

"Yes, sir, I do. Kruger didn't have a lot of friends and most of them are glad to see him gone. This includes both his BKA associates *and* his non-BKA operatives. With your letter of introduction, I've been able to step in and hold his organization together."

"And what about his BKA duties?" asked Edwards.

"Oh, they'll find another director soon enough. Right now the BKA is scrambling to deal with the scandal and that's giving our organization a little extra freedom to operate. It actually looks like our revenues might be up for the week, sir!"

"Really!" replied Edwards, raising his eyebrows. "And what about this Schmidt guy?"

"Apparently he's disappeared off the radar. Kruger had the entire Munich office of the BKA looking for him and they never turned up a trace. However, I've brought in some specialists and we'll find him soon. But there's actually more to that story, sir. We've learned that the agent who served as Kruger's special assistant has also disappeared, along with a graduate student he was investigating. But I assure you, we'll round them all up very soon."

"Schröder, you impress me, and you always have. I've been keeping my eye on you for a while, now, and that's why I called on you in this time of need. How would you feel about working on a couple of extra projects for me?"

Schröder's eyes widened and he cracked a broad smile.

"Of course, sir!"

"These would be projects that we wouldn't want to discuss in front of the other Committee members, do you understand?"

"Uh, yes, I think so," stammered Schröder. "You can count on me!"

"I thought so. There are some loose ends that I need tied up and I think you're just the man for the job. Let's meet in my office after lunch and we'll continue this discussion then. In the meantime, learn all you can about an organization called NWIDI and pay particular attention to the group's scientist, a former university professor named Jim Barnes."

***

The NWIDI team discussed "first contact" scenarios for nearly an hour before agreeing to table the matter and give it more individual thought. Tony, of course, was for a direct and to the point approach. Jim, on the other hand, pushed for a subtle, drawn out process to gain their trust before entering into any serious dialog. Linda, Javier, Susan and Fitz each had their own opinions that fell somewhere in between the two extremes.

Finally, Jim suggested they move on to another topic and revisit the message another time.

"Okay, so assuming we can eventually come to some agreement about what to say, let's discuss a plan for making contact. As you know, I have two acquaintances that have actually 'seen' *the Teachers*: Professor Karl Schmidt, who originally gave me the dossier in Munich, and a graduate student named Sophie Hoffman. Both of them are associated with the Ludwig Maximilian University in Munich and I met them when I was there attending a conference. I suggest we contact one or both of them and see if we can get an introduction. If either one is willing, this would be the easiest way for us to make first contact."

"I agree," nodded Javier. "Are you still in touch with either of them?"

"Well, I haven't seen or talked to Schmidt in almost a month but I talked with Sophie by cell phone just a few days ago. She called me last Friday night with this wild story about going to the *'Other Side'* with Schmidt and a BKA agent named Becker so I called her back the next morning to make sure she was okay and not on some drug. She stuck to her story and when I tried to get her to come to the U.S. until things cool down she refused, saying that she would be more useful in Munich. I have no idea what that means and I haven't heard from her since, but things have been a little hectic for me since you guys showed up."

"Assuming you can reach her, will we need to travel to Munich to make contact?" asked Tony. "Because I'm guessing we can't just catch the next bus into town and zip over to Germany."

"I don't know, but I don't think location has anything to do with it. She was fairly vague about her experience but I got the feeling she didn't have to leave the room. She talked about being transported, but I don't think she meant in a normal way."

"You mean like teleportation or something?" asked Linda. "This is starting to sound spooky."

"Maybe it was some kind of mind control," offered Tony.

"No, I don't think it was that, either, because she described being there among *the Teachers*. She even delivered some photos of the triangles that I had sent to her. And the next day the triangles were missing from my lab, replaced by a note giving me the exact GPS locations of you and Linda. I would never have found either of you without that information and somehow *the Teachers* knew that."

"If they knew where we were," frowned Linda, "they've probably been watching us the whole time! That's pretty creepy."

Jim smiled. "I've had a bit longer to consider all of this than the rest of you, and I prefer to think of them as watching *over* me, rather than simply watching me. I know the distinction is a fine one, but my version is a lot less unsettling."

"Okay, so let's give your little friend a call, shall we?" suggested Tony. "And if we *do* have to be physically in the same room, I'll bet our hosts have the means to go grab her and bring her to us."

"Fine, but as you pointed out, Tony, cell phones don't seem to work around here, even topside, so I'll have to find out how to make outside calls before I can attempt to reach her. I'll work on that and let you know what I find out when we meet for lunch. In the meantime, there's something else I think I should share with you as a group."

Jim paused and took a deep breath before continuing.

"Back at NRL, when we had our initial meeting and talked to the President, I handed you each a menu from the base cafeteria—do you remember that?"

Everyone nodded.

"Do you also remember that when you all so eagerly accepted this mission I told you that I had some reservations and I wondered out loud what Frank might do?"

This time only a few heads nodded.

"Well, I did. And when I got to the door to hand those menus to the orderly, there were seven in my hand."

"So?" asked Tony, growing impatient with Jim's dramatics.

"So, when I entered the room I was only carrying six. There was one for each adult: Linda, Javier, Susan, Fitz, you and me."

Slowly, Jim removed a square of paper from his shirt pocket, unfolded it and held it up for all to see. On the back, in black printed letters, were the words "I would have voted with the majority, Jim."

It took a second for the significance of the message to settle in and Linda was the first one to connect the dots.

"That's a message from Frank!" she screamed.

Chapter 2

As they entered the dining room, the NWIDI team members were still talking about the mysterious message Jim had revealed two hours earlier. Even Tony was caught up in the speculation that the message might have come from the long lost—and presumed dead—Frank Morton.

"But how else *could* it have gotten there?" he challenged Javier as the group took their usual places around the large, rectangular table. "There's just no other way!"

As everyone was getting settled, Jim entered the room from the door normally used by the kitchen staff. He took his seat and held up his hand for silence.

"Folks, we need to put this conversation on hold until after lunch for security reasons. However, I'm happy to report that we will soon have telephone access to the outside world. I just came from the Communications Center and they're installing a secure land line in our conference room right now, so as soon as we're done eating we can try contacting Sophie and Professor Schmidt. And Tony, since you first raised the communications issue, you can make your call first."

"My call?" asked Tony from the other end of the table.

"Yes, didn't you say you were trying to use your cell phone and couldn't make it work?"

"Oh, that!" smiled Tony. "No, I was just going to call my ship and let them know that I would be delayed, but that can wait."

"You mean the dive boat you told us about?" questioned Linda. "Are they expecting you to meet them somewhere?"

"Yes, I'm afraid so," laughed Tony. "Jim's little bomb this morning about Frank's message was quite a shocker, but I have a story about a message of my own that I'll tell you about over lunch."

Once the food had been served and the staff had left, Tony told the others about the message that had been delivered by dolphins while he and the crew of the boat were diving off Norman Island in the British Virgin Islands.

"The exact translation of the message was: '*Your assistance is urgently requested at 24°30.74' north, 77°43.23' west. One of us will serve as your guide when you arrive. Bring your ship and crew. AF18674201.*' We were all blown away, of course, and I ordered the ship to prepare to sail as soon as possible. They should be about half way there by now and I'd like to give them a heads up but there's no rush."

Tony's story resulted in questions from everyone at the table except Mariana, and they all tried to talk over one another. Now it was Tony's turn to hold up his hand for silence.

"Are you suggesting that we now have a technology that allows us to communicate directly with dolphins, in *their* language?" stammered Linda.

"Well, it's still pretty crude, but yes, that's the general idea."

"Wait, I don't get it. When those dolphins delivered the message to you, how could they have known that you'd ever figure it out?" asked Susan Fitzgerald.

"That's something that's bothered me a little, too," nodded Tony. "But there was no question in my mind that they were trying to communicate something very important to me, and there was also no doubt that they assumed I would understand. Fortunately, the boat's divemaster had the presence of mind to record the message on a little underwater camera he was carrying and that's how we were able to transmit the message back to the research center in Belize for translation. It was almost like the dolphins knew…"

Tony paused and scratched his head.

"Like they knew what?" prompted Linda.

"Well, I was going to say it was almost like they knew we would be able to translate it, but that's not possible because the technicians had only made the translator breakthrough a couple of days earlier."

"That's some amazing coincidence, my friend," said Fitz.

"I know, and it's actually even more bizarre, because the breakthrough occurred accidently due to incorrect parts being received and subsequently used in the assembly of a prototype. If the correct parts had been installed, the translator wouldn't have worked."

"Divine intervention?" shrugged Linda.

"It sure sounds like some kind of intervention," mumbled Tony. "So anyway, as a result of the message, we immediately began preparing to leave for the specified coordinates, which just happen to be a place called the Guardian Blue Hole on Andros Island. I was hijacked by the Feds and dragged to Washington D.C. the day before we were to depart."

"Sorry about that," smiled Jim sheepishly, "but you were all in far more danger than you realized and the President felt it was urgent that we pull you all in. And once we had your locations, we…"

"Another fortunate coincidence," interrupted Fitz. "This whole thing—and I mean everybody's experiences—is starting to sound pretty weird. But I'm curious, Tony, why didn't you mention this dolphin message before now?"

"Well, there's just been too much else going on. The dolphins' message—and the recent scientific breakthrough that allowed us to translate it—is exciting stuff but it doesn't really have any bearing on our mission here, so I thought I'd save the story for a slow day. But with Jim's revelation this morning, I decided we should chew on this, too."

"What does this have to do with my communication from Frank?" asked Jim.

"Remember those letters at the end of the dolphins' message? *AF18674201*. That just happens to be Frank's old Air Force Serial Number!"

***

Edwards motioned Schröder to a straight-back chair in front of his desk and waited for the other man to be seated.

"I trust you had a satisfactory lunch," began Edwards. "The caretaker staff we have down here is doing their best, under the circumstances, but I'm making arrangements to secure some additional help and food preparation is one of the areas I hope to improve on."

"Lunch was fine, Mr. Edwards. I'm a man of simple tastes and I could probably live for months on dark bread, cheese and wine."

"Well, let's hope it doesn't come to that! I won't keep you long because I know you have your hands full in Germany but, as I mentioned, I could use a man of your skills to help me with a very special project. As I also mentioned, this project is strictly off the record and is not to be discussed with anyone else, is that clear?"

"Yes, sir, I understand," replied Schröder. "How may I help?"

"Somewhere within your extended organization there are one or more individuals who were involved in an assassination attempt on a person named Jim Barnes. He used to work with a small group called NWIDI. Were you able to find any information on Barnes or this group?"

"Yes sir, I found a few things around the Internet and I have one of my people back in Berlin taking advantage of some unauthorized access into the BKA database. By this time tomorrow, we'll know everything they knew about him."

"Good, good! Let me fill you in on some details that you won't find on the Internet or in the BKA system.

"Barnes was associated with a group called NWIDI, which was the brain-child of a guy named Frank Morton. Morton was from Seattle and that's where the group was based, but they spent a lot of time poking around in what seemed at first to be useless pseudo-scientific investigations. I first encountered this group when they showed up in Nevada with some curious artifacts. When Morton and Barnes took off for the Yucatan Peninsula, I followed them and it was soon clear that they were on to something huge.

"Using my position within the Department of Defense, I was able to keep a lid on what they turned up and to this day there are only a small handful of people in the world that know about their discovery. The same is true of a discovery they made a few months later in Japan. This, too, involved some very special artifacts and once again I was able to lock down the information and prevent Barnes and his friends from publishing anything about their find.

"At this point I should probably tell you about the connection between the small, black spheres they discovered in Nevada and the jewel-studded clay disks they found in Japan. In both cases the objects were very old but more importantly, they were of alien origin."

Edwards stopped to let his last sentence sink in. When Schröder's eyebrows popped up, Edwards continued.

"Their third, and final, mission was actually a task I sent them on, although I had no idea at the time that it would end up so linked to their first two missions."

"You mean they found more alien objects?" interrupted an engrossed Schröder.

"Yes," smiled Edwards, "and this time I think they also found the aliens. At least they came close. Then there was a diving accident in the Bahamas and Morton went missing, along with one of my very best operatives. The bodies were never found and the whole accident had to be hushed up, but the last communication I had from my guy indicated that they were very close to making contact. Shortly after the diving incident Barnes slipped through my fingers and ran back to a high-security Navy research facility on Andros Island in the Bahamas. I couldn't touch him, but at least I didn't have to worry about him being a loose cannon. He and his buddies had found yet another set of alien artifacts off the northwestern tip of Cuba and the Navy allowed him to work at the facility so they could keep tabs on the artifacts."

"What about the others in this NWIDI?"

"I grabbed Morton's long-time friend, a guy named Tony Nicoletti, and locked him up in a place very much like this."

Edwards gestured to the ceiling.

"The female member of the team, Linda McBride, and her new husband, a Mexican who had become an unofficial member of the team, disappeared off the map and we still haven't located them. Unfortunately, some now-deceased agents in Cancun allowed Nicoletti to escape a couple of months ago and he's also still currently missing. However, I suspect that they will all try to reunite at some point."

"So this NWIDI group was just four—make that five—people? Morton, Barnes, Nicoletti, a woman named McBride and her husband. That doesn't sound like much of a threat, sir."

"You wouldn't think so, but this is the luckiest bunch of individuals I've ever run across. And there are two more you should know about—a husband-and-wife pilot team. After my first encounter with Morton and his team I made arrangements to acquire a confiscated Learjet for them. The deal was done through official channels and Morton had to pay for the aircraft, but he got it for an incredible price. What he never knew was that I had it bugged before he took delivery so I could monitor their movements whenever the NWIDI team left Seattle. I'm proud to say that those bugs are still providing valuable information. I actually had Fitzgerald—the husband, at least—in custody for a short time but I kicked him loose in the hopes that he would lead me to the others. Unfortunately, we ended up down here before I could track Fitzgerald back to Barnes."

"And the plane?" asked Schröder.

"Ah, well Fitzgerald had the presence of mind to fly directly to the nearest military installation, which happened to be a Naval Air Station in southern Florida. The plane is still there, although I suspect that the pilot is long gone."

"The U.S. Navy seems to keep coming up, Mr. Edwards. Don't we have any connections there that we can use?"

Edwards frowned.

"Not at the highest levels, I'm afraid. If they were being handled by any other branch of the military I'd know their every move but Barnes has apparently made some friends at the very top. And that's where you come in, Schröder."

"How so?"

"I want the whole NWIDI organization destroyed. I know this won't be an easy task, but I want it done at any cost. They—and especially Barnes—are the reason I'm down here in this hole and I want him and everybody associated with him eliminated. I realize that my fellow board members may object on the grounds that it could draw attention to our little group, and that's why you must never breathe a word of this to anyone in this facility. Use whatever resources you need from your own organization, but keep you efforts contained."

"I understand, sir, but even if we can locate them, it seems likely that your government will have them *very* well protected."

"I agree, but I know these people and I think you can draw them out if you chip away at any of their associates my government doesn't have in protective custody. Learn as much as you can about every individual and then cast your net wide. Anybody is fair game as long as it will bring you closer to Barnes. And when he finally steps out of the shadows, take him down. Is that clear?"

"Very clear, Mr. Edwards. And thank you for your confidence in me. I won't let you down."

"I know you won't, Schröder. Keep me posted and call me directly anytime you have good news. That will be all for now."

And with that, Edwards reached for his telephone, obviously finished with the current task and on to the next.

Schröder saw himself to the door and quietly left the office without another word. As the door closed behind the German, Edwards looked up and smiled.

***

When the NWIDI team reconvened in the conference room, they found a black, star-shaped device in the middle of the table.

"Is that our new telephone?" asked Tony.

"Yes, and it's designed specifically for conference calls," replied Jim. "The Captain back at NRL had one just like it in his office the first time I ever spoke with the President."

"I see," teased Tony. "So just how chummy are you two?"

Jim blushed.

"I'm not a big fan, actually," he replied. "I don't trust any of them and that's why I was against taking on this mission. But that's water under the bridge, as they say. Here, let me show you guys how this thing works."

Soon the device on the table was dialing the telephone number Jim had entered using the keypad on one of its legs. After about five rings, a male voice finally answered.

"Hello?"

"Hi, who is this?" asked a puzzled Jim. "I thought I called Sophie Hoffman's cell phone number."

"This sounds like Dr. Barnes," replied the voice on the other end of the line.

"It *is* Dr. Barnes. Who is this and why do you have Sophie's phone?"

"Dr. Barnes, this is Manny. Boy, am I glad you called! The police just left here and they've taken Sophie with them."

"On what charges?" demanded Jim. "And which agency has her?"

"It was the BKA and they were very vague about any charges. Something about an ongoing investigation into the assassination of Kruger, but they wouldn't get any more specific than that. I don't even know if they've arrested her or if they've just hauled her in for questioning."

"I'll see what I can find out and get back to you but before I go I need to ask you something. Do you know if she's done any traveling lately?"

There was a long pause on the other end.

"Dr. Barnes, if you're referring to her visits to the Other Side, I know about that and she made me swear to never discuss it with anyone."

"I don't think she would mind you discussing it with me, Manny, especially under the circumstances. What about Professor Schmidt? Have you seen him lately? Can you put me in touch with him?"

"No, I haven't seen him since he left with Max Becker about a week ago."

"By left, do you mean..."

"Yes, I mean to the Other Side. Max and Sophie have been back and forth several times, but I think Max has gone to stay this time. Sophie was really bummed out after he left this last time. I think she was finally starting to like him, even after the bad start the two of them had."

"Manny, this is very important. Do you know how they do it? Do you know how they move back and forth to the Other Side?"

"No, I don't have a clue and I don't really want to know. I know Sophie is really into it, but it freaks me out and I want no part of it."

"That's too bad," replied Jim. "Listen, it's very important that I speak to Sophie as soon as possible, but I'm not where she can call me. I'll try to see what I can find out on this end, but if it is just routine questioning, please let her know I called. I'll call this same number tomorrow afternoon and let you know what I've found out. If she returns before then, please ask her to wait for my call."

"I will, Dr. Barnes, and I'm really glad you called."

Jim poked the End button on the communications device, tapped out another number and pressed Call. A man answered on the first ring.

"Bill Blass here!" he said.

"Bill, this is Jim Barnes. Listen, I need a huge favor. Are you someplace where you can talk?"

"Yes, I'm actually still working out of our old office for the time being. Everything was already set up so I asked if I could hang around for a while. What's up?"

"Sophie has been picked up by the BKA and I'd like you to find out everything you can about it. If it's just routine questioning, that's fine, but if there's something else going on, we need to get her out of there fast. The BKA is probably a mess right now and it's hard to say who's in charge."

"I'm on it," replied Blass. "I assume I can't call you, so give me a couple of hours and then call me back."

The line went dead, and Jim slumped back into his chair.

"Who was that?" asked Tony.

When Jim had composed himself, he looked at the others around the table.

"That was Bill Blass, the best resource the U.S. intelligence community ever had. He was part of my team back at the Naval Research Laboratory. We only worked together for a few days, but he's the absolute best. If anybody can find Sophie, he can. He's the one who eventually exposed Edwards and his cronies."

"I agree," added Fitz. "I met him at Jim's office and he seemed like a straight up guy. I wonder if they kept your whole crew together."

Jim shook his head.

"I doubt it. But I have the feeling that Blass could stay as long as he wanted to. Or at least until the President sends him off on another special assignment."

"There's that 'P' word again," scowled Tony. "So this Blass knows the big guy, too, huh?"

"On a first name basis," smiled Jim. "And as you heard him say, there are no call-backs to this telephone, so think about that before you reach out to any friends or relatives. You can't tell them where you are or why you are here and they can't call you. If you think those conditions will raise concern, it might be better not to make the call.

"Okay, moving on. We can't talk to Sophie until we find her, but we *will* find her so let's go back to the topic of what our initial message will be once we make it over to this place they keep calling the Other Side."

***

Edwards was still getting used to his new office, but one thing he had caught onto right away was the building security system. His desktop computer was equipped with a special program that allowed him to tap into the network of video cameras in the facility and view a live feed from any camera right on his monitor. Using the camera at the end of the hallway outside his office, he watched Schröder leave and studied his walk. The man appeared unshaken after receiving his covert mission. He walked with a purpose, his head high and steady. This was a person who was going to go far, Edwards thought to himself. He was also a person to be watched very carefully.

The telephone rang and Edwards glanced at the display to see who might be calling. He had one of the few outside lines that still worked but this call was from the Mexican representative.

"Good afternoon, Gomez. What can I do for you?"

"Sorry to bother you, Mr. Edwards, but I just received some news from one of my agents in western Mexico and I thought you should know about this before tomorrow's meeting. We've been running a communications network to support the Pacific fleet for some time now and I just learned that the Federal Police have disabled the entire system by destroying several critical relay stations on the Baja Peninsula.

It will take us months to rebuild and the reconstruction will only be possible if the *Federales* leave us alone."

"How did they find out about your network? I thought those sites were all unmanned."

"They are! However, we had an unfortunate incident a couple of weeks ago when our Chinese friends sent in a technical team to upgrade the primary site near La Paz. They were sent ashore in a powerboat but there was an explosion before they reached land and the Navy picked them up before they could execute their termination orders. They were subsequently forced to talk by the Federal Police and they probably gave up the location of the site they were supposed to upgrade."

Edwards frowned.

"But you said that several sites were taken out. Would they have known anything about the rest of the network?"

"No, they would have had no knowledge of the rest of the network to prevent situations like this from happening. And the other towers that were taken down were the next three in line. They cross the Peninsula from the shores of the Sea of Cortez to a beach on the Pacific side. There's no way to route radio traffic around the disabled towers because of the mountains. What this means, of course, is that we have lost contact with the entire Pacific fleet."

"These are mostly Chinese vessels, right?"

"Yes, and that's why I thought you should hear about this now. Mr. Chen is going to be hopping mad by tomorrow morning."

"You let me take care of Chen," replied Edwards confidently. "You get me some intel on how the Federal Police learned about these other towers. If we have a leak, we need to close it, even though the damage has already been done. And be prepared by tomorrow's meeting to offer a workable plan to restore communications to the ships in the Pacific."

"But..."

"No buts, Gomez! There must be a way and I expect you to find it. Cost is not an issue—just be prepared to present a plan so we can keep the Chinese happy. Is everything else going okay in your part of the world?"

"Yes, things are pretty normal. There's the constant in-fighting among rival gangs and the usual turf wars between the major players, but nothing out of the ordinary. Well, I'd better get busy if I'm going to have a plan ready by 9:00 a.m. I'll see you tomorrow."

"Goodbye, Raul, and thanks for the heads up."

Edwards put the receiver back in its base and reviewed what he'd just been told. If the Chinese technicians didn't know about the other towers, then somebody else on the Baja Peninsula did!

Edwards scrolled back through his news feed archives until he found a headline about a Chinese ship that had been boarded near Ensenada on the northern Pacific coast of the Baja Peninsula. In the ship's holds the authorities had found more than one hundred refugees being smuggled into the United States as part of a human trafficking operation. He jotted down the date, May 5th, and continued scrolling back in time. Just three days earlier, on May 2nd, two huge drug busts had been made in the Pacific Northwest that involved Chinese crewed ships that had sailed from South America.

Suddenly, Edwards slammed his fist down on his desk and yelled, "Those are all our ships! Somebody's been intercepting our radio transmissions!"

Chapter 3

The NWIDI team discussed, debated and argued over the message they would deliver if, and when, they ever made contact with *the Teachers*. By breakfast Thursday morning, the best they could come up with was a compromise that no one really liked.

'*The U.S. Government has recently become aware of a dangerous organization known as the Six. We believe they pose a serious threat to the American way of life and we also believe they are aware of your existence and that they intend to bring harm to you.*

'*We respectfully request that you agree to a meeting to discuss ways in which we might work together to disarm the Six and end their interference in the lives of our citizens and their lawful government.*'

And adding to the group's frustration was the fact that they still hadn't been able to contact Sophie Hoffman, Jim's German connection to *the Teachers*.

"Well, boss man, what's our next move?" asked Tony. "Your intelligence guy hasn't turned up anything; your Professor Schmidt seems to be on a permanent vacation to the Other Side; and we don't seem to have any options. I don't know about you, but I think I'd be a lot more useful if I flew over to the Bahamas, rendezvoused with my boat and kept that appointment at the Guardian Blue Hole."

Jim shook his head.

"I don't think that's an option any more, Tony. We were pretty much under 'protective custody' back at the Naval Research Lab and once we accepted this assignment, we signed on for the duration. I thought you understood that back in D.C."

"Oh, I get the whole 'duration' thing, Jim, but I'm not accomplishing a thing here, whereas out there I'd be fulfilling a pretty bizarre request. You've got to admit that being asked to move my ship and crew to a specific place by a pod of dolphins is out of the ordinary. That request might have even come from *the Teachers*."

There was a long silence around the breakfast table as each team member considered what Tony had just said and then everyone started talking at once.

"He's right!" exclaimed Fitz, finally out-shouting the others. "He's absolutely right! We've all gotten so used to strange events in our lives that when Tony told us a story about receiving a message from dolphins we didn't even challenge the significance of it. But he's right—what else could explain his story?"

There was another moment of silence.

"It's a bizarre story, I'll grant you that," nodded Jim. "But the ship is already headed to the rendezvous point and it can check out whatever might be there. There's no need to expose ourselves to any unnecessary danger."

"But that message wasn't delivered to the ship or its crew," blurted out Tony. "That message was delivered directly to me. Whoever sent that message requested that I make the rendezvous. The ship and crew part was like an 'oh, by the way' addition to the primary request. I should be there in person. The message said 'one of us will serve as your guide' so I assume that means that a dolphin will be my guide. I have to be there, guys. Besides, I spent the better part of the last five years in an underground bunker similar to this one and I'm going to go crazy if I don't get out of here soon!"

"If you can get the Learjet released and moved to D.C.," offered Fitz, "Susan and I could fly Tony over to Andros, drop him off and be back here in about six hours."

"No, come on, guys, this is crazy!" objected Jim. "First of all, I doubt if the powers that be are going to let any of us out of here, much less in a plane that's already been hijacked once."

"Will you at least ask?" pressured Tony. "I feel very strongly about this and I think you'll all agree that those dolphins didn't just show up in the Virgin Islands by chance. Someone—or something—sent them there. You guys can pursue the meeting with *the Teachers* from here and I'll check out this Guardian Blue Hole lead from there. Maybe we'll meet up on this Other Side, wherever it is. But time is of the essence because the Dolphin Diver should be reaching the rendezvous site today or tomorrow and I'd really like to be there when it arrives."

After yet another heated debate, Jim finally caved to group pressure and agreed to push the idea up the chain of command.

After he had left the room to make his call, Linda said, "What's up with him? Jim used to be such an easy-going guy but now he's really up tight."

"Maybe it's the result of living with the Navy for five years," replied Javier. "But you're right—that's not the Jim I remember, either. Tony, if they let you go back out into the real world, you have to promise to be careful! There are obviously folks out there who would like to see us out of the way."

"Hey, you know me," laughed Tony. "Careful is my middle name!"

Linda frowned.

"Seriously, Tony. No macho, risky behavior. I don't know what this meeting on Andros is all about, but has it ever occurred to you that it might be a setup? A trap they knew you couldn't resist?"

"Yes, that thought has crossed my mind," replied Tony in a more serious tone. "But whoever sent the message to me already knew where I was, more or less. If they just wanted to grab me and stuff me back into MX-2, they could have done it without creating this whole dolphin thing. This is no kidnap attempt. Whoever sent that message knew where I was but couldn't get to me in person. And yet they can apparently communicate with dolphins and even get them to cooperate. It was a week ago today that I received the message and it's just about all I've thought about ever since. Why me? Who sent it? And then there's the whole issue about how it was decoded by a device built from the wrong parts and...well, you've heard the story. It's just too incredible to be true, and yet it is. If Jim can't talk me out of here, I might have to make a break for it on my own."

"Now, see, that's exactly the kind of behavior…"

Linda was interrupted by Jim's return to the room. He was scowling as he returned to his place at the table.

"Well?" prodded Tony. "What did they say?"

"Against my advice, they seem to agree with you, Tony. Once I laid out all the details you've shared with us, they couldn't move fast enough."

As the room went up in cheers, Jim turned to Fitz.

"Sorry, guys, but they nixed the Learjet idea. It seems that they found some bugs in the plane and they don't want to risk the possibility of there being more that they haven't yet discovered. Tony's going to get a ride to Andros courtesy of the Navy and if he gets to ride in the same plane that brought me up here, he's going to have a great time!"

"Wait, did you say *bugs*?" questioned Susan. "Are you saying that they found bugs in our Learjet? Was this done while they were holding Fitz in Cuba?"

"They appear to be much older than that," replied Jim. "In fact, they may even date back to a time before Frank acquired the aircraft from…"

"From Edwards!" shouted Linda. "So he's been tailing us the whole time!"

"They don't know who actually installed them, but apparently it was a very sophisticated job. So sophisticated that Fitz and Susan never found them in six years of aircraft maintenance. As you know, that plane has a sordid history and the bugs could have been planted anywhere along the line."

"What kind of history?" asked Javier. "It was already an integral part of NWIDI when I came along and I don't think I've ever heard the history."

"As I remember it," began Jim, "the former owner…"

"Hey! Can we save the history lesson for later and get back to me?" scolded Tony. "When do I leave?"

"Oh, yes, Tony!" smiled Jim. "You will be picked up topside by a helicopter at 0600 hours tomorrow morning and transported to Andrews Air Force Base. From there you will be flown to the Andros Town airport that we've all traveled in and out of several times. You will be met by a security detail from AUTEC and they will take you to a waiting Navy patrol boat that will get you out to your boat."

Tony smiled and then frowned.

"And then what?"

"What do you mean?"

"I don't want the Navy shadowing me once I'm on board the Dolphin Diver. Besides, they might spook whomever I'm supposed to be meeting at this Blue Hole place."

"Tony, as you can plainly see, I don't make any decisions around here. If you don't want your transfer to be visible from the rendezvous point, I suggest you get on the telephone to someone on your boat and arrange a meeting place. As for the Navy's plans, I have no idea what they will be instructed to do. They are now aware of the significance of your meeting, so I doubt if they're going to just drop you off, hand you a lollipop and say 'have a nice day.' They're a player in your game now and you're going to have to deal with it."

"Great!" shouted Tony. "That's just what I need! I'm going to go make a call and then start packing. I'll see you all back here later."

And with that, Tony was gone.

"Jim, you were telling me about the history of the Learjet," prompted Javier.

"Oh, yes. Well, before it was the NWIDI company plane, it was used by some infamous Central American drug dealer. The U.S. Government confiscated it when they busted him but he only had the plane on loan from its real owner."

Jim paused, leaving Javier on the edge of his seat.

"And who was that?" demanded Javier.

"A little-known Arab named Qusai Hussein."

Javier thought for a second. "Never heard of him."

"Probably not, but I'll bet you remember his father, Saddam Hussein! So you see, the bugs in the plane could go all the way back to the original owner. In fact, they may have been installed at the orders of our own government when they found out who the plane's first owner was going to be."

"How come we were never told any of this?" asked Fitz.

"I think Frank told us the story on our first official flight, somewhere between Seattle and Adak Island, and I'm guessing you two were probably both in the cockpit. I don't think Frank was trying to hide anything from you, but the lineage of the plane was classified, if I remember right, and I don't remember him ever mentioning it again."

"No, I don't either," added Linda. "In fact, I'd completely forgotten about all this until just now. So the bugs could date back to before the plane was delivered or they could be as recent as when Frank took delivery. Personally, I'm betting that Edwards had the plane tagged before he turned it over to NWIDI so he could track our long-distance moves. He had already seen us in action in the Yucatan and he knew we would probably turn up more alien artifacts. The bugs were a way to keep tabs on us without our knowledge."

"But that means he might have been tracking every flight we've made since Tony signed the plane over to us more than five years ago!" gasped Susan.

"So what is the Navy doing with these bugs?" asked Fitz.

Jim smiled.

"They've moved everything they've found so far into a highly secure warehouse down on the Miami waterfront. If whoever is on the other end of those things comes looking for them, they will get a mighty big surprise!"

***

After discovering that at least three ships from the Pacific fleet had recently been put out of commission,

Edwards had pondered several courses of action before finally opting to test his new understudy's resourcefulness. He summoned Hans Schröder to his office and detailed the facts as he knew them.

"Here's a list of the ships I know about. They're all Chinese-crewed vessels that would have been getting regular updates from the Baja, Mexico, radio system. How fast can you have someone from your organization on the ground over there to investigate?"

Schröder thought for a minute before responding.

"The closest operative I have would be half a world away, Mr. Edwards. I have access to some agents in Thailand but I think Germany is actually closer."

Schröder tapped something into the iPad he always seemed to be carrying and frowned.

"Yes, Thailand is almost nine thousand miles from the Baja Peninsula and Germany is only about six thousand. If I issued the orders right now I could have someone there in about eighteen hours, taking into account airport layovers and plane changes."

Edwards shook his head.

"No, that's too long. I'm going to temporarily assign one of my southern California operatives to you. I'll get him moving now and have him check in with you as soon as he lands in La Paz. I want to know who leaked the information and I want that mess cleaned up permanently."

"Of course, Mr. Edwards, but wouldn't the Mexican representative be in a better position to handle this? He probably has personnel in La Paz right now."

"Yes, I'm sure he does. But the problem could be within his own organization and I don't want any cover-ups. The problem could also be on the Chinese side, so tomorrow morning I'll bring this up at the meeting, but I want you working on it long before then, understood?"

"Yes, sir!"

"Good. I'll email you the agent's name in a few minutes."

The next morning Edwards patiently listened to twelve status reports that each painted a "business as usual" story. When it was his turn, he made direct eye contact with Raul Gomez, the Mexican representative.

"I've recently learned that two large shipments to the Pacific Northwest have been confiscated and the ships impounded by the U.S. Coast Guard. Do you know anything about that, Mr. Gomez?"

Edwards' question caught Gomez off guard, but he recovered quickly and replied defiantly.

"No, but the United States is not under my control. I wouldn't have access to that intelligence."

"No, perhaps not," replied Edwards. "What about a ship full of Asian illegals that was boarded by the Mexican Navy ten days ago in Ensenada? Would you happen to have any knowledge about that?"

"Yes, I am aware of that incident. We are still investigating, but it appears that the Navy just got lucky on that one."

Edwards shifted his attention to Chen Yong.

"Mr. Chen. Since all three ships in question were manned by Chinese nationals, I assume you can shed some light on this for us. Do you have any idea how the authorities in two different countries might have learned about the cargos these ships were carrying?"

"No, I don't, Mr. Edwards, but on the twenty-ninth of last month, seventeen days ago, we had another ship impounded while it was tied up in Seattle. The ship was being loaded with legitimate cargo bound for the Far East but the authorities received a tip about five Chinese nationals who had entered the United States illegally and then fled back to the ship."

Edwards' face began to redden.

"Another ship?" Why aren't these losses being covered in your morning reports?"

"In my case," replied Chen, "the incident occurred many days before we were brought here and I had already reported the incident to you in a regular weekly update. It was my understanding that you wanted our morning status reports to cover only current activities since the convening of this Committee."

Others around the table nodded their heads in agreement.

"What were these five operatives doing in Seattle without my knowledge, Mr. Chen?"

"Actually, they were there on your orders—or at least the orders of someone in your organization. They were part of an assassination team sent to Seattle to terminate a member of this NWIDI group you've mentioned several times. Someone by the name of Tony Nicoletti, I believe."

Edwards clenched his teeth and was silent for a moment.

"Well, we have a problem, folks, and beginning immediately I want your reports to include any unresolved issues that might relate to this problem. I recently learned that sometime yesterday we lost all communications to the Pacific fleet because the authorities in Baja, Mexico, destroyed our radio link from the east side of the peninsula over to the west side. This network has operated without detection for several years and suddenly the Mexican Navy takes out four transmission sites in a single day! And I should point out that the four ships we've been discussing all received one or more communications from that same radio network.

"There's a leak somewhere, and I want it plugged fast. Mr. Gomez and Mr. Chen, get me some answers, even if you have to pound them out of each other! And I want the rest of you to reexamine your own organizations' recent events in detail and look for *anything* that seems out of the ordinary. And if you find something, I want to know about it immediately. Is everybody clear on that?"

There was vigorous nodding of heads—all except Chen's.

"Mr. Chen, do you have a problem?"

"Yes I do. Are we going to discuss the fate of the seventeen vessels currently plying the waters of the Pacific Ocean waiting for instructions that they will never receive? It seems to me that the cargo aboard those vessels is far more important than a witch hunt to exterminate a bunch of amateur detectives. At least one of those ships would still be free if it hadn't been carrying five high-value resources on a foolish mission."

Edwards glared at Chen.

"That boat would be free if your agents hadn't allowed themselves to be caught. And they also failed in their mission, if I remember correctly!"

"Only because they were given bad intelligence," mumbled Chen. "They were sent to Seattle to kill a man who hadn't been there in more than five years."

"That will be enough, Mr. Chen! I remind you that it was a team of Chinese technicians that first brought attention to our Baja radio network so I suggest you take a long, hard look at your organization. We have other ways to communicate with the vessels and we'll repair or replace the radio network as soon as possible. In the meantime, you all have work to do. That will be all for today."

Edwards turned his back on the group and when it became obvious that the meeting had been abruptly dismissed most of the board members collected their papers and began to make their way to the door.

"Mr. Chen, stay," said Edwards without turning around.

When Edwards turned to face Chen, his expression was hard and stern.

"Chen, if you ever challenge me again it will be your last day on this planet, do you understand me? If you have a problem with an order I've issued, I expect you to bring it to me privately, not in this forum, and *especially* not when the provisional members are present. These are difficult times and those of us that are senior members of the Committee must show solidarity or we will soon have chaos—both in this room and in the world outside it. Good day, Mr. Chen."

Edwards turned back around without waiting for a response from the Chinese representative.

Out in the hall, Chen was joined by Raul Gomez and Aleksey Mednikov. Both men had remained close enough to the door to overhear Edwards' words.

"He's obsessed with these Americans," commented Gomez when the three men were far enough away from the conference room that Edwards wouldn't hear.

"I agree, and for what reason?" replied Mednikov. "If he hadn't been misusing his organization's resources to hunt them, we wouldn't be confined in this hole in the ground."

"I don't understand," said Chen, stopping dead in his tracks. "Did this group have something to do with the U.S. Government learning our identities?"

"Of course! I thought everybody knew that," replied Mednikov, turning to Gomez for confirmation.

"I didn't know either," frowned Gomez. "Let's go someplace more private and you can fill us in, because this is the first I'm hearing about why I'm not at home with my wife and children."

Seated in the cramped living room of Raul Gomez' living quarters, Mednikov explained.

"I really thought everyone knew about the events that forced us to retreat into this underground command center. Maybe it's just because Russia is closer to Germany, but it's pretty common knowledge in our organization. One of these amateurs that Edwards keeps referring to made a trip to Munich about a month ago to speak at a university function. While he was there, a Professor named Schmidt slipped him a file that contained, among other things, a list of the six major players in our group. You all remember Colonel Kruger, right? Well, our illustrious former German representative attempted to recover the file but his agents were arrested on a U.S. military installation and during their interrogation they identified Kruger. Edwards had Kruger killed, of course, but somehow the Americans learned the identities of all of us, including Edwards. He keeps hammering on us for these stupid daily reports, but it's really his operation that's in shambles. I've heard that dozens of his senior operatives have been arrested—perhaps more."

"But I don't understand," said Chen. "How can a small group of amateurs create so much havoc with the most powerful organization in the world? Why weren't they just eliminated long ago?"

"That's a very good question," nodded Mednikov. "I've heard that the group is less than a dozen people—maybe even as small as four—and that they actually worked for Edwards at one point. Maybe he's been protecting them for some reason and got caught off guard when they turned on him."

"He certainly seems intent on eliminating them now," observed Gomez. "In fact, Chen and I have to go out behind the bunker and have a fist fight to determine which one of us lost those ships!"

The three men laughed and Gomez poured another round of tequila.

"You mentioned Colonel Kruger," said Chen. "He was never one of my favorite people, but what do you think about his replacement? Schröder, I think his name is. Doesn't he seem just a little too eager to please?"

"If you mean too eager to please Edwards, then I agree," replied Gomez. "In fact, I ran into him in the corridor yesterday and I'm sure he had just come out of Edwards' office. I think we need to keep a close eye on him because he strikes me as the ambitious type."

"So, when are you two having this fist fight?" asked Mednikov. I'd like to get some photos for the company newsletter."

"Well, let's discuss that," replied Chen. Holding up his hand to fend off Gomez' objection, he continued. "Seriously, he's obviously trying to pit the two of us against each other and draw attention away from his own mess. He must know that I don't hand pick every electronics technician in my vast organization, so to blame that incident on me was just a diversion. And the same is true of his attack on you, Gomez. Does he think you personally monitor that one radio tower every minute of the day? I think he's hiding something and I think we need to be very careful until we figure out what he's up to. After all, it was his orders that forced us to leave our homes and come here."

"I agree," grunted Mednikov. "Who knows what he's doing out there while we're down here for 'our own safety,' to use his words."

Chapter 4

At 5:45 a.m. the next morning, Tony was surprised to see Linda, Javier, Jim, Susan and Fitz all walking down the concrete apron from the topside bunker blast door. Tony, of course had been pacing the parking lot for thirty minutes, even though he knew that his pick-up wasn't scheduled until 6:00 a.m.

"Hey, guys, you didn't have to get up so early just to see me off!"

"Come on, big guy! You didn't think we'd let you get out of here without a hug, did you?" teased Linda. "Besides, I figured one more caution about being careful wouldn't hurt, either."

The group gathered around Tony and either shook hands or hugged him, as appropriate. Susan noticed the single, small carry-on Tony was clutching and commented.

"You're certainly traveling light. Are you planning to be back here tonight?"

"No, but I have some clothes and personal items on board the Dolphin Diver. Remember, I'd been living on board for three weeks when Jim's buddies kidnapped me and brought me up here. There's no sense hauling a lot of stuff back and forth."

Fitz turned and looked to the eastern sky.

"Well, have fun at your 'summer place'—I think I hear your ride approaching."

Soon a helicopter was visible and the group backed away from the helipad as a black machine came in swiftly and settled down on the large concrete pad marked "M1."

"Wow," whistled Fitz as the rotors quieted enough to talk. "You must be important cargo, Tony. That's a fully armed AH-6 Special Ops attack helicopter. Check out the air-to-air missile launchers on each side!"

The pilot was waving to the group, obviously anxious to get underway so Tony waved to his friends, ducked his head and ran to the helicopter. As he approached, the pilot signaled for Tony to get into the back.

Tony instinctively reached for the safety harness and buckled himself in behind the co-pilot's seat so his weight would offset the pilot's. Once he was secure, he gave a thumbs-up signal. The pilot returned the sign and then pointed to a headset that was on the seat next to Tony.

"Good morning," greeted the pilot through Tony's headphones. "My name is Lieutenant Rogers and I assume you're Tony Nicoletti. Judging by the way you handle a military-style safety harness, I'm guessing this isn't your first ride in a helicopter. Hang on, we're off!"

The engine whined as it increased rotational speed and the machine gradually lifted up and away from the helipad. Tony waved to his friends again and then focused on the instrument panel at the front of the aircraft.

"I was a forward air traffic controller in the Army back in the day. I've been in and out of these things more times than I can remember. Never anything quite this sophisticated, though."

"Vietnam?" asked the pilot, trying to guess the conflict by Tony's apparent age.

"Sort of," replied Tony. "Ever hear of the TLC Brotherhood?"

"As a matter of fact, I have," smiled the Lieutenant. "My father was a Huey pilot in 'Nam but he also flew a number of missions into Laos and Cambodia. Hey, you might have been on one of his insertions!"

"Or extractions," added Tony. "I was part of a joint Army/Air Force task force assigned to bring back our F4 pilots shot down behind enemy lines."

"Well, it's a pleasure to know you, friend. Are you Special Ops these days?"

"Me?" laughed Tony. "No, I'm strictly a civilian and have been for a long time."

"Oh," replied the pilot apologetically. "I just assumed from the special transportation order—and given the pick-up and drop-off points—that…"

"I understand," smiled Tony. "I'm a little confused by all of this, too, but I'm currently part of a team that's doing a little job for the President, so I guess that's why I'm getting the royal treatment."

"Very good, sir. It was improper of me to inquire and I apologize. That's Washington, D.C. off the starboard side. We'll be touching down at Andrews Air Force Base in a few minutes and it's going to get pretty busy up here as we pass through restricted air space, so sit back and enjoy what's left of your ride."

Tony took that to mean that he should shut up and leave the pilot alone, so he focused on the landscape below. When he and the others had been transported up to the Meriwether Mountain complex it had been dark and they were all chatting so he took advantage of his first daylight helicopter flight over the nation's capital.

The pilot brought the helicopter smoothly down on a large patch of concrete in front of a hanger marked "U.S. Air Force Civil Air Patrol." When the rotors spun down, he gave Tony the thumbs-up sign again, indicating that it was okay to unbuckle and exit the aircraft. By the time Tony climbed out, the young Lieutenant already had his flight helmet off and was waiting. He held out his hand to shake.

"It was a pleasure, sir. Maybe I'll see you on another flight sometime. Someone from the CAP will be right out to take you on the next leg of your trip."

The Lieutenant started to walk away but Tony stopped him.

"Wait! Isn't the Civil Air Patrol a civilian search and rescue group?"

"Yes, that's correct. Here they come now, in that blue pickup. Good luck!"

An older model Air Force blue pickup pulled up and the driver called through the open passenger's window.

"Jump in, Mr. Nicoletti. We have a few minutes before takeoff. Would you like a cup of coffee?"

Inside the CAP hangar, Tony was surprised by all the people in uniform. As he sipped his coffee, he questioned his host.

"So, I thought the Civil Air Patrol was a civilian agency. What's with all the Air Force personnel around here?"

"Oh these aren't Air Force uniforms, Mr. Nicoletti—these are CAP uniforms. It's a little hard to tell on these fatigues, but on our dress uniforms the buttons are different and the words "U.S. Air Force" over the pocket are replaced by "Civil Air Patrol." We're actually as much a part of the Air Force as the Air Force Reserve is, except that we can't be called into combat situations."

"Really!" acknowledged Tony. "So why am I here, anyway?"

"I'm only aware of our portion of the mission, of course, but I assume you need to get from Point A to Point B and we've been ordered to transport you from here—Andrews Air Force Base—over to an airfield on Andros Island in the Bahamas. I know the orders came from the White House, but other than that I'm just a pilot doing my duty."

"So you are going to fly me over?" questioned Tony as he scanned the hangar full of small private planes. "In what?"

"In that twin-engine Beechcraft over there," replied the man proudly. "By the way, my name is John Hodson. It's a pleasure to meet you."

"Ah, thanks, same here. But I don't understand. My friend was flown up here in some fancy Navy trainer jet and I'm going to travel in *that*?"

"Sorry, my friend, but no Navy trainer that I know of is going to land at the Andros Town airport and especially if you want to arrive anonymously. Planes like that beauty over there are in and out of Andros Town all day long so nobody will even notice us. There aren't any restrooms on my Beach, so maybe you should hit the head and then let's go get saddled up."

Although disappointed that he didn't get the ride Jim had told him about, he thoroughly enjoyed the four-hour flight almost due south. The plane had space for six passengers in the main cabin, but Tony elected to take the co-pilot's seat so he could chat with Hodson. By the time they reached the northern end of the Bahamas, the pilot knew almost everything there was to know about Tony and his NWIDI friends—the part that hadn't been classified, anyway.

"We're coming up on the Bimini Islands right now," announced Hodson. "If you look just to your right, you should be able to make out a feature called Bimini Road. Do you see it?"

"Is it kind of a 'J' shaped thing?"

"Yes, that's it. It was first discovered in the 1960s and theories about it have been all over the map. However, current research indicates that it's a man-made structure designed to protect a harbor."

"I don't see any harbor."

"Well, that's because the harbor is now under water but several thousand years ago the sea levels were much lower and there was a harbor just east of the structure you can see. It's all been verified by scuba divers."

"Really? So how much lower *was* the water?"

Hodson thought for a minute before answering.

"If I recall, the folks who are doing the research around here believe that during the last ice age the oceans were about three hundred feet lower than they are now. All of these tiny islands that make up the Bahamas were much larger back then and many of them were even connected. I've seen a map that shows what they think it looked like and it's amazing. You could almost walk from the Bahamas to Cuba!"

Tony was barely listening.

"Did you say three hundred feet lower? Could it have been even lower than that?"

"Well, those are just estimates, of course, so I suppose it could have been lower, why?"

"Remember the friend I told you about who went missing during a dive? I have reason to believe that he was exploring something we had found on an earlier dive—at a depth of more than three hundred feet. Can we swing around the end of South Bimini a mile or two?"

"That will take us a little east of our scheduled route but sure, if we can see the bay where your friend disappeared. Did you say his name was Martin?"

"Morton," Tony corrected. "Frank Morton. And the spot we're looking for will be just south of the southern island."

"Roger that. I'm going to bring her down as low as I can but there's an airstrip in that area so keep your eyes open for other planes."

As the Beechcraft banked left around the end of South Bimini, Tony immediately recognized the area known as Nicholas Harbor.

"There! We did a shore dive from right down there and I'm sure that's the spot Frank went back to the day he disappeared."

Hodson flew the area twice in each direction before resuming his southward course and leaving Bimini behind.

"We'll be landing on Andros in a few minutes, but this has been a fascinating trip, my friend. I don't know where you're off to, but if any part of your mission requires small plane air support, you call me, okay? I can be here in less than 5 hours!"

Just as Jim had promised, a Navy staff car was waiting for Tony as he exited the small building that served as the general aviation terminal and airport administration headquarters.

"Mr. Nicoletti?" asked the sailor behind the wheel. "Hop in and I'll get you to the patrol boat. They're waiting for you at the base pier."

A few minutes later, Tony was standing on the aft deck of a small Navy patrol boat racing out into the Atlantic Ocean in search of the Dolphin Diver. He had arranged a rendezvous off the coast of Big Wood Cay, about sixteen miles south of the mysterious meeting place specified in the message delivered by the dolphins. As the patrol boat passed Man of War Sound, one of the officers pointed to an undistinguishable point along the shore.

"You'd never know it, but your Guardian Blue Hole is right over there. The pools that serve as its only two entrances are hidden from here by the grass, but that's where it is."

Very soon, Tony was going to find out just who had brought him here and why they had scheduled a meeting in such an unusual place. He nodded, but suddenly he wished he were back on Meriwether Mountain behind those thick blast doors that were protecting his friends.

***

At the following morning's briefing, the main topic of discussion was once again the alleged "leak" on the Baja Peninsula and what was being done to fix it. Edwards challenged both Gomez and Chen for answers but neither could provide anything definite.

"The man who was leading the Seattle assassination team has dropped off the radar, but even if he's talked to the authorities that would only account for the first vessel," explained Chen. "He had no knowledge of the other ships and he was out of circulation by the time they were impounded.

"I've checked the communications logs from the two ships carrying our product and both reported in just a few hours before making port—one in Seattle and one in Tacoma. We haven't been allowed to speak to the crew yet, but the Seattle newspaper accounts indicate that the ships were allowed to enter their respective ports and tie up before being boarded. That suggests that the authorities had prior knowledge of their cargo and were waiting for them."

"And the same is true of the ship that was taken in Ensenada," nodded Gomez. "It had reported in less than ninety minutes before boarding and it reported nothing unusual."

"What does this tell us?" demanded Edwards. "What's the connection here?"

"I think you put your finger on it yesterday," replied Chen. "All four of the ships containing cargo—human or otherwise—would have received their last set of orders via the Baja network. And those orders would have included the coordinates of their final destination. That information is withheld from the captains until the very last minute in case they run into trouble at sea. They truly don't know exactly where they are going until the last possible minute. Or in this case, until they pass our northernmost radio relay station."

"Gomez, I want a diagram of that radio network—all of it—on my desk this afternoon. And I specifically want to know where those messages originated. I assume that's not on the Baja, correct?"

"That's correct. I don't know all the details yet, but I have someone working on that diagram as we speak. I do know that the tower the Chinese technicians were sent to upgrade connects the Baja Peninsula to the Mexican mainland, but I don't have the rest of the story yet. The network was carefully segmented and the information was highly compartmentalized on purpose. I'm afraid I can't promise anything by this afternoon, but I will get you the information just as soon as possible."

"I can relate to Mr. Gomez' position," interjected Peter Fleck, the representative from South Africa. "We operate a similar network that spans the entire continent, from Liberia, on the Atlantic to Somalia, on the Arabian Sea, and all I really know about it is that it works. I couldn't tell you a thing about the exact route it takes or who maintains it. Our organizations are simply too huge, Mr. Edwards. It's impossible to know every detail."

Edwards scowled.

"Do you know what your network is used for, Mr. Fleck?"

"Not exactly," replied the South African, "but I suspect it's very similar to the Baja system. Oh, I do know that it's bidirectional, unlike the Baja network. I assume it's to allow ships in the Atlantic to communicate with ships on the Arabian side of the continent."

"Wrong!" shouted Edwards. "The African network, which also includes a leg up to Libya, on the Mediterranean, has a hub in southern Chad where there is a very sensitive satellite receiver, allowing us to beam down messages and get them to ships in three oceans. I suggest you do a little studying, Mr. Fleck!

"And, Gomez, I think you will find that the Mexican network extends all the way across the country to the Yucatan, where it connects the Pacific and the Sea of Cortez to the Gulf of Mexico and the Caribbean Sea. And I believe your satellite link is in the mountains of northeastern Oaxaca."

"I wasn't aware that we even had a satellite in orbit," challenged the Russian, Mednikov. "When did this happen?"

"Well, technically, we don't have a satellite, Mr. Mednikov, we're just *borrowing* it. It's something I arranged a few years ago—I'm sure I mentioned it at one of our annual meetings. At any rate, this very high-tech downlink service feeds into several very low-tech networks due to the nature of the terrain that hosts them.

"But enough about this! The bottom line is that we have made absolutely no progress in our quest to find the leak in Baja and the only reason we still aren't broadcasting information to the authorities is because they blew up our towers in Baja!"

"Mr. Edwards, if I might offer a thought?" asked Hans Schröder, softly.

"Yes, Mr. Schröder?" replied Edwards, his tone immediately changing.

"To recap just a bit, the first vessel lost was carrying a team of assassins sent to Seattle to eliminate Tony Nicoletti, a member of a group called NWIDI. The team eventually learned that he wasn't there, but when they returned to their ship, it was boarded and apprehended. Then the second and third vessels were boarded and impounded, also in the northwestern United States. The information that led to these losses could only have come from a network that terminates in Baja, Mexico. Is it possible that Nicoletti or some other member of the old NWIDI group is—or was—operating in the La Paz area and stumbled onto our transmissions?"

There were mummers around the table and several heads nodded affirmatively.

"That's an interesting theory, Mr. Schröder, but I doubt if it was Nicoletti because until a few weeks ago he was in my custody. Unfortunately he escaped from MX-2 and hasn't surfaced yet but he has no connection to the Baja area. Neither does the only female member of the NWIDI team, Linda McBride, although she did marry a Mexican national. The last time we saw either one of them, they were living in Cancun but they disappeared shortly after their wedding and we've never picked up their trail. I wonder if..."

"It's a long shot," frowned Gomez, "but I'll have someone check out all the Americans living in the La Paz area and see if we can turn up anything. Can you send me a photograph of her and her husband?"

"Of course," replied Edwards. And thank you for that suggestion, Mr. Schröder. You might be onto something there."

Silently, Edwards wondered what Schröder was up to with his comment. He was already in contact with a man Edwards had hand-picked and assigned to the young German. If Schröder's temporary agent had discovered a link between the NWIDI group and the Baja, why would he put Gomez on the trail?

The briefing dragged on for another thirty minutes but as soon as it adjourned, Edwards went straight back to his office and called Schröder.

"Get over here!" he said before abruptly hanging up.

When Schröder entered the room, Edwards lashed out at him.

"What's the matter with you? I assume you know something about the Baja situation so why did you give

Gomez an opportunity to mess things up? If he sends his goons out knocking on the doors of unsuspecting Americans, he'll run afoul of the local authorities and we'll never learn anything."

Schröder smiled and took a seat in front of Edwards' desk. Feeling suddenly awkward, Edwards also sat down.

"Well?"

"Mr. Edwards, my comments were designed as a small test for our Mexican comrade. My guess is that he will do nothing, but regardless of what he does, the problem has already been taken care of and your agent is on his way back to California."

While Edwards and Schröder were enjoying a celebration drink in Edwards' office, another meeting was taking place in another wing of the underground complex.

Gomez, Chen and Mednikov were huddled in Gomez' place again, and Gomez had some news of his own.

"We didn't find out in time to stop him from killing a Mexican national, but my men caught up with him at the La Paz airport and before they killed him he confessed to being involved with a southern California group we know to be under Edwards' direct control."

"And you think Edwards sent him down there to take care of the leak?" asked Chen. "Then why did he agree to your offer to check out all the Americans in La Paz?"

"I don't know. Maybe he didn't find out until after the meeting or maybe…"

"Maybe he's testing you," said Mednikov. "And if that's the case, then that German is in on it!"

"Well, tomorrow's meeting should be very interesting, because I'm going to beat him at his own game," laughed Gomez. "I'm going to announce that we have not only 'plugged the leak,' as Edwards likes to say, but that we also captured the leak's Gringo accomplice. And then I'm going to identify the Gringo and let everyone in the room know about his connection to Edwards. That should start some fireworks!"

***

When everyone was seated for supper, Jim tapped his spoon on the edge of his water glass to get the group's attention.

"I have some good news, for a change. When I made my regular twice-daily call to Bill Blass a few minutes ago, I learned that he has finally located Sophie Hoffman and he's arranging a teleconference for early tomorrow morning. As you know, she can't call us, but she's going to call Bill at 9:00 a.m. our time. We're going to call him as well, and he'll conference us all together."

"Cool!" exclaimed Linda. "I was afraid Tony was going to beat us to the punch."

"Speaking of Tony," smiled Jim, "I have some good news there, too. Last night I gave him Bill's telephone number and asked him to check in as soon as he could. Apparently the communications black-out we are subject to doesn't extend to the Bahamas, because Tony called Bill about 4:00 p.m. and told him that he was safely aboard the Navy patrol boat and headed out to the Dolphin Diver. He had already talked with someone on board and apparently the crew is preparing a big 'welcome home' party for him tonight. The plan right now is to attempt the rendezvous at the Guardian Blue Hole sometime tomorrow morning. There's a storm in the area, so that may delay things, but at least he's arrived safely and they're working on a plan. He also asked Bill to look into the whereabouts of someone named Carley Quinn. Apparently she had something to do with the Dolphin Diver and she's gone missing but if she's out there, Bill will find her."

Chapter 5

As the U.S. Navy patrol boat sped away, Tony turned to greet his former crewmates. Even the ship's master, Captain Braydon, was in the salon as Tony reached the top of the ladder leading up from the dive platform.

"Hip, hip, hooray! Hip, hip, hooray! Hip, hip, hooray!" cheered the crew as Tony stepped into the ship's main assembly area.

Tony greeted each of his friends with a warm handshake and, in some cases, with a man-hug. Rob Jefferies was at the end of the line and Tony nodded, acknowledging an unspoken question. When he had called Rob from the AUTEC pier, he had inquired about Carley Quinn, the ship's former cook, and Rob had said that he hadn't heard from her since saying "Goodbye" at the Miami airport several days earlier. Tony had promised to have someone look into it and his nod signified that he had already done so.

In addition to Rob and the Captain, he was greeted by Cesar Acosta, the ship's divemaster, Rigo Mejia, the ship's engineer, Nicolas Banks, the first mate, and Terry Hedges, the new cook who had joined the crew in Road Town, British Virgin Islands, when Carley had suddenly decided to return to Belize via Miami.

Stepping back slightly, Tony scanned the semi-circle of men and smiled broadly.

"I can't begin to tell you how good it is to be back on board!" he laughed. "But I do have one question—who's driving this thing? I don't think I've seen both Captain Braydon and Mr. Banks in this salon at the same time since we pulled away from the dock in Belize City nearly a month ago."

"You're not going to believe this," answered Rob, "but Anne has been taking a regular shift on the bridge. With you gone, we had to fill your spot in the security schedule so Captain Braydon and his shotgun volunteered and Anne took over part of his shift up front. She seems to love it and, according to the Captain, she's really catching on."

"Well, listen guys, I really appreciate this welcome but we have a lot of work to do and I think…"

"Oh no you don't!" shouted Cesar. "We're having a party tonight and you're the guest of honor! There will be plenty of time for work but we've been at sea for five days! Terry, get Tony a cold beer and let's get this party started!"

The words were no sooner out of Cesar's mouth when Terry started lining beers up along the service bar that separated the small galley from the rest of the salon. The beers were followed by trays of snacks and bowls of chips.

"Okay, I guess it's party time!" laughed Tony as the crew converged on him.

A few minutes later the first mate disappeared and Anne appeared in the salon. When Tony saw her, he rushed over to say hello.

"I'm sorry I didn't get up to the bridge, Anne, but these guys have been holding me hostage. So I hear you're taking over my ship!"

Anne smiled and hugged Tony.

"The last I heard, this ship belonged to the Turneffe Wild Dolphin Institute, Tony. It was donated to the Institute by a really generous guy, but it *was* donated, wasn't it?"

Anne was referring to a series of transactions her husband, Rob, had put together to recover more than eighteen million dollars that Tony had deposited in an off-shore account. The money had been his share of the proceeds from the liquidation of the NWIDI organization after Frank Morton's death and it had remained undiscovered for the entire five years that Tony had been held captive by Edwards. Using his background in the banking industry, Rob had engineered a series of untraceable transfers that liquidated the single account in the Cayman Islands and dropped the funds into a host of smaller accounts at institutions around the world. During the time that Tony was sequestered, his money had earned more than enough interest to purchase the Dolphin

Diver, so he had instructed Rob to work that transaction into his financial "magic." It was the least he could do to say "Thank you!" for liberating his money without attracting the attention of Edwards and the Six.

"Yes, Anne, you are correct," replied Tony with a smile. "And it was the smartest thing I've ever done. With the breakthroughs the folks back at the Institute have made, this ship will soon be traveling the world doing incredible things and bridging the gap between man and dolphin."

Due to a bizarre, still unexplained mistake at the Institute, a technician had accidently assembled a working version of a dolphin-to human-to-dolphin translating device that had been in development for years. With it, the team had translated a message delivered to Tony by a pod of dolphins in the British Virgin Islands, and that message had set the ship on its present course.

"So I take it you finished your business in Washington, D.C.?" queried Anne.

"No, not exactly," laughed Tony. "But that project seems to be stalled at the moment, so I talked them into letting me come back out here. As you know, the message we received specifically requests that I make this rendezvous at Guardian Blue Hole and I convinced the powers-that-be that I would be more useful out here than sitting around a conference table. Fortunately, they agreed."

"Oh, I didn't realize that your business in Washington was related to the dolphins' message. I thought Rob said it had something to do with your old NWIDI group."

"It does, but this isn't really the place to talk about it. Could I chat with you and Rob in private a little later?"

"Of course, Tony! The guys are really excited to see you back and they were also getting a bad case of cabin fever, but maybe the three of us can slip away from the party a little early and have a glass of wine in our state room?"

"Perfect! And if you'll excuse me, I need to talk to Cesar about the plan for tomorrow."

Later that evening, Tony, Rob and Anne met as planned and the topic of conversation immediately turned to Tony's trip to Washington, D.C.

"So what was so important that they had to send someone out to escort you back to D.C. if they were only going to keep you a few days?" asked Rob.

"It's complicated, and mostly classified," replied Tony, "but I'll tell you what I can. However, even what I can tell you must never leave this room."

By the time he was done, Tony knew he had said too much because he had mentioned *the Teachers* twice. Both Rob and Anne had been polite enough to let it slide, but the implications were obvious.

"Wow," Anne said when Tony finally stopped talking. "That's unbelievable—and I mean that in the nicest possible way."

She smiled, but all three of them knew what she meant.

"Backing up for a minute to something that probably *isn't* classified, are you suggesting that this group called the Six is some kind of super-cartel?"

"That's as good a term as any," nodded Tony. "From what the authorities know right now, if you look at any group of bad guys—any group on Earth—you will eventually find a connection between that group and some element of the Six. They have infiltrated the governments of several countries—six that we know of—and they control vast resources. I can't explain how they managed to gain administrative control over some top secret underground facilities, but they did—including MX-2, where I was held in Mexico. When Jim's team exposed the identities of the leaders, they vanished and the assumption is that they went underground—literally."

"This has probably already occurred to you, but if I were Edwards, I'd be pretty upset with the NWIDI folks right now. First you escape and then Jim and his cohorts expose the leadership of the most powerful criminal organization in the world."

"Yes, that's occurred to me, Rob, but it also occurred to the government and that's why they rounded us all up and took us to…well, to a safe place. Unfortunately, it's so safe that I don't think anything is going to get accomplished there and that makes our mission here even more important. Not that being summoned by a pod of dolphins isn't important enough, but…"

"Yes, we've been talking about that since we left Road Town," interrupted Rob. "And by 'we' I mean the entire crew. We've tried to figure out what we would do if we got this far and you still hadn't returned. Cesar was willing to jump into this blue hole, of course, but then what? Would whoever or whatever he met be willing to communicate with him or would they take his presence as an act of aggression? In their message the dolphins said they would act as *your* guide but would they accept a substitute if you were unavailable? That's just one of the many reasons why they were all so glad to see you tonight, my friend!"

"It's good to be needed," laughed Tony, "but I'm glad we don't have to find out the answers to any of those questions. Cesar doesn't think we'll be able to pull the dive off in the morning due to the storm but the weather looks like it will clear by mid-day. Since the entrance to the blue hole is really an inland pool, we don't need the ocean to cooperate—just the sky."

"I'd love to be a frog in that pond tomorrow," replied Rob, "but I know this is something you have to do alone. Besides, it's probably classified!"

After a good laugh, the conversation turned to Carley.

"Still no word from her, huh?" asked Tony.

"None," replied Rob. "While we were bouncing around in the open sea it was nearly impossible to use my satellite phone, but I did try to reach her several times. And if she were trying to contact me, I would have had voice-mail but there's been nothing."

"Well, Jim knows this guy named Bill Blass who's supposed to be a wizard at finding people. In fact, he was the one who flushed out the leaders of the Six. He's working on it and he promised to call me as soon as he knows something. I assume we have normal cell service this close to land, right?"

"Yes, the crew's regular phones started working again this afternoon."

"As usual, I've said way too much, so I think I'll go get settled back into my room—I do still have a room, don't I?"

"It's just the way you left it," nodded Rob. "I put the new guy in Carley's old room just in case you decided to surprise us."

"Then I guess I'll see you both at breakfast," yawned Tony. "I hope it's not my last meal."

***

As Edwards waited for everyone to settle down, he watched Gomez and Chen whispering at the far end of the table. For two guys who were supposed to be "pounding the truth out of each other" they sure looked friendly. Edwards made a mental note to check into that and called the meeting to order.

"This is our fifth day in this makeshift command center and I hope everyone is settling in. There will be several new staff members arriving later today and I hope that will improve our standard of living somewhat. For one thing, we're getting a real chef and he'll be accompanied by a fresh supply of food."

The announcement was met with sounds of approval and a few smiles.

"Okay, let's get down to business, shall we? Gomez, you're up and I hope you have some good news for us for a change."

Gomez cleared his throat and ran through the normal numbers regarding inventory levels and revenue from his geographic area of control. When he was finished, he took a deep breath—just long enough to get Edwards flustered—and then he continued.

"I'm also happy to report to the group that the security issue in Baja has been taken care of, once and for all. My men…"

Edwards was irate and couldn't stand it anymore.

"Your men?" he shouted. "Are you suggesting that you or your men had anything to do with putting a stop to the radio message leak?"

Gomez tilted his head as if trying to understand what Edwards meant.

"Oh, is that the issue you were referring to? No, sorry, I didn't have anything to do with that because an outsider from southern California showed up in La Paz yesterday and killed a Mexican civilian before my team had a chance to interrogate him. But I'm very happy to report that the unauthorized shooter was captured on his way to the airport and after an extensive interrogation he was disposed of."

Edwards' face went white but Gomez had his attention focused on Schröder. If the man had been involved in Edwards' plot, he certainly didn't show it.

Playing the devil's advocate, Mednikov put the question to Edwards that everyone had on the tips of their tongues.

"Mr. Edwards, did an agent from your organization break one of the few rules this group has? Did someone from north of the border interfere in Gomez' territory?"

"Of course not!" replied Edwards sharply. "At least not at my orders, and how dare you make such an accusation?"

Gomez cleared his throat loudly to regain the attention of the others.

"Mr. Edwards, before you go any further, you should know that my men convinced the shooter to reveal not only his affiliation, but also the name of his handler."

This time there was a slight squirm from Schröder—enough to convince Gomez, Chen and Mednikov that the truth was hitting a little too close to home.

Edwards' face was red and his eyes were locked tightly on Gomez.

"Sir, I suggest you choose your next few words very carefully. There is no room in this organization for traitors or troublemakers and when you get voted out of this group, you leave in a body bag."

"I'll remember that, Mr. Edwards, but I have a digital video recording on which the agent from the U.S. clearly states that he is—or was—a member of the East L.A. Latin Lords, a gang closely connected to your west coast operations, I believe. After a little more coaxing, he also explained that his orders to travel to La Paz came down through the usual chain of command."

The room broke out in a buzz of murmurs.

Trying to regain control of the meeting and of his own emotions, Edwards pounded the table for silence.

"Enough! There's clearly been a gross misunderstanding here, and I will get to the bottom of it immediately. You are all dismissed, but I want everyone back here at 1:00 p.m. In the meantime, I'm going to find out what really happened in La Paz, Mr. Gomez, and I hope, for your sake, that your story holds up."

Edwards watched the room quickly empty. Someone was going to pay for the embarrassment he had just endured!

***

The entire NWIDI team, minus Tony, of course, was assembled around the conference room table the next morning. At exactly 9:00 p.m., Jim dialed the number Bill Blass had given him and waited for the speaker of the communications device to come alive.

"Jim, can you hear me?" asked the voice on the other end.

"Loud and clear, Bill," replied Jim.

"And Sophie, are you still with us?" they heard Blass ask.

"I sure am. Good afternoon, Dr. Barnes. Oh, I guess it's still morning where you are. Well, anyway, it's very good to hear your voice."

"Hi, Sophie, and likewise. You've been a hard person to track down. Bill, thanks for all your efforts!"

"All in a day's work!" replied Blass. "Should I drop off the line now?"

"No, Bill, please stay with us. We may have questions regarding logistics or we may need to schedule another conference call. Sophie, are you okay? We heard that the police had hauled you in."

"I'm fine, Dr. Barnes. The BKA did show up at the apartment building and demanded that I accompany them to their offices for questioning, but it was mostly routine stuff and I was out of there in a couple of hours. They're a pretty disorganized bunch since their infamous Colonel Kruger was taken out."

"Well, I'm glad you're okay, but I have to ask where you were all this time. You haven't been answering you cell phone and poor Manny has been worried sick!"

"I'm terribly sorry, Dr. Barnes, but shortly after I was released by the German police I was called away and my cell phone was inoperative until I returned late last night."

"Sophie, as you can probably tell, I'm on a speaker phone and there are others in the room with me, but let me assure you that we are in a very secure location and all of the others here know about the Other Side and *the Teachers*. In fact, that's precisely why we've been so anxious to speak with you. So let me ask you directly—were you on the Other Side? Is that why we couldn't locate you?"

There was a long pause before Sophie replied and when she did she sounded more like a scolded school girl than a twenty-six year old graduate student.

"Yes, Dr. Barnes."

Okay, good. Sophie, we need your help. My friends and I have been given a very important task by the President of the United States and I don't see how we can accomplish it without you. But before we get to that, we need to know more about your trips to the Other Side. Are you in a place where you can speak freely?"

"Yes, I'm in my apartment in Munich. What is it that you need to know?"

"First, let me introduce the others and have them each say a word or two so you can hear their voices."

Jim went around the table, introducing Linda, Javier, Susan and Fitz.

"There's one more member of the team, but he's away at the moment. His name is Tony Nicoletti. Together, we are the remaining members of the NWIDI group I told you about when I was in Munich. Now here's the problem."

Jim outlined the recent events regarding the Six and then described in detail the President's request.

"So you see, my friends and I have been asked to represent the United States and to facilitate a dialog between our leaders and *the Teachers* that will lead to an alliance strong enough to destroy the Six once and for all."

There was another long pause from Sophie's end.

"You'll excuse me if I find this all rather incredible," she finally replied. "First of all, anyone who lives outside the United States knows that if the USA wants to give you something it's because they want to take something of greater value while you're not looking. And secondly, if *the Teachers* wanted an ally, they could pick any country on the planet. What makes your President think they would pick the United States?"

"The United States has the military strength and technical know-how to be a strong partner. And the United States is asking for their help, Sophie, and I doubt if any other country is. All we're asking for is a chance to plead our government's case to *the Teachers*. After that, it's up to the two parties to work things out—or not—on their own."

"I don't know how I can help, Dr. Barnes, or if I even want to. And I'm certainly in no position to bring five or six strangers over to the Other Side. I can't even make the journey on my own yet. I have to be invited and guided."

"Will you at least ask?" pleaded Jim. "You're our only chance to make contact."

"I'll make some inquiries, Dr. Barnes, but I can't make any promises."

"Fair enough, Sophie, fair enough. Now if you don't mind, we have some questions about what actually happens when you make the journey. Assuming we get to go, some of us are curious about what to expect."

"This is Linda, Sophie, and he's talking about me! I'm very concerned about this whole thing because I have a little girl and I don't want to come back with my molecules all scrambled up."

"I don't know how to explain the process. That is, I don't know what actually happens. I know you physically leave this side and go to the Other Side, but I can't put that into scientific terms, Linda. I can tell you that there's no sensation—that is, it doesn't feel good or bad or anything. One instant you're here and the next instant you're there. I've made the journey, if you can call it that, several times and I've never felt any ill effects."

"I have a question, Sophie. This is Fitz Fitzgerald, by the way. Do you always return back to the same place that you left?"

"Yes," replied Sophie. "At least I always have. I've departed from—and therefore returned to—several different locations, so there doesn't seem to be any magic spot that you have to stand on."

"What about arrival points on the Other Side?" asked Fitz. "Are they always the same or have there been different places?"

Sophie laughed out loud before replying.

"It sounds like you are trying to make a comparison to the transporter room on the old Star Trek show, Mr. Fitzgerald, but I don't think it's anything like that. It's very difficult to describe the Other Side but I believe that I've been in a different place each time, if place is even the right word to describe it. In my case, I've ended up very near the person—or *Teacher*—that summoned me and I don't think the locations were ever the same."

THE TEACHERS

"Sophie, it's Jim again. You said that you have to be invited over. You can't just go whenever you want?"

"No, not yet. But that's probably because I'm a novice at this. I'm pretty sure Professor Schmidt was able to initiate the jump at will, but he's been at this for a long time—several years, anyway."

"You said 'jump'—is that your word or theirs?"

"Actually, it's Professor Schmidt's," replied Sophie, pausing to think about Jim's question. "I don't know if I've ever heard anyone else refer to the process. To them, you're simply 'here' or 'there.' Man, you guys are asking some really hard questions!"

"Sophie, this is Susan Fitzgerald. So it sounds like you've seen and talked with these *Teachers*. Can you describe them to us?"

"Wow, another tough question! I remember my first experience very clearly and I remember thinking to myself that they were 'light beings' because while they have a vaguely human outline, their bodies are more fluid, as if made of light or a glowing gas. They always remain at a distance— maybe five or six feet away, but it's hard to tell due to their composition. And I've never made actual physical contact with one. Somehow I instinctively knew that it would be harmful to me or to them or maybe to both of us."

"And when you communicate," continued Susan, "do you speak to them in German?"

"Ah, yes, I guess so, although I've never really thought about it. I speak a number of languages, but German would be my natural choice, I guess. But they don't reply vocally. Their response just ends up in my head without the use of sound or ears. It was very unnerving at first, but now that I'm used to it, it seems quite natural. And I know they can target specific brains because when Becker and I went over with the Professor the very first time, I could hear the Professor asking questions but I couldn't hear the answers. But when I asked a question, I did hear the answer. And sometimes we would all hear the answer to a question. Weird, huh?"

"It sounds like some form of ESP," replied Jim. "Sophie, it's very important that we have a chance to speak with them and specifically with one that can make important decisions. And we need this to happen as soon as possible but based on what you've just told us, I don't understand how you signal them. Do they just zip you away whenever they want to speak with you or do you have some way to initiate a request?"

"So far, I've just been a pawn in this chess game, Dr. Barnes. I don't have a secret bat signal or a magic ring. However, I sense that they are aware of my actions, as if they are watching over me now that I've peeked into their inner sanctum. I'll pass your request along at my first opportunity, but, like I said, I can't promise anything."

"Understood, Sophie, but let me stress again how important this is. Maybe you can remind them that I was the one who provided the triangles they seemed so anxious to get. And please contact Mr. Blass as soon as you hear anything. I will stay in frequent contact with him."

"I'll do that, Dr. Barnes. Goodbye for now and I hope to meet you all in person soon."

Jim punched the End button on the communications device and leaned back in his chair.

"Well, I guess we just wait," he frowned. "I hate this part because we have no idea how long it will be before they contact her again. She's having fun because she's just along for the ride but we have a job to do! I'll call Bill every few hours during the normal work day and I'll let you know the second I hear something. In the meantime, I guess we just enjoy the hospitality of the U.S. Government."

Jim opened the manila folder on the table to add the page containing Bill Blass' telephone number but his eyes widened as he glanced at the top of the mostly blank sheet.

"Guys, take a look at this!"

He turned the folder so the others could read the neatly printed message.

"Your request is being considered."

Chapter 6

Tony's first full day back aboard the Dolphin Diver began with a thunderous boom that startled him out of a deep sleep. As he sat up, a bright flash outside his porthole reminded him that a storm system was scheduled to pass through the area this morning. Since there would be no diving until the storm passed, he considered sleeping in but the smell of fresh coffee from the deck above changed his mind. After a shower and a shave, he dressed and headed up to see what the new cook had planned for breakfast. When he entered the salon, Cesar greeted him from one of the large tables.

"There he is, the man of the hour! I was just coming down to rouse you."

"Why?" asked Tony with a yawn. "I might be crazy, but I am *not* going out in that!"

"No, of course not," laughed Cesar, "but we need to check out the equipment and before we can do that we need to decide what we're going to need."

"We? I thought this was going to be a solo mission?"

"Nobody dives alone on my watch," frowned Cesar. "You will have the lead, of course, but these blue holes—and this one in particular—are very dangerous dives. It would be foolish to jump into that thing alone, especially when you don't know what awaits you once you drop below the surface. Who—or what—are you meeting? Do they understand human limitations under water? No, I'm going along as your wing man and that's that. At the very least, I can carry spare air cylinders in case something goes wrong. Now have a seat and let's figure out what extras we're going to need."

Tony shrugged, poured himself a cup of coffee and joined Cesar just as Rob entered the salon from the bridge.

"So, is this really going to happen today?" he asked, as he refilled his cup at the large coffee urn. "I've been awake half the night worrying about all the things that could go wrong down there, Tony. Are you sure you want to do this?"

"Absolutely! In fact, I'm looking forward to it. This is truly a step into the unknown and I'm eager to find out what this is all about. Sit down and keep us on the right track here."

Two hours later, Caesar had all the equipment assembled on the Dolphin Diver's special dive deck and he was carefully inspecting the rebreather devices. These units would be their best bet on the upcoming dive because they had no idea what depths were going to be involved. He had already checked Tony out at more than two hundred feet and he was confident the older man would be okay down to the limits of the equipment but deep dives presented many risks that a novice could easily forget, especially in the excitement of whatever might be happening underwater. Cesar had never lost a diver, but this event was so off the charts that he was very, very concerned.

"Hey, check this out," yelled Tony from the starboard side of the platform. "It looks like our guides have arrived already!"

Cesar looked over his shoulder and when he saw the dolphins bobbing almost vertical in the choppy water, he grabbed his camera and joined Tony.

"I think they're trying to tell me something again," said Tony, pointing to the nearest dolphin. "Can you record it?"

Cesar held up his camera to show Tony and pressed his finger to his lips to signal for silence. After listening to songs from three different animals, Cesar clicked off the camera and hurried up the ladder to the main deck

"I'm going to get this to Rob for translation. Will you stay here with the dolphins until I get back?"

Tony nodded but when he turned around the dolphins were gone. He scanned the dark waters for several minutes but he couldn't see any sign of them. When Cesar returned, he explained.

"As soon as they saw you leave with your camera, they disappeared. I guess they somehow knew their message had been delivered."

"Could that be? Well, they would be right because Rob is transmitting the recording to the lab back in Belize right now. He has his laptop connected to his cell phone which is somehow connected to the Internet."

"Any estimate on when we'll have the results?

"Rob says it will be a couple of hours, at least. Shall we finish checking out the gear now or do you want to wait for the translation?"

"Let's do it now, I guess, although I don't see any sign of this storm letting up. What's our latest entry time if we want to be back on the Dolphin Diver before dark?"

Cesar thought for a minute and then poked at the rectangular dive computer he was wearing on his wrist.

"Assuming all the worst case scenarios, I'd say we should be dropping below the surface of the Guardian Blue Hole no later than 1:00 p.m. so that means we need to leave here by noon. And you're right, I don't see any signs of this storm lifting. I don't mind getting rained on, but I don't want to get struck by lightning on the way to shore!"

"I guess we'll just keep our fingers crossed and hope for the best," replied Tony, as he returned his attention to the dive gear.

***

After the aborted morning meeting, Edwards went directly to his office and called his southern California regional coordinator. Although the man could not substantiate Gomez' claim, he did confirm that the agent in question should have checked in hours earlier and that his whereabouts was currently unknown.

Next, Edwards called Schröder to get the cell phone number the agent had provided.

Schröder read out the number and then said, "But I've already tried the number a couple of times and I get a message stating that the phone is out of service. He could be in an area where there's no service or the phone could be off."

"When was the last time you heard from him?" questioned Edwards.

"Yesterday, right after he finished the job. I received a text message saying "It's done. Heading north on the next flight."

"Yeah, well it looks like he missed his flight, because he hasn't checked in up north!" replied Edwards.

"So is it possible Gomez' men really did get to him? I assumed Gomez was bluffing during the meeting because there's no way he could have known about our man."

"You mean *your* man!" replied Edwards. "If they have his cell phone, his calls are going to point to you, not to me."

Schröder was silent for a minute.

"I see. Well, I guess it's a good thing I took special precautions before he contacted me. Since I have no other connections in either Baja or southern California, I'm afraid I can't help much with your investigation. Is there anything else I can do?"

"No, I'll handle this. Don't forget the rescheduled meeting at 1:00 p.m." replied Edwards curtly before hanging up.

After spending some time considering his options, Edwards called Gomez. He let the telephone ring a dozen times but there was no answer. He slammed the receiver down, realizing that Gomez had probably anticipated the call and was intentionally staying away from his quarters. Remembering that Gomez and Chen had been acting unusually friendly before the meeting, he tried Chen's quarters but there was no answer there, either. This just strengthened Edwards' belief that the Mexican and Chinese agents were working together—a dangerous situation, since they headed up two of the most powerful arms of the Six.

Meanwhile, in Mednikov's quarters, Gomez and Chen enjoyed another shot of Russian vodka, poured by their host.

"Did you see the look on his face when I told him I had killed his agent?" laughed Gomez. "I thought his eyes were going to pop right out of his head!"

"Yes, and I'm positive that the new German guy was somehow involved. His body language gave him away," added Chen. "Did your men get any other useful information out of the agent before they killed him?"

"No, not really. They have his cell phone, but it appears that he did a reset on it while he was being transported from the airport to the interrogation site because everything was wiped out—the contact list, the call logs, everything!"

"Too bad," frowned Mednikov, "but since Edwards doesn't know that, you should be able to make him squirm a little more by suggesting you have a record of the agent's last calls. Ultimately, though, he's going to claim he had nothing to do with this and the only real link you have is that the man belonged to a group Edwards controls. You can't prove that Edwards had anything to do with sending him to Mexico or that Edwards put out the hit on the civilian. And he's going to make you pay for this morning. I don't know how or when, but he's going to come after you, Gomez."

"I don't care! I've had it with this *imbécil* and I think we should start making some contingency plans."

"Like what?" asked Chen, suddenly very serious.

"Like a Committee without Edwards! I've met his second-in-command a couple of times and he seems like a reasonable person. Besides, he would be the junior member of the Inner Circle, so the leadership role would pass to the next most senior member, whoever that is."

"That would be me," smiled Mednikov.

Both Gomez and Chen stared at Mednikov for a second before all three broke out in laughter again and toasted each other with another round of vodka.

***

After the revealing conversation with Sophie Hoffman, the conference room was abuzz for nearly an hour. The details Sophie had shared about *the Teachers* had piqued everyone's interest and imagination but the note Jim had found in the folder was even more interesting.

"How do they do that?" Jim had asked soon after the note had been discovered. "How do they slip a piece of paper into a folder that was sitting right here in front of us all, without anyone seeing it being done?"

No one had an answer to Jim's question, of course, just as they couldn't explain the mysterious appearance of the GPS coordinates that had led Jim to Linda and Javier, on Mexico's Baja Peninsula, and to Tony's live-aboard dive boat in the British Virgin Islands. These were topics of conversation at almost every meal but the NWIDI team never seemed to get any closer to an answer.

"Let's ask them when we get over to the Other Side," suggested Javier, only half joking. And then, as an afterthought he added, "In fact, maybe we should make a list of all the things we want to ask them. I have a feeling that we're all going to be so caught up in the experience that we might forget why we're there. Maybe we need a script, so to speak."

"An excellent idea," agreed Fitz. "And how they do the little trick Jim mentioned would be a good first question. We need to know what the ground rules are and I, for one, would like to know if they are spying on us twenty-four-seven. If we're really going to work as ambassadors, we need to be able to have private discussions among ourselves to consider all options."

Jim pulled a pad out of the worn, leather portfolio he always seemed to have with him and made a notation.

"Check. That's question number one. Anybody else?"

"Where are they?" asked Linda. "Or if we're over there when we ask, I guess the question should be, where are *we*?"

Jim scanned the table and everyone seemed to be in agreement, so he scribbled down question number two.

"Where did they come from?" added Fitz. "Based on Sophie's description, it's pretty clear they aren't from around here, so where did they come from? And when?"

Jim scribbled some more and then looked up questioningly.

"I guess I'd like to know why they are here," added Susan. "What is their intent, motive or objective, as the case may be?"

Jim scribbled again and then looked around. When no one offered any additional thoughts, he said, "I'd like to add one of my own. I'd like to know what message was carried by those triangles and why it is—or was—so important to them."

Everyone agreed, so Jim added his question to the list before tearing the sheet off the pad.

"If you don't mind, I'll hang on to this, but if you think of anything you want to add, please let me know. It will be in here," smiled Jim, patting his portfolio, "and this is never very far away from me."

"I've noticed that," laughed Linda. "A person might wonder just what's so important that you never let it out of your sight."

"Well, for one thing, the file I received from Professor Schmidt is in here," replied Jim. "It's what got me into this whole mess in the first place and it's become my primary working document. It contains information about the Six and *the Teachers* but there's also a document titled *Those Who Know* that happens to include my name—and I've never understood why."

Fitz pointed to the leather bag and said, "Maybe you should add that to our list, Jim. Why are you on the list of Those Who Know?"

Jim hastily retrieved the sheet of paper and jotted down some text.

"And what is it I'm supposed know?" he laughed.

***

It had been nearly three hours since Rob had transmitted the message to the technicians at Turneffe Wild Dolphin Institute and Tony was growing impatient. The gear for the dive was all checked out and ready to go and the sky was beginning to clear in the south but the window of opportunity, as defined by Cesar, was beginning to close. As

Tony paced the length of the salon for the hundredth time, Rob burst into the room waving a piece of paper.

"Got it!" he shouted.

Tony, Rob and Cesar convened at one of the tables as Rob read the translation.

"Please join us tomorrow morning, one hour after sunrise, at the previously indicated location. You will not need your recording device nor will it be permitted. Others may accompany you to the site, but only you may enter the water. You will be back on the surface in less than an hour and your underwater breathing device will be adequate. We advise you to travel light."

"That last sentence is my own interpretation," added Rob. "The actual message used a lot of words to say it, but that's what they all boiled down to."

The salon was quiet for a minute while the group digested the content of the dolphins' message.

"Well, I guess we're waiting until tomorrow," shrugged Tony. "And it sounds like you're staying topside, Cesar."

"I don't like this," replied Cesar. "But at least I can be suited up and ready to go. We'll take the full-face masks so you can yell for help if something goes wrong."

"Hey, this sounds like a piece of cake," laughed Tony. "What could possibly go wrong?"

Cesar wasn't amused.

"We have no way of knowing whether or not your hosts understand the human body's need for decompression," he replied angrily. "The message says you'll only be below the surface for an hour, but if you drop down to three or four hundred feet, which you could do in just a few minutes, you'll need hours to return to the surface."

"Relax, Cesar. I'll be fine. And if I need hours, then I'll take hours. Like you said, we'll be in constant communication and I'll call out my depth every ten meters as I descend so you can begin planning my exit strategy while I'm meeting with whomever it is I'm supposed to meet."

"I think you should have a larger support crew than just Cesar," said Rob. "If he has to enter the water to help you there will be no one left on the surface for support. The message says 'others may accompany you to the site' so I think I should go and maybe Rigo, too. That would still leave Captain Braydon, Nick and Anne aboard the Dolphin Diver for security."

"I agree," nodded Cesar. "And in light of the change of plans I need to make some equipment changes. Rob, with two more people in the Zodiac space is going to become an issue so would you let the Captain know that we need to get the Dolphin Diver as close to the blue hole as possible? He might want to start looking at his charts now and we should probably reposition the ship this afternoon to save some time in the morning."

Rob disappeared towards the bridge and Cesar turned to Tony.

"What about a practice dive this afternoon? It's been quite a few days and you're going to be on your own."

"A little bottom time might be a good idea," replied Tony. "Besides, there's really nothing else for me to do until tomorrow. But won't that mean reloading and rechecking the rebreathers before morning?"

"We'll use the backups today. Let's go see the Captain and decide whether we dive before or after he moves the ship."

***

Gomez had felt pretty feisty during the brief morning meeting of the Committee but he was not looking forward to the rescheduled afternoon session. Edwards would have had time to verify that one of his agents was, indeed, missing and he was going to be a very unhappy man. Mednikov had suggested that the three comrades not give any indications that they were working together and Chen had hastily agreed. Gomez knew both other men were distancing themselves from him in case things went bad, but he would do the same thing under similar circumstances.

Gomez waited until the last possible moment to enter the conference room, knowing that the others would already be seated. When he finally dashed through the door, he was surprised to discover that Edwards was not in the room. Normally, Edwards was the first one to arrive and everyone assumed this was to monitor when—and in which order—the others arrived.

Gomez took his seat quietly, placed his thin report folder on the table in front of himself and folded his hands on top of it without making eye contact with anyone else.

Seconds later, Edwards entered the room and closed the door.

"I apologize for being late, but I had to attend to a very important matter that could not wait. Let's begin, shall we? I would like to hear status reports from each of the junior members first, followed by each of the senior members. I will hold my report until last. Mr. Purnama, will you begin by telling us what's happening in Indonesia?"

One after another, the junior representatives gave their reports and Gomez was surprised at how calm Edwards seemed. When the Venezuelan finished his brief report on the situation in South America, Edwards turned his attention to the senior members, beginning with Peter Fleck, of South Africa. When it was Gomez' turn, he rattled off the standard facts and figures and then closed with a simple statement.

"As I mentioned this morning, the situation in Baja has been resolved and we are actively pursuing ways to restore the radio network as soon as possible."

"Thank you Mr. Gomez," replied Edwards without emotion before nodding for Mednikov to begin.

Following the Russian's report, Edwards provided routine figures on how the U.S. operation was fairing and then closed with a summary.

"It appears that things are proceeding more or less as usual, even though the governments of most of our countries are now aware of our existence. Perhaps they are trying to figure out what to do about us or perhaps they have reconciled themselves to our presence. Regardless, I see no signs of increased activity against our day-to-day operations and I'm encouraged by that. I suggest we continue to meet briefly each morning in case the situation changes, but for now I think we can resume all normal production and delivery schedules. That is all, gentlemen, and since tomorrow is Sunday, I suggest we forego our meeting and reconvene here on Monday at our regular time. Oh, and don't miss dinner tonight! I hear our new cook has something special planned for us."

While the twelve Committee members filed out of the room, Edwards remained at the head of the table, smiling.

As the group made its way down the hall, Mednikov pulled alongside Gomez.

"Be very careful," he whispered so no one else could hear. "He's up to something!"

***

When the NWIDI team met for their evening meal, Linda, Javier and Mariana were conspicuously absent.

"They received some very bad news this afternoon," explained Jim, as Susan and Fitz took their normal seats at the table. "They've decided to have dinner in their apartment tonight."

"What happened?" asked a concerned Susan. "Are they all right?"

"Yes, they're all fine, physically, but Linda made a routine call to La Paz today and she learned that a close friend of theirs named Carlos had been found shot to death this morning."

"How terrible!" gasped Susan. "Isn't he the man Mariana calls Grandpa?"

"I think so, but he was really just a close friend. Both he and Javier volunteered at the same non-profit and that's where he was found. The police think the murder actually happened yesterday but the body wasn't discovered until this morning when some of Carlos' co-workers arrived for work."

"Do the police have any leads? What about a motive?"

"Not that I know of, but the first day we were here Linda mentioned something about work she and Javier had been doing to thwart the Six. Maybe Carlos was also involved in that."

"Yes, I remember!" added Fitz. "They were intercepting and decoding radio messages of some sort and forwarding the information on to a reporter in Seattle. And that means that whoever killed Carlos might also be looking for Linda and Javier!"

***

Captain Braydon pointed to the navigational chart and explained what he had discovered.

"According to this data there appears to be a very narrow channel right here. I discovered it when I was looking for a spot deep enough to anchor the Dolphin Diver near the shoreline. I was looking for a natural area twenty to thirty feet deep, but this channel is more than sixty feet deep and it extends out from the coastline until the ocean becomes that deep naturally."

"But why?" asked Tony. "Does this suggest that some vessel needed that much draft? And for what purpose? The channel ends at the shoreline and there's no sign that there was ever a dock there, right?"

"That's correct," replied the Captain. "The settlement of Behring Point is about four miles south and there are several fishing lodges in the area, but nothing very old and certainly nothing that would require a sixty foot draft."

"Could it be the work of the Navy?" asked Rob. "That point is pretty close to the Tongue of the Ocean, where the Navy does a lot of underwater testing."

"I suppose that's possible," agreed the Captain. "About a mile and half offshore the sea floor suddenly plunges from sixty feet down to several thousand feet by the time you get over here."

The Captain indicated an oval area further south that was marked on the chart.

"May I offer another possibility?" asked Cesar, as he laid a straightedge on the chart table.

He placed it so that one edge split the channel the Captain had pointed out and he let it extend inland. It was immediately apparent what he was suggesting.

"It could be a tunnel that passes under the edge of the island and opens into the Guardian Blue Hole!" exclaimed Tony, stating the obvious.

Chapter 7

Tony glanced at his watch for the hundredth time and decided that he might as well get up. It was only 4:00 a.m. and sunrise was still more than an hour away but at least he could do something useful instead of tossing and turning. After a shower and shave, he dressed in his swimsuit and a lightweight set of sweats. Without really knowing why, he tried Carley's cell phone again but he received the same out of service message he'd been getting since leaving the Meriwether Mountain facility two days earlier.

He retrieved his dive log book from his desk, opened it to the first blank page and filled in the date at the top of the page: May, 18, 2008. On the line labeled "Location" he wrote, "Guardian Blue Hole, Andros Island, Bahamas." He closed the small book and put it back in the desk. If things didn't turn out well, at least that much of his dive would be recorded. He hadn't slept much during the night and a variety of morbid thoughts had crossed his mind—including the possibility that this could be his last dive ever.

Tony hadn't felt so apprehensive about a mission since his days in Southeast Asia and he knew he needed to settle himself down before he entered the water so he sat on the edge of his bed and tried to remember some of the breathing exercises he had learned in the Far East.

Some minutes later, there was a light knocking on his door.

"Tony, it's Rob. It's almost 5:00 a.m. and we should probably start loading up the Zodiac."

Tony opened the door and greeted Rob.

"Good morning. I'm all ready. In fact, I've been up for quite a while."

"Yeah, me too," replied Rob, "and I'm only going along for the ride. Are you ready for this?"

"As ready as I'll ever be, I guess. Let's go grab a quick cup of coffee and then we can get this show on the road!"

Captain Braydon had decided against anchoring the Dolphin Diver in the channel he had discovered the night before because of the depth and the uncertainty of what might lie on the bottom. He had opted, instead, for a shallower spot just north of the channel with a white, sandy bottom devoid of coral and other fragile marine species. Since they had arrived at low tide, the Dolphin Diver could ride out the changes in water level without any fear of running aground.

As the Zodiac pushed away from the dive platform, Tony looked over his shoulder and waved to Captain Braydon, Anne Jeffries and Nickolas Banks before turning his attention back to the task at hand. Cesar was piloting the Zodiac with Rob and Rigo on the widest seat, directly behind him. Tony had opted to take the point position on the smaller seat near the front and he now focused all his attention on the approaching shore. With hand signals, he directed Cesar to a small patch of sand along the otherwise grassy area of the coastline.

Using a human chain, the equipment was quickly transferred from the Zodiac to a spot above the high tide line and then the four men heaved on the bow line to haul the inflatable boat as far out of the water as possible. Cesar tied the line around a large rock and the group began the short, ten-minute hike to the Guardian Blue Hole. Tony glanced at his watch. It was 5:45 a.m. and the orb of the sun was now partially visible above the horizon.

Cesar helped Tony into his dive gear and checked everything thoroughly before they reversed roles. Even though Cesar wasn't planning to dive, he wanted to be ready in case the need arose.

"Now what?" shrugged Tony as they looked at the large fresh-water pool that was the main entrance to the famous blue hole. The words were barely out of his mouth when a dolphin cleared the surface in a high, arching jump and then splashed back into the water.

"I guess that's my queue! I'll see you guys back here real soon. Don't leave without me!"

Tony lowered the full-face mask and adjusted the straps. After a quick sound check with Cesar, he flashed his friends the thumbs up sign and slowly waded out into the water. Within just a few steps he came to a sudden drop off and found himself floating head-up thanks to the buoyancy of his rebreather BC. After one more thumbs up, he pressed the BC's purge button and began a slow descent into the unknown.

***

Linda, Javier and Mariana had stayed in their quarters and out of touch the remainder of Saturday so the other NWIDI team members were surprised when they entered the dining room for Sunday morning breakfast. Since none of the others had known Carlos, it was awkward, but they expressed their sympathies and Linda accepted graciously before changing the subject to a less somber topic.

"Have we heard from Tony recently? I can't wait to find out how his meeting with the dolphins went."

"Actually, I was going to bring you all up to speed as soon as our food was served, but there's no need to wait. He checked in with Bill Blass yesterday afternoon and told him that the dive had been moved to early this morning. Apparently the dolphins delivered another message yesterday and rescheduled the rendezvous for one hour after sunrise today so with any luck Tony has already had his meeting and he's back on that boat of his."

"So when do we get a report?"

"He told Bill he would check in after the dive and when he does Bill is going to set up a time for us to call Tony direct. I'm hoping we can make that call right after lunch."

"Not being able to receive calls is becoming a real inconvenience," said Fitz. "When we thought we were all going to be here together I didn't think much of it, but now, with Tony in the Caribbean and your friend Sophie in Germany, it's a real pain. Are you sure those hot-shot intelligence folks can't find a solution for us?"

"I'll ask again," replied Jim, "but they weren't too happy when I asked for this outbound line and they reminded me several times that there would be no incoming call service."

"Maybe it's time to go up the chain of command a ways," smiled Fitz. "Like all the way to the President himself. If he can carry a secure cell phone, I don't see why they can't rig up something that makes it look like our calls are originating in D.C. or anyplace other than here."

Jim shrugged again. "All I can do is ask, but you're right—it's a real pain right now."

"Speaking of Sophie," said Susan, "has Bill heard from her? I wonder if she's any closer to arranging that meeting for us."

Before Jim could answer, one of the food service workers that normally took care of the team entered from the kitchen area pushing a serving cart full of covered plates. He placed a plate in front of each team member, removing the heat-keeping covers as he did so. He served Jim last but before he stepped away from the table he handed Jim a small, brown envelope.

"Sir, I believe this is for you."

While Jim was examining the envelope, the worker pushed the cart back through the door and disappeared.

"What's that?" inquired Linda as she served Mariana from a special plate the kitchen always prepared for her.

"I don't know," he replied, opening the sealed envelope with his table knife. He unfolded a piece of matching brown paper, studied it for a minute and then said, "Huh!"

Without another word, he pushed back his chair and rushed through the kitchen door, leaving his teammates surprised and silent. A couple of minutes later, he returned with a very puzzled look on his face.

"What's the matter?" asked Susan Fitzgerald. "You look like you've seen a ghost."

Jim held the small brown note so the others could see it.

"All it says is '*Conference room at 9:30 a.m.*' but do any of you recognize the lettering?"

There was a brief silence before Linda blurted out, "The paper you found in your file!"

"That's right," nodded Jim. "I think this matches the printing on the paper that was mysteriously placed in a folder while it was closed and in plain view of all of us."

"*The Teachers*?" asked Javier to no one in particular. "So where did this note come from?"

"Well, that's a good question! Joe says he found it on the food cart after he loaded it up and he's sure it wasn't there when he put the last plate on. He went across the room to get silverware and when he came back it was on top of one of the food covers."

"What does the envelope say?" asked Linda.

"Just my name—Dr. J. Barnes," replied Jim, as he examined the envelope again before handing it to Linda. "I guess we'd better eat up and be in the conference room at 9:30 a.m. to see what this is all about. Maybe they've approved our request for a meeting!"

***

Since the regular morning meeting had been canceled for Sunday, most of the Committee members hung around the cafeteria after breakfast and enjoyed an extra cup of coffee and a brief break from the intense feeling that seemed to accompany Edwards and his demands. Edwards never joined his comrades for breakfast and today had been no exception, but his name had certainly been mentioned many times. Now, in smaller groups, his behavior was being discussed again.

"Maybe he's bipolar," suggested Gomez, only half joking. "Yesterday morning he was a raving lunatic and by afternoon it was as if the whole 'Baja hit man' incident never happened. I don't get it."

"Like I told you yesterday, he's up to something," warned Mednikov. "Between yesterday's two meetings he hatched some sort of plan and I have a feeling none of us is going to like it—especially you, Gomez!"

"Well it sounds like we're not the only ones who are concerned," whispered Chen. "I sat between the members from North Korea and Pakistan this morning and they are both frustrated and concerned. As junior members, they haven't had to deal with Edwards in person very much and they've already had enough of his attitude."

"Same here," nodded Gomez. "Iran and Venezuela would throw him overboard in a minute if this were a ship! I wonder what the feelings are among the other senior members."

"It's about the same," offered Mednikov. "I've been trying to poll them informally and none of them are happy with this situation. In fact, Daniel Manchester, the Englishman, thinks all this underground bunker stuff is nothing more than personal paranoia on Edwards' part. There's no doubt that Edwards is in trouble in his own country, but Manchester thinks we would have all been fine if we would have just kept a low profile for a few days. He also thinks that the longer we stay down here, the more we risk losing control of our own organizations. Apparently his Number Two is already making noises about taking over."

"I trust my own Number Two," stated Chen, "but there are a few further down my chain of command that I always keep my eye on—or at least I did until I ended up here. So I guess I'm a little concerned, too."

"And you know, all we really have is Edwards' word that our identities have been comprised," hissed Gomez. "Nobody in my organization can confirm that this NWIDI group actually fingered me, by name. What if Edwards set this whole thing up so he could move in on our territories? Or take over our entire organizations? Like you, I trust my closest deputies, but if they thought I were dead there would be a mad scramble for the top and there would be chaos in Latin America for a while. My organization would be ripe for the picking!"

"Where does Fleck, the South African, stand?" Chen asked of Mednikov.

"I haven't heard him express any real opinions one way or the other. He's a tough one to read and I suggest we be careful what we say around him until he speaks out on his own. I wouldn't be the least bit surprised if Edwards has a spy in our midst."

"You mean other than Schröder?" smiled Chen.

"I'm not yet convinced that the German is anything more than an overly ambitious status climber. But even if that's all he is, we need to be extra careful around him. Let's mix a little while there's an opportunity, but don't be too opinionated. It's more important that we get a sense of how the others feel right now. And when this little gathering breaks up, let's meet in my quarters and compare notes some more."

In his office, Edwards watched the morning's events unfold—as he did every morning—thanks to his private interface into the facility's extensive system of hidden security cameras. Later, he would have this recording transcribed by a lip-reader but he had already learned some useful information. While Gomez, Chen and Mednikov had managed to keep their faces turned away from his cameras, Edwards now understood why he had been unable to contact Gomez and Chen the previous day—they had been hiding out in the Russian's quarters! He had never trusted the former KGB agent and now his suspicions were being confirmed. But Edwards smiled, because he had the advantage—he had eyes on them!

***

Tony kept a close watch on his digital depth gauge as he slowly submerged below the surface of the Guardian Blue Hole. However, the first thing he noticed about his surroundings was how clear the water was. From the surface, the entrance to the blue hole appeared to be a shallow, miniature pond surrounded by grasses and small bushes. But once Tony had stepped off the ledge, it was apparent that at least a portion of the pool was very deep. In the distance, he could see the vertical surface that made up the opposite wall of the cave he was descending into. As he called out "forty feet" to Cesar, he caught a glimpse of something below and to his right. When he turned his head, he was almost face-to-face with a large dolphin that had apparently been behind him during his entire descent!

The dolphin chattered something and then swam straight down.

"I think I was just told to get a move on," commented Tony.

"You're doing just fine," replied Cesar from the surface. "Maintain your current rate of descent and keep an eye on your rebreather console."

"Roger that. I'm just passing fifty feet now."

As Tony continued to descend and call off depths, he scanned his surroundings with interest. Here and there, long stalactites hung from outcroppings indicating that this part of the cavern had once been above the surface.

"One hundred feet," reported Tony. "My aquatic friend is still circling below me, so I guess we have a ways to go. The console is showing all systems normal."

"Understood," replied Cesar. "Steady as she goes."

When Tony reported in at one hundred ninety feet, there was a distinct change in his voice.

"One ninety, Cesar, but something's happening because several more dolphins have joined the party."

"You'd better check your console in case things get busy down there."

"I just did and everything seems to be fine. Hold on, I think I see something shiny below me!"

"*You may stop your descent now*," Tony heard someone say.

"Cesar, was that you?"

"I didn't say anything, Tony," came the reply from the surface.

"Well I did! Who else is on this comm line?"

"Please relax, Mr. Nicoletti. We are communicating with you mentally so your associate on the surface won't be able to hear us. You may respond mentally or by vocalizing your thoughts but if you choose the later your associate will hear only your side of the conversation. Do you understand?"

"Yes, I understand," stuttered a confused Tony.

"You understand what?" replied Cesar. "I didn't say anything!"

"Cesar, I believe the meeting has started. Either that or I've gone completely mad. At any rate, please ignore anything you hear from me unless I specifically say your name. I'm hearing the other side of the conversation but apparently you can't. Please stand by."

"Roger that!"

"I think this will work best if I speak out loud," stated Tony to whoever was listening.

"As you wish. First of all, we would like to thank you for responding to our request. There have only been a few times in history when we have requested the assistance of human beings and you are the first to ever respond so again, thank you."

"You're welcome, I guess," replied Tony. "Who are you? And where are you?"

A shiny metallic sphere slowly rose into Tony's field of view.

"We are here," came the reply. *"And you can call us by any name you are comfortable with. We don't really have names in your context."*

"Well, you can call me Tony. Are you inside this sphere?"

There was a pause and then, *"That's a difficult question to answer, Tony. The object you see is an extension of our senses, but we are not physically enclosed within it."*

"Ah, like a submersible drone! I get it. Okay, since I have a limited amount of time at this depth, let's get right to it. How can my crew and I help you?"

"We, too, have an issue with depth. We cannot function properly any closer to the surface. That's one of the reasons we specifically requested your help—you have the technology and skills necessary to meet us at a mutually acceptable pressure. We selected this location because it offers the necessary depth for us and protection from the ocean for you.

And now for our problem. We have a facility nearby that has remained hidden since its creation but it is now under threat of exposure. It was you and your friends that first discovered it, Mr. Nicoletti, and over the past few years various bits of information have leaked out. Now, we fear that our secret will be exposed to the world and that would be a very bad thing."

"You mean the site off the coast of South Bimini!" shouted Tony, hurting his own ears in the process. "The site where Frank disappeared!"

"That's correct. Your naval forces have received a number of complaints that suggest their charts of the sea-floor bottom are incorrect and they are planning to re-survey the area very soon. When they discover that their charts are, in fact, wrong, there will be an investigation and that will bring many curious visitors to the area. We need you to provide a cover while we evacuate the facility and destroy any evidence that it ever existed."

"But how can one small boat keep the U.S. Navy away? At best they will arrest us and at worst they will blow us out of the water!"

"We have a plan that should not involve the destruction of your vessel. It takes advantage of your existing involvement in dolphin research and it will also provide the human species with several significant benefits. Our plan will force your Navy to postpone their survey until we have left. Once we are gone, they can examine the area all they want."

"I will do whatever I can, of course, and I'm sure my crew will agree. What's this plan of yours?"

"There are too many details to provide here. Our dolphin friends will begin delivering instructions to your ship

tomorrow but in the meantime we request that you move your vessel to the vicinity of our facility and begin making routine dives. It's important that you appear to be conducting some type of research in case your Navy has observers in the area."

"Okay, we can be underway as soon as my team and I get back onboard but you do realize that communicating through the dolphins is cumbersome, right? We have to make a recording, transmit it to Belize and then wait for the translation to be transmitted back to us."

"We understand and that situation is about to change. As soon as you reach your ship, contact your research facility on Turneffe Atoll and ask them to send you their most recent prototype by the fastest possible means. It has some capabilities that even they haven't discovered yet and it will help with the coordination efforts. You should begin your ascent now. Your teammates will be getting worried."

"Wait! I must ask you about my old friend, Frank Morton, who went missing near the facility you're asking us to protect. What happened to him?"

"We think it would be better if you ask him that question in person."

"What? When?"

"Soon. Now please begin your ascent."

And with that, the oxygen alarm on Tony's rebreather console sounded. He momentarily panicked and quickly began his ascent but as soon as he did the alarm went silent.

"What was that?" Cesar yelled through Tony's earpiece.

"Just a friendly nudge," replied Tony, smiling to himself. "I'm on my way back up."

***

Jim, Linda, Javier, Fitz and Susan sat huddled around the conference table anxiously waiting for 9:30 a.m.

"I wonder how they will contact us?" asked Linda. "Do you think they will suddenly appear on the table the way the notes have?"

Before anyone could answer, the conference calling device in the middle of the table emitted a sharp tone followed by a brief silence and a second tone.

"*Greetings,*" said a metallic-sounding voice from the device. "*We have chosen to address you as a group using a device you are familiar with. Our normal method of communications can be unnerving to your kind and it is difficult to manage when there are so many of you. Mr. Barnes, are you present?*"

"Yes," replied Jim, still in shock. "Yes, I'm here along with Linda and Javier Reyes and Fitz and Susan Fitzgerald. And we thank you for agreeing to meet with us."

"*We understand you have something you wish to discuss with us, Mr. Barnes, and this is an initial interview to determine if we should move forward with that discussion. Please elaborate.*"

Jim grabbed a piece of paper from the folder in front of him and read the text he and his teammates had drafted.

"Ah, yes, well, we have been asked by our government to explore the possibility of establishing a formal dialog between their representatives and yours to discuss matters of mutual concern."

"*And what might those matters be?*"

"In summary, they involve the Six and the threat they pose to both of our species," replied Jim.

"*We believe we are capable of protecting ourselves from all adversaries. Why would we need the help of your government?*"

"To be honest with you, my associates and I have wondered the same thing. Nevertheless, we have been asked to pose the question and we agreed to do so. Just for the record, I was the one who provided you with the five lost triangles, so maybe you could agree to an initial meeting as a favor to me."

There was a long pause and Jim was afraid he had angered the mysterious voice and it had disconnected.

"Hello?" he asked.

"Yes, Mr. Barnes, we are here. We were discussing your statement and we have decided to grant your request for an initial meeting in return for your discovery and care of the triangles."

"Great!" exclaimed Jim. "Where and when shall I tell our government's representatives to meet you?"

"No, you misunderstand. We are only agreeing to meet with you and the others in the room, not with your government. We still see no reason to do that."

Jim pushed back a bit.

"Perhaps we can convince you to talk with our government when we meet."

"Perhaps we can convince you not to return to your government when we meet. Please be in this room at the same time tomorrow morning. And you may bring the small one, if you wish."

There was a single short tone from the communications device and it went dead.

Chapter 8

The NWIDI team waited silently for more than a minute after the communication terminated, but there was no further sound from the device—apparently the "conference call" with *the Teachers* was over.

"Well, that's a little rude," Javier finally said. "They didn't even say good-bye."

"Dealing with these creatures is going to take some getting used to," agreed Jim, "but it will be worth the effort. Can you believe that by this time tomorrow we'll be face to face with alien beings? I've waited all my life for an opportunity like this!"

Jim was obviously on a high and in the best spirits any of the others had seen since their reunion seven days earlier.

"I'm excited, too," replied Linda, "but I have no intention of taking Mariana with us. They clearly extended an invitation to her, but that's not going to happen."

"Yes, and I can't help wondering what the motivation was behind that," frowned Javier. "Do they really think they can convince us not to come back?"

"I don't know, but it certainly is a bit troubling," said Susan. "However, leaving Mariana here should make it obvious that we have no intention of staying. This whole idea of traveling to this Other Side is beginning to sound like a bad idea to me."

"Oh, come on!" exclaimed Jim. "They were just being friendly, that's all!"

"I know you're on Cloud Nine, Jim, but I didn't sense anything that I would call friendly from the voice we just heard and I'm not sure these aliens are even capable of emotion. I find it a little strange that they always refer to themselves as 'we' as if they are speaking as a collective. Susan is right—we need to be on alert and not let our guard down until we know their true motive. I also suggest that we stay together and not let them separate us."

"Strength in numbers?" smiled Javier. "Somehow I think that once we're on their turf we will be totally and completely at their mercy."

Jim held up the note he had received earlier.

"I think we may be at their mercy even here because they seem to be able to visit us any time they wish. I, for one, can't wait for tomorrow's visit, but I'm also anxious to know what Tony learned this morning. Let's call Bill Blass and see what he's heard. Anybody need a break first?"

Blass had, indeed, received a call from Tony and he passed along Tony's cell phone number to the NWIDI team. Jim dialed the number and the team waited for Tony to answer.

"Tony Nicoletti here. Who is this?"

"Tony, it's Jim and the gang. We're all dying to know how your meeting went. Can you give us an update?"

"Oh, hello, guys! My phone's caller ID says 'Blocked' so I didn't know it was you. The dive and the meeting both went very well, and I have some interesting news to share with you. Is everybody there?"

"We're all here and we have some big news for you, too, but please tell us all about your adventure this morning"

"Okay, well it seems that the mysterious things Frank, Jill and I saw on our dive off the south coast of Bimini are actually part of a facility built and used by *the Teachers*. Bits of information from our dive apparently leaked out and resulted in a number of complaints about the Navy's charts of the area. There have been so many inquiries, in fact, that the Navy is being forced to re-survey the entire southern coastline. When they do, they will rediscover the three-hundred-fifty foot wall and this time the public scrutiny will prevent them from hiding the truth. Our new mission is to keep them out of the area until *the Teachers* can evacuate the site and destroy any evidence that it ever existed. Once that has been accomplished, the Dolphin Diver will head back to Belize and the Navy can survey all they want."

"How the heck are they going to destroy the facility without creating a huge tsunami?" asked Jim. "And why would the Navy have hidden the truth in the first place?"

"I didn't ask and they didn't say but I don't have all the details yet. We are supposed to receive further instructions from the dolphins once we reach the site. *The Teachers* asked us to air freight a translator from the research lab in Belize and it should be here tomorrow. They're going to provide the necessary modifications to allow us to communicate with the dolphins in real time!"

There was excited murmuring around the table at Meriwether Mountain before Linda finally addressed Tony.

"Tony, that's incredible! My head is spinning just thinking about this device. The things the dolphins can—and probably will—tell us about our oceans will completely change the way we interact with our environment."

"I agree," replied Tony, "but before we can start doing any real research we have to get past our task of confusing the Navy."

"I know you're proud of that ship of yours, but how do you plan to stand up to the U.S. Navy?"

"A very good question," laughed Tony. "The best I could get out of them was that their plan *probably* wouldn't result in the destruction of the Dolphin Diver! But at this point we're committed to the mission and we're proceeding at full speed to the south Bimini coast to await further instructions."

Jim glanced around the table to see if anyone had anything more for Tony but everyone seemed to be lost in their own thoughts.

"Tony, it appears that your news about the prospect of communicating with dolphins has caught everyone here by surprise—a very pleasant surprise—and I'm sure we'll have a million questions for you later. Can we set up a regular time to call you each day?"

"Sure, that would be great. I'm an hour ahead of you, so how about if you guys call each morning right after your breakfast? That would be about 10:00 a.m., my time. If necessary, we can schedule a second call in the afternoon. By the way, didn't you say that you had some big news, too?"

"Yes we do but it doesn't hold a candle to your news. It seems that we have been granted an audience with *the Teachers* tomorrow morning at 9:30 a.m., our time. Maybe we should wait to call you until after we get back. What do you think?"

"Absolutely!" replied Tony. "The number you have is my cell, so call anytime. Maybe I'll have some more news about the dolphin translator by then, too. Hey, it's been a good day all around, team! The Captain wants to see me on the bridge so I have to run, but I look forward to hearing about your trip tomorrow. Talk to you then!"

Jim pressed the End button and leaned back in his chair smiling.

"Well, it sounds like things are going to get exciting in the Bahamas and Tony is right in his element. However, I wouldn't trade places with him for a second!"

"Not even to talk to a dolphin?" frowned Linda.

"Well, okay, maybe I'd trade places for a few minutes, but I have a feeling that our own meeting with *the Teachers* is going to be just as exciting. I don't know what we've gotten ourselves into, Linda, but I think the rules, as we know them, are about to change. Let's take a break until after lunch and then meet here to go over our plan for tomorrow one more time. And then I guess we should place a call to the President and bring him up to speed."

"I disagree," objected Fitz. "You were the one who originally questioned the Government's motives, Jim, and tomorrow's encounter is just a trial run. Let's wait until we've had our first meeting and we have a better sense of the mood of *the Teachers*. If you call the President now we're going to get a lot of pressure to do and say specific things. I'd rather be able to play it by ear for now."

"I agree," added Javier. "After tomorrow's experience we can develop our own agenda and then notify the officials."

"Don't you think they'll get a little suspicious if we all disappear at the same time?" challenged Jim.

Javier nodded.

"Sure, if they even notice, but they won't be able to question us about it until we get back and maybe by then we'll have a plan. I'm not saying that we shouldn't tell them—I'm just saying that we should wait until we have something significant to report. Maybe you can pass the word to the local staff that we're going to have an extended meeting in here and that we need to be left alone for the morning. We could even order an urn of coffee and some bottled water for 9:00 a.m. to make the cover story believable."

"That sounds like a good plan," replied Jim. "I'll go take care of the arrangements for tomorrow now and then I'll see you all at lunch in a couple of hours."

***

Gomez, Chen and Mednikov hung around the CV-13 cafeteria until all the other members had wandered off to spend the rest of their Sunday relaxing, as best they could, in the underground complex. As they passed the small recreation room, Gomez noticed that only a few of their comrades were making use of the facility and he couldn't help wondering what the rest of them were up to.

In Mednikov's small apartment, the three men settled down to compare notes from the morning.

"Did anybody pick up anything of value?" asked the Russian.

"Not me," replied Gomez, "but I may have branded myself a rebel because most of them didn't really want to talk to me."

"Well, you did have a pretty serious showdown with Edwards a couple of days ago. What about you, Chen?"

"The only real piece of information I picked up was a comment by Rivera, from Venezuela. He questioned out loud whether or not Edwards had—and I quote—'outlived his usefulness.' That's a pretty bold statement for someone from a country that isn't even a formal member yet."

"It certainly is," replied Mednikov. "Let's make an effort to stick close to him and see if his comment was a serious sentiment or just tough-guy talk. I've been reviewing the original agreement that was signed by our predecessors back in the late sixties and it won't be easy to get rid of Edwards. There's no established policy for removing a Committee member, especially the Chairman. Even if his own organization wanted him out, they would be foolish to do so now and surrender the seniority they enjoy. They would almost certainly wait until their Chairmanship rotation is up next year. However, I don't intend to spend the next year of my life in this hole."

"And Edwards would never give up control, even if we voted him out," said Chen. "He told me the other day that if I ever challenged him again it would be my last day on the planet, or something to that effect."

"I wouldn't expect him to give up control without a fight," replied Mednikov, "but without the support of the others we run the risk of being on the losing side of a power struggle. And that's especially true for me, since I'm next in line to become Chairman. As for removing Edwards, I think we all know that there's only one way to do that."

"What about an accident?" questioned Gomez. "A tragic but fatal accident would eliminate him without exposing our personal feelings."

"Yes, but under those circumstances his Number Two would simply move up to fill his remaining term as Chairman. As I said earlier, I think that would be a big improvement, but I'd rather see a vote of no confidence because that would end his term and begin mine. Edwards is a problem at the individual level, but American leadership in general has not been good for our organization and it's time for a change."

"I agree," replied Gomez, "but if the Committee isn't willing to take action or if we can't get a majority you should know that I will pursue other options because I don't intend to spend the next year down here, either."

"Understood," acknowledged the Russian.

***

As soon as the "away team" had returned to the Dolphin Diver, Tony had called a meeting of the full crew to explain the new plan. Although the Captain had expressed some reservations about taking on the U.S. Navy, the anchor had been hoisted in a matter of minutes and the boat headed northwest, towards South Bimini Island.

After the call from his teammates at the Meriwether Mountain complex, Tony had retired to his room to rest and ponder the new mission. The one-hundred-forty mile trip would take the Dolphin Diver about sixteen hours, so he had plenty of time to do both.

He was awakened by a knock on his door and the sound of Rob's voice.

"Tony, are you going to join us for dinner?"

Tony looked at his watch and was surprised to see that it was already 6:00 p.m.

"Yes, I'll be right there," he called back as he slipped on his sandals and ran his fingers through his graying, wavy hair.

Upstairs, everyone except Captain Braydon was seated at the large table in the salon when Tony arrived. As was his style, Terry Hedges had served the food family style and tonight's spread included meatloaf, mashed potatoes, corn and fresh baked bread.

"Wow, that looks good," commented Tony as he slid between divemaster Cesar and first mate Nick. "I don't know what happened to me, but I guess I slept all afternoon. Does anyone know where we are?"

"The Captain really has his foot in it and we're making excellent time," replied Anne. "When I came in for dinner we were just about to make the left turn at the top of Andros Island."

"So we've already passed the AUTEC facility, then. Was there any reaction from the Navy?"

"No, but the Captain didn't really expect any. We had already cleared Bahamian customs before you came aboard so they're probably aware that we are in the area, but the Dolphin Diver is just one of many research vessels in this part of the Atlantic and we should be able to stay anonymous for a while."

"I'll bet the Captain has been at the wheel ever since we left the blue hole, right?"

"That's right," frowned Anne. "Nick and I take turns riding shotgun with him, but he insists that he's going to pilot us all the way to our destination. It's almost like he's obsessed with it."

"Well," laughed Tony, "I think I know how he feels. We're both a couple of old warriors who have been given the unexpected gift of one final mission and we both want to experience every minute of it. The Captain's part of this job is to get us there as quickly and safely as possible. After that, he'll pretty much be on stand-by and I think he knows that. This is his time to shine and we need to let him enjoy it. Just continue to keep an eye on him and make sure fatigue doesn't become a factor."

"And what about you?" asked Rob. "You slept all afternoon—you must have been exhausted from the dive."

"Yes, but I also didn't get much sleep last night. In case you guys hadn't noticed, I was more than a little concerned about how things would go. As it turned out, the dive went exactly the way Cesar had planned it, but when I started my descent this morning it was all I could do to make myself breathe in and out. I haven't felt that way since my days in Southeast Asia and that was a *long* time ago."

"And yet your voice sounded perfectly normal over the intercom," said Cesar. "I didn't detect the slightest hint of anxiety until the oxygen alarm went off just before you started back up. I checked your gear, by the way, and I couldn't find anything out of order. It must have been a false alarm."

"I don't think it was an equipment malfunction, my friend. I think it was their way of telling me that the meeting was over. And once I stopped my descent and began communicating with them, I felt completely at peace. I didn't realize it at the time, but now I remember it as a very calm, logical conversation."

"I know we're supposed to get further instructions tomorrow after we have the translator onboard, but we're going to have a minor problem before then," said Rob. "If the water where we're headed is really three hundred feet deep, we won't be able to set an anchor. I suppose we could cruise around in a circle, but that's going to look pretty odd, don't you think?"

"Uh, yes, it certainly is. And now that you mention it, why haven't other boats discovered the same problem over the years? We can't be the first boat in history to anchor in that area and everyone would expect the bottom to only be about seventy-five feet down."

"At our current speed, we're going to arrive about 2:00 a.m." said Anne. "Maybe we should get the Captain to slow it down a bit and postpone our arrival until after the sun is up."

Tony nodded his agreement.

"I'll go talk to him as soon as we're done eating. In fact, I'll take him a plate so he doesn't starve up there. Will you or Nick follow about five minutes behind me? I'd offer to stay with him, but I have no idea how to drive this thing. I'm afraid you two are going to have to alternate with each other until we reach South Bimini."

Later, when Tony went to the bridge, he discussed the issue of anchorage with the Captain, who listened with one ear, ate with one hand and still managed to keep the other hand on the wheel.

"So here's what I was thinking," explained Tony. "What if we put the extra four or five hours we have to good use by changing our direction now and entering Bimini waters from the northeast rather than from the south? If there are any Navy observers around, we'll look like just another trawler coming down from Freeport. It won't fool them for too long, but maybe it will give us a slight advantage."

"That's not a bad plan, Tony. I'll need to do some calculating to determine just how far east and north we can travel to still reach our destination at sun-up, but I'll do that when one of my shadows returns to the bridge. They're awfully worried about me, you know—like I've never sailed for sixteen hours at a time."

"Captain, we old guys have to keep proving ourselves, over and over again. I had the same problem with Cesar when we were prepping for the dive. You would think I'd never jumped into a bottomless blue hole with a bunch of aliens before!"

Tony and Captain Braydon had a good laugh before Nickolas Banks reached the bridge. When he took over the wheel, the Captain shifted his attention to the large nautical chart spread out on the map table and Tony returned to the salon.

"Well?" inquired Rob.

"Well, I convinced him that we should sail east and north as far as time allows so our arrival at daybreak will appear to be from Freeport rather than Andros. He's doing the math right now and then we'll be changing course. Our new arrival time is 7:00 a.m. and I'd like it to look like we sailed in with a plan in mind. Cesar, let's get a small dive party in the water as soon as we arrive. We may have to drift dive if the boat can't be anchored, but at least we'll appear to be just another live aboard spending the day in the area. Hopefully we'll have a better plan before the end of the day."

"Okay, I'd like to get the gear set up now so who's going to be in the dive party?"

"How about you, me and Rob? Anne and Nick are going to be up all night keeping the Captain company and I think Rigo may need to spend some time in the engine room since the Captain has run the engines so hard."

"Very well. I'll excuse myself, then, and go get things ready. I assume you and I will use the rebreathers again?"

"Sounds good to me. What about you, Rob?"

"I'm already a little concerned about killing time for an hour in three hundred feet of water, so this probably isn't the best time to learn a new technology. Standard scuba gear for me, please."

Rigo also excused himself from the table, leaving just Tony, Rob and Anne in the salon.

"So how soon can we expect this new translator?" asked Tony. "Apparently I slept through the arrangements this afternoon."

"It left Belize City about 2:00 p.m. on its way to Miami and from there it's being flown to the South Bimini airport on an island hopper that's scheduled in about 9:00 a.m. tomorrow. Once it reaches the island, I've made arrangements to have it sent by courier to the beach, where one of us will pick it up in the Zodiac."

"Wow! How did you put that all together from here?"

Rob tapped his head with his index finger and said, "Kidneys!"

"What about the necessary modifications? Who is going to do that—and when?"

"I have no idea," shrugged Rob. "You're the dolphin whisperer, my friend! I was hoping you would have that answer."

"Not yet, but I guess we have to trust *the Teachers* to know what they're doing. As long as we follow instructions, the rest is up to them. Maybe we'll run into a dolphin wearing a tool belt during our dive tomorrow!"

"Yeah, maybe *that* will happen," laughed Rob. "Listen, Anne needs to nap before it's her turn back on the bridge and I was up before dawn myself so if you don't mind, we're going to retire early. Anne, or whoever is on watch at the time, will wake us all up before we reach our destination tomorrow morning. Until then, I think it's good night for me."

"Okay. Hey, I appreciate all you two have done to hold this thing together. And Anne, your help on the bridge is way beyond the call of duty—especially for an honored guest! Thanks, you guys."

"Are you kidding?" replied Anne. "We are on the trip of a lifetime, about to communicate directly with dolphins and who knows what else. I wouldn't miss this for *anything*!"

Tony sipped another cup of coffee and chatted with Terry Hedges for a few minutes before grabbing a cold beer out of the galley refrigerator and heading off to his room. As he opened the door, Tony noticed that the light was on and he cursed himself out loud for being wasteful.

"That was my fault," said a familiar voice from behind the door. "I was afraid that if I sat here in the dark I'd scare you to death when you came in."

"Frank!" shouted Tony, at the top of his lungs. "Where have you been for the last five years?"

Chapter 9

Immediately after lunch, the NWIDI team moved to the conference room and placed a call to Sophie Hoffman. Even though it was after 9:00 p.m. in Germany, she answered on the first ring.

"Good evening!" greeted Jim. "You are on the speaker phone with the whole gang, minus Tony. Sorry for such a late call, but we have some exciting news to share with you. We've been informed that we will be meeting with *the Teachers* tomorrow morning!"

"Wow, that is exciting news!" replied Sophie through the communications device. "You're going to be blown away with the place, so be prepared. I was so awe-struck on my first visit that I could barely speak—if speak is even the right word. Anyway, you'll see what I mean when you make the jump. Just try to relax and take in everything you can. Once you get back you can process the experience and try to make some sense of it. I'm really happy for all of you!"

"Sophie, this is Linda. You make this sound so wonderful but I have a concern. They suggested that we bring my four-year-old daughter along and implied that they might try to convince us not to come back. Do you think they might hold us against our will?"

"Absolutely not!" replied Sophie emphatically. "And they won't need to convince you to stay—you'll come to that conclusion all by yourselves and I'm sure that's all they meant. As for your daughter, I can't imagine what the experience would be like for a child, but I'm guessing it would be like her first trip to Disneyland only a hundred times better. However, I understand your concern, so I would suggest leaving her behind on your first trip. Once you've experienced the Other Side first-hand, I'm sure you'll want to share it with your daughter."

"Sophie, it's Jim again. You said something a minute ago about speaking to *the Teachers*. Will there be a language issue or do they speak English?"

"Once you're on the Other Side, they will communicate in a manner I can only describe as mental telepathy. Their words will just be in your head without actual words being spoken. I don't have a clue how it's done, but that's been my experience. At first I replied by speaking out loud because that's how I'm used to conversing, but I'm slowly learning to reply mentally. It takes a lot of concentration and effort but I'm working on it because it seems to be what they prefer."

"So will we be able to speak to each other?" asked Javier.

"Ah, good point! Yes you will, but only if you speak out loud. And it gets a little weird if they address just one member of your group. The rest of you won't hear *the Teachers'* side of the conversation but they *will* hear your side. I think you should ask about the protocol right away and let them explain how it's going to work."

"Is there any chance they will try to separate us?" asked Fitz.

"I have no idea. When Becker and I made our initial jump we were with Professor Schmidt on this side, but he wasn't present once we completed the jump. I assumed he must have had other business because when we returned to the basement of my apartment building he was with us again and one of my associates later told me that the room had been empty while we were gone."

"Sophie, you keep using the word 'jump' to describe the travel." noted Jim. "What do you mean by that?"

"Oh, sorry. That's their word for the process of traveling to or from the Other Side. It seems to happen instantaneously but to be honest I've never asked about the technical details of the process. However, if you're curious, don't hesitate to ask them because nothing I've asked about so far seems to be off the table. I haven't always understood the answers I've received, but they don't seem to have any secrets, so ask away! They actually seem to enjoy providing information—maybe that's why they call themselves *the Teachers.*"

"I have one more question for you," said Jim. "You said you made your first trip with Becker. Have you ever seen anybody else you know over there? I mean someone obviously from this side that you didn't travel with?"

There was a pause while Sophie thought about Jim's question.

"No, I guess not, Dr. Barnes. I hadn't really thought about it until you asked, but I don't remember seeing *any* other humans on the Other Side except for Becker and I only saw him the time we went together. It's odd that I didn't realize that before."

"Is there anything else you think we should know before tomorrow morning?"

"Dr. Barnes, I made my first jump with no prior information whatsoever—just a keen interest in finding out what it was all about. I survived and you guys will, too. Just relax, enjoy and try not to over think this. There's no way you can prepare yourselves for what you are about to experience, so don't waste any time trying."

***

While the other members of the Committee enjoyed their first day off since entering the underground complex known as CV-13, Buzz Edwards spent the day sequestered in his private office working out the final details of his plan.

Although it was patterned after the twelve facilities scattered across the world and owned by their respective host countries, CV-13 had been engineered to even higher specs. The other facilities had been hardened to protect occupants from the sudden attack of a rogue nation but CV-13 had been designed to withstand prolonged siege by the entire free world. In addition, CV-13 had a sophisticated communications center that connected to the outside world through a major hub in Havana. This underground link provided the occupants of CV-13 with untraceable telephone and Internet connections to any place in the world.

It was over one of these secure telephone circuits that Edwards was speaking to his next-in-command back in Washington, D.C.

"Have things back there settled down at all?"

"Yes, a little," replied Tom Danielson. "But the FBI really made a mess of your office and most of your staff members are still in custody. So far, they haven't linked your department to mine, so we're able to function more or less normally. However, we are keeping our heads down and spending a lot of time doing the work the government actually hired us to do. It's cumbersome, but necessary. How are things there?"

"A little tense, but I'll manage. Do you have any news on the whereabouts of those do-gooders I asked you about?"

"Nothing new, I'm afraid. It appears that the Navy has jurisdiction, but I haven't been able to get any more information than that. The location where they're hiding those people is a very closely guarded secret but we'll figure it out soon. I just need a little more time."

"You can have all the time you need but I don't want you to let up on this. Destroying that group—every single one of them—is my number one priority. And beyond that, we need to hunt down anyone who has knowledge of that file that came out of Munich. Until we have this contained, our organization remains in real danger."

"I understand, and I assure you we won't rest until we've taken them all down and reacquired the file."

"Good," replied Edwards. "I also have another task for you. Although I'm being told otherwise every morning, I believe some of our friends are beginning to lose control of their operations. In particular, I think our Mexican friends are losing control of the cartels again. The last time that happened, our deliveries were disrupted for months, so I think we need to prepare for the worst. I'd like you to start making some quiet inquiries into the possibility of purchasing directly from South America and eliminating the middle men in Mexico."

"But what about the transportation logistics, Buzz? We've looked at this option many times in the past and it's always been more economical, in the long run, to let the Mexicans move the product across the border."

"I'm working on that problem," replied Edwards. "When you make your inquiries, just preface them with the phrase, 'Assuming we can solve the transportation issue' and don't elaborate."

"Okay, I'll see what I can find out but I'm surprised to hear about the cartels because I thought they had a pretty tight network."

As Edwards, replaced the telephone handset, he smiled broadly.

"Yes, and the Mexicans will be pretty surprised, too," he said out loud.

***

"Hello, to you, too, Tony," smiled Frank Morton when he saw the surprised look on his old friend's face. "Pull up a chair—I think we have a lot of things to talk about."

Tony plopped down in his desk chair and stared in disbelief. Frank waited patiently for the other man to process what he was seeing.

"I can't believe it's really you. How have you been— and *where* have you been? We all thought you were dead. In fact, I'm not sure what I'm seeing right now is *real*."

"I know, Tony, and I'm really sorry, but it's complicated. I'll try to explain where I've been for the past five years but some of it isn't going to make sense and you're just going to have to take my word for it. But let me assure you that what you see is really me—the new me, that is.

"The day Miles Adderly and I made that dive off the coast of South Bimini, we discovered a portal, of sorts, that led into an alien facility deep beneath the island. We both communicated with the beings that created the portal and they asked us to help them protect their secret. When Miles made it clear that he intended to return to the surface immediately and report our discovery to the Navy I had to do something so I pushed him out over the portal where he was sucked in and disappeared. The aliens thanked me and assured me they would take good care of him, but, for reasons I still don't understand, I felt compelled to follow him. So I swam into the same portal and I, too, vanished."

Tony considered Frank's statement for a minute before replying.

"Okay, let's assume I buy your 'the aliens made me do it' tale to explain why. But *where* have you been, Frank? Have you been down there in that facility all this time?"

"No, we were only there for a few days, actually, while *the Teachers* decided what to do with us. Miles was pretty unhappy about what I had done and we were separated immediately. I haven't seen him since but I heard that he finally came around. I, on the other hand, was on Cloud Nine! I have embraced the possibility of aliens on Earth all my life and you and I even searched out evidence that they really existed. But to be there, to interact with them—it was unbelievable, Tony! Returning wasn't ever an option for me and apparently *the Teachers* saw something of value in me because I was soon shipped off to another facility for training and I've only recently returned."

"What kind of training?" asked a dumbfounded Tony. "Do you have super powers now?"

With that, Frank disappeared. Tony blinked his eyes but Frank was definitely gone. Beginning to suspect his own sanity, Tony crossed the small cabin and waved his hand through the space that Frank had just occupied but there was nothing there. When he turned around, Frank was sitting in his desk chair, smiling.

"Would you call that a super power?" asked Frank.

Tony stopped dead in his tracks and then began to laugh.

"I've finally gone crazy!" he told himself. "All this talk about ancient civilizations and alien beings has driven me right over the edge."

"You're not crazy, Tony. You asked me about my training and I tried to show you because I knew you'd never believe me if I just told you. This is part of the 'new me' I referred to earlier. I've learned how to initiate jumps on my own. More importantly, I've learned to control the process so I end up where I want to be—like moving from over there back to the Other Side and then back to here. It actually takes a great deal of control to perform that small feat of magic. Here, you can have your seat back."

Frank disappeared and as Tony spun around Frank reappeared more or less in his original spot behind the door. Tony stepped forward and cautiously reached out to touch Frank's arm. He half expected it to pass right through the apparition but it didn't.

Frank smiled and said, "Yes, it's really me and I occupy real space regardless of which side I'm on."

Finally accepting the fact that his long-time friend really was in the room with him, Tony slapped Frank on the back and smiled.

"It's good to see you again," he said through a broad smile. "I was—we all were—devastated when you disappeared and I blamed myself for not being on that dive with you. As it turns out, I guess I couldn't have made any difference anyway."

"No, probably not, Tony, although you might have decided to join Miles and me on the Other Side."

"I doubt it. And instead, I returned to Seattle and liquidated all the NWIDI assets, per your instructions. Linda, Jim and I each took a third of the resulting cash but now that you're back…"

"You did exactly what I asked, Tony, and I appreciate it. And I don't want or need any of that money. I don't know how they do it, but I seem to have a no-limit debit card that was provided by *the Teachers* when I returned from my most recent training, so my needs are being well taken care of. Now take a seat and grab a pencil and paper—I have some information to pass on before I have to go back."

Tony did as he was told and when he was ready, Frank began.

"Ask your captain to take the boat to latitude 25.694895 North, longitude 79.271905 West and orient it with the bow pointed due north. Once there, he is to lower exactly seventy-three feet of anchor chain and wait."

"But the water there is hundreds of feet deep!" interrupted Tony.

"Yes, and that's why I'm giving you these specific instructions. A cable will be attached to your anchor and one of our seabots will secure the ship to the bottom. I can tell by your face that you doubt me, but we've been doing this for hundreds of years. Trust me."

"We?" questioned Tony. "Frank, you've only been gone a few years. And what the heck is a seabot?"

"Sorry, I should have said that *they* have been doing this for hundreds of years. It's very common for *the Teachers* to refer to themselves collectively, and I've fallen into the pattern myself, I guess. Anyway, the boat will be fine. A seabot is a metallic sphere about the size of a basketball—I believe you saw one on your dive this morning, right?"

"Yes, I did!" replied Tony, suddenly remembering the shiny, metallic sphere that appeared just as his conversation with the beings started. "But I thought those things couldn't operate above two hundred feet?"

"They can't. A dolphin will snare your anchor in a loop at the end of the cable and the seabot will handle the rest. You have to learn to trust us, my friend."

"And then what?" challenged a doubting Tony. "This morning I was told to put divers in the water to make it look like we were doing something meaningful. Is that still the plan?"

"Yes, that's still the plan. You and your crew are going to make some very interesting discoveries over the coming days—discoveries that will force the Navy to postpone their side-scan sonar mapping until after we have evacuated and destroyed the facility. Once that process is complete, we will help you move off the site in a reasonable and convincing manner so the Navy will never suspect what your real mission was."

"So why all the fuss about the translator if you are here to provide instructions?"

"I only returned from training this morning and I wasn't made a part of this mission until just a few hours ago. And I can't be here for the entire length of your mission, Tony, so your primary source of information will be the dolphins. I'll pop in when I can, but I also have to attend to several other tasks. In fact, I need to return now, so please be sure to get those coordinates to your captain and then get some rest—you look terrible!"

"Who's going to make the necessary modifications to the translator?" asked Tony, almost as an afterthought.

"I am. I'll see you in the morning," replied Frank just before he disappeared.

Tony sat in his chair for many long minutes, wondering what had just happened. Had he been hallucinating? Was he drunk? Was this all a dream from which he'd soon awaken? Anything made more sense then what had really happened. Tony looked down at the notepad on his desk and spotted the GPS coordinates. Even in a drunken stupor he couldn't make up eight-digit numbers! He tore the sheet off the pad and headed up to see the Captain.

"How are we doing?" he asked as he entered the bridge.

"We'll be in the area about 6:30 a.m., if my calculations are correct," replied the Captain without looking around.

"Great! Hey, I need your help with something. I have some coordinates that I'd like you to punch into one of your electronic gadgets and locate on a map for me."

"Nick can help you with that. Where did you get them?"

"Captain, if I told you that you'd have me locked up for the duration of the voyage. Let's just see where this place is first and then I'll tell you where they came from!"

Nickolas Banks took the sheet of paper from Tony and entered the coordinates into a laptop that was perched above the map table at the rear of the bridge. On the monitor, an image of a globe spun and zoomed in, finally placing a set of cross hairs in the center of a screen full of blue. Nick manually zoomed out until some land began to show at the top of the screen.

He turned to Tony, handed back the sheet of paper and smiled.

"I think Tony's afraid we're going to get lost, Captain! These coordinates are very close to our destination, just off the coast of South Bimini."

"Tony?" questioned the Captain over his shoulder. "What's up?"

"Okay, but you two have to promise me that you won't think I've gone crazy! A few minutes ago I went down to my cabin to get some rest and I found Frank Morton sitting on the bench behind my door. He told me to write down those coordinates and give them to you. That's where you're supposed to position the Dolphin Diver in the morning."

"Who's Frank?" asked the first mate before realizing who Tony was referring to. "Oh, *that* Frank!"

"You mean this is the spot we're supposed to circle?" asked the Captain. "We certainly won't be able to drop an anchor in the deep water, but I suppose it doesn't matter which point we pick to circle. Tony maybe you should go lie down for a while. You've had a big day."

"No, Captain, this is the point where you are to drop the anchor, releasing exactly seventy-three feet of chain. According to Frank, *the Teachers* will take over at that point and secure the Dolphin Diver as if we were in much shallower water. I know it sounds crazy, but that's what Frank told me!"

"Seriously, Tony, you've probably just had too much excitement for one day. Nick, will you fetch Rob? Tony, please sit down and have some water. I insist!"

Tony was already very confused and suddenly sitting down seemed like a very good idea. He opened the water bottle and took a long drink. When he lowered the bottle, both Rob and Anne were on the bridge.

"What's this I hear about a visit from Frank?" asked Rob in a soft, even voice.

"That's right. I think I just spent several minutes talking to Frank Morton. I know it sounds crazy—it sounds crazy to me, too—but he gave me this position and specific instructions about what we are to do when we arrive in the morning. I couldn't have possibly made up all those numbers and Nick just confirmed that the location is in the same vicinity where we are headed."

Tony repeated to Rob and Anne what he had told the Captain about the anchor and chain and then added Frank's comments about the seabots. He decided to leave out the more bizarre details, like how Frank could jump from one side of the room to the other.

"I saw one of those seabots just this morning, so I know they exist. I can't explain any of this, but it all seems to make sense to me. And besides, we'll know for sure tomorrow morning when Frank comes back to make the modifications to the translator."

"What was that?" asked Anne. "Frank told you he was coming back tomorrow?"

"Yes. We're supposed to get most of our mission instructions from the dolphins and the translator will need to be modified in order to make it work in real time. Frank is coming back tomorrow to take care of that for us and then he has to leave to take care of something else. That's why we have to be able to work directly with the dolphins."

Tony inhaled deeply and tilted his head back onto the chair. When he closed his eyes briefly, Rob nodded his head towards the door.

"Tony, you look exhausted. Why don't you come down to our room and take a short nap. After you've rested for a few minutes, you can tell us all about your visit from Frank."

"Yeah, I guess I am pretty tired, but I can make it to my own room." He pushed the sheet of paper towards the Captain. "Here, you'll need these coordinates in the morning."

As he stood up, Rob took his arm and steered him down the stairs and into the master suite. Tony protested, but Rob prevailed and helped him onto the large king sized bed in the spacious stateroom. Tony was asleep almost before his head hit the pillow.

Back on the bridge, Rob and Anne conferred with Captain Braydon.

"What do you make of our friend's story?" asked Rob.

"Well, like I told him, I think he's had too much excitement. Today was extraordinary, to say the least, and I think his imagination is just picking up where some pretty bizarre reality left off."

"That's certainly possible," agreed Anne. "His story has a lot of fact woven into the fantasy and maybe his mind is just trying to fill in the blanks, so to speak."

Rob nodded. "He's struggled with Frank's death since the day it happened and maybe the fact that we're returning to the site where his friend vanished is more that he can deal with. At any rate, we need to keep an eye on him tonight. In the morning, when Frank doesn't reappear, he'll probably come to his senses and be himself again. If not..."

"Is there any chance he's suffering from side effects of the dive?" asked Anne. "I don't mean his conversation with *the Teachers* and the whole alien aspect of today but I mean from the dive itself. He was pretty deep and breathing exotic gas mixtures. Could it be some sort of dive-related hallucinations?"

"That's a good point," said Rob. "If you'll stay with him for a few minutes, I'll go talk to Cesar and see what he thinks."

As Rob and Anne turned to leave the bridge, the Captain held up Tony's sheet of paper and asked, "What about this?"

"Let's do exactly what he said," replied Rob. "Tony's coordinates are no worse than any we would have come up with on our own and if nothing happens, we can pull up the anchor and go back to our original plan."

Cesar confirmed what Anne had postulated on the bridge: nitrogen narcosis is a very real threat to divers, especially at depth. However, he also discounted it as an explanation for Tony's behavior.

"Tony was certainly deep enough, but the fact that he was using a rebreather would make narcosis almost impossible—that's the very reason we use them on deep dives. Of course, the complex system that mixes the gases and keeps the diver safe can fail, but I examined Tony's gear very carefully after his dive this morning and the digital log shows absolutely no issues."

"Can you think of anything else that could explain this wild story of his?"

Cesar shrugged.

"Maybe Frank Morton really did visit him tonight."

Chapter 10

Jim didn't get much sleep during the night and he doubted if anyone else on the NWIDI team did, either. At the first smell of coffee, he showered, dressed and made his way to the dining room. When he pushed open the door, he was surprised to see Linda seated at the large table, helping Mariana with her breakfast.

"Morning," he said sleepily. "Are you ready for our big day?"

"Actually, I need to talk to you about that, Jim. I've decided to pass on today's trip and stay here with my daughter. Javier and I talked about it until the wee hours this morning and we think it's best if one of us stays behind in case something goes wrong. Neither of us has any close relatives. If we weren't able to get back, poor Mariana would become an orphan. After we know a little more about this jump thing then I'll consider going and maybe Javier can stay behind with Mariana."

"Wow," replied Jim, raising his eyebrows in surprise. "After our work together in southern Japan I'm surprised you'd pass up a chance to meet the beings responsible for what we discovered over there, but I appreciate your concern. I'm pretty sure today's trip will just be an orientation so we can probably manage without you but I think you're missing the opportunity of a lifetime."

"I know, but I feel very strongly about this, Jim. In fact, I tried my best to talk Javier into staying behind, too, but he wouldn't hear of it. He even suggested taking Mariana with us so we'd all be together but I just can't bring myself to do that. I know I'm letting the team down, but the four of you can handle this, right?"

Jim frowned but nodded.

"Yes, I'm sure we can handle it, but I really think you should reconsider. There's still some time before we leave so if you change your mind, just meet us in the conference room.

I'm going to grab a mug of coffee and head back to my room but I hope to see you a little later."

Jim was reviewing the list of questions he and his team had prepared when Javier entered the conference room—alone. Jim shrugged and Javier shook his head.

"I tried my best, Jim, but I couldn't talk her into going. She says it's all about not leaving Mariana alone here but she's terrified about this. In fact, she's so terrified that she has me a little spooked. You don't really think there's any danger, do you?"

"No, I don't and I'm sorry Linda is having such a problem with it. Have you talked to the Fitzgeralds this morning?"

"No, I haven't seen them, but..."

Just then Fitz and Susan came through the door. When Susan asked where Linda was, Jim explained her concerns about leaving Mariana alone.

"She's scared, isn't she?" Susan asked Javier.

He nodded.

"I think we all are," said Susan, glancing at her watch. "I know we're not the first humans to do this, but it's still a scary situation. And in about ten minutes we'll know whether or not we had any reason for concern."

Jim looked at his three teammates as a group and smiled.

"I just thought of another question we should have asked Sophie. We should have asked her what to wear!"

Jim was dressed in khaki pants, a long-sleeved black shirt and an explorer-type vest with a number of pockets. Javier was wearing jeans, a t-shirt and gym shoes and the Fitzgeralds were dressed in light-weight business casual clothes.

When they realized what he was talking about, nervous laughter broke out around the table. If the "climate" on the other side turned out to be arctic, they were all going to be in trouble!

The mood was broken by a single, loud tone on the communications device in the center of the table.

"*Not all of you are present,*" said a monotone, metallic voice.

"All of us who will be joining you are here and we are ready," replied Jim.

"*Interesting,*" said the voice without emotion. "*We are disappointed but we shall proceed as planned.*"

Jim felt a cold chill that made him blink his eyes and when he opened them his jaw dropped. The chill was gone and the scene around him reminded him of a scene from a National Geographic photo spread. Javier, Fitz and Susan were still standing a few feet away, facing him, but the conference table was gone. In fact, the whole conference room was gone, replaced by a grassy hill that gently rolled off into the horizon.

Jim sensed a presence to his left and turned, ever so slightly. He was shocked to see…he couldn't really put a label on it but it appeared to be a tenuous, shimmering object that looked like a tall, thin human with a sheet over its head—except that it was softly glowing and seemed to have a very fluid surface.

"*Welcome to what others of your kind call the Other Side,*" said a warm voice of indeterminate sex. "*Please take a moment to adjust to your surroundings and then we believe you have some questions for us.*"

Fitz was the first to speak.

"Is everybody else seeing what I'm seeing?" he marveled. "It looks like we're in a boundless meadow and the aromas are incredible."

"That's what I see, too," replied Javier. It's beautiful and it feels so…peaceful!"

"I wonder where we are," said Susan. "Is it alright to ask them, Jim?"

"I think so," muttered Jim, still in awe of the being to his left.

"*We will answer all your questions in due time,*" said the voice, "*but we suggest that you take a few minutes to allow your senses—all of them—to take in your surroundings. We understand that humans often return so overwhelmed by what they see here that they cannot describe it to others. We would like to avoid that today, if possible."*

Jim knelt down and tentatively touched the soft surface they were standing on. It looked like lush, dark green grass and that's what it felt like, too. A gentle breeze was blowing and it carried with it sweet fragrances, like those from a thousand kinds of flowers. It reminded Jim of his last trip to Butchart Gardens, near Victoria, Canada, and the aroma invoked a pleasant memory from his past.

"It feels like grass," said Jim, stating the obvious.

Remembering a question they had posed to Sophie, Jim looked around himself in a full circle but there were no signs of any other creatures—just the four of them and the single being to his left. He inhaled several deep breaths of the aromatic atmosphere and addressed his teammates.

"Have you taken in all you can?"

Everyone concurred, so Jim turned to "face" the light being that he assumed was communicating with them.

"I believe we are all ready to proceed."

"Very well. You have prepared a list of questions for us. Let's begin there."

Jim held up the piece of paper he had been studying in the conference room.

"Yes, as a matter of fact we did, so I guess I'll just dive right in."

He glanced down at the sheet to jog his memory and he was suddenly very glad they had prepared the list in advance because he would never have been able to recall the questions now.

"Well, one thing we would like to know is how you've been able to communicate with us in the past. I'm referring to the messages that seem to appear out of nowhere like the sheet of paper you somehow slipped into a folder the other day when it was in plain sight of all of us."

"The answer to that question is complicated but it will be easier to explain once we describe how we brought you here. Let's move on and come back to that question later."

Jim was caught off guard by the non-answer but he shrugged and referred to his sheet again.

"Okay, here's a simple one: Where are we?"

"It's difficult to describe our current location in terms you can understand, but you are in what you might call a parallel universe. Our space exists independently of yours but we share a common time line so while you are here you are not there, and vice-versa."

"Are there other such parallel universes?" asked Javier.

"Not that we are aware of, but they are theoretically possible."

"Well, I guess our next question is irrelevant. We wondered where you are from, but the answer is that you are from 'here,' right?"

"Yes, but your question still has merit. We did not always exist in a part of our own universe that coincided with your part of your universe. And, of course, we did not always possess the ability to move between universes."

"Of course," shrugged Jim, not really following the explanation. "So how long ago did you come here?"

"We first traveled to this part of our universe several hundred thousand of your years ago and we first traveled to your part of your universe shortly thereafter."

"So, before the dawn of civilization, huh?" asked Javier. "That must have been an interesting trip."

"There have been many 'dawns' as you call them— thirty-seven, in fact, counting your present one. But the others all failed, for one reason or another, and yours seems to be on the same course. But we can discuss that later. Please continue with your list."

"Well, our next question was 'when did you arrive?' but you've already covered that so that brings us to the question of why you are here and what you want."

"We came to this part of our universe as explorers of the unknown. We stayed because we were fascinated by the existence of other beings so different from us that showed so much potential. We hoped that by helping your development process along, we could create a partner on the 'other side'— your side—but so far we have been unsuccessful."

"You mentioned the number thirty-seven," challenged Fitz. "Are you suggesting that you've interfered in human development thirty-seven times in an effort to create a culture worthy of being your partner?

"We have provided specific assistance at certain critical times in an effort to stabilize an already emerging civilization but, so far, we have been unsuccessful."

"Yes, yes, you mentioned that," said Fitz impatiently. "But what type of assistance? Are you talking about advanced technology or something like that?"

"Sometimes our assistance has been in the form of technology and sometimes it has been in the form of basic knowledge. An example you might be familiar with is the advanced mathematical and astronomical understanding enjoyed by your own Maya race. We helped them gain a better understanding of their universe, but they squandered the knowledge, using it instead to plan cyclical rituals. In the end, it was another unsuccessful experiment and the knowledge we shared died with their culture."

"Experiment?" challenged an increasingly agitated Fitz. "Is that what we are to you? Just an experiment?"

"Easy there," interrupted Jim. "We're here to learn, not accuse! And that brings us to the last question on our list. What is the significance of those triangles we found buried in the sand near Cuba and what was the message they were carrying? They were obviously very important to you and we'd like to know why."

There was an uncharacteristic pause from the being who had thus far responded to questions with what seemed like practiced answers.

***

Using a private, encrypted telephone circuit, Buzz Edwards was talking to a contact in Havana.

"Yes, I understand the difficulties, Valdes, but I've done the math and I've studied the maps and I think we can make this work. Our current route takes our product from the Pacific coast of Columbia up the western side of Central America and Mexico by narco-sub. We offload along the Sinaloa coastline, where the product is transported overland into the western United States. That trip is more than three thousand miles long and almost all of it is by sub.

"If we shift our transportation routes east, we can shorten the distance to less than seventeen hundred miles and eliminate the Mexicans altogether. And we still make use of our sophisticated submarine technology. It means moving the facility where we assemble the subs, but I think that's doable. And on the up side, we can enter the U.S. through one of the southern Gulf port cities like New Orleans or Mobile and be that much closer to our major markets on the east coast. Besides, the authorities are capturing more and more of our subs in the Pacific and changing our route will throw them off, at least for a while."

"I don't know, Buzz. Shifting our operations from the west coast of Columbia to the east coast is going to be a bigger job than you imagine. There are facilities to acquire and officials to bribe. And my biggest concern is that we have to duplicate the sub manufacturing capability somewhere on the northeastern coast—an area we don't know much about. On the west coast we have the benefit of dense jungle cover to hide our activities, but the eastern side is more barren. The risks could be substantially greater."

"You let me worry about that detail, my friend. I would like you to concentrate on the land transportation logistics necessary to move the present capabilities to a new location in the northeastern part of the country. Find me a location that will provide the necessary cover and locate an overland carrier willing to play ball with us. I realize we'll have to make a substantial initial investment, but it will be returned in very short order if we can reduce our travel time by one third. I'll check back with you in a couple of days and see what you've found out."

Edwards replaced the handset and leaned back in his simulated leather desk chair. One thing his voluntary exile to CV-13 had done was give him more time to focus on the operations side of the Six's global empire. As he contemplated the route changes, he wondered how many other inefficiencies he could correct now that he didn't have the distractions that came with a senior position in the Defense Contract Administration Agency.

***

"Tony, we're about thirty minutes away from the GPS coordinates you gave Captain Braydon last night. Do you want to be on the bridge when we drop the anchor?"

Rob had let Tony sleep as long as possible but he was sure the other man would not want to miss their arrival. Soon they would all know if Tony's "visit" with Frank was fact or fiction.

"I'll be right up," called Tony through his cabin door.

Tony couldn't remember ever seeing the entire crew assembled on the bridge before, but when the Captain gave the order to release the anchor, eight people collectively held their breath. Watching a digital display on the starboard side of the instrument panel, Nickolas Banks called out the depth. Ten, twenty, thirty feet. Tony scanned the surface for any sign of activity, but the water around the ship was calm.

"Seventy-three feet, sir," called Banks, as he pressed a large red button to stop the release of anchor chain.

"Thank you, Mister Banks," replied the Captain. "Stand by."

The Captain held the Dolphin Diver in position, per Tony's instructions. After a minute or two, he slipped the engines into reverse and eased the throttle up ever so slightly.

In a normal anchoring procedure, this act would "set" the anchor into the sandy sea floor.

"Well, I'll be damned!" shouted the normally unemotional Captain. "We're hooked on something!"

Captain Braydon returned the engines to idle and took one more look at his instruments before switching the throbbing diesels off. With the constant vibration of the powerful engines gone, the ship seemed suddenly helpless, bobbing in the Atlantic.

Turning to face the others, the Captain caught Tony's eye. "So when do the rest of us get to meet this Frank of yours?"

Thirty minutes later, they had divers in the water, although Cesar, who was leading the dive, had no idea what he was supposed to be doing. The boat was "anchored" in relatively open water, so there weren't any nearby reefs to explore and he knew that the bottom was far more then seventy feet below them. For lack of a better plan, he took his fellow divers, Rob Jefferies and Rigo Mejia, on an inspection tour of the Dolphin Diver's hull. Tony had tried to talk his way onto the dive team but Cesar had vetoed the request for fear that Tony was still too fatigued. They had all seen him nearly collapse the evening before and three hundred feet of water was no place for a tired diver!

Using hand signals, Cesar pointed out several areas near the stern of the ship where the bright blue paint was severely scratched. Closer examination didn't reveal any structural damage but it was clear that something had contacted the hull.

As the trio moved forward along the port side to examine the bow, they came face to face with an Atlantic Bottlenose dolphin. Surprised, Cesar stopped and signaled for the others to do the same. The dolphin bobbed its head and slowly approached Cesar, who held his position. The dolphin gently placed the tip of its snout against Cesar's full-face mask and emitted a series of whistles and clicks before slowly turning and moving away.

Cautiously, Cesar followed, motioning for the others to stay behind him. The dolphin led the group around the front of the vessel where they were met by several other dolphins who greeted the leader with a variety of vigorous sounds. After what sounded to Cesar like a heated debate, the leader moved down the starboard side to the anchor chain and waited for Cesar to join him. He then dove quickly down the chain, disappearing out of site. Seconds later he returned and repeated the process.

Cesar signaled for his fellow divers to make their way along the starboard side to the dive platform on the rear of the ship. Once he was sure they understood what he wanted, he returned his attention to the dolphin. He nodded his head up and down, not knowing if that meant anything at all to the dolphin, and then began to slowly follow the anchor chain down into the depths.

Cesar had started using the rebreather at all times so he was prepared to descend all the way to the anchor, if that's what the dolphin intended, but he kept a close eye on the unit's digital monitor. When they reached a depth of fifty feet, the dolphin stopped and hung, motionless, for several seconds before continuing on. Cesar noted the behavior—humans would be stopping on the way up, not down, and the stop would be minutes long, not seconds.

As the anchor came into view, Cesar could see that a large loop of steel cable had been placed over the bulk of the anchor, which hung free in the water. The taut cable continued down, disappearing into deeper water. The dolphin swam around the anchor several times while Cesar examined the connection. When he had a good mental picture of the situation, Cesar extended his hand, palm up, hoping that his new friend would understand his gesture to mean "It's your move."

Immediately, the dolphin dove down the cable and, after a quick check of his display, Cesar followed, breaking all his own safety rules about diving alone, especially at this depth.

After several long minutes of descent, Cesar spotted a ghostly object below him that appeared to be attached to the cable. As he got closer, the object resolved into a metallic sphere about a half-meter in diameter. Cesar stopped his descent and examined the sphere, which now appeared to have a shiny bronze-colored surface. The cable seemed to flow into the surface of the sphere rather than being attached by a hook and he couldn't see any blemishes or markings on the object's surface.

The dolphin swam around the sphere, watching Cesar carefully. Cesar was puzzled by the fact that the sphere just seemed to be hanging motionless at a depth of two hundred ten feet. There were no signs of propulsion or thrust and yet the sphere appeared to be keeping tension on the cable and, indirectly, on the Dolphin Diver's anchor chain. When Cesar started to move below the sphere for a closer look, the dolphin interceded and physically pushed the diver back away from the sphere. Cesar tried one more time and was again rebuffed.

"Okay," he thought to himself, "I guess you don't want me to go down there. You win!"

After a final look at the cable/sphere interface, Cesar began a slow assent, staying within arm's reach of the steel cable. The dolphin swam around him but never got more than a dozen feet away until they reached the anchor. When Cesar grabbed onto the device to stabilize himself for a long decompression stop, the dolphin once again approached his mask, made some sounds and then disappeared. Thirty minutes later, when Cesar finally climbed onto the dive platform, he was met by an angry Tony Nicoletti who was dressed in a wet suit and wearing a rebreather. Above him, on the deck, stood the rest of the crew.

"Where have you been?" demanded the elder man. "I was just about to come looking for you—or your body!"

"Sorry, man, but a dolphin insisted on showing me our anchoring system and I just couldn't say no. There's some sort of cable looped over our anchor and it's attached to…"

"...to a metallic sphere at a depth of about two hundred feet! Frank told me all that last night. You didn't have to risk your life to find out something I already knew!"

"Well, I didn't know it and I think they were just trying to reassure us that the ship was safe. I'm also pretty sure this dolphin was trying to communicate with me and it even pushed me away from the sphere at one point. I tried to examine the bottom and that clearly wasn't acceptable."

"Following a fish down to two hundred feet by yourself isn't acceptable, either," barked Tony, clearly angry. "You're supposed to be the expert here and set a good example for the rest of the crew. Taking off on your own like that is totally irresponsible!"

"Chill out, Tony," replied Cesar, calmly. "What I did doesn't even begin to compare with your blue hole dive yesterday, and I'm the younger, stronger, *better* diver! We're in uncharted waters here —no pun intended—and we're going to have to trust each other to make good decisions as new situations arise. In this case, I felt that the goodwill gesture from our new friends warranted a certain amount of risk. But I know my abilities—and my weaknesses—and I would have aborted the dive if there had been the slightest hint of trouble. However, I appreciate your concern. Now you know how the rest of the crew felt yesterday when you stepped into that blue hole and dropped out of sight."

Tony was silent for a minute as he processed Cesar's comment.

"He's right, you know," said a voice behind him. "I've seen you do some pretty risky things but the risk was always warranted by the situation at hand."

Tony was still lost in thought as he turned to face the speaker who had suddenly become the center of attention.

"My name is Frank Morton, by the way. Tony, be a sport and introduce me to your friends."

Chapter 11

"I know you all thought I was crazy last night, but there he is!" stammered Tony.

"Who?" replied Rob, trying to keep a straight face. "I don't see anybody."

"What? He's right there beside you! Don't tell me you can't see him!"

At this point, Rob couldn't stifle the laugh any longer and he cracked up. He turned to the newcomer and extended his hand.

"I'm Rob Jefferies and this is my wife, Anne. As you can probably imagine, we've heard a lot about you."

Frank shook hands with Rob and Anne.

"I'm pleased to meet you and I promise most of the things this scoundrel told you about me aren't really true."

Frank shook hands with the remaining crew members as they each, in turn, were introduced by Tony.

"I'm terrible with names, so please excuse me if I have to ask a couple of times before I catch on, but I'm very pleased to meet you all. I understand you've all been helping keep Tony out of trouble and I'm grateful for that. Unfortunately, I'm going to have to ask you to shoulder that burden a while longer, because I have a number of chores to take care of before I can return to collect my old buddy here."

"How do you do that, Frank? How do you just pop in whenever you want to?" exclaimed Tony.

"Yes, I was wondering the same thing," added Rob. "I just shook your hand, so I'm pretty sure you are real, but I'm also sure you weren't there just a minute ago."

"That's true, Rob. I can't explain the mechanics of it, but I've been taught this technique we call a 'jump' which enables me to move around more or less instantaneously. When I leave here I momentarily travel to a very special place that's hard to describe and then I shoot myself back here—or wherever I want to go. Just before I showed up on your deck

I was in the underwater facility we're all trying to protect until it can be evacuated and destroyed."

"Teleportation?" asked Nickolas Banks, in awe of what he had just heard.

Frank thought for a minute and then said, "Well, that's actually not a bad analogy. In the old Star Trek movies, individuals were always beamed to or from the Enterprise and never directly from one place to another so I guess this place I mentioned is like our transporter room."

"Is it on the Other Side?" asked Tony weakly.

"Yes! How do you know about the Other Side?"

"Jim, Linda, Javier and the Fitzgeralds are supposed to be making their first trip today. I'd be going with them if I hadn't decided to return to the Dolphin Diver."

"Fantastic! Then I don't need to bore you with all the details about that place. And let me say that I, for one, am very glad you decided to come back to the ship because if our facility is discovered..."

"Wait a minute!" interrupted Cesar before realizing what he had done. "Sorry, Mr. Morton, but if Tony knows about a place called the 'Other Side' he hasn't shared any of that information with us. Can you please elaborate?"

Frank looked at Tony and shrugged.

"Okay, but I don't have much time so I'm going to be very brief. Maybe Tony can fill in the details later.

"As I understand it, the Other Side is a region of space in a parallel universe that happens to coexist with a region of space in our universe. With the right training, it's possible to move back and forth between these universes more or less at will. That transit is called a 'jump' by the beings who taught me how to do it."

"*The Teachers*?" asked Tony again.

This time Frank's eyebrows indicated surprise. "You know about *the Teachers*, too? Wow, you are way ahead of the game, my friend!"

"Not so much," mumbled Tony. "It's actually Jim who has all the info—or at least whatever is known by our team.

He has a friend in Germany who has made several jumps and when I left she was trying to set up something for the team back in D.C. We are on a mission for the Pres..."

Tony halted in mid-sentence, realizing that he had given away far too much information already.

"Oops," he finished.

"Please continue," insisted Rob. "I believe you were about to tell us something about the President. So that's why you were hauled off the ship back in the British Virgin Islands!"

"Come on, guys, I shouldn't have said anything at all. It's all very top secret, hush-hush stuff. But, yes, I was flown back to Washington, D.C. to be reunited with all my old NWIDI teammates—except Frank, of course—and we were given a very special mission. However, I got tired of waiting around for things to happen, so I talked them into letting me rejoin the Dolphin Diver just before the meeting at the Guardian Blue Hole. And that's all I can tell you!"

"Wow!" said Frank, shaking his head. "I guess I have a lot of catching up to do, too. I didn't know the team had been reunited and I didn't know you were clued in to *the Teachers*, either. So I suppose you must also be aware of the Six and how they fit into the puzzle."

"No," replied Tony. "I'm aware of them, but not how they fit in. Their name was mentioned in a file that Jim ended up with—a file that also mentioned *the Teachers* and included a hand written foot note mentioning you. But I don't think Jim ever figured out how it all fits together."

"Well, it's a long story, but suffice it to say that the reason I was brought back early from my training is to deal with the Six. But first, we have to deal with this Navy sea floor survey and make sure they don't find our facility. So when is this translator going to show up so I can get out of here?"

Rob checked his watch and then removed a small piece of paper from his shirt pocket.

"If everything goes according to schedule, it should be here in about an hour. The charter flight is due in about fifteen minutes and then I figure it will take them about thirty minutes to get it couriered over to the beach, where we will meet them in the Zodiac and then another fifteen minutes to get it back here."

"Can you contact someone at the airstrip and cancel the courier?" asked Frank. "If you can, I'll pick it up in person as soon as the plane touches down and have it back here in a flash—literally!"

Confused, Rob wrinkled his forehead before realizing what Frank was suggesting. He reached for his cell phone and dialed a number he had written on the piece of paper. A minute later, he slid his cell phone back into his pocket and smiled.

"Done! And the plane is actually running a little ahead of schedule—it's on final approach right now!"

"I'll be right back," said Frank just before he disappeared.

"Now that's a trick I'd *really* like to learn," commented Rigo, who had been silent in the presence of the newcomer.

During the lull, Tony climbed down onto the dive platform and helped Cesar stow his gear while the rest of the crew chattered noisily about the appearance—and disappearance—of the infamous Frank Morton. When they were all assembled on the rear deck behind the salon, Rob addressed Tony.

"How much of what he was talking about do you really understand?"

"A little, but not all of it. Like I told Frank, Jim Barnes is really the expert on all this stuff, but I picked up a little bit during the week I spent with him in D.C. The file I mentioned was given to Jim by a German professor while Jim was attending a conference in Munich and that apparently started a whole sequence of events that included an attempt on Jim's life by this group known as the Six. Jim had assembled a small team of experts in D.C. and they were able to use information from the file to identify the group's leaders, who have now gone into hiding. The U.S. Government has a big push on to find and eliminate them but I get the feeling they don't have a clue where to look."

"Is this the reason you were called back to Washington?" asked Rob.

"No, I think that's in the hands of the intelligence community. Our mission was to…oh no you don't! Nice try, but I already told you I can't talk about that!"

"So who or what is this group called the Six?" asked Anne. "Is this the same bunch we ran into back in Jamaica?"

"Yes, I think so. With your help we were able to track that guy in Kingston back to the Defense Contract Administration Agency, a part of the Department of Defense. When Jim's people connected Buzz Edwards to the same agency, things really began to unravel for the Six and that's when Edwards and his associates went into hiding.

"As for what they are, all I know for sure is that they are international in scope and they control most of the bad stuff that goes on in the world. We're used to thinking of individual crime syndicates such as the Mexican drug cartels, the Russian mafia, organized crime in the U.S. and the Triads from China. Regionally, these groups operate independently, but Jim's people think they all answer to a small group of people who have wiggled themselves into positions in six major governments around the world. However, there's also some evidence that this core group now has a number of minor members."

"Wow, they sound powerful and very dangerous," said Anne. "But I don't see the connection to what we are doing here or to your friend Frank."

"Jim's file also included a section about a group called *the Teachers*. They are apparently a group of aliens who have been trying to manipulate human development—in a good way—for a very long time. There's some evidence that the Six has learned about *the Teachers* and the U.S. Government is concerned that a battle between good and evil—pardon the cliché—would result in a global catastrophe."

Rob snapped his fingers.

"I remember now! Didn't you tell me that Frank had asked you to protect some group? Does that mean that Frank is…"

"I don't know," replied Tony softly. "But I can assure you that he didn't have this 'super power' of his when I last saw him on Andros Island six years ago."

Before anyone else could pursue the subject of *the Teachers*, Frank reappeared on the deck holding a device about the size of a small laptop computer. His sudden appearance startled everyone.

"We're going to have to tie a bell around your neck!" scolded Tony.

"Sorry, folks, but there's no easy way to do that. If someone can get me a small Phillips screwdriver, I'll get this modification completed and be out of your hair."

Rigo disappeared down the stairway to the engine room and was back in less than a minute with a small tool kit.

Rapidly, Frank removed the back of the device, replaced several components with similar items he had in a shirt pocket and then replaced the back.

"That should do it. Let's give it a try."

Handing the device to Tony, Frank climbed down the ladder to the dive platform and then reached back up for the translator. After placing the unit on the platform, he carefully connected one end of a cable to the box and dropped the free end into the water. When he slid a switch on the side, several small lights blinked to life on the top surface.

Leaning close to the device, he said, "This is a test from the vessel Dolphin Diver. Please respond if you are able to hear this message."

From a small speaker on the unit's top surface came the weak reply of a mechanical sounding voice.

"Message received. Please increase the gain, if possible."

Frank adjusted a knob on the translator and then tried again.

"How's this?"

"Much better." The response was stronger this time. "Please address us as Station Alpha in future communications. We will have some specific instructions for you later today. At that time we would request that you place a diver in the water with underwater photographic equipment. Will that be possible?"

Frank looked up to Cesar, who was still on the deck above.

"Yes, of course. I have both still and video equipment in my room."

Frank repeated the response into the translator.

"Single frame equipment will be sufficient, but please be sure it is set to include the date and time on each image. Your diver will be met near the back of the vessel by a small pod of rare striped dolphins. Please take a number of photographs and then return to the surface. These photos should be communicated to the local authorities along with your exact location. Please include a warning that all other vessels must stay out of the area until the pod moves on. Are those instructions clear?"

Frank scanned the crew to see if there were any questions.

"Understood," he said loudly.

When there was no reply from the translator, Frank stood and said, "Well, I guess my work here is done. Good luck with your distraction project. I need to return to help shut things down but I'll look in on you guys whenever I can."

"Frank, what about this shut down process? How do you plan to destroy the facility without blowing us out of the water up here?"

"I don't know how they do it, but I'm told the area will experience what feels like a very minor earthquake and then it will be all over. All that will remain is a large underwater cave system like the rest of the blue holes in this area. You've already been in one of their former facilities—it's called Guardian Blue Hole now, but before civilization came to Andros Island it was a major training center. At least that's what I'm told. Hey, gotta run! See you later."

And with that, Frank disappeared, leaving the crew of the Dolphin Diver staring at empty space.

"Yup! I definitely need to learn that trick," repeated Rigo.

***

Jim's question about the importance of the triangles seemed to have caused some confusion or disagreement among *the Teachers*, but an answer finally emerged.

"*The triangles are, indeed, very important to us and we would like to express our gratitude again for finding them and returning them to us. When a female of your species first showed us the photograph we were very 'pleased' I think you would call it.*"

"That would be Sophie," Jim told his teammates.

"*Yes, Sophie. She was introduced to us by Professor Schmidt and it has turned out to have been a very fortunate introduction. It is, in fact, the primary reason we granted your request for an audience.*"

"You still haven't told us why they are so important," pressed Jim.

There was another pause before the reply.

"*We travel within our own universe in a way that you could never understand and the objects you refer to contain the information necessary for us to return to our place of origin,*" replied the voice.

Now it was the humans turn to ponder.

"Wow," said Jim, finally breaking the silence. "So you were trapped here with no way home until Frank found those things? You know his discovery was a complete accident, right?"

"Yes, but had your associate not been in the area that day we might never have recovered our lost information. He has become something of a legend with us."

"Frank?" asked a shocked Jim. "Frank Morton is a legend with *the Teachers*? I can't believe it! Then why did you allow him to drown?"

"Frank Morton did not drown. He joined us voluntarily and he has chosen to remain with us indefinitely. In fact, he is meeting with the one you call Tony right now."

"Where has he been for the past five plus years? If he's alive, why didn't he try to contact us?" demanded a frustrated Jim.

"He has been in extensive training far from here and it was not possible for him to communicate with you from that location. He returned today to assist us with several tasks, including the evacuation of a facility we operate near the place you call Bimini."

"The place where he originally disappeared?"

"Yes, although he did not 'disappear'—he simply chose to exist in another place."

"So you've said! How is Tony involved in all of this?"

"Tony and his vessel are going to provide information to the authorities that will force a delay in the marine survey of the area around our facility until we can evacuate and destroy it, but that is of no concern to you."

"What if Tony had decided to stay in Washington with us, rather than return to the Dolphin Diver?"

"We would have found another way to accomplish our objective. Do you have any additional questions on your list? If not, then today's visit is concluded."

"You never answered my question about interfering in human events," said Fitz. "Are we just an experiment to you?"

"We sense anger in your question but it is not justified. It is true that we tested various theories regarding the developmental process of your species but we never caused any harm or pain. Our work was certainly nothing like your experimentation on the lesser species of your own world."

"What about the thirty-six failed cultures you mentioned?" replied Fitz sharply.

"They would have failed anyway, and most of them would have failed much sooner without our involvement. This is also true of your own culture. It seems that the human species can't survive in a stable and permanent environment. You seem to thrive on turmoil, pain and suffering. Each time you reach the brink of success, you find it necessary to fall back into your own misery and you will probably continue repeating that pattern until you eventually destroy yourselves. We do not wish to witness your demise, so we are making preparations to return to our place of origin. We would have left long ago if the 'triangles' hadn't been lost."

Jim suddenly realized the finality of what the being was saying.

"What if humans changed their ways? What if we learned to live together in peace and harmony and started taking care of our planet and..."

"Jim, what are the odds of that?" interrupted Javier. "It hasn't happened in the five thousand years of our own civilization and apparently it didn't happen in any prior civilizations, either. I don't blame them for giving up on us."

"We are not giving up completely," replied the being. *"We are preparing a small group of humans to continue our efforts once we leave but our time here grows short."*

"Wait!" pleaded Jim. "There are those among us who would desperately like to change things and they actually have the power to make those changes—they just need some help from you. They have asked us, specifically because of our triangle discovery, to engage you in a dialog that might lead to cooperation between our species. I beg you to listen to them before you depart."

"We are aware of many individuals who have the qualities necessary to make positive changes, but they are few against the sea of humanity. The odds are just too great."

"No, that's not true! Those who have asked us to secure your help are in control of the United States of

America—the most powerful nation on the planet. I'm not talking about a small group of radicals here—I'm talking about an entire nation!"

There was another pause in the conversation, which Jim now interpreted as an offline discussion by whomever the collective "we" represented.

"*Your proposal interests us,*" came the eventual reply, "*but we need more time to consider the implications. Would you be willing to meet with us again at a later time?*"

"Yes, yes, of course!" exclaimed Jim. "Our government has authorized us to meet with you whenever and wherever you wish to further this conversation!"

"*Very well, then. We will return you to your side now and contact you when we are prepared to discuss this subject again.*"

Jim and the others felt a chill again, and found themselves standing around the table back in the conference room at Meriwether Mountain.

"That was certainly interesting," commented Susan Fitzgerald. "And congratulations to you, Jim! I think you may be on the road to the first intergalactic peace conference in history!"

Jim glanced at his watch. It was 9:45 a.m. The visit to the Other Side had only taken fifteen minutes and yet he felt like they had been gone for hours. He filled a Styrofoam cup from the large coffee urn in the corner of the room and returned to the table.

"Let's take a break, collect our own thoughts and then meet back here. Obviously, we have to report in and advise the President, but I think we should discuss our own feelings first. Does everyone agree with that?"

"Yes, I certainly do," replied Fitz. "Because I don't think we should be as trusting as you apparently do, Jim."

"I picked up on that," smiled Jim. "And I think we should include Linda in our discussions. Maybe the process of relating our experience to her will help us understand our own feelings better. Since we have no idea when *the Teachers* will contact us again, we need to get busy so we're prepared when the call comes."

"Well I, for one, can't wait," smiled Susan. "I don't know what it is about that place, but I felt an inner peace over there that I haven't felt in a long time. I can't wait to get back."

"I know what you mean," nodded Javier. "It's almost addictive. And yet I don't feel like I was being manipulated because I think I still had the ability to reason and even disagree at times."

"You mean like my husband?" replied Susan. "What was up with all that negativity, dear?"

"I guess I'm just disappointed, Fitz frowned. "I expected extraterrestrials to be smarter and kinder than humans, but I didn't expect them to treat us like lab rats."

"And yet you know humans would do the same thing—only much worse!" replied Susan. "They mentioned our treatment of our 'lesser species' but what about our treatment of our fellow human beings? How do you justify the inhumanities done throughout our own history?"

"I can't, of course. I guess I just resented their suggestion that humans are also a 'lesser species.' I'll try to be a better ambassador on our next trip. However, I do have one more question before we break. Did any of you pick up on their comment about preparing humans to remain behind after they leave? What do you suppose 'preparing' means?"

Chapter 12

After the team meeting, it was obvious that Jim, Javier, Fitz and Susan had each come away from their first alien encounter with widely different opinions. During their brief stay on the Other Side, Susan had felt a sense of security and inner warmth that she hadn't experienced in a long time while her husband, Fitz, had felt agitated, distrustful—even angry. Javier had been more neutral during the visit but had returned with a sense that the human race was doomed to fail by its own actions. Jim, much to everyone's surprise, returned hopeful that *the Teachers* could still save humanity from itself and he seemed intent on bringing *the Teachers* and the U.S. Government together in a meaningful dialog. Since the others agreed that this was probably the best course of action, they had chosen to omit *the Teachers'* comment about "preparing" humans to stay behind after they left.

For his part, the President seemed pleased with the NWIDI team's first contact. He had agreed that the team should return when summoned and he even suggested that they could commit his Government to formal negotiations if the opportunity presented itself. It wasn't until the very end of the call that Jim and the others had sensed a hidden agenda.

"Once my team makes contact, we will make our demands known," the President had said, "but until then, please continue on your present course."

The following morning at breakfast, the call to the President was the main topic of discussion.

"Well, I guess you were right all along," sighed Linda as she sipped the last of her coffee. "You expressed trust issues the day we were reunited in Washington and it appears you were right. We're just being used to soften up *the Teachers* and then a government team is going to swoop in and take advantage of the relationship we have developed."

"I expected nothing less," frowned Jim, "but up until yesterday I had held out hope that I was wrong. Somehow we have to make this work, but it's going to be tricky. And we need to be very careful from now on because we never know who's listening to our conversations. *The Teachers* have been in and out of here like ghosts and the government will probably have this whole place bugged now that they know we're getting close. Any ideas?"

"I don't know if it will prevent *the Teachers* from eavesdropping," offered Javier, "but we should be able to beat any facility bugs by meeting outside in the parking lot. I don't know about you guys, but I could stand to get more fresh air, anyway."

"I suppose it's worth a try," agreed Jim. "After breakfast, let's take an hour of personal time and then reconvene topside in the main parking lot. We can discuss future meetings and our immediate course of action then."

When they were assembled in the parking lot, Fitz suggested that they walk a few laps around the large paved area to provide the impression that they were doing some form of group exercise. On the far side of the lot FEMA had been thoughtful enough to install a large wooden picnic table, which Fitz pointed out during the first lap. After passing it two more times, the group stopped on the third pass and sat, as if resting.

"Wow, the walking really feels good!" puffed Linda as she sat down next to Javier. "I sure miss Baja right now."

Jim, who had been bringing up the rear for most of the last lap, flopped down opposite Linda and heaved a huge sigh of fatigue.

"Let's bring this meeting to order before I have a heart attack," he laughed. "As the first order of business, I'd like your thoughts on our phone call. Susan, you didn't say much yesterday. What's your take on it?"

"Well, I don't have any experience in these matters, but I guess I agree with Linda's statement—we're obviously being used. Their intention isn't to make us ambassadors. They just want us to crack the door open and then they're going to storm in and they'll probably trample us in the process."

"Yes," agreed Javier. "It's one thing to be used, but it's another thing altogether to know you're being used and just go along with it."

"I take it no one is happy with the idea of being used as a pawn," said Jim. "So what do we do about it? If we don't get the two parties together, there's no hope for mankind but if we do get them together, we do so by deceiving *the Teachers*."

"Not necessarily," said Fitz. "Maybe there's a way to tell *the Teachers* about our concerns without causing them to reject the idea of a meeting altogether. Put them on alert without putting them off."

"I like that idea," replied Jim, "but I don't know how we can pull it off."

"You got their attention yesterday when you mentioned that they would have the collective ear of an entire nation by speaking to the President's representatives. You continue to push that angle and I'll continue my tone of negativity and warn them against such a meeting. I just have to back off soon enough for you to win the debate. Hopefully they will take my losing arguments to heart and go into the negotiations with their eyes wide open."

"Something like good cop, bad cop?" asked Javier.

"Yes, exactly! It has to look like all of you agree with Jim and that I'm the maverick of the bunch. That way, when I eventually drop out, it will appear that right triumphed over wrong."

"That's better than anything I can come up with," said Linda. "Fitz' plan gets my vote."

There were no dissenting votes, so Jim pretended to gavel the table with his fist and said, "The motion is approved by unanimous vote. Is there any other business?"

"Can we discuss Frank and Tony and their roles in all this?" asked Linda.

"Of course, but I think we've already told you everything we know," replied Jim. "*The Teachers* told us

Frank isn't dead, which is something you've maintained all along. They also said he had been in extensive training and that he'd recently returned to assist them. We don't really know any more than that, Linda. As for Tony…"

"Wait! You also told me they said he had joined them voluntarily and that he had chosen to remain with them indefinitely, right? What do you suppose that means? Do you think we'll ever see Frank again?"

"I don't have a clue, Linda, but that would certainly be a good question for our next visit with them. As for Tony, they said he was going to be used in some plot to deceive the authorities but they also mentioned a marine survey, so those 'authorities' might be our own Navy. Since the Navy is also our current host, I suggest we not discuss Tony or his mission anywhere except up here. Anything else? Anyone?"

When no one spoke up, Jim slowly stood up and untangled his legs from the picnic table seat.

"Ouch! Then I guess we should go back down into our hole and wait for our summons from *the Teachers*. But let's move a little slower, please! These legs are really feeling the results of too little exercise."

***

The crew of the Dolphin Diver had waited all afternoon for the "further instructions" that had been promised by the voice from the modified translator, but the device had remained silent. A guard had been posted overnight, just in case, but by breakfast of the next morning, Tony was beginning to wonder if there was an equipment problem.

Half way through his meal, he couldn't stand the waiting any longer so he excused himself and made his way down to the dive platform where Cesar was currently standing watch.

"Hey, Station Alpha, can you hear me!" shouted Tony. "What's going on down there?"

"There was no reply at first but just as Tony was about to yell again, the odd sounding voice from the previous day replied.

"We hear you loud and clear. There was a slight delay, but we are almost ready for your diver. Please stand by."

"Roger that," boomed Tony sarcastically, "and thanks for letting us know about the delay!"

Quieter, he said to Cesar, "If you're going to have breakfast you'd better go grab something now because it sounds like we might be getting ready to roll."

"No thanks, I'll wait until after the dive. I put my gear together while I was killing time down here, so as soon as they give the word I'm in the water. It shouldn't take long to shoot a dozen or so photos and then I'll grab something to eat."

"You be careful down there, and stay in touch. I'll be right here in case you need a hand."

Minutes later the translator announced that the pod of striped dolphins had arrived and were circling the stern of the vessel. Cesar did a quick communications check with Tony, who was now wearing a headset, before slipping quietly off the dive platform. By now, most of the rest of the crew was peering over the railing of the aft deck. Cesar gave his teammates a thumbs-up and disappeared below the surface.

Almost immediately, Tony heard Cesar shout, "Wow!"

"What is it?" asked Tony.

"They're right here! They were under the boat so I didn't see them at first, but they are here. There's…um…five of them, it looks like. No, make that six! There's a young one that I didn't see! I'm starting my photo session now, so if I don't talk it's because I'm concentrating."

"Roger that! Have fun."

Tony cupped his hand over the microphone portion of the headset and updated the others, one deck above him, on Cesar's progress.

About ten minutes went by before Cesar checked in again.

"Tony, is that translator still on?"

"Yes, it is."

"Well, I think I have all the photos I need, but could you ask them if there's anything else before I surface? Also, ask them if we're going to do this again. If so, it would help to know when they want me in the water."

"Roger. Please stand by."

Tony repeated Cesar's questions to the translator and waited for a reply but the box remained silent.

"Cesar, are they still with you? I'm not getting any response to my questions."

"Yes, they're here, but there seems to be a problem because when sound came out of the hydrophone, they zoomed away as if they were afraid of it."

"Maybe something's gone wrong with the device. Let me try again.

"Station Alpha, this is the Dolphin Diver. Do you read me?"

Below the surface, the striped dolphins had begun to relax but when Tony spoke from above, they scattered again. Suddenly Cesar saw one of the Bottlenose dolphins shoot out of the darkness and approach the dangling hydrophone.

"This is Station Alpha. Is there a problem?"

"We are trying to ask the pod a couple of questions but they don't seem to be responding. Is there something wrong with our equipment?"

"Your equipment is working, Dolphin Diver, but it isn't sophisticated enough to handle multiple species yet. It is tuned for our ears only. Please repeat your questions."

Tony did as requested and then asked, "By the way, who *can* we communicate with?"

"For the time being your device is limited to Bottlenose dolphins from this immediate area only. Perhaps in the future additional capabilities will be added but that decision is not ours—nor yours. Regarding your questions, we wish to repeat the photography sessions at least once per day at approximately the same time until further notice. It's important that your authorities be aware that the pod is still in the area until we are ready to let them begin their sonar scans of the bottom."

"I understand," replied Tony, "but we could manually adjust the date and time in the camera and take a week's worth of pictures in one session if you would like."

"We prefer that the photographs show the actual water conditions and lighting of each day. We do not know how much analysis these images will undergo but it's better to supply accurate photos than to have our diversion exposed."

"Okay, whatever you say," replied Tony. "Every day at the same time until further notice. But do we really need to post a sentry at the translator twenty-four hours a day or is there some other way you can get our attention when you want to talk?"

There was a short pause.

"We will signal you by knocking on the hull of your vessel when we wish to have you activate the translator. Until then, you may secure it safely aboard. Is that all?"

"Ah, yes, I guess so," replied Tony.

"Please transmit the photos as soon as possible. Station Alpha is now terminating communication."

"Did you get any of that?" asked Tony, realizing that he had left the mic on his headset active during the entire dolphin conversation.

"I got enough to know that I get to make at least one dive a day with these beautiful creatures," replied Cesar. "I'm coming up right now."

A minute later Cesar's head broke the surface and he handed Tony his bright yellow underwater camera.

Once the photos and the prescribed message had been transmitted to the Navy's Marine Mammal Programs office in Norfolk, Virginia, Tony returned to the galley for more coffee and to graze the large fruit bowl cook Terry kept on the counter between meals. With the ship at anchor, the rest of the crew had settled into a more relaxed routine. Tony had already suspended the security lookouts and this morning the Captain had eliminated the requirement that someone be on the bridge at all times.

"We have a whole security force swimming just a few meters below us," he had said at breakfast. "I think we can relax for the time being and catch up on some minor maintenance projects."

Rob and Anne wandered into the salon from outside and joined Tony.

"Why so glum?" asked Tony, noticing the unusually somber faces of his two new friends. "It looks like we're on vacation for a while—relax and enjoy the scenery!"

"We received some unsettling news a few minutes ago," replied Rob. "We got an email from Carley indicating that she plans to shut down the bar effective the end of this week."

"That's only three days from now," frowned Tony. "I can see why you would be upset about the short notice, but didn't you offer her a job at the Turneffe Wild Dolphin Institute?"

"Yes, but that's not why she's closing it—she's decided to return to Guatemala. Apparently you told her during one of your 'counseling' sessions that she should follow her heart and she's decided to pass on our job offer and instead return to the jungles where she was a guerilla soldier fighting against the government. We're very disappointed and concerned about her decision. Tony, if you could have seen the condition she was in when we found her behind the bar the last time she returned from Guatemala, you'd understand why."

"Yes, she told me a little about her experiences in the jungle and she also told me that you two had literally saved her life. I certainly never thought she would go back to that. She still has enemies in Guatemala, you know."

"No, we didn't know that," replied Anne, "but that's all the more reason why she shouldn't do this. Rob and I have been talking about it and we think that one or both of us should go back and try to talk her out of this crazy plan.

It seems as though things have calmed down here and you even said that once this mission is complete the Dolphin Diver would be returning to Belize, so…"

"I agree," nodded Tony vigorously. "You will both be missed, but if you can stop Carley I'm willing to make the sacrifice here. Did she say when she's planning to leave Belize City?"

"Only that she is closing the bar effective the end of the week," replied Rob. "But knowing Carley, my guess is that she'll be gone the next day."

"Then you two need to get moving as soon as possible! The island hopper that services South Bimini has already come and gone for today, but maybe we can get you on tomorrow's flight back to the mainland. From there you can catch a commercial jet to Belize. By the time you get home you'll be down to two days, at best, to talk some sense into her. I would go myself, if I thought it would do any good, but the way things ended between us…"

"No, you're needed here, Tony. You're the bridge to *the Teachers* and it's absolutely essential that you see this through. We'll keep you posted and the minute this is over you can fly back to Belize, too. We'll collect the Dolphin Diver when it's convenient."

"Right! Listen, will you be leaving the short wave radio on board? It might come in handy. I've noticed that the cell coverage is pretty spotty up here."

"Absolutely," replied Rob. "And I insist that you move into the forward stateroom as soon as we've off the boat. It's never been an issue with these guys, but after dinner tonight we'll have a crew meeting and I'll appoint you the owner's official representative. We need to do the paperwork anyway, in case you're ever boarded by Bahamian maritime authorities."

That night the crew was informed that Rob and Anne would be departing the following day to take care of a family emergency. Since they all knew that Anne had recently been in Miami caring for her sister, no one even asked what the emergency was and Carley's name was never mentioned.

***

When they returned from their topside "exercise workout" the NWIDI teammates retired to their respective quarters to rest and freshen up. After a long, hot shower, Jim flopped across his bed and instantly went to sleep. When he awoke, he glanced at the clock on his night stand and realized that he was five minutes late for lunch! He dressed quickly and as he dashed out of the room he noticed a piece of paper that had been slipped under his door.

He opened the folded sheet and read the simple message aloud. *"Today. 1300 hours. Conference room."*

There was no signature, but the unique font suggested that this message was from *the Teachers*. The next meeting was less than an hour away!

"I thought we would have more time to prepare," said Javier after Jim showed the others the note he had received.

"Yes, me too," frowned Jim, "but we don't so let's just go with the plan we discussed this morning. Our primary objective is to get them to the table for talks."

"And to make sure they are adequately prepared," added Fitz with a thin smile.

The rest of the team had convinced Linda that it would be very advantageous to get her take on the events and that she should make the jump with them this time. She had reluctantly agreed and it was Linda who uttered the first words after the jump.

"Wow, this is amazing! And it feels so…peaceful!"

"We are pleased that you decided to join us," said a voice in everyone's heads. *"Perhaps you will bring the little one next time."*

"Well, I don't know about that," replied Linda, suddenly brought back to the reality of the situation.

"As you wish. We would like to continue our previous conversation, if you don't mind. You suggested that the

leaders of your government are interested in meeting with us. Is this correct?"

"Yes, yes!" replied Jim, exhibiting a little more enthusiasm than he really felt. "As I explained, they asked us to make initial contact because of the connection they think we have with you."

"We have considered the implications of such a meeting and we see merit in the proposal. How do we proceed?"

"Well, first you need to load all your big guns," sneered Fitz, as if to himself.

"What was that?"

"You know, your big guns. Because our 'leaders,' as Jim calls them, are all scoundrels. Me, I wouldn't turn my back on them for an instant!"

There was a brief silence.

"Perhaps we should reconsider this meeting."

"No!" exclaimed Jim. "Don't pay any attention to Fitz—he's just a malcontent. He's had a couple of bad experiences with our government in the past and now he mistrusts them all. Just ignore him."

"Bad experiences? What kind of bad experiences?"

"Like I said, just ignore him. The next step would be for us to arrange a meeting between you and the representatives of our government. I assume this meeting would take place here, right?"

"That is correct. You must all assemble together in a single location from which we can initiate the transport."

Jim started to speak but stopped in mid-word.

"Wait, what? As I mentioned, our job is to facilitate a meeting with our government's representatives but I don't think we will be in attendance ourselves."

"Then there will be no meeting."

"That's a smart move, my friends," snorted Fitz. "Nothing good can come from this meeting, anyway. They're just a bunch of liars and cheats."

"Fitz! Please stop interrupting," shouted Jim in mock anger. "Now, back to this meeting. You see, we can't actually speak on behalf of our government, especially not with you. We can only arrange the meeting and then our job is finished."

"We will listen to your leaders, but only with all of you present. If that's not acceptable, then there will be no meeting."

"Wow, why do you insist on having *us* present? I'm sure our government won't allow us to take part in such high level discussions and we really have nothing to offer or contribute."

"You will serve as witnesses to your government's actions and words. With you present, they will refrain from 'lying and cheating' as one of you described it."

"Oh, I think you way overestimate our worth to them," laughed Fitz. "If they want us out of the way, they will just…"

"What Fitz is trying to say," interrupted Linda, "is that our presence wouldn't change their behavior. However, we have every reason to believe that without your help our government—our civilization—will fail. That gives you the advantage in any discussions and you really don't need the five of us as insurance."

"There are six of you, of course, but the decision has been made and it is non-negotiable. If the five of you here now do not attend, there will be no meeting. Please deliver that message to your leaders and advise us of their decision."

"Okay, but I'm not very optimistic. How do we notify you?"

"Write your reply on a sheet of paper and place it under your door where you found the message this morning. We will see it and—if there is to be a meeting—we will notify you of the time. Remember, all attendees must assemble in a single location so please indicate in your reply where that transport location will be."

"Well, that's not going to work!" said Fitz, this time in all seriousness. "We are not allowed to leave the government facility where you found us. The government says it's for our own safety, but I suspect otherwise!"

"Then they must come to you, but it is absolutely essential that you all be in the same place at the same time or we can't execute the jump."

"If they agree to the meeting, we'll make the rendezvous happen," stated Jim confidently. "Don't pay any attention to our friend. He doesn't always have his facts correct."

"Yes, we know. After all, he mistrusts us, too. But that's precisely why he must attend any meeting that takes place. We will return you now. Prepare to jump."

Chapter 13

Early the next morning Tony, Rob and Anne made their way to the southern shoreline in the Zodiac, where Rob had arranged for a shuttle to meet them and take them to the small South Bimini airport. Tony wanted to accompany them to the terminal, but Rob was concerned about leaving the Zodiac unattended, so Tony reluctantly said his good-byes on the tiny, deserted beach.

"You guys let me know as soon as you get home," insisted Tony. "I'll monitor that radio frequency you gave me on the sixes and the twelves, my time. You can try my cell, too, but I haven't had any service all morning, so I doubt if that's going to work. The radio will be a more reliable way to communicate."

"I have a little going away present for you," said Frank, as he suddenly appeared beside Tony and extended his right hand toward Rob.

"Man, I wish you'd stop doing that!" shouted Tony with a start. "And how did you know we'd be here, anyway?"

"One of your crew members told me that I could either find Rob and Anne here or at the airport, so I tried here first. I guess I got lucky."

Rob accepted the small brown envelope from Frank and peeked inside.

"Those are the parts you will need to modify a second translator," explained Frank. "There's also a flash drive in there that contains the instructions your technician will need to make the necessary changes."

"What about the localization?" asked Tony. "Yesterday we tried communicating with the pod of striped dolphins and I was told our unit on the boat was limited to a single Bahamian species."

"Hey, I'm just the delivery boy," replied Frank. "But I imagine *the Teachers* thought of that—it would be very uncharacteristic of them to make such a boneheaded mistake. Is this your van?"

Rob and Anne glanced over their shoulders to see a small, white minivan bouncing down the dusty dirt road towards the beach.

"That's our guy," confirmed Rob. "Well, I guess this is good-bye for now. We'll see you soon, Tony, and we'll talk even sooner. And Frank, it was a real pleasure to finally meet the man we've heard so much about. Good luck with your current mission and wherever your travels take you."

Frank and Tony shook hands with Rob, kissed Anne on the cheek and then walked them to the arriving vehicle.

The two former NWIDI teammates waited until the shuttle van was out of sight before returning to the Zodiac.

Tony eyed Frank with curiosity as he reached for the side of the inflatable.

"I'll ride back with you, if you don't mind the company," smiled Frank as he climbed into the boat.

Once the Zodiac was under power and headed back to the Dolphin Diver, Tony said, "So, are you going to teach me how to do that?"

"What? You mean jumping? No, I'm afraid not, my friend. I can barely do it myself and I'm certainly not qualified to teach it. Besides, it requires some modifications to your brain that I'm not sure you'd want done."

"Are you kidding me?" exclaimed Tony. "Don't tell me you let them rewire your head! Is that where you've been all this time?"

"I've been in training, yes, but not just so I can jump. I've also learned to communicate with *the Teachers* on their level—without words, that is. And I've picked up a few other tricks along the way, too."

"Is all this stuff permanent? Are you now some kind of half man—half machine?"

Frank laughed.

"No, I'm physically the same old human I always was. But my mental abilities have been significantly enhanced. You know that old saying that we only use ten percent of our brains? Well, that's pretty close to the truth but with the help of *the Teachers* I've been able to learn how to use more of what I already had."

"So now you're some kind of genius?"

"No, it's not like that, Tony. I probably know more than I did before just because of my exposure to many new experiences, but what I meant was that I've learned to use parts of my brain that weren't doing *anything* before my training—like speaking without words, for example. We used to call it mental telepathy or ESP, but it's a perfectly valid method of communications once you have the right tools and the right training."

"But why do you need to do that? Jim's friend, Sophie, told us that she had visited the Other Side and talked with *the Teachers*, so apparently they can understand us without this special power."

"That's true, but when we communicate with words, we only use one medium—sound—to transmit our ideas. Imagine how rich this conversation would be if I could send you my thoughts directly, including all the images and emotions that go along with them. Not only could I tell you that the sun feels warm on my back but I could show you and you would actually feel it! It's such a rich, complete way of communicating."

"Well, I don't know about that! We've been getting along just fine for a long time. Maybe where these *Teachers* come from this is important but..."

"Tony, it's how dolphins and whales communicate right here on Earth! In some ways, they are much more evolved than we are. That's why *the Teachers* developed relationships with them first. But the old 'opposable thumbs' issue kept rearing its ugly head and eventually *the Teachers* sought out creatures that were better adapted to land activities."

"Like humans?"

"Yes, and a few others, but that's a story for another day. Well, here we are. Listen, you said you tried to talk to the striped dolphins yesterday. How about if I pimp up your translator before I hit the road? I'm going to be busy for a while, so I might not see you again until after the facility down below is wiped clean. But I will be back, I promise. If you talk to the other team members, give them my best, okay?"

Frank completed his adjustment, showed Tony which dial to turn to alter the dialect of the translator and then said good-bye to the crew. He had told Tony he would be back, but his parting words to the other crew members sounded pretty final.

When Frank was gone, Tony found himself filled with an odd mixture of emotions. He was glad Frank was alive, of course, but he wasn't sure he really knew this 'enhanced' version of his old friend. In the brief time they had been together, Tony had recognized some of his old buddy's characteristics, but other things had seemed and sounded strangely out of place. For one thing, the Frank that Tony had known in the jungles of Viet Nam had been fiercely independent and would have never let anyone tinker with his brain!

***

Immediately after returning to the Meriwether Mountain Operations Center, Jim initiated a request to speak with the President. He had been given a protocol to use and somehow his request got passed up the chain of command all the way to the White House. When the President was available, an aide notified Jim, who rounded up the gang and assembled them in the conference room. Jim dialed a special number he had been given and seconds later the President was speaking to them on the conferencing device.

"Good afternoon, Dr. Barnes," greeted the now-familiar voice.

"Good afternoon, Mr. President. The rest of the team is here with me and we are just back from our second visit with *the Teachers*. I think we have some good news for you, sir."

"I could use some good news today, Dr. Barnes. Please go on."

"*The Teachers* have agreed to meet with your people as soon as possible. However, there's one small catch."

"There always is," sighed the President. "What do they want in exchange?"

"Well, it's not so much an exchange, but they insist that we—all five us—be present at the meeting. Otherwise, it's no deal."

There was a pause before the President replied.

"No offense, folks, but this will be a diplomatic mission at the highest levels. You really have no place at such a meeting. The very fact that it ever took place will be classified way beyond Top Secret. I'm sorry, but I can't allow you to attend this historic—and critical—session."

"They were very clear, Mr. President. If we don't accompany your representatives, there will be no meeting. And to ensure that, they insist that everyone attending must gather in a common location for transport. So I assume your folks will have to travel here so we can all make the jump together."

After another pause, the President cleared his throat and spoke, a tone of frustration creeping into his voice.

"I'll get back to you, Dr. Barnes. In the meantime, please suspend all communications with *the Teachers*. Is that understood?"

"Yes, sir!" replied Jim. "But…"

"I'll get back to you as soon as possible. Until then, just sit tight."

And with that, the connection went dead.

"That went well," remarked Fitz sarcastically. "I have a very bad feeling about this whole process."

"What do you mean?" asked Linda. "Either they include us or they don't get their meeting. It sounds pretty straightforward to me."

"That part is certainly true, Linda, but you heard what he said. The very fact that the meeting took place will be ultra-classified. Do you think they're just going to let us walk away from here with that knowledge?"

"Well, they can't keep us here forever, dear," replied Fitz' wife, Susan.

"That is also true. It would cost the government a fortune and there would be too many risks involved. But they have a much cheaper option that I think we should consider a real possibility."

"Let's take a walk!" insisted Jim, pointing to the surface nearly two hundred feet above them.

When they were assembled at the picnic table, Jim returned to Fitz' last comment in the conference room.

"Fitz makes an excellent point," began Jim. "If the government is forced into allowing us to attend this meeting with *the Teachers*, there's no way they're going to let us walk away from here—ever! We have to contact *the Teachers* ahead of the meeting and get our names taken off the guest list."

"But the President specified no contact," objected Linda. "Either way we're in trouble."

"I'd rather be in trouble than in a box! But we need to do this right away, while the government is mulling over their options. We were told to leave a note under my door and I suggest we do that now. I'll explain the situation and let *the Teachers* decide how to handle the government threat."

"But what if they don't see a problem?" asked Fitz. "What if they decide the meeting is important and we're expendable? I'm not sure we should spill our guts to *the Teachers*, Jim."

"Do you have a better suggestion?"

"Why don't we just make a run for it? I know our chances aren't great, but they're certainly a lot better than they will be if we just sit around here and wait to see what happens. We're up here, out in the open, more or less, so it's just a matter of getting to the perimeter fence and sneaking away."

"But if we get caught..." said Javier.

"We'll be dead!" interrupted Fitz. "But no deader than we'll be if *the Teachers* decide to sacrifice us for the sake of this meeting. I say we make a run for it."

Jim held up his hand to stop what was destined to become a heated argument.

"Fitz, we don't even know which way to run! And we probably don't have much time to figure that out. Let me contact *the Teachers* first. If we don't like the response, then we'll revisit your idea. In the meantime, why don't you see what you can find out about this place and the surrounding countryside? For example, how far away is the nearest population center? Maybe there's some info available online that will help."

As Jim and Fitz stood to leave, Linda objected.

"Hold on just a second, you two! You do realize that I'm not leaving my daughter behind, don't you? If you're thinking about running off through the woods, keep in mind that Javier and I will be carrying a four-year-old! This is insanity and even if we did get away from here they would hunt us like animals for the rest of our lives. Jim, I can't believe that you—of all people—are actually entertaining such an idea!"

"It's not our first choice, Linda, but you must agree that if we're forced to attend this meeting we are essentially signing our own death warrants."

"Maybe, but not immediately. The government will have to keep us around for as long as they want to continue meeting with *the Teachers* and that will give us time to come up with a better plan than Fitz'. What if you make our concerns known now and they decide to cancel altogether? We already know what will happen—*the Teachers* will pull out, we'll be eliminated and our civilization will be doomed. Let's see how this first meeting goes and then decide on a course of action. Maybe we'll find some way to save the negotiations *and* our own skins."

Jim thought about Linda's idea for a minute and then nodded.

"Okay, I'll hold off for now but I think it's prudent to prepare an escape plan, just in case we need it. Is everyone okay with that?"

Reluctantly, Fitz agreed to the delay and the picnic table conference adjourned. On the way back to the underground facility's entrance, Fitz urged Jim to hold back a short distance and Linda noticed the two of them carrying on a very animated discussion.

When the NWIDI team stepped out of the large elevator deep below the surface, a young man in a dark suit greeted them.

"Dr. Barnes, the President would like you to call him at sixteen hundred hours. Please use the same number you used last time."

Once Jim had acknowledged, the man vanished into the maze that was Meriwether Mountain's "Section 2"—the vast, underground portion of the complex.

Jim glanced at his watch and sighed. It was already 3:30 p.m.

"That was quick. I guess we'll know our fate soon enough."

"My people are already on their way to you and they will arrive within the hour," stated the President thirty minutes later. Please take whatever steps are necessary to convene a meeting as soon as possible, Dr. Barnes."

"Yes, sir, but I can't guarantee that the meeting will take place today."

"I'm only sending three people, Dr. Barnes, and that facility was designed to hold more than two thousand. I'm sure my folks will survive. Please make the arrangements. We'll talk again soon."

Again, the line went dead without even a "good-bye" from the President. Jim scanned the table and noted looks of concern on every single face, although probably for different reasons.

"Okay, it sounds like we're going to have company soon, so if you have anything you need to take care of, now would be the time to do it. I assume we'll be notified when the others arrive. In the meantime, I'll be in my quarters."

As soon as he reached his room, Jim drafted a message to *the Teachers* reiterating what the President had said. He placed the folded piece of paper under his door and went into the bathroom. When he came out, he noticed that the paper had been moved and he raced to the door to retrieve it.

"Please have everyone assembled in your conference room at exactly eighteen hundred hours."

The President's team included two middle-aged men, Wayne Grogan and Sam Reid, and a thirty-something woman, Carol Dover. Grogan seemed to be the leader of the group and during his curt introductions he had described himself and Ms. Dover as negotiators and Reid as a legal specialist. Jim thought it odd that the government's initial contact with aliens would include a lawyer, but then what did he know about these things?

At exactly 6:00 p.m. those who had experienced it before knew the jump was beginning by the sudden chill on their bodies. Seconds later, eight humans found themselves on the Other Side to begin the first intergalactic diplomatic talks in the history of the human race. Jim, Linda, Javier, Fitz and Susan acknowledged their host—or would that be 'hosts?'— and then remained silent for the duration of the thirty-minute conference. They could hear the government side of the conversation, of course, but *the Teachers* excluded them when replying, so it was difficult to get a feel for exactly how things were going. The government team seemed to be skilled at their trade, though, never raising their voices or displaying any negative emotions. Based on the questions being asked by Grogan and Dover, things seemed to be progressing in a generally positive direction, but Jim would have loved to have been privy to *the Teachers'* responses.

When the group was returned to the conference room, the newcomers huddled for a second before Grogan addressed the five NWIDI teammates.

"We need your conference room again, so if you will excuse us for a few minutes, we'll catch up with you in the dining area. And thank you for your help. Our new friends speak very favorably of you all."

Feeling a bit shut out, Jim and the others shuffled out of the conference room and heard the door lock behind them.

"It must have gone well," commented Linda as the group moved down the hallway. "Hopefully they will be a little chattier at dinner. I'm going to pick up Mariana from the nanny and I'll see you in a few minutes."

Mariana had been spending a lot of time with her government-supplied baby sitter lately and Linda felt guilty about her own absence, but her daughter seemed to enjoy her time with Connie and the woman seemed to genuinely care about Mariana. Connie also looked after the Fitzgeralds' dog, Sandstrom, and Mariana had grown quite attached to him. If and when they ever left this compound it was going to be a very difficult transition for Mariana.

A few minutes later, Linda and Mariana entered the dining room to find the other members of the team laughing and embracing each other.

"Linda!" greeted Jim. "You're just in time for the celebration—come on in and join the party!"

"What's going on?" asked a skeptical Linda as she helped her daughter onto the booster seat in the chair next to her father. "I haven't seen any of you this happy in years."

"Grogan just stopped by and told us the President has accepted *the Teachers'* offer of a limited alliance with the U.S. Government! There are still a lot of details to work out but they have an understanding, at least in principle. And the best news is that *the Teachers* are sticking to their guns when it comes to us. One of us must be present at every meeting with the negotiating team and the rest of us will have the opportunity to explore more of the Other Side while the meetings are taking place. We're supposed to develop a rotation schedule and take turns monitoring the negotiations, which begin tomorrow morning. I've already volunteered to take the first watch, so you'll get to experience something new and awesome tomorrow."

"Ah, okay," smiled Linda, thinly. "I'm not quite as excited about that as you obviously are, but this is certainly good news for us—at least in the short term. But what happens when the negotiations conclude? Aren't we right back to the dilemma we discussed earlier?"

Jim shot a glance at Mariana to see if she had heard Linda's comment but she was being entertained by her father and was oblivious to everything else.

"Yes, that problem still exists, but now we have some time to work on a solution that's suitable to all of us—both big and small."

Linda laughed at Jim's obvious attempt at a cover-up.

"Jim, she's only four—she has no idea what you're talking about. But I want to be involved in the planning, as an official representative of the 'small' faction."

"That's fine," replied Jim, glancing at the ceiling. "You and Fitz can work together on our long range plan but it actually wasn't Mariana I was concerned about overhearing us."

Linda caught on and realized this was a subject better discussed outside, away from the prying ears and eyes of their government hosts.

"Oh! Well, we can discuss this more later. Right now let's celebrate the good news. Any chance we can get the kitchen to throw together a cake?"

***

Just as the crew was sitting down for their evening meal, a U.S. Navy patrol boat pulled alongside and hailed the Dolphin Diver. After asking—and receiving—permission to board, a young naval officer named Benson came aboard and asked to speak to the Captain. Sensing that this might be a response to the striped dolphin photos, Tony accompanied the Captain and the Navy man onto the bridge.

After introductions and a quick review of the ship's documents, the officer turned to Tony who was now designated as the representative of the ship's owners.

"Let me come right to the point, Mr. Wykes. Your vessel has reported sighting some very rare dolphins in this area and I've been asked to confirm that sighting. If verified, we will be forced to declare this area off limits until the pod moves on. We can't take the chance that a ship might activate sonar equipment that might harm the dolphins. But before we get to all that, may I ask what the Dolphin Diver is doing in this area?"

"Of course," replied Tony cautiously. "We're associated with a dolphin research organization from Belize and we're here doing an informal survey of the marine mammal populations. We were very surprised when our divemaster happened across the small pod of striped dolphins this morning and we thought we'd better notify someone right away. Since we're aware that the U.S. Navy has a presence in this area, we decided you folks were the best ones to contact. Apparently we were right, huh?"

The officer studied Tony for a minute and then smiled broadly.

"Yes, Mr. Wykes, I believe you were. The Navy has a research facility nearby which includes a number of vessels, so we were able to respond rather quickly. If you had contacted the Bahamian government, you might *never* have been paid a visit. Tell me about this research institute you mentioned."

Tony summoned everything he could remember about the Turneffe Wild Dolphin Institute and parroted it back to the naval officer, trying to sound as authoritative as possible. He concluded with a disclaimer that he was relatively new to the project.

"Unfortunately, our expert in this area was called away on a family emergency just this morning, but I think I've covered all the important facts," he said.

That would be, er, Mr. Jefferies?" asked the officer, scanning the ship's roster that the Captain had provided.

"Yes, that's correct. And as you can see from our log, we've made several similar survey stops since leaving Belize and this was to be our last before beginning the long voyage home. We really didn't expect to see such a rare find on our very first dive."

"Yes, well some folks have all the luck," smiled Benson. "Listen, how tight is your schedule? Would you be available to remain here for a few days until this pod moves on? The Navy doesn't really have the equipment or manpower to conduct a station-keeping mission right now and since you're in the dolphin research business anyway, I thought…"

"We'd be happy to help out!" interrupted Tony with a broad smile. "We're not really equipped to do any policing, but we would be delighted to keep an eye on the pod and let you know when they leave the area."

"Please leave any police work to us. If you have issues with anyone, hail us on your marine radio and we'll get someone out here in a hurry. We'll instruct the local maritime authorities to notify any arriving vessels of the situation and we'll also let them know that your presence here is authorized. Your services will be a big help to us and you will have exclusive access to a very rare species, Mr. Wykes. A win-win, it would seem."

"Yes, and the dolphins win, too, because they won't be tortured by any pesky sonar equipment while they're here," replied Tony, his smile fading.

Chapter 14

The captain was jolted awake by a sharp thump on the hull of his small, fiberglass vessel. He had been napping restlessly against one of the bulkheads that separated the crew's cabin from the much larger cargo holds fore and aft. It was hot and cramped inside the sixty-foot semi-submersible submarine and there were no bunks, so he and his three crew members slept sitting up when they weren't on watch. Normally there wasn't much to do on the twelve-day voyages from the northwestern coast of Columbia to the rendezvous point just off the coast of Mexico's state of Sinaloa. Except for the single refueling stop near a small fishing village in central Oaxaca, the only exercise any of the men received was alternating between standing and sitting. During the refueling process, they were allowed to board the converted fishing trawler and walk around the deck to stretch their legs before returning to their cramped quarters for another six days.

There was another thump, and then another.

"What's going on?" demanded the captain, knowing that no one else onboard had any idea either.

Suddenly the boat rolled violently to the right, knocking down the two crewmen who were standing and spilling the captain and another crewman off the overturned five- gallon plastic buckets that served as chairs.

"We've been hit!" bellowed the captain, as the boat returned to the upright position. He threw a lever that dumped the ballast and the boat rose the few feet to the surface. "Open the hatch! Everybody out!"

Assuming that they were under attack by a patrol boat from either the Mexican Navy or the U.S. Coast Guard, the captain was carrying out his orders to evacuate himself and the crew and then scuttle the boat and its cargo. Current maritime laws required that drug smugglers be caught "red handed" and that meant they had to be in possession of an illegal substance at the time of their arrest. When the captain bobbed to the surface in his life jacket, the narco-sub had already begun its rapid descent to the bottom, carrying nine tons of cocaine with it. Scanning the horizon to locate the would-be attackers, he was shocked to find nothing but open sea in every direction. To the east he could just barely make out the coastline but there were no vessels anywhere in sight and that meant there was no chance of being picked up.

"Where are they?" yelled one of the crewman floating nearby.

Just then the captain spotted several dorsal fins breaking the surface a dozen yards away and pointed.

"Dolphins!" he yelled back. "We were attacked by a pod of dolphins! Make your way to shore, men, but take it slow because it's a long ways. And stay together!"

***

Edwards finished reading the email message and slammed his fist against the top of his desk. He had just been informed about another lost shipment off the coast of Mexico. Some losses were expected, of course, but this was the fourth one in the past month and this time the crew hadn't even been picked up by the authorities. Normally, the arresting agency fished the narco-sub's crew out of the water, held them for a few days and then turned them lose due to lack of evidence. The sub and its cargo were lost, of course, but the crew was eventually returned to Columbia after being deported by the Mexican government. However, in two recent cases the crews had been lost and this time the crew had eventually washed up on the shores of western Mexico two hundred miles south of their destination. When the captain had finally reported in, he had related a strange story of being "attacked" by a pod of dolphins—an encounter he had mistaken for a naval boarding. The rest of his crew had disappeared into the jungle and he was currently stranded in a tiny fishing village south of Puerto Vallarta.

Edwards couldn't understand why dolphins would suddenly begin attacking the small, slow moving subs. There hadn't been a single incident like this in the eight years the subs had been serving as the primary mode of transportation for Columbian cocaine and yet here was one confirmed case and at least two other possible cases. And while he couldn't understand the new situation, he knew it had to stop immediately! Compared to the two hundred million dollar cost of the cargo, the single-use subs were relatively inexpensive to build but they took a significant amount of time to assemble and there weren't any "extras" in the manufacturing pipeline to make up the lost shipments.

Edwards used his private, encrypted line to follow up with Valdes, in Havana. He had asked the other man to look into a new route for the cocaine and the sudden increase in lost subs on the Pacific side of Latin America might be enough justification to get his plan implemented.

"So what's the verdict?" asked Edwards when Valdes came on the line.

"It's more positive than I would have expected," replied the Cuban, "but there are some big obstacles to overcome."

"I expected that. What about a suitable site? Were you able to locate anything useful?"

"Yes, that was actually the easy part. I found an abandoned banana plantation south of Necoci, on the road to Turbo, and it looks very promising. It would mean moving the assembly facilities overland about one hundred fifty miles, but it's located in the province of Antioguia, where some of your product is already grown. It's also connected to the nearby Gulf of Uraba by a wide, meandering river so new vessels could be launched right at the assembly point if the tides were right."

"It sounds perfect!" exclaimed Edwards. "So what are the obstacles you mentioned?"

"As I've already mentioned, we would have to move the submarine assembly plant overland, by truck. That will take some time and there will be security issues on the highway. And then there's the issue of relocating your existing work force. Many of them are locals who are established on the west coast."

"Can't we just find new workers on the east side?"

"To some extent, yes, but the skilled laborers are a different matter. You have diesel mechanics, plumbers, electricians and fiberglass workers that would be very hard— and very time-consuming—to replace."

"Can it be done?" asked Edwards, impatiently.

"Yes, it can probably be done, but it's going to be an expensive move."

"I've lost eight hundred million dollars in cargo in the last month—that's 1.6 billion dollars, at street value—can it be done for less than that?"

There was a hearty laugh on the other end of the line.

"My friend, you could buy the entire country for that much money!"

"Okay, then I want you to put the wheels in motion as soon as possible. I assume you will go to Columbia and personally oversee the project, right?"

"Of course, but my fee..."

"Your fee will no doubt be outrageous, Valdes, but I will pay it all up front and throw in another fifty percent bonus when this job is complete. As soon as we hang up I'll call my associate, Tom Danielson, and ask him to contact you regarding the transfer of funds. You can provide him with the necessary banking information then. But this project must be completed in the shortest possible time and with the least amount of publicity, is that clear?"

"Of course. I take it you haven't told your friends in Sinaloa about this change and that will probably introduce some additional complications, you know. They won't take too kindly to losing all that revenue."

"Well that's *their* problem! I can't stand to lose any more product and they don't seem to be able to protect the subs. I'll deal with the cartel—you just worry about getting the facility moved and operational on the east coast. I have to run to a meeting, but I'll talk to you again soon. Expect a call from Danielson later today."

Edwards collected his notes for the morning Committee meeting and made his way to the conference room. When he entered the room, he immediately noticed the empty chair.

"Where's Gomez?" he demanded as he stomped the length of the room to his own seat at the head of the table.

When there was no answer, he slowly scanned the table, his eyes stopping on the Chinese representative, Chen.

"Well?"

"Last night at dinner he mentioned that he wasn't feeling very well, but I haven't seen him this morning. Maybe he's sick."

"Maybe," frowned Edwards, "but he hasn't checked into the infirmary so when we're done here I'd like you to stop by his room to make sure he's still alive. If he is, tell him to call my office immediately. Now let's get to the business of the day."

After each of the representatives had presented their daily reports, Edwards pointed at the empty chair.

"Since Mr. Gomez couldn't be with us this morning, let me bring you up to date on some events that I find very troubling. Earlier this morning I learned that another one of our narco-subs was lost at sea off the coast of Mexico and I don't need to tell you how that's going to impact sales, especially in the United States and Canada. A couple of weeks down the road we're going to have a severe product shortage in that part of the world so I need each of you to review your inventories and be prepared to ship anything you can spare to North America. This is our biggest market, so we need to pool our resources to weather this storm. And when Mr. Gomez decides to return to our daily meetings, I'll expect him to provide us all with a detailed explanation of the problem in the Sea of Cortez. That's all for today, but come prepared to present your surplus numbers tomorrow morning. That is all."

The room cleared quickly, except for Aleksey Mednikov, of Russia.

"You wish to speak to me, Mr. Mednikov?" asked Edwards, looking up from his notes.

"Yes, I do. I would like to discuss with you the terms of this product transfer you mentioned."

"You will be compensated at your original cost for any product you make available to help relieve the North American shortage. That's how we always do it."

"Yes, but I, too, have periodic supply line issues and I can't put my own organization at risk just because you lost a boat in Mexico. I'm afraid I won't be able to provide any product—at least not at cost."

Edwards flushed.

"Are you suggesting that you expect to profit from this misfortune?"

"Cost plus twenty percent—take it or leave it," smiled Mednikov as he stood to leave. "Otherwise, I'll be reporting a zero inventory surplus at tomorrow's meeting."

"You won't get away with this!" shouted Edwards, lurching to his feet.

"Oh, I think I will, because if you challenge my report I'll let the others in on my offer and then you'll be paying all of them an inflated price, too! Have a good day, Mr. Edwards."

Mednikov marched out of the room before Edwards could calm himself enough to retaliate.

***

While the others were having their morning meeting in the main conference room, Gomez was in Edwards' office. He had waited in an adjacent room for Edwards to leave and then he had picked the lock on the door connecting the two rooms using some skills he had honed earlier in his life.

With a specially modified cell phone, Gomez photographed several documents he found on the desk, including some hand-written notes about a place in Columbia called the Gulf of Uraba. But that wasn't his primary reason for the covert operation. Gomez lifted the handset of Edwards' telephone and skillfully installed a bug. Surgical gloves ensured that he didn't leave behind any fingerprints or DNA samples that would betray him later.

After a quick look around the office, Gomez silently slipped back into the makeshift computer room and sat down in front of one of the monitors. In a matter of seconds, Gomez had edited the digital file associated with the hallway camera, erasing any evidence of his arrival a few minutes earlier and replacing the cut portion with video of an empty hallway. He also keyed in some new code that would give him time to leave the area before restarting the camera. Satisfied with his work, he ducked out of the room and disappeared.

***

By the time Chen knocked on his door, Gomez had changed from his black sweats into pajamas and a robe. He had also applied just enough makeup to his nose to make it appear that he was suffering from a severe head cold. On his way to the door he faked a cough. Even Chen was almost fooled by the show that had been staged for the benefit of anyone who might happen down the hallway at that minute.

"Edwards asked me to check on you, but you seem to be alive. Is there anything I can get you?"

"Yes, I'm alive, but I'm not very well. I could sure use some soup from the kitchen, if they have any. I was going to call down there, but I haven't gotten around to it yet."

"Speaking of calling," replied Chen, "Edwards wants you to call his office right away. He was on a rampage about another lost submarine, so that's probably what's it's about. Why don't you take care of that call while I see what I can do about your soup?"

Gomez closed the door and padded across the room to the telephone. He was getting into his sick character so much that he even walked like he was sick!

"Sorry, I tried to call a couple of times this morning but the line was busy," lied Gomez. "And I've been back and forth to the bathroom so many times that I couldn't hang out by the telephone. Chen was just here and gave me your message."

"Why haven't you been to the infirmary?"

"It's just a simple cold," Gomez lied again. "Besides, I didn't want to take a chance on infecting the whole place. I'm sure I'll be fine by tomorrow."

"I certainly hope so," replied an uncompassionate Edwards. "Because I want you to explain to me—and to the group—what's going on with our narco-subs. We lost another one, you know."

"No, actually, I didn't know, but I haven't been in contact with anyone in my organization for more than twenty-four hours. I'll look into it and have a full report for you by tomorrow morning."

"See that you do!" replied Edwards. "Losses like this hurt the entire group and they must stop immediately."

The line went dead and Gomez slammed the phone into the cradle. Just what he needed now was another sub incident! It would focus attention on him at a time when he really needed to keep a low profile here in Cuba and stay focused on his organization back in Michoacán.

When Chen knocked again, Gomez quickly opened the door, checked the hallway to make sure it was clear, and then ushered him in.

"These large Styrofoam containers were all they had available, so you should have enough soup for a week!" laughed Chen. "How's your tequila holding out?"

"I have plenty, thanks," replied Gomez, setting the container on the counter and motioning Chen to the small sitting area of his unit. "I don't even like chicken soup, but it will help reinforce my cover.

"You were right about Edwards. He wants a full report by tomorrow morning on the most recent sub loss and I have a feeling he's going to use this to discredit me with the

Committee and somehow further his own interests. Take a look at this."

Gomez handed Chen a sheet of paper and a map of Columbia.

"The hand-written notes are from a photo I took in his office this morning. They mention a place called the Gulf of Uraba, which I've circled on the map. As you can see, it's a very large bay on the extreme northeast coast of Columbia."

"So what does this mean?" asked Chen, shrugging his shoulders.

"I don't know, but in the past I've always been the point of contact with the Columbians. Why would he be poking around down there? And why on the east coast? All our operations are over on the Pacific side. That's where the subs are built and loaded and that's where the bulk of the product is produced. There is some production in the northeast, but it only represents a small percentage of the total."

"Well there you go," said Chen, standing to leave. "He's probably trying to find more product to replace the recent sub loses! And speaking of that, you need to get busy on your report for tomorrow morning and I need to get out of here so my stay doesn't look suspicious. Since you were able to photograph his notes, I assume the bug is securely in place, too."

"Yes, and I covered my tracks in the surveillance system, just as you instructed. I thought I'd review the voice recording from the phone bug every evening after he's left his office for the day. I'll prepare a quick summary and slip it to you and Aleksey just before the morning meeting each day. If there's anything significant that we need to discuss in the daily summary, we can get together after lunch."

"That sounds good. I'll pass the word to Mednikov and we'll see you tomorrow at breakfast. Good luck with that report!"

Gomez locked and bolted the door behind Chen and then placed a call to one of his lieutenants in Mazatlán, Mexico.

***

After the morning meeting, Edwards spent some time going over the daily reports that had been submitted by the other Committee members before making a quick stop at the facility's cafeteria on the way back to his office. He had them prepare a cold sandwich to go so he could skip lunch and spend the rest of the day refining the details of his new Columbia plan. While he was waiting, he casually asked about Gomez and he was informed about the recently delivered container of soup.

"Maybe he really is sick," thought Edwards, as he accepted the brown paper sack and headed for his office.

When he keyed his access code into the small digital pad hidden behind a painting inside the office near the door, a tiny red light flashed rapidly on the pad. Edwards quickly spun and scanned his office for signs of entry but everything seemed to be in place. He closed the door and went immediately to his desk. After signing into the security system, he scanned the system logs for unusual events and found three that stood out. He had enabled the system when he left for the morning meeting and less than ten minutes later the outer door to his private, connecting conference room, had been opened and closed. Less than a minute after that, the door between the conference room and his office had been opened and it had remained open for nearly six minutes before being closed again. Another nine minutes later the conference room outer door was opened and closed again. It was obvious that someone had broken into his office via the connecting conference room, but whom? And why? Who in this ultra-secure facility would have the audacity to stoop to breaking and entering?

The answer, of course, was on the digital camera files in the next room and that's where Edwards headed at full speed. He took special care unlocking and opening the door in case the perpetrator had been stupid enough to leave finger prints behind but he didn't expect to need that evidence. He rolled the video back and forth at high speed through the sixteen minutes in question several times without spotting any activity on the camera that was mounted just down the hallway from his own office door. Finally, he returned the video to the point where he had left the office and watched it non-stop for thirty minutes at normal speed.

When he finally clicked pause on the monitor, he was frustrated, furious and left with one of two possibilities: either three separate sensors in his state-of-the-art security system had failed in a very specific order or someone had managed to alter the digital file he had just reviewed!

Edwards double-checked the outer doorway lock on the conference room, returned to his office and secured the lock on the door between the two rooms. After making a thorough examination of his office, he was satisfied that nothing important had been disturbed so he gathered up the materials he would need for the rest of the day and stuffed them into a brief case he had brought when he fled Washington, D.C. Before leaving for his living quarters, he reset the alarm system. But this time he enabled the Claxton horn mounted in the ceiling just outside his office door. If anyone tried to enter his office or the adjacent room again, they would have fifteen seconds to locate the hidden keypad and enter the proper code. If they didn't, the entire facility would know about the security breech!

***

Gomez had spent most of the afternoon on the telephone with a variety of staff members, from his top field personnel along the west coast of Mexico to his most trusted associates in Michoacán. He had made it quite clear that if another sub were lost, heads would roll, too, but he knew that there was only so much that could be done to protect the barely-submersed, slow-moving vehicles. In fact, too much protection would give away the existence of the very vehicles they were trying to conceal.

In the end, he agreed to a plan that included a "shadow" trawler, posing as a working fishing boat, and fly-overs by two different light planes working out of two separate airports—one out of Manzanillo International Airport, south of Puerto Vallarta, and one out of Mazatlán International Airport. Both facilities were busy airfields with a lot of private aircraft activity and these two cities bracketed the coastal area where the last four sub losses had occurred.

After carefully documenting his counter-measures in a report suitable for the Committee, Gomez decided to try the soup before settling down to his next task. It turned out to be pretty good, especially after he added a teaspoon full of the hot sauce he had brought with him from central Mexico. Returning to the living area, he hoisted a hard plastic instrument case about the size of a laptop onto his coffee table and opened the lid. The screen mounted into the cover came to life and displayed a counter, much like that on the front of a home DVD player. The numbers indicated that the unit had been recording continuously for just over nine hours and forty-five minutes. Gomez didn't begin to understand the technology that allowed this box to communicate with the bug he had placed inside Edwards' telephone handset, but he had been given enough training to operate the record and playback controls in front of him. He pressed the Rewind button and watched the digital display race backwards to zero. Slipping a set of headphones on, he pressed a button labeled Seek and waited for the unit to automatically detect the first hint of sound on the recording. Soon, the display stopped at 01:15:23. Gomez jotted down the elapsed time and pressed Play. He heard a door close, followed by a series of six faint beeps. There was a short period of silence and then he heard the distinct sound of a door being unlocked.

Edwards must be entering his conference room that housed all the electronics Gomez had seen earlier in the day!

He listened for more than forty minutes before he heard the door being re-locked. Several more minutes passed before the sound of rustling papers broke the silence and shortly after that he detected the faint beeping again, followed by the sound of a door closing. And after that, there was nothing! Gomez put the system into seek mode again and it didn't stop until the display read 09:45:27—the end of the recording.

Edwards hadn't been in his office all day long and the bug had recorded nothing of value!

Chapter 15

Friday morning Cesar and Tony made another routine dive, photographed the striped dolphins and sent their photographs off to the Navy before joining the rest of the crew for breakfast. Life aboard the Dolphin Diver had become very relaxed since its arrival off the coast of South Bimini and Tony was happy to see everyone getting a little down time but he was feeling suddenly lonely. Carley had been gone almost three weeks and Rob and Anne had been off the ship for more than forty-eight hours and Tony missed the opportunity to discuss some of the things he had kept secret from the rest of the crew. No one currently aboard the Dolphin Diver even knew his real name!

Tony took meals with the crew and did the dolphin dives with Cesar, but otherwise he spent most of his time in the forward stateroom that had been vacated by Rob and Anne. Cell phone coverage on the boat was intermittent and Internet access was non-existent so he passed the time reading some of the books Rob had left behind. He had just started the best seller *Einstein*, by Walter Isaacson, when the short-wave radio on the desk crackled to life.

"V31DK Mobile, this is V31DK Base, do you copy?"

Tony grabbed the microphone and pressed the button on the side of the small device.

"V31DK Base, this V31DK Mobile. I copy you loud and clear, Rob, and it's good to hear your voice. How are things going back there? Over."

"Not so well, I'm afraid. We had several travel delays and didn't get into Belize City until late yesterday so we stayed in town overnight. We stopped by the bar but the 'Closed for Remodeling' sign was still in the window and there were no signs that Carley had been there. When we finally got to the island this morning we found an envelope she had sent over a week ago. Inside were a short letter and the keys to the bar. I'm afraid she's gone, Tony. We were too late. Over"

"Gone? You mean back to Guatemala? Over."

"Yes, I'm afraid so. Apparently after she got back here she contacted an old friend who's still living in the jungle and he convinced her to join his group. I have his name here somewhere but she didn't provide many other details—she simply said she'd contact us when she could. I'm sorry. Over."

"Yes, me too, but I think this is what she's wanted to do for a long time. She told me once that she felt like her life was just marking time, with no purpose or direction. Maybe she'll change her mind once she gets there and realizes that the good old days weren't so good after all. So what are you guys going to do? Are you coming back to the Bahamas? Over."

"I don't think so, Tony. We're both pretty upset about this situation with Carley, but we need to do *something* with the bar—I'm not sure I want to look for another tenant, so maybe we'll just sell the whole building. But that means we have to be here in case we find a buyer. If you need one or both of us, we'll certainly come back, but I assume you'll be heading back here once your dolphin monitoring job is finished, right? Over."

"Yes, that's the plan. The crew is enjoying their little vacation right now, but it won't be long before boredom sets in and I'd like to have the Dolphin Diver headed for Belize before that happens. Besides, they're all excited about the prospect of working with you and Anne at the Dolphin Institute. Over."

"Yes, and that's another thing. The boys in the lab are working as we speak to get the translator modified and I expect that by tomorrow the Institute will shift into overdrive! I can't wait to see the reaction from Emma and the other dolphins we've been working with when they find out that we can finally communicate with them! Over."

"I wish I were going to be there to see that, too, but I'll see you soon, I hope. Give Emma my regards and tell her she can thank me for the translator when I get back. And please let me know if you hear anything from Carley. Over."

"Will do, Tony. Anne sends her love. This is V31DK Base signing off."

"Ditto from V31DK Mobile."

Tony clipped the microphone back onto the side of the small transceiver and flopped back in the chair. He had hoped to have a chance to talk Carley out of returning to Guatemala but given the way things had ended between them, he wasn't surprised that she hadn't contacted him about her decision.

"Be safe, Carley," he said out loud, wiping a single tear off his right cheek.

***

The negotiation team had departed for Washington, D.C. soon after their return from the last meeting with *the Teachers* and there had been no communications from either them or the President's office in almost thirty-six hours. The NWIDI team had been present during the meeting, so they had heard everything the government team had said, but they also knew that *the Teachers* had the ability to address a subset of the group privately. At breakfast, Fitz had raised the possibility that *the Teachers* might have secretly arranged their next meeting with the President's people and cut the NWIDI team out of the process.

"If that happened," he had observed, "then our days here are numbered. The President and his cronies could be plotting our demise right this minute!"

Linda, Javier and Susan had defended *the Teachers* but, surprisingly, Jim had expressed a real concern that Fitz might be on to something. This restarted the debate about an escape plan and that had sent Fitz hustling off to his quarters to continue work on his plan.

As the group began to gather in the dining room for lunch, the debate from earlier in the day was reignited when Linda spotted an aerial view of the Meriwether Mountain facility on the table in front of Fitz.

"I thought we were going to work on this together!" she exclaimed. "Where did you get that, anyway?"

"It's from Google Earth," replied Fitz, sliding the sheet across the table to Linda. "And I actually brought it for you. There are some things I think you should review and then we can get together and discuss a plan. I made some preliminary notes on the back but I'm sure you will spot those issues on your own and you'll no doubt find some things I've missed."

"Oh," replied a slightly subdued Linda. "Thanks. I'll check it out after lunch. But I still have faith in *the Teachers*. I just can't believe they would throw us to the wolves, especially since they were the ones who requested our presence at the meetings in the first place."

"You can believe whatever you wish but I think it's pretty strange that we haven't heard from anybody yet. And where's Jim? I haven't seen him all morning, have you?"

Just then Jim burst into the room waving a folded piece of paper.

"Good news, team! *The Teachers* have called another meeting for tomorrow morning and specifically requested that one of us be present to monitor the event. Since I've already volunteered to take this one, the rest of you will get that grand tour they promised. By the way, the negotiation team will be returning early this evening."

Jim took his place at the table and the kitchen staff immediately began serving the food. The team remained silent while the facility employees were in the room but as soon as the last one returned to the kitchen, the table was buzzing.

"When did you find out about this?" questioned Fitz. "I stopped by your room a couple of times this morning and you didn't answer the door. I was afraid you'd gone off and left us."

"Your paranoia is really starting to bug me," Javier shot back. "But yes, Jim, where were you?"

Holding up the folded piece of paper again, Jim replied.

"I received this about 10:30 a.m. and went to the conference room to alert the President. That call lasted about fifteen minutes and then I hung out there catching up on some paperwork until just now. The desk in my room is so small that I have a hard time working on it and I can really spread out on that big conference room table. Did you need to see me for something?"

"Well, it's probably a moot point, now, but I did have some questions about the escape plan that I wanted…"

Fitz stopped in mid-sentence when he saw Jim vigorously and repeatedly drawing his index finger across his throat.

"What?" he asked angrily. "Man, you talk about me being paranoid! If they really had this place bugged, you wouldn't have to call the President; you could just hold your note up to one of the apparently invisible cameras and let him read it for himself!"

Mariana looked up from her plate and asked, "Mommy, why is Mr. Fitz angry?"

The child's innocent question effectively put an end to the argument and the conversation turned to more pleasant topics, such as what new tricks Sandstrom had learned in play school that morning. For his part, Fitz chose to remain silent during the rest of the meal but when he pushed his chair back to leave the table, Linda shoved the paper containing the overhead shot of the facility back in front of him.

"I guess I won't need this for a while," she smiled sarcastically.

With nothing to do but wait, the team went their separate ways for the remainder of the day. Linda and Javier spent the afternoon topside with Mariana and Sandstrom, who were becoming inseparable. Fitz took off by himself to the underground facility's workout room and Susan spent the afternoon in the dated but well stocked library/reading room.

In his room, Jim watched a documentary on the Discovery Channel about whales and then flicked the television off with the remote. Spotting the note from *the Teachers* on his small desk, he decided to try something he had been curious about for several days. Under the brief message from *the Teachers*, he wrote a single question. He then refolded the paper, slipped it part way under his door and flopped onto his bed to read.

Periodically during the next hour he glanced to his right to check the status of the note but it was always there, exactly as he had placed it. Or was it? Straining his eyes, Jim suddenly realized that the fold, which had been facing his direction when he placed the note, was now facing the opposite direction!

Scrambling off the bed he retrieved the paper and opened it. He had written, "Are my associates and I in danger as a result of our participation in your meetings?"

The reply, printed below Jim's question was simple and to the point.

"No."

Satisfied, Jim settled back onto his bed and smiled before drifting off into the first peaceful sleep he'd had in weeks.

***

Edwards arrived for the Friday morning meeting early and he was seated at the head of the long table when members of the Committee began arriving. He greeted each by their last name as they took their place. When there was just one empty chair, he frowned and looked at his watch.

"We'll wait one more minute and then…"

Edwards was cut off by Gomez flashing into the room and sliding to a stop behind his chair. He checked his own watch, waited a few seconds and then took his seat at exactly 9:00 a.m.

"Are you feeling better, Mr. Gomez?" asked Edwards, taking note of several smiling faces around the table.

"Yes, sir, I am, thanks to some excellent chicken soup the cafeteria provided." He nodded to the group in general and added, "I highly recommend it, by the way."

"Good. Then let's start with the special report I asked you to prepare for the group, shall we? Can you tell us why we have lost nearly a billion dollars' worth of drugs in the last thirty-three days, Mr. Gomez?"

Gomez' face took on a serious expression and he nodded as he opened a folder in front of him.

"Well, I'm not sure I can tell you why, but I do have some updated information on how. And I think you will be as surprised as I was when you hear the details I've recently learned. Let me start with the most recent incident, which took place three days ago.

"According to the captain, the trip had been routine, with a normal refueling stop and no indications of what was to come. Then, as the vessel reached latitude twenty point forty-five north, the crew felt a series of sharp thumps on the hull and the boat rolled a full ninety degrees before righting itself. Assuming they were under attack by one of the maritime authorities, the captain ordered an immediate evacuation and, as he exited the vessel himself, he sent her to the bottom. For those of you not familiar with our narco-subs, this is standard procedure. The captain did exactly what we expected of him. However, the captain soon discovered that there weren't any law enforcement boats in the area. All he saw was a pod of dolphins swimming away from the site.

"Thanks to their life jackets, the captain and his men managed to make their way to shore, which was more than a mile away. The three crewmen apparently decided they had had enough sea travel and disappeared but the captain contacted a telephone service we have set up for just such occasions and he is already on his way back to Columbia. In fact, I spoke with him personally just minutes ago."

"That's all very interesting," interrupted Edwards, "but I find it very hard to believe that a group of dolphins would attach a sub in the open sea."

"I did too, but that's the captain's story and I believe him. And the sub wasn't exactly in open water. The location I mentioned is just north of the lighthouse at Cape Corrientes—

the closest land approach the sub makes once it leaves Columbia. The cape marks the southern end of a huge, extended bay that contains Puerto Vallarta and that area is teeming with dolphins of several different species. However, the attack on the sub is unusual, to say the least, and completely out of character for dolphins. We haven't been able to turn up even one case of this ever happening before."

"The U.S. Navy has been training dolphins for years," said Hans Schröder, the new member from Germany. "Is it possible that they are using them to intercept subs and force unnecessary sinking rather than sending their patrol boats out to do the job?"

"I suppose that's possible," replied Gomez, "but the Americans are so hung up on statistics that I doubt if they would miss the opportunity to take credit for a cargo loss. And as Mr. Edwards has already pointed out, this is our fourth loss in just over a month. One of them was a boarding by the Mexican Navy but two others were unexplained. Both vessels and their crews were lost. And by lost, I mean they just never showed up at their rendezvous points. There's no indication that the authorities were involved because there are no reports of contact and the crews were never formally arrested. My belief is that these two missing boats were also victims of dolphin attacks and that the crews didn't survive the swim to shore. Maybe they didn't grab their life jackets or maybe they were attacked by sharks before they reached land—there's no way to know what happened to them except to say that all eight men have disappeared."

"So, what's being done to reduce future losses?" asked Edwards.

"We've revised our captains' operating orders, effective today. From now on they won't scuttle the vessel until they have personally seen the Navy or the Coast Guard. This means that the sub will come all the way to the surface before the captain exits and initiates the sinking, but this new procedure will eliminate situations like the one we just experienced."

"Won't this increase the possibility of the sub being spotted?" asked Edwards. "Once it surfaces it will be clearly visible from both sea and air."

"True, but if there's a patrol boat waiting, then it's already been spotted. If there's no patrol boat nearby, the captain simply gathers his crew and they submerge again. He's on the surface for no more than five minutes and the chances of being spotted by a random aircraft patrol are minimal. It seems like it's worth the risk to save a cargo from unnecessary loss."

Edwards thought for a minute before replying.

"Okay, I'll buy your plan, for now, but I want a serious investigation into this dolphin thing, if that's really what happened. And check out Schröder's idea about trained dolphins. If that's what's going on, someone in the area will know about it and we can put a stop to it. But we need answers and we need them soon. Otherwise, we'll have to look for other ways to move our product from Central America to the United States. Now let's go around the table for your daily reports and don't forget to include the surplus quantities you can make available to help out the U.S. supply situation."

While the others were speaking, Gomez was lost in thought. Edwards had just uttered the words "other ways to move our product." Was that why he was interested in eastern Columbia?

***

Tony was soaking up some late afternoon sun on the rear dive platform when he spotted a small pleasure boat headed directly towards the Dolphin Diver. There were always boats coming and going due to the nearby settlement of Port Royal, but none had approached the Dolphin Diver since the visit by the Navy patrol boat two days earlier. As a precaution, Tony took a spear gun out of the equipment cabinet, loaded it and placed it on the deck beside his chair.

"Ahoy, there!" shouted a large, bearded man on the bow of the approaching boat. "How's the fishing?"

Tony stood to get a better view of the other vessel.

"We're not fishing. We're just doing some diving and amateur dolphin research," replied Tony. "You'll have to check with someone else about the fishing."

"Dolphins, huh? I hear they taste like chicken!" laughed the man sarcastically. "Is that a Belizean flag you're flying?"

"Yes," replied Tony, intentionally avoiding a prolonged conversation with the stranger. "This vessel belongs to a dolphin research institute in Belize."

"Wow, you're a long ways from home, dude! Looks like you've got a pretty nice setup, though. Well, we're off in search of those famous bone fish everybody talks about, so have a nice day!"

As Tony watched the other boat reverse engines and slowly move itself away from the Dolphin Diver he noticed a glint off something inside the smaller boat's cabin. The windows were tinted so he couldn't see anything other than the sharp flash when the sun angle was just right but he suspected that someone was watching him through binoculars or some other optical device.

Crossing the dive platform to the other side, he watched the boat until it was out of sight. As he did so, he repeated the name on the stern over and over so he wouldn't forget it. When the other boat was barely visible, he quickly made his way to the bridge, where he found Captain Braydon staring in the direction of the now vanished boat.

"Who was that?" he asked.

"I don't know," replied Tony, grabbing a note pad off the captain's chart table and scribbling down the name. "But the boat is called Black Jack III. Is there any way to find out who owns it?"

"Not with just a name," replied the captain, shaking his head. "If you had the hull number and the country of registration we could probably dig up something but otherwise it would be a long shot."

"What about asking the local harbor master or whatever they're called around here? Maybe it's a local boat and the name would be enough."

"I suppose that's worth a shot. I'll give him a call on the radio, if you want to hold on a minute."

As it turned out, the local port captain *did* know the Black Jack III. It was a U.S. registered charter fishing boat currently working out of the Port Royal Marina. He remembered the boat's name because of several recent run-ins it had with local authorities. Apparently the skipper of the Black Jack III wasn't too particular about who he took fishing or whether they had valid permits.

"So what did they want?" asked the Captain.

"They just asked about the fishing and I told them we weren't fishing. But I'd swear that someone inside was either watching me or photographing me. It's probably nothing, but it sure seemed as though they came around the point and headed directly for us, as if they were on a mission."

The captain smiled and held up his own digital camera.

"We have some pictures of them, too," he laughed. "I'll print out a couple of the better ones and pass them around to the boys in case these guys decide to pay us another visit. Maybe we should start posting a guard again."

"I think a nighttime watch might be a good idea," nodded Tony. "Besides, the guys need something to do to stay sharp or they will be useless once we start back to Belize. I'll draw up a schedule and you can present it at supper tonight."

There was a loud groan when Captain Braydon announced the reinstatement of security watches, but when he explained that everyone on board was going to participate and that each shift would only be two hours long, the idea received better acceptance. And when he passed around photos of the Black Jack III and described it as a potential threat, the security duty suddenly had a sense of purpose.

In deference to his seniority—and to his age—Tony had given the 6:00 pm to 8:00 pm shift to Captain Braydon, followed by Cesar, Rigo, Nickolas, Tony and, finally, the new cook, Terry. Terry was always up early to prepare breakfast, so it made sense to put him in the 4:00 a.m. to 6:00 a.m. slot and Tony had taken the 2:00 a.m. to 4:00 a.m. shift because he suspected that if there were any trouble, that's when it would happen.

Tony climbed up to the custom "crow's nest" lookout position he had designed for the long open water journey from Belize to the Virgin Islands and checked to make sure everything was still in order. He opened the special horizontal compartment mounted in front of the seat and checked the high-powered, telescope-equipped rifle that was stored there. The weapon had never been fired, but it was ready if needed. The cabinet also included a hand gun, for personal defense, and a pair of large military-style spotting binoculars. The large swiveling chair, a modified fighting chair like those used on big game fishing boats, was equipped with a racing-style safety harness and surrounded by a covered tubular frame that could be fully enclosed with clear plastic panels in case of bad weather. A compartment built into the left arm of the chair contained a small, hand-held walkie-talkie that communicated directly with a matching unit located on the bridge.

In addition to the fire power available in the crow's nest, Tony had concealed an arms locker into a special storeroom on the lower deck and he had stocked it with various weapons he had come to appreciate during his days as a member of the U.S. Army's Special Forces. The Dolphin Diver wasn't looking for a fight, but it was certainly prepared to defend itself, if necessary!

Chapter 16

At precisely 9:30 a.m. the next morning, the government negotiating team, plus Jim, vanished from the underground conference room. On the other side of the table, Linda, Javier, Fitz and Susan watched in amazement as the "disappearing act" took place right before their eyes. They had been part of the process several times but this was the first time they had seen it from an observer's point of view.

"Amazing!" commented Linda to no one in particular.

Jim's instructions for this "trip" had been very specific. *The Teachers* had stipulated that all who were attending the meeting should stand on the north side of the table and all those not attending should stand on the other side. Seconds after watching the meeting group disappear, the others felt the tell-tale chill that told them they, too, were in transit. Sixty miles away the President and several of his most trusted advisors watched the event courtesy of a recently installed hidden video camera.

"I want that technology!" exclaimed the President. "I don't care if anything else comes from these meetings, but I want that technology!"

"Our team has your orders, Mr. President," replied one of the others, "and I'm confident they will be able to deliver."

***

Not used to being disturbed in his living quarters, especially at 7:00 a.m. on a Saturday morning, Edwards reached for the telephone in an unusually bad mood.

"What!" he yelled into the handset. "And this better be really important!"

Only a very small group of people knew the number of his direct line so he assumed it was his Number 2, back in Washington D.C.

"It is, Buzz, and I didn't think you'd want me to sit on this information for even a second."

The voice on the other end of the line was, indeed, his deputy, Tom Danielson. His interest piqued, Edwards slid up against the headboard and shook his head to wake himself up.

"Go on."

"Buzz, I just got off the phone with one of our operatives in the Bahamas. You asked me to keep an eye on two areas over there and yesterday afternoon our man in Bimini spotted a fairly large vessel sitting out in the bay just off the southern edge of South Bimini Island. This is roughly the same place where Frank Morton went missing so our guy went out to investigate. I've just seen the photos personally and there's absolutely no doubt about this—Morton's ex-partner, Tony Nicoletti is on that boat!"

Edwards was silent for several seconds as he processed the words. He had been conducting a global search for Nicoletti ever since he had escaped from another underground facility in Cancun and he'd almost given up hope of ever finding him.

"There's no doubt?" questioned Edwards. "You're absolutely positive about this?"

"I am," replied Danielson firmly. "I've studied the photos and our man over there even had a face-to-face conversation with Nicoletti. The vessel is an eighty foot dive boat named the Dolphin Diver and it was recently purchased by a research group in Belize. I'm betting that when Nicoletti slipped away from MX-2 he fled right down the coast and across the border into Belize. He's probably been there the whole time!"

"I knew he would turn up in Bimini sooner or later! You said the vessel was owned by a research group. What kind of research group, do you know?"

"Not yet, but I have people working on all the details right now. As soon as I have more information I'll get back to you, but I didn't think you'd want me to sit on this breaking news."

"No, you did the right thing! In fact, you just made my whole day! Get back to me with those details when you have them, but, in the meantime, make sure somebody keeps eyes on that boat every second. If it pulls up anchor, follow it! I'll have a more specific plan the next time we talk, but for now just make sure Nicoletti doesn't get away from us again!"

Edwards replaced the handset, leaned back against his pillows and smiled broadly. This was going to be a very good day, indeed. First he had to follow up on his plan to move the narco-sub routes from the Pacific side of Mexico over to the Caribbean side, but then he would focus his attentions on a much more personal project—the elimination, once and for all, of Tony Nicoletti!

***

Although Jim trusted *the Teachers*, something Fitz had said the previous day caused him to pay particular attention at this fourth meeting with the government negotiators. Fitz had suggested that *the Teachers* could, if they wanted to, communicate with a subset of the group without the others knowing. But since none of the negotiators—or Jim, for that matter—could reply using the Teachers' telepathic technique, they were forced to verbalize their questions and answers for all to hear. Aware of this fact, Jim listened carefully during the forty minute meeting to see if any of them uttered words or phrases that seemed to be out of context with what he was hearing. While he didn't detect any one-sided conversations, he was caught off guard when Wayne Grogan, the lead negotiator, seemed to demand that *the Teachers* give up their 'jump" travel secret in exchange for protection from the Government. *The Teachers* suggested that they weren't the ones who needed protection and that even if they were inclined to share their technology, teaching it to even a select few humans would take years. *The Teachers* then countered by suggesting that they work together to locate and destroy the Six and *then* discuss exchanging ideas and technologies.

As the meeting was winding down, Jim was very surprised when he heard *the Teachers* say, "Dr. Barnes, you seem extremely focused on this conversation. If something is troubling you, please acknowledge by taking one step backwards."

It took a second for Jim to realize that the very type of secret communication he'd been listening for was actually taking place with him. Silently, he took one step back.

"We understand. We will contact you privately after this meeting concludes."

And with that, the formalities of any high-level meeting played themselves out and the four humans were returned to the conference room. When they arrived, they found the rest of Jim's NWIDI team seated on the other side of the table talking and laughing. As soon as the negotiators excused themselves, Jim sat down and listened, waiting for a place to jump in.

"I know!" Linda was saying to Susan. "That was the most incredible place I've ever been! And the colors—I can't even describe them—so vivid and bold. Jim you won't believe…"

As Linda turned to address Jim, he vanished as quickly as he had just appeared.

"They've taken him again!" she shouted, bringing silence to the room.

"What?" asked her husband, who was in another heated debate with Fitz about the pros and cons of aligning themselves with *the Teachers*.

"Jim! He was just here and now he's gone! *The Teachers* must have snatched him back."

"I'm sure he's fine," replied Javier. "Jim seems to have a special bond with these beings and I don't think they would harm him. It's probably just a post-meeting debriefing to get his take on whatever our government offered—or demanded."

"But I had the feeling he was about to say something to us. He didn't look like he expected to be jumping again," worried Linda.

"And that's precisely why we need our own plan," insisted Fitz. "Susan and I have been talking about this, and we don't think it's a good idea to trust either the government *or the Teachers*. We need to get out of here before one or both of them decide to toss us in the trash."

At this point, he launched into the details of a plan that was so incredible that Linda and Javier couldn't help listening. Ten minutes later, the two men were locked in a heated debate over the merits of Fitz's plan when they were interrupted by the reappearance of Jim.

"Are you here to stay this time?" asked Fitz sarcastically.

"Yes, I think so," laughed Jim. "Near the end of the meeting they said they wanted to talk to me privately 'later' but I had no idea it would happen that soon. During the few seconds I was here earlier it looked like you guys really enjoyed your stay wherever you were and I can't wait to hear about it."

"It was certainly incredible," smiled Linda, "but maybe we should hear your report first. Once we get started, we probably won't stop until bedtime!"

Jim agreed and suggested they adjourn to their regular picnic table on the surface. Once they were all settled, he summed up the meeting between *the Teachers* and the U.S. Government in as few words as possible. Fitz pounced on his statement about the government demanding *the Teachers'* "jump" technology and everybody laughed at *the Teachers'* reply about who really needs help.

"The negotiators were almost arrogant," added Jim. "They basically insisted on the technology handover or there would be no further meetings, as if they were actually in control of the situation. I wanted to remind them that if it hadn't been for us there would have been no meetings at all but I didn't. I just kept my mouth shut and listened. Eventually, the tone subsided and they all agreed to table the request until the next meeting, two days from now.

"I also listened closely for evidence of any side conversations, but the only one I heard was the one *the Teachers* had with me. Apparently, I looked too intense and they asked me if something was bothering me. I signaled yes and that's why they pulled me back right after the negotiators left the room."

"So what was bothering you?" asked Susan. "Just the tech transfer thing?"

"Yes, I guess. However, once back there I took advantage of the opportunity and explained our concerns regarding what might happen to us when this whole negotiation process wraps up."

"And..." demanded Linda, impatiently.

"And they told me not to be concerned—that we would be protected. I pressed for details, but they wouldn't elaborate. Instead, they kept bringing the conversation back to why the Government wanted their jump technology and I kept telling them that I had no idea."

"Because it would give them a huge strategic advantage over everybody," replied Fitz. "Not just the Six, but everybody! *The Teachers* must be made to understand that they can never share that ability with *any* government."

"I agree," nodded Javier. "It would change the world order overnight and make slaves of anyone who didn't possess the ability. Jim, you have to make *the Teachers* understand that before they do something stupid!"

"We only have two days to plead our case before the government folks meet with them again but fortunately I know how to initiate a dialog with them. Let's get together up here after lunch and draft a statement. Once we agree on the words, we'll go back down to my room and I'll show you all how to get a message to *the Teachers* in a matter of minutes."

***

"Tony, do you copy?"

The hand-held radio startled Tony awake and he glanced at his watch. It was 11:45 p.m. and he wasn't due to go on watch for more than two hours. He reached for the radio and replied.

"This is Tony, go ahead."

"Tony, it's Rigo. I'm sorry to bother you, but there's something up here I think you should see."

"I'll be right there," replied Tony, rubbing the sleep out of his eyes.

Five minutes later Tony was standing next to the lookout post he had designed and Rigo was pointing into the darkness towards the coastline.

"It's not regular, so I don't think it's a navigational buoy. To me, it acts more like a ship riding the swells. It's dark, except for one light that's only visible when the sea and the ship's angle with us are just right. There! Did you see it?"

"Yes, I did," replied Tony, whispering for no reason. "And your analysis makes sense. But what's so unusual about a ship anchored for the night? They're probably all asleep and somebody just left a light on."

"Well, they're definitely not all asleep, because when I first saw that light it was over there." Rigo pointed to his far right. "Now it's way over there." He pointed to his left.

"So if it's a boat, it's under power with no running lights!" exclaimed Tony. "Seems pretty stupid, doesn't it?"

"Very stupid, unless you're trying to remain hidden," replied Rigo.

Just then, first mate Nickolas Banks reached the top of the ladder that led from the deck below and startled both Tony and Rigo.

"What's up, mates?" he asked in his Cockney accent.

"Come on up here, Nick," waved Tony. "Rigo has spotted something that I want you to keep a close eye on during your shift. Look out over the third railing support from the bow and try to focus as far away as you can. You're looking for a light that will appear and then disappear again after just a couple of seconds."

All eyes remained focused on the darkness until Tony finally whispered, "There! Did you see it?"

"Got it!" acknowledged Nick. "Looks like a boat anchored near the shoreline."

Tony repeated the discussion he and Rigo had just completed, arriving at the conclusion that something wasn't right and this boat, or whatever it was, needed to be watched closely for the remainder of the night.

Two hours later, when Tony returned to the lookout post to begin his own shift, his first question was about the light.

"About ninety minutes ago it started back to the right and now it's just about straight off the port rail," said the first mate.

"So it's obviously under power, as opposed to being adrift, and it's moving very slowly on a predetermined course."

"I think so. I've done some rough calculations and I'd say it's traveling at about 1 or 2 knots—barely idling. But it's definitely under power."

"Has it moved any closer to us?" asked Tony.

"I don't believe so. I've been trying to pay attention to things like that and it seems to be traveling on a pretty predictable course. Shall I alert the captain?"

"No, there's no need to bother him now. We'll discuss it with the whole crew this morning at breakfast. In the meantime, I've got the watch—you go get some sleep. And thanks for your observations."

Tony spent the next two hours monitoring the mysterious light. He had brought a notepad and calculator up from his room and he estimated that the object carrying the light was about a thousand yards away at its closest approach. It appeared to be traveling back and forth over a course of about a mile and this route had a thirty-degree angle at about the center point. Checking a nautical chart he had grabbed from the bridge, Tony realized that the shoreline made a bend directly opposite the Dolphin Diver's position, which accounted for the bend in the path of the light.

About an hour into his shift, Tony observed the light change direction again, moving back to his left, which was west. Curious what would happen at sunrise, Tony excused Terry from his shift when he reported for duty at 4:00 a.m.

"Sorry, but I didn't have any way to contact you from up here," apologized Tony, holding up both radio units. "We have a potential situation brewing and I'd like to stay here and monitor it."

"Sounds like fun," yawned Terry. "How about if I go brew us a pot of strong coffee and come back up to watch?"

"Sure!" smiled Tony. "Coffee sounds great and I could use another set of eyes when the sun starts to come up."

When the ship's cook returned, Tony brought him up to speed and pointed out the current location of the ever-moving light.

"If it sticks to its pattern, it should be turning and heading back east in about thirty minutes. If it does, it should be about there at dawn and maybe we can get a description to pass on to the Navy."

Terry produced a small flashlight from his pocket and studied the nautical chart briefly.

"But there's nothing over there," he remarked as he turned the light off. "The east end of the island is almost deserted."

"I know," smiled Tony, "and that should make them pretty easy to find! As soon as we have some daylight, Cesar and I are going to jump in the Zodiac and do a little investigating."

As the time passed, Tony and Terry chatted about each other's pasts. Hedges, who was now thirty-eight, had been at sea since the age of seventeen and had learned most of his culinary skills on the job. Starting as a lowly kitchen helper, he had worked his way up to cook and eventually to head cook on a ship that resupplied cruise ships during their longer, fourteen-day Caribbean voyages.

Tony described his Army days behind enemy lines in Southeast Asia and explained how he had first met Frank Morton in Cambodia. When he stopped for a moment, Terry was silent.

"But I thought you were from Belize? At least that's what the captain told me."

"Oops! Well, this mission is almost over and I intended to tell the others then, anyway, but I guess I did blow my cover, didn't I? It's been really hard to pretend to be Anthony Wykes for so many weeks. Please keep this to yourself until I have a chance to tell the others, but my real name is Tony Nicoletti and I'm from the United States, not Belize. It's a complicated story that I hope to share with everyone very soon, but suffice it to say that there are some bad dudes after me and the only way I could get out of Belize was with a false identity."

"Bad dudes like those guys?" asked Terry, pointing in the direction of the light's last observed position.

"Yes, that's certainly a possibility," mumbled Tony as he gazed into the darkness. "I don't see it anymore, do you?"

Both men stared for long minutes, but there was no further sign of the mysterious light.

"So it didn't turn after all!" shouted Tony. "It continued west and either ducked into a cove or it's just too far away to see anymore. What's the geography look like in that direction?"

Terry unfolded the chart again and ran his finger along the coastline.

"Here! Port Royal has two, long canals and the one closest to us has a back entrance right here. It would take someone with a lot of knowledge of the area to navigate this area in the dark, but this must be where they went."

"Well, so much for ever finding them. Those canals probably have dozens of boats tied up along the edges and we'd never be able to pick out our observer."

"Do you think they will be back tonight?" asked Terry as he poured another cup of coffee from the thermos he had brought up from the galley.

"I'm sure they will, but this time we'll be waiting for them!"

***

After two hours of heated debate over the wording of a single paragraph, Jim, Linda, Javier, Fitz and Susan returned to the underground bunker and squeezed into Jim's small room. He removed a sheet of paper from the center drawer of the room's writing desk and printed the final version of their warning to *the Teachers* on it.

"It is imperative that you NOT share your technology with the U.S. Government or with any other government on Earth. To do so would upset the delicate balance of power that currently exists and this would almost certainly lead to a global crisis. You must find some other way to help resolve the issue with the Six."

Jim passed the sheet around so each of his teammates could verify that he had written the agreed upon words. When everyone had given their nod of approval, he folded the sheet in half and slid it part way under his door to the hallway.

"Now we just wait," he announced.

"What?" scoffed Fitz. "Do they just stop by and pick it up?"

"Not exactly, but I suggest you memorize the note's exact position and then ignore it for a while. Linda, if you'll switch on the television, we'll give them some time to process the information and prepare a reply.

The television was set to CNN, the only station Jim had watched since arriving at the facility, and the current story was of yet another mall shooting in southern California. Nearly five minutes had passed before anyone thought to check the note.

"I think it's moved!" shouted Linda, pointing towards the door.

Jim retrieved the note, opened it and placed it on the desk as the others gathered around. He read out loud the neatly printed response from *the Teachers*.

"We have no intention of sharing anything with anybody, but we appreciate your concern. Please assemble in

your conference room tomorrow morning at 0930 hours for a private meeting to discuss your concerns further."

"Crap! Now we've done it!" exclaimed Fitz. "Now we have them questioning our motives!"

Jim stared at Fitz and shook his head.

"What are you talking about? They just want to know why we don't think they should share their technology. We have legitimate reasons and although we don't agree on the all details we all have our reasons. We'll just tell them what we think."

"And what if our guys find out about this off the record meeting of ours?"

"Hey, we were called and we went," replied Jim. "We didn't think that at this delicate point in the negotiations we should tell *the Teachers* 'No!' Besides, it will be the perfect opportunity to bring up our concerns about what happens to us when this process is all over."

"Okay, but I want it understood that I'm speaking my own mind and asking my own questions," insisted Fitz. "No more group politics for me."

Jim frowned and scanned the faces of the others.

"Is that okay with everyone else?"

Linda and Javier seemed concerned but didn't speak out and he didn't expect Susan to veto her own husband, so Jim nodded.

"This time, it will be every person for himself or herself, so speak your mind and get your questions answered, because this may be out last chance."

That evening, alone in his room, Jim wondered where it had all gone wrong. What had started out as an opportunity to lead the first peace mission with an alien intelligence now found him caught between his own government and the aliens with no trust for either side. And as Fitz was quick to point out, the NWIDI team was soon going to become a huge liability, regardless of how the negotiations turned out.

Chapter 17

Edwards began his Sunday morning with a breakfast of Eggs Benedict, orange juice and black coffee. Since arriving at the underground CV-13 facility he had opted to dine alone, in his quarters, and today was no exception. What *was* different about today was the broad smile that replaced his normal scowl.

He had learned the previous afternoon that the vessel now carrying Tony Nicoletti belonged to a dolphin research group based in Belize and suddenly a lot of pieces fell into place. If Nicoletti were mixed up with dolphin research, that might explain the recent attacks on the narco-subs in the Sea of Cortez. And even if there weren't any real connection, the mere possibility of one would give Edwards enough justification to eliminate Nicoletti without being accused of conducting a personal witch hunt at the expense of the Six. Several Committee members had taken issue with his determination to strike down the NWIDI team and Aleksey Mednikov, the member representing Russia, had even called his goal an unjustified obsession.

Rather than reacting to the dolphin research news hastily, Edwards had spent the previous afternoon and evening considering a variety of options and plans before sleeping on the problem. This morning, as he sipped the last of his coffee, he settled on a plan.

He dialed the cellphone number of Tom Danielson and waited for his top Lieutenant to answer.

"Good morning, Buzz! How's your Sunday going so far?"

"Very well, thank you," replied Edwards. "And that's mostly because of the news you brought to me yesterday. I've been mulling over some ideas and I'd like to run one by you. Are you where you can talk freely?"

"I'm alone in my car, so yes—go ahead."

"Okay, well, my first instinct was to just have our boys in the Bahamas board this research vessel and put a bullet in Nicoletti's head but then we have a boat full of witnesses to deal with so here's what I think we should do. Interrupt me if you hear any flaws in my thinking."

For the next thirty minutes Edwards and Danielson hashed out the details of a sophisticated plan that could not be traced back to either Edwards or the Six. Once both men were in agreement, Edwards gave the order to execute the plan as soon as possible.

Replacing the handset, he turned his attention to his other current project—the relocation of the narco-sub base from the Pacific coast of Columbia to the northeast coast. He had spent hours considering various routes and he was amazed that somebody hadn't suggested this change a long time ago. Launching from the Gulf of Uraba would cut the trip by more than a thousand miles and shorten the delivery time by five days. Initially, the Mexican coast had probably been considered a safer route but the recent losses now made that argument invalid. The main issue to be resolved was how to get the cargo onto U.S. soil without arousing the suspicion of the authorities and he had put that problem in the hands of Danielson, who had come up with what seemed like a workable plan. Within a few days the Six, under a legitimate corporate name, would become the new owners of a large, abandoned oil rig off the coast of Tambalier Island, about sixty-five miles southwest of New Orleans. The rig would be rehabbed just enough to make it look like an investor was in the process of restarting it but it would actually serve as a transfer point where the sub cargo could be transferred to a seaplane and flown inland to any one of a number of locations. Because the rig was well inside U.S. territorial waters, the plane—and its valuable cargo—wouldn't have to clear customs and the subs would have a protected place to unload by positioning themselves directly under the platform. What's more, Edwards' branch of the Six wouldn't have to deal with any Mexican middlemen—they would buy directly from the source and handle their own transportation.

So, all in all, this was shaping up to be one of the best Sunday mornings Edwards had experienced in a very long time.

***

Meanwhile, two hundred miles northeast of the CV-13 facility, just off the southern coast of South Bimini Island, Tony and Cesar had just completed their regular morning dive and dolphin photo op.

"They're amazing creatures, aren't they?" asked Cesar as he lowered his gear into the fresh-water dunk tank. When there was no reply, Cesar turned to find Tony sitting with his feet dangling in the water, lost in thought.

"Tony, is something wrong?"

"Huh? Oh, sorry, Cesar, I was just thinking about our visitors last night. I'd sure like to know who they are and why they're watching us."

"So let's go pay them a visit!" replied Cesar with a grin. "Later today we can jump in the Zodiac, motor on over to shore and wait for them to show up. After dark we can pay them a little visit and get all your questions answered."

"No, I don't think so. If they have a lookout posted on the hill over there, the Zodiac would be spotted and the boat would be alerted. We'd just be walking into a trap."

"Well, it's too far to swim all the way over, Tony. If I had some propulsion units onboard, we could use the rebreathers and slide in under the boat after dark. Unfortunately, I didn't bring anything like that."

Suddenly, Tony jumped up, smiling.

"Propulsion devices! That's the answer, Cesar, and we *do* have some! We have a whole pod of them right below the boat! Help me set up the translator and let's see what we can arrange."

Before Tony was ready to transmit, a low rumble that seemed to be coming from all directions sent the entire crew running to the salon for answers. The normally calm seas around the Dolphin Diver suddenly picked up a significant chop that dissipated almost as fast as it had materialized.

"Relax," smiled the Captain as he emerged from the bridge. "What you just felt was a small, underwater earthquake and I'd guess it was fairly close. I'll verify that with the local maritime authorities, but it seems to be over, so you can relax, gentlemen!"

Not completely convinced that they were out of danger, Tony and Cesar returned to the dive platform and the task at hand.

A few minutes later, the transportation issue was resolved. Tony had learned that the pod of striped dolphins would be moving out of the area by mid-day but several of the Bottlenose dolphins had agreed to help out. It took a lot of explaining to get the concept across to them, but once they understood the mission, the dolphins were eager to take on a new challenge.

As they were packing up the translator, Cesar had a thought.

"Hey, if the striped dolphin pod is moving on, that means our job here is done, right? Does that mean we can head for home soon?"

Tony smiled, realizing that the "earthquake" was probably the destruction of *the Teachers'* nearby underwater complex.

"Way ahead of you, pal! Let's go up and talk to Captain Braydon and see how soon he can be ready to set sail. We'll need to coordinate with the Navy, but I think we should be able to get under way soon!"

The Captain was ecstatic about the developments. He was completely out of his element on a stationary boat and he could see boredom in the faces of his entire crew.

"Are you sure about this deal tonight?" he asked. "If we're going to be leaving the area anyway, why do we care who they are or why they're watching us?"

"Because they might follow us or dispatch another boat to engage us and if we're going to take them on in open waters I want to know who we're dealing with. Besides, we need some time to get everything stowed and get the ship ready to travel so we couldn't leave until morning anyway. If we're going to need supplies, we should try to arrange that somewhere on Andros, before we head west. Let's call a quick crew meeting and get the boys to work."

The Captain agreed and soon the crew was assembled in the spacious salon of the Dolphin Diver. One of the issues that had to be worked out was how to tell the Navy about the pod's pending departure without disclosing the existence of the translator.

"We haven't sent today's pictures off to them yet, so what if we just report 'no dolphins sighted' and let it go at that. We can make another dive after lunch, our little adventure this evening will serve as a third 'no dolphins' dive and then we'll make an early dive tomorrow morning. At that point there shouldn't be any doubt in the Navy's mind and we can ask to be released from duty. As soon as they agree, we're out of here!"

Tony scanned the salon for any objections and, when there weren't any, he slapped the table and said, "It's a plan! Let's get to work and get this tub ready to travel! I'm going to go check in with Rob and then I'll be back to help."

When Tony sat down at the desk to turn on the radio, he spotted a note scrawled on the pad that Rob kept nearby.

"*Sorry, but I have an urgent matter to deal with and I can't stay. Apparently you're off diving somewhere but I wanted to let you know that the facility will be disposed of shortly. I've asked them to wait until you and your buddy are out of the water, but I can't guarantee anything. You'll definitely know when it happens and once it's over you can let the Navy do all the scanning they want to because all they'll find is an extensive underwater cave system that will appear to be many thousands of years old. Thanks for your help with this matter and please extend my best wishes to the entire crew.*

I'll catch up with you as soon as I get this other problem under control."

The note was signed simply "Frank." Tony was disappointed, but at least Frank had taken the time to provide an update. He put the note in his shirt pocket and turned back to the radio.

"So the translator has turned out to be useful already," replied Rob after Tony explained the evolving situation. "We've been hard at work with our resident dolphins, including Emma, and we have made some truly amazing progress. With the communications barriers mostly gone, our current task is to answer their questions about why humans have behaved the way they have in regard to the environment and our planet's other creatures."

Tony laughed. "And how's *that* going?"

"It's tough, Tony. I leave the lab at night ashamed to call myself a human but we're doing what we can to mend the fences with our small group here. They have agreed to carry the message but of course they won't make any promises about how it will be received. So when do you think you'll be arriving in Belize City?"

"The Captain put together a rough route just a few minutes ago and it looks like we might pull in as soon as Thursday afternoon. We're going to take the most direct route possible, which is about 700 nautical miles, so we're estimating our travel time at four or five days. Interestingly enough, our path will take us very close to that underwater city off the tip of Cuba that I told you about, but we don't have any gear that would make stopping worthwhile. Maybe another time."

"You have the translator. If there are dolphins in the area, you might have some 'tools' after all. Anyway, Anne and I look forward to seeing you all very soon. We hope you will agree to stay with us here on Turneffe until you figure out your next move."

"I appreciate that, Rob. I suppose my next move will be out of your state room and back to my old cabin—if I still have a place on the permanent crew. Carley and I actually talked about that one night before she left and she thinks I'm too old for ship life. Have you heard from her?"

"Not a peep. We don't even know if she arrived at her destination. I'm really sorry about the way things turned out, but she clearly had her mind made up before she ever left the Dolphin Diver."

Tony was silent for a minute, as his mind revisited his time with Carley.

"Yes, I'm sure that's true. If she does contact you, try to get a phone number or address or something. I'd like to wish her well personally when I get back to civilization where there are telephones. I guess that's all for now. I'll try to check in during the voyage home, but probably not every night. We have to go back to a round-the-clock lookout schedule once we hoist the anchor here and with the smaller crew size it's going to make for some long days. This is V31DK Mobile over and out."

When Tony returned to the salon, Terry Hedges was busy taking inventory of the galley and everyone else was apparently off tending to their own duty stations.

"Did you see which way Cesar went?" asked Tony.

"Yes, as a matter of fact he asked me to let you know that he could use a hand down on the dive platform but do you have a second before you go?"

"Sure, what's up?"

"Well, I hope I'm not out of line here, but I was sort of wondering about my future with the Dolphin Diver. We'll soon be heading to Belize and I know that my predecessor left the boat to return there. I've heard rumors that you two were close and I was wondering if she will be rejoining the crew when we reach home port. I would understand fully if she does, but I'm not sure I want to be unemployed in Belize. It might make more sense for me to leave the ship here and find my way back to the British Virgin Islands."

Tony suddenly realized that no one else onboard knew about Carley's recent decision, but he decided to leave it that way in case he could convince her to change her mind.

"Terry, as far as I know, your job is safe. Carley has absolutely no interest in returning to ship life, so even if she does accept a position with the Turneffe Wild Dolphin Institute, it definitely won't be as a cook aboard the Dolphin Diver. I can't make commitments for the institute, but I think there would be a mutiny onboard if they were to let you go so don't worry about it. And I suspect that the next few months aboard the Dolphin Diver are going to be very exciting times. Rob just told me that, thanks to the second translator, they are now having an ongoing dialog with their resident dolphins back in Belize. Imagine the questions we'll be able to ask—and the answers we'll finally have—in the near future!"

Terry frowned and picked up a pad he had been writing on.

"I guess I'd better take fish off our menu for a while," he mumbled.

When Tony reached the dive platform, Cesar had gear laid out everywhere.

"What's up?" greeted Tony.

"Oh, there you are!" replied Cesar, looking up from his work. "I decided this would be a good time to check out every piece of gear we have and make sure everything is in good working order. Some of this stuff has never been used or was only used once and it's a lot easier to do it while we're still in calm waters and gentle breezes."

"That makes sense. What can I do?"

For the next two hours, Tony and Cesar unpacked, inspected and repacked all the diving gear. Everything went into dry bags or water-tight cases except for the equipment they would need for their afternoon dolphin dive and the additional equipment they would take on their covert mission that night.

"Well, I guess that's it," observed Cesar as he looked over the gear that remained. "I'll get the flashlights on chargers and then it will be time for lunch."

After lunch, Tony went to the bridge to confer with the Captain about the upcoming voyage until it was time to make the afternoon dive. Tony and Cesar didn't expect to see the pod of rare striped dolphins, but even if they did they didn't plan to take any pictures or report any sightings. However, Cesar insisted on carrying the camera just in case the Navy was also secretly watching them.

As they were donning their rebreathers, Tony had a thought.

"These things are fully charged, right?"

"Of course!" insisted Cesar.

"Rather than just jumping in the water and pretending to look for dolphins, I'd like to do something a little more constructive. How about if we run down the anchor line and check out the sphere that's been holding us stationary for the past week? I know you've already seen it, but I'm curious and it beats just swimming around in circles."

Reluctantly, Cesar agreed to the deep dive after warning Tony about keeping a safe distance from the sphere when they reached it.

"My dolphin escort physically pushed me away when I tried to check out the bottom side, so don't do anything impulsive, okay?"

Once in the water, Cesar and Tony conducted a routine communications check and then descended to a depth of twenty feet before making their way around the Dolphin Diver to her anchor chain.

"Okay, easy does it," said Cesar into his full-face dive mask. "You take the lead and stay within arm's reach of the chain. When you reach the anchor itself, hold up and we'll discuss our next move."

"Roger that," replied Tony. "Slow descent to the anchor and then stop."

When the Dolphin Diver's anchor finally came into view, Tony checked his depth gauge—seventy-one feet. He could see that a steel cable was looped over the anchor and that the cable continued on down into the darkness below.

"I'm at the anchor," he reported seconds later.

"I'm right behind you," replied Cesar. "The sphere is still another one hundred thirty feet down—are you sure you want to do this?"

"Why not? It's either this or sit around all afternoon waiting for dark. I'm curious to see if this one is similar to the one I ran into back at the Guardian Blue hole a few days ago."

"Okay, then let's continue down with the same plan. Stay close to the cable and stop as soon as you see the sphere. And remember, don't touch it!"

"Got it, boss," replied Tony as he gave his gauges a once over and began descending again.

At a depth of one hundred eighty feet Tony was startled by the sudden appearance of a dolphin. When he yelled in surprise, Cesar responded immediately.

"What is it? Tony, what's wrong?"

"Just a friendly Bottlenose checking us out," laughed Tony. "But he gave me quite a start. We must be getting close because he's circling me."

"I'm about ten feet above you so let me catch up, okay? We should show the dolphin that we're together."

"Holding my position," replied Tony.

When Cesar dropped down beside him, Tony extended an open palm towards the dolphin, which caused the mammal to abruptly back away.

"Okay, so I guess that's not the sign for friend," snorted Tony. "Let's ease on down to the sphere and take a look around and then leave this guy in peace. He doesn't look like he expected any visitors, anyway."

A couple of minutes later, Tony and Cesar were hovering just above the sphere.

"So, does it look like the one you saw at Guardian?" asked Cesar.

"Yes, except for the cable that seems to flow out of it. That's amazing—they seem to be a single unit and yet when this thing is done here it couldn't possibly move away dragging more than a hundred feet of steel cable, could it?"

"No, I wouldn't think so, but I don't see any other explanation. Watch yourself, that dolphin is inching closer and closer."

Tony turned his head to the left and the dolphin made a quick move to close the distance. With only inches separating man and beast, the dolphin broke into a rapid, staccato dialog which, of course, meant nothing to Tony.

"He's definitely trying to tell me something," remarked Tony when the dolphin moved back a couple of feet.

"The translator!" exclaimed Cesar. "They think we can speak their language because of the translator!"

"Of course! Man it's a good thing we figured this out before our trip tonight. As soon as we get back to the boat we need to set up the translator and make sure our rides for tonight understand how this all works. I guess I've seen all I need to, so let's head back to the surface and leave this guy alone. How long can he stay down here, anyway?"

As the two divers began their slow ascent to the surface, Cesar told Tony what little he knew about Bottlenose dolphins.

"They normally hang out very close to the surface and breath several times a minute, but I've heard that they can hold their breath for as long as twenty minutes. Typically they don't venture much below one hundred feet, but they have been trained to dive as deep as a thousand feet. I'd say this guy has been trained by somebody—or something."

"Yes, that's one big difference between this sphere and the one I encountered at the blue hole," replied Tony. "That one communicated with me on a very high level. It was weird, too, because it spoke using some sort of mental telepathy or something."

"That's right! I remember listening to this very strange, one-sided conversation through the dive communications system. Well this one seems to be of the strong, silent type. And at least I didn't have any strange thoughts pop into my head, did you?"

"No, not this time. Maybe they have workers and talkers, just like humans."

Back on the Dolphin Diver, Tony set up the translator while Cesar rinsed their dive gear and recharged the rebreathers for the upcoming night mission.

"I'm ready to do this," called Tony. "Anything special you want me to tell them?"

"No, just make sure they understand that we won't have the translator and therefore won't be able to understand or speak with them. Maybe you can work out some hand signals or something. Oh, and ask them how we disengage the anchor tomorrow morning. The Captain asked me about that earlier and I forgot to mention it to you."

Tony had a difficult time conveying the concept of a translator but he was pretty sure he had made them understand that he and Cesar would not be able to hear or speak once they left the boat. Agreeing on a time was also a real challenge when Tony realized that the dolphins had no idea what an hour was. They finally settled on "when the sky becomes dark" which narrowed it down to an eighteen minute window beginning at sunset and ending at dusk.

"Close enough," laughed Cesar. "We'll be ready early and wait as long as we have to. It sounded like they got the concept of shoreline, so hopefully we'll end up approximately where we want to go but I'm a little concerned about whether or not they understood that we want them to wait there until we're ready to come back."

"Yea, I'm not sure about that either," nodded Tony. "I'll take a two-way radio in a dry bag and if we get stranded we can call for the Zodiac to come and pick us up. By then we'll have the information we need and the element of surprise will be lost anyway."

As the disk of the sun disappeared below the horizon at 6:44 p.m., Tony and Cesar sat on the dive platform in full dive gear. Twenty minutes later, as total darkness enveloped the Dolphin Diver, a splash near the back of the boat signaled the arrival of their "transportation" to shore. Tony gave Cesar the standard "thumbs up" sign, lowered his dive mask and giant-stepped from the brightly lit dive platform into the dark water. As the rest of the crew watched from the rear deck of the salon above, Cesar flicked on his hand-held light and followed Tony. Less than a minute later, both divers were churning through the water clutching for dear life to the dorsal fins of their respective "propulsion units" and laughing out loud.

In the distance, on the bridge of a darkened vessel that had arrived unnoticed, a large man with powerful binoculars watched the activity with interest.

"They have divers in the water!" he yelled. "Everybody stay alert!"

Chapter 18

Sunday morning, right after breakfast, the NWIDI team assembled in the conference room to wait for *the Teachers* to transport them to the meeting that had been scheduled as a result of their warning of the previous day. Jim and the others had secretly urged *the Teachers* not to share any technology with the U.S. Government—or any other government—at the risk of upsetting the delicate balance of world power. Surprisingly, *the Teachers* had insisted on discussing these concerns in person with the entire group.

Individually, they each felt the chill that indicated the transport process had begun and by the time their brains finished processing the thought, they were gone. A surveillance camera that monitored the room through a tiny hole in the face of the military-style wall clock recorded the event. A powerful image processing computer in a room not far away detected the anomaly and silently issued the appropriate alerts.

Jim, Linda, Javier, Fitz and Susan found themselves standing in a gray fog. There was no visible horizon in any direction and the place was strangely silent.

"Where are we?" asked Jim.

"You are on the Other Side."

Jim sensed, rather than actually heard the reply and, by the expressions on the faces of his comrades, he gathered that they had sensed the reply as well.

"But the last time …"

"Those environments were artificially created for your amusement. Today we wish to have your undivided attention to discuss a matter of some concern to us."

"Artificial, huh?" shot Fitz. "So what does your real world look like?"

"Our world would seem very confusing to you. In fact, you probably wouldn't be able to comprehend it at all. May we begin?"

"Ah, yes, I guess so," stammered Jim. He felt like a child that had just been told Santa Clause doesn't really exist.

"Very well. We are confused by your statement of yesterday. We know you were instructed to persuade us to meet with your government, which we have done. But it was also our understanding that you personally believed such a meeting would be beneficial for both sides. Is this no longer the case?"

"I'd like to respond first, but then I encourage any of my teammates to add their own comments," said Jim, looking directly at Fitz.

"Everything you just said is correct. We believe that some level of cooperation between you and our government is necessary to stop the growing influence of an international group called the Six. The activities of this group are damaging legitimate societies all over the world and they must be stopped. We don't believe our government can stop them alone and history tells us that a consortium of world governments would be even more helpless. So, yes, we feel that your help is necessary.

"However, if action is required that makes use of your advanced technology, then you must take that action. We encourage you not to teach agents of our government how to use your technology and then expect them to do so wisely."

Jim scanned the faces of his team but no one seemed to have anything to add.

"Interesting. So you don't actually trust this government that you seem to care so much about. Why would you continue to live in such circumstances?"

"Because it's the best option available!" exclaimed Fitz without waiting for Jim to respond. "With all its faults, American democracy is still the best system humans have come up with and, for many of us, moving to another country isn't an acceptable alternative."

"Are you suggesting that it's not the form of government that you distrust, but rather the individuals who

administer the government? If that's the case, then why not just replace those individuals who are causing you concern."

"You make it sound so simple," snapped Fitz. "Unfortunately, the system doesn't work that way."

"If I may," interjected Jim. "By the constant use of the pronoun 'we' I've come to believe that your species operates as a collective of some sort. When you say 'we' you don't mean you and a couple of close friends, do you? You think and decide as a much larger unit."

"Yes. We function as a unit"

"May I ask how many entities make up your current unit?" asked Linda.

"All of us who are here, in this remote portion of our universe, are a single unit and we number about four billion sentient beings."

"Wow! That's half the population of our entire planet. Except humans don't function as a unit. We function as individuals—more than seven billion of them. And each of us has his or her own idea about every minute detail of our individual existences. The more of us that are involved in a decision, the harder it is for us to reach a consensus."

"We view that as a very inefficient system. So, regarding the current situation, did you expect us to get directly involved in this conflict between your government and the other group?"

"Yes, I guess we did," replied Jim. "Of course, we didn't understand the nature of your physical existence then. Personally, I pictured classic little green men all carrying phasers or other deadly weapons. An alien army that could swoop in, clean out the Six and then ride off into the sunset, so to speak. I realize now that my vision was a bit naive, but I'm hoping there's still some way for you to intervene without putting dangerous technology into the hands of inherently untrustworthy humans."

"Perhaps there is a way for us to intervene. We have a small force of human beings who have elected to work with us

on a permanent basis. These are carefully selected and highly trained individuals in whom we place a great deal of trust."

"Abductees?" exclaimed Fitz in shock. "Wow!"

"No, not abductees—volunteers. Volunteers who spend most of their time on your side and who are free to stay there permanently, if they wish. However, most of them are much more interested in furthering our cause and they help us with tasks our physical form makes difficult."

"Cause? And what exactly is your cause?" jabbed an increasingly distrustful Fitz.

"Our cause, since we first arrived here, has been to ensure the survival of all sentient species on the planet. That is our cause wherever we go, and this place is no different."

"How do you do this?" asked Linda, cutting Fitz off and trying to change the tone of the conversation from adversarial to something a little more civil. "And why? Do you think humans deserve to survive?"

"Of course! All sentient creatures deserve that chance. In many cases, a civilization such as yours just needs to reach a certain level of awareness before they realize that the only way to proceed is through peace and cooperation. We try to push civilizations in that direction without directly interfering with the natural evolutionary process of the culture. Unfortunately, humans have proven to be a particularly difficult challenge and we have experienced many failures."

"Wait, you have worked with other civilizations besides our own?" asked Jim. "How many?"

"There have been thirty-six other Initiatives, as we call them. We monitor a civilization's progress and try to encourage positive survival behavior. If our efforts fail, we help a new culture emerge from the remains of its predecessor. But yours must be our last attempt in this region. In fact, we had already given up and were preparing to move on when you suggested that your government might be able to make a significant change here. That now appears to have been wishful thinking on your part."

"The artifacts!" shouted Jim. "They were from you! The spheres, the tsubutes and the triangles were all from you!"

"*That is correct, and there are many more examples waiting to be discovered. They represent our efforts to pass information or technology along to a struggling civilization. Except for the triangles, of course. As we have already told you, they contain important navigational information that we need to return to our place of origin.*"

"So what's next? Will you continue to talk with our government or are you just going to let the human race self-destruct?"

"*We are considering our options and this meeting is an important part of that process. When you first approached us we had renewed hope but your comments of yesterday have given us reason to reconsider. We have invested a great deal of effort in this project, but we are also anxious to return to our home.*"

"Project?" shouted Fitz. "Is that what the human race is to you? Doesn't it matter whether we live or die?"

"*Of course it does. Although time has no real meaning to us, we have invested hundreds of thousands of your years into our efforts to establish a permanent, self-sustaining civilization on this planet. However, we can neither create nor destroy life and when a race of beings is intent on self-destruction, it almost always succeeds. It appears that humans are just a few generations away from that event. However, we will continue to negotiate in good faith with your government as long as there is some chance of a positive outcome. Thank you for the information. We will certainly take your comments and concerns into consideration. We will now return you to your facility.*"

The surveillance camera hidden in the conference room recorded the return of the NWIDI team and the computer once again detected the anomaly and issued its obligatory alerts.

***

Tony and Cesar struggled to retain their grips on the dolphins' dorsal fins as the animals made their way towards the South Bimini shoreline. Normally the dolphins would cruise just below the surface and catch a breath every minute or two, but with the extra weight and drag of a "passenger" their lungs were working overtime. Eventually, the dolphins did stay submerged for a period of several minutes but it was clearly a strain for them. By the time they reached their destination, both divers and dolphins were exhausted.

Cesar had spotted the ocean floor rising to meet them and alerted Tony.

"Time to drop off! I'll meet you on the bottom."

As he settled onto the bottom, Tony activated his backlit depth gauge.

"Seventeen feet," he said out loud. "Perfect call, Cesar!"

"I'm right behind you," replied the other diver. "Keep the lights on until I get there."

Kneeling on the sandy bottom in total darkness, Tony and Cesar rested almost face mask to face mask. Their communications equipment had a range of many feet, but they stayed close together so they wouldn't need to use their lights while they discussed their next move.

"After we catch our breaths, I guess we should surface and see where we are and figure out where we need to go," suggested Cesar.

"Roger that," replied a gasping Tony. "If the boat isn't in sight yet, I vote for a rest on the beach. It's so dark that I don't think we would be seen."

Several minutes later, two black-hooded heads broke the surface and scanned the surroundings.

"We're closer to shore than I had expected," commented Tony as he stared at the shoreline a short distance away.

"Maybe, but turn slowly and take a look behind you," said Cesar.

The two divers bobbed shoulder-to-shoulder in the dark water not more than a dozen yards from the hull of the boat they had observed through binoculars the previous night.

"When did they get here?" asked Tony rhetorically. "Do you suppose they saw my light?"

"I don't know," replied Cesar, "but now I understand why the dolphins stayed down for so long just before we let go. They had obviously seen the boat and tried to bring us in as quietly as possible. Let's hope it worked!"

"The boat looks totally dark," observed Tony. "My guess is that there's only a skeleton crew—maybe even just a single individual. Let's move a little closer and check it out. And we'd better observe radio silence so they don't hear us talking."

The divers dropped down to a depth of fifteen feet and slowly swam in the direction of the vessel while staying close enough together so they wouldn't get separated in the darkness. Suddenly a hand grabbed Tony's arm and he jerked away before realizing that it was just Cesar indicating that it was time to stop. If he strained his eyes, he could just make out the hull of the boat just a few feet away. Obviously, Cesar's younger eyes had seen it first. Tony felt a gentle tug towards the surface and cautiously made his way up. Since the rebreathers emitted no bubbles, he hoped their arrival had gone undetected.

Once they were on the surface, there was just enough ambient light to use hand signals. Tony had already told Cesar that one of his primary objectives was to get enough information about the boat so they could track down the owner and whoever might be chartering it. Using two fingers, Tony pointed to his eyes and then to the back of the boat, indicating that he wanted to circle around and try to find out what name, if any, might be back there. Cesar signaled his understanding with a thumbs up and the two men slipped silently below the surface again.

When they reached the rear of the hull, Tony continued on for several feet before surfacing so he would be well away from the props in case they were started unexpectedly. As his head broke the surface, he strained to read the name painted on the transom. It was the Black Jack III, the same boat that had pulled alongside the Dolphin Diver three days earlier! Tony quickly ducked below the surface and returned to the place where he had left Cesar bobbing next to the hull on the starboard side. He flashed "two-zero" with his fingers and pointed down before reaching out to grab Cesar's rebreather so they wouldn't get separated.

Tony reactivated his backlit gauges and they began their descent. At twenty feet, both men reestablished neutral buoyancy.

Tony, still clutching Cesar's rebreather, spoke as quietly as possible.

"It's the Black Jack III, the same boat that stopped to chat with us a few days ago. The same one the local port captain cautioned us about. So they've been watching us almost since our arrival. What I don't understand is why they aren't cruising back and forth like they did last night. The boat hasn't moved at all, as far as I can tell. They must have her anchored."

"But why would they do that tonight?" asked Cesar. "Unless…"

"Unless there's nobody on board!" whispered Tony. "Maybe they've gone ashore."

"Or maybe they're in the water with us!" exclaimed Cesar. "Either way, we need to find our ride home and get out of here."

"I haven't seen our dolphin friends since we dropped off their backs, have you?"

"No. I assumed they would stay nearby but maybe they didn't understand that part of our instructions. Maybe we're out here on our own. Any suggestions?"

"Not really," replied Tony, "but under the circumstances I don't think going ashore is a good idea and hanging here takes too much energy. Let's move forward and see if we can stumble across their anchor chain. If we find it, we can hang there until our aquatic friends show up to take us home."

After swimming back and forth near the bow for more than fifteen minutes, they finally located the anchor chain and descended to an even thirty feet to wait for the dolphins. The worst case scenario was that the crew would return to the Black Jack III and hoist the anchor, in which case Tony and Cesar would simply back away until it left the area and then swim ashore and call for the Zodiac.

For the hundredth time, Tony pressed the button on the side of his dive watch to check the time. It was 10:17 p.m. and they had been hanging onto the anchor chain for almost three hours.

"Well, it seems pretty clear that our dolphins have abandoned us and who knows what's up with whoever was on this boat. Let's go aboard and take a look around."

"I don't know, Tony. We're not very well prepared to defend ourselves if we run into these guys. Maybe we should just stay here until they pull out. We have several hours left on our air scrubbers."

"I'm more of a proactive guy," laughed Tony, "and not a patient one, at that. Let's go see what we can find. Once we're out of the water, I'll dig out the two-way radio and hail the Dolphin Diver."

Reluctantly, Cesar followed Tony but he didn't have a good feeling about this plan.

***

Captain Braydon's lip and nose were bleeding and he was clutching his mid-section in obvious pain. The remaining members of the Dolphin Diver's crew were being held at gunpoint at the rear of the salon.

"This is the last time I'm going to ask you, old man. Either tell me where they went or I'm going to start putting bullets in your mates until you do!"

The large, burly man grabbed the Captain's white hair and yanked his head back to make sure he had heard the threat.

"Well?"

"I told you, I don't know where they went. They are both experienced divers and they decided to do a night dive. That's all I know."

"Crenshaw, bring me that scrawny one."

One of the other gunmen snatched Rigo Mejia up off the bench that stretched across the back of the salon and shoved him towards the larger man.

When he was in reach, the leader of the boarding party wrapped his large hand around Rigo's throat and squeezed. He pulled a handgun out of his waistband and pressed the muzzle against Rigo's forehead.

"You have about five seconds to tell where they are or this one dies on your watch!"

Before the Captain could reply, the two-way radio clipped to his belt crackled to life.

"Captain, this is Tony. Do you read?"

The Captain instinctively reached for the radio but the larger man shoved the gun into his waistband and grabbed the radio out of the Captain's hand without releasing his grip on Rigo's throat.

"The Captain is busy right now, Mr. Nicoletti, but I suggest you get yourself back up here before I'm forced to kill him and the rest of the crew."

The man released the talk button on the radio and moved his face within an inch of Rigo's.

"I want you to tell him exactly what's going on here, do you understand? Any funny business and you die."

"Captain, what's going on?" Tony replied.

The large man pressed the talk button and held the radio close to Rigo, loosening his grip just enough so the other man could speak.

"Tony, it's Rigo! Some men have taken over the boat and they're apparently looking for you. They're threatening to kill us all if you don't return to the Dolphin Diver immediately.

"Put him on!" demanded Tony.

"You have five minutes before bodies start hitting the floor, Mr. Nicoletti. Five minutes."

"Well, that's going to be a little tough, you see, because I'm currently standing on the bridge of your boat. It will take me half the night to swim back to my vessel."

There was a pause as the large man processed the information.

"If you think I'm bluffing, you are sadly mistaken and your time is running out. You now have four minutes and forty-five seconds."

"Look towards your boat," replied Tony.

Still clutching Rigo, the man moved to the port side of the Dolphin Diver. When he saw the lights in the distance blinking on and off, he yelled a string of obscenities.

"Do you believe me now?" came Tony's voice from the radio.

"Mister, I'm getting real tired of playing games with you! Hoist the anchor and get over here right now, if you value the lives of your crew. And if I see even the slightest deviation from a straight line to me, I'm going to kill someone, do you understand?"

"Yes, I understand, but I'm all alone over here, so it may take me a few minutes to figure this bridge out."

"Your captain said you were diving with another crew member," countered the man suspiciously.

"I was, but he had equipment problems and he went ashore to sort them out," lied Tony. "I can wait for him to return, if you'd like, but it might be a while."

"No! You get here soon or people die."

The radio clicked off and the large man slid it into his pocket.

"Okay, everybody sit right where you are and keep your mouths shut." The man gave Rigo a violent shove towards his friends. "And that goes for you, too, little man.

Crenshaw, watch them! Captain, you get over there and sit down, too. I'm going topside to make sure this Nicoletti character doesn't try anything. If there are any problems down here, shoot somebody."

Aboard the Black Jack III, Cesar was visibly shaking.

"What was that all about? Why did you tell them I had gone ashore?"

"Because now they're only expecting one person to be aboard when we pull alongside. And that gives us the element of surprise. I want you to get the anchor up but don't get underway until I tell you to go. I'll be right back. And leave the lights on in here."

Tony quickly slipped on his rebreather, grabbed his mask, fins and the dry bag and disappeared down onto the main deck. It took Cesar more than five minutes to free the anchor and get it out of the water. Just as he had completed his task, Tony reappeared on the bridge.

"All set?" he asked as he tossed his fins and mask into a corner.

"Yes. Where did you go, anyway?"

"I just gave us a little insurance. I'll explain it later. Head directly for the Dolphin Diver as fast as this thing will go."

Tony retrieved the two-way and keyed the transmit button.

"I'm underway. It took longer than expected to shake the anchor loose but I'm on my way. There's no need to hurt anyone."

"I'm watching your every move. No funny business!"

In a matter of minutes the two boats were tied together with lines and Tony was standing on the aft deck of the Black Jack III with his hands over his head. Meanwhile, Cesar had slipped over the far side of the smaller boat and was making his way under the two boats to the far side of the Dolphin Diver.

"Go aboard and search our boat," the large man told his henchmen. "If that other guy is onboard, find him and bring him to me."

While his men began their search, the leader kept his pistol pointed at the crew on the bench.

"Mr. Nicoletti, it seems that your crew owes you their lives. Too bad you aren't going to fare so well. On your knees, hands behind your head!"

Tony complied and watched the large man struggle to keep his balance as he moved from the larger Dolphin Diver to the smaller sportfisher.

Soon the two boats were unlashed and the Black Jack III was drifting away from the stationary Dolphin Diver but Tony kept his gaze focused on the Dolphin Diver and he remained completely motionless when he saw Cesar flash him the thumbs up from the bridge.

Soon the henchmen returned.

"There's nobody else here, boss. He must have gone ashore just like this one said."

"Alright, then get us out of here!" He glanced at his watch. "We only have five minutes to clear the area."

A minute later the charter boat was plowing through the surf with the throttles wide open.

"Say goodbye to your boat and crew, Mr. Nicoletti. I had one of my men rig it with explosives while you were taking you sweet time coming to me. In about one minute it— and your crew—are going to suffer a catastrophic explosion. We should have a very nice view from here."

"I'm afraid not. You see, my divemaster—who did not actually go ashore—has found and disarmed all your charges. But you're still going to get to see that fireworks show, because earlier I did a little explosives work of my own."

In a move that took the large man completely by surprise, Tony leapt to his feet and dove over the side of the boat in a single, smooth action. Just before he reached the water, his hand found the detonator in his wetsuit pocket and he pressed the button.

The air was filled with an intense flash of light just before the boat disintegrated. Tony dove straight down as fast and as deep as his bare feet would carry him but the explosion still rocked him violently. His last thoughts before losing consciousness were of the Dolphin Diver and her crew.

Chapter 19

The NWIDI team's private meeting with *the Teachers* had left everyone feeling a little uneasy because it wasn't clear how *the Teachers* planned to proceed. They had said they would continue to negotiate as long as there was hope but no one had come away with a strong sense of commitment and there was a feeling of impending doom among the team members. Only Fitz seemed energized because the meeting had reinforced his belief that escape was their only hope and he had convinced Susan to help him finalize a plan. Linda and Javier spent the afternoon with their daughter, Mariana, and Jim disappeared into his room and skipped both the mid-day and evening meals.

The next morning, breakfast was a sullen and quiet meal, partly because Fitz and Susan were no-shows.

"Has anyone seen them this morning?" asked Jim, indicating their empty spots at the table.

"No, but you went missing most of yesterday, too," replied Linda. "Maybe they worked late into the night on that wild plan of theirs."

"I thought you were going to get involved in that process to make sure it was appropriate for Mariana."

"Yes, so did I," snapped Linda, "but they made it clear yesterday that my input wasn't needed. When I left, they had maps and diagrams spread out all over the table in the conference room. They may still be in there, for all I know."

"No," replied Jim, shaking his head. 'I checked in there on my way over here to make sure it was presentable for our guests when they arrive and it was empty and clean. Well, I guess they'll show up for the jump—they know the meeting is scheduled for 9:30 a.m."

"Jim, about the meeting—is it really necessary for Javier and me to do that today? Now that we know it's all a show put on for our benefit, there doesn't seem to be any point. I understand that you need to make the jump to monitor the negotiation, but we don't need to go, do we?"

"Ah, no I guess not," stammered a surprised Jim. "Would you rather attend the negotiations in my place?"

"No thanks!" replied Linda with a smile. "You've attended all the other sessions and you know what's going on. If one of us were to go, we would have a lot of catching up to do and we might not pick up on subtle inconsistencies. I know the original plan was for us all to take turns, but I think you should see this through."

"Yes, you're probably right," frowned Jim. "And I guess Fitz and Susan should have the same option. I don't think either of them is too interested in going back either. I'll come and find you guys when I get back and give you an update if there's anything of interest to report."

At exactly 9:30 a.m. Jim and the three negotiators disappeared from the conference room to meet with *the Teachers*. Elsewhere in the underground complex, Linda and Javier were watching Mariana play fetch with Sandstrom and the Fitzgeralds were angrily pacing the floor of a holding cell in a remote section of the facility.

***

The explosion that vaporized the Black Jack III and filled the sky with light also sent a powerful shock wave through the water and violently rocked the Dolphin Diver. Just seconds after the blast, Cesar was on the dive platform launching the Zodiac.

"Rigo, give me a hand! If Tony survived that stunt, he's going to need our help."

Rigo leaped into the already moving Zodiac and dropped to one knee to keep from being pitched into the water.

"Grab my dive light and start looking for him!" shouted Cesar.

Although the other boat had been a quarter of a mile away, Cesar had no idea how soon before the explosion Tony had been able to jump clear. Tony had explained his plan while he and Cesar had moved the Black Jack to rendezvous with the Dolphin Diver but Tony hadn't figured on being held at gunpoint in the middle of the open aft deck.

As Rigo waved the intense beam from the dive light back and forth over the water in front of the Zodiac, the full meaning of Cesar's words finally sank in.

"Hey, are you suggesting that Tony blew up that boat on purpose?" he shouted above the roar of the outboard motor.

"Yes! He attached underwater charges to the hull just before we started over to the Dolphin Diver. He wasn't in the water more than five minutes, so he must be an expert at it. Maybe it's something left over from his military experience."

"But where did he get the explosives?" asked a stunned Rigo. "And why would he blow up a boat he was on?"

"We found the devices on the Black Jack when we went aboard and he said it looked like some had been removed from one of the boxes. He correctly assumed that they were going to be used against us, so just before we tied up to the Dolphin Diver, he took over on the bridge and I slipped off the back and under water. While he was stalling the bad guys, I found and disarmed six charges they had attached to our boat. What Tony hadn't counted on was being taken hostage and trapped aboard the Black Jack. He must have figured that they would come back when the devices they had planted didn't go off, so he took them out to protect the Dolphin Diver and her crew—us. If he's still in one piece, he's going to need our help."

Rigo returned to his task more committed than ever to find Tony alive. However, by the time the Zodiac reached the debris field that had once been the Black Jack III, both Cesar and Rigo were losing hope.

"There isn't much left," called Cesar, as he throttled the outboard down to an idle and grabbed another light. "It looks like Tony did a first-rate job, unfortunately."

After several minutes of scanning the surface, Rigo suddenly called out from the front of the Zodiac.

"Over there! I think I saw something off our port bow!"

While Rigo held his light beam on a fixed place in the water, Cesar slowly moved the Zodiac closer to the spot. Both men were startled when a bottlenose dolphin arched out of the water just a couple of feet from the small boat.

"Dolphins!" shouted an exasperated Cesar. "It's just dolphins!"

"No, wait!" replied Rigo. "Move us forward a bit more. I think I see something."

As Cesar complied, Rigo suddenly pointed to the water straight off the bow.

"It's him, Cesar! He's floating just ahead."

Soon the two crewmates could see that Tony's motionless body was riding high in the water, face up. Seconds later they realized that Tony was being supported on the backs of several dolphins that were swimming slowly, side by side. The dolphins started a large arc towards the Zodiac and Cesar skillfully maneuvered the Zodiac alongside the living raft. As soon as Rigo and Cesar had each hooked an arm under Tony's armpits, the dolphins dove, leaving Tony's body hanging vertically in the hands of his shipmates. Seconds later, they had Tony in the Zodiac. As a divemaster, Cesar had taken numerous first aid and lifesaving courses, so he bent to Tony and did a quick damage assessment.

"He's breathing, but just barely, and he's unconscious. Grab the wheel and get us back to the Dolphin Diver as fast as you can."

***

When Jim and the government negotiators reappeared in the conference room, Linda was pacing one end of the room and she had obviously been crying. If the negotiators noticed, they chose not to say anything and instead exited the room in haste to report the results of their latest meeting to the President.

"Linda, what's wrong?" asked Jim as he rushed to her.

"Everything!" she shouted, bursting into tears again. "Jim they just came to tell us that there's been an accident in the Bahamas and Tony…"

Linda's voice trailed off as she sobbed again.

"What kind of accident?" demanded Jim. "Linda, what kind of accident?"

"There was an explosion. I don't have all the details, but Tony was on a boat that exploded. They recovered his body and transported him back to a hospital in Miami, but it doesn't look good. Apparently the explosion was so violent that it collapsed both of his lungs and he hasn't regained consciousness since it happened last night. I asked if I could go to the hospital to be with him, but they said it would be too much of a security risk. Jim, you've got to do something!"

Jim was stunned and at a complete loss about what to do so he put his arm around Linda's shoulder to comfort her.

"Where's Javier?" he asked for no real reason. "And do Fitz and Susan know about this?"

Linda sobbed again and stepped back.

"And that's the other thing!" blurted Linda. "Both Susan and Fitz have been detained and are being questioned about that escape plan of theirs. I suppose we'll be next, but they were grabbed early this morning—that's why they didn't show up for breakfast!"

"How do you know all this?" asked Jim, mentally fatigued by the news.

"The same Marine that came to tell Javier and me about Tony also told us about the Fitzgeralds. Javier's in our room with Mariana, but I'm really upset and I didn't want her to see me like that. She wouldn't understand what's happening and it would scare her."

"It certainly scares me. Let's go get Javier and figure out what we're going to do. Maybe we can go topside and let Mariana play where we can keep an eye on her but where she won't directly overhear us."

When Mariana and the three adults reached the elevator that led to the surface, there was a guard posted in front of the door.

"What's this all about?" challenged Jim.

"I'm sorry, sir, but you and your associates are temporarily confined to the lower level."

'Get out of our way," demanded Jim, "or my next call will be to the President himself."

"This temporary confinement is by his order," replied the young Marine calmly. "Please return to your regular facilities and wait for further instructions. I'm sorry, Dr. Barnes, but those are my orders."

Jim's face turned red with rage but he knew there was no sense arguing with the guard. He did an abrupt about face and started back in the direction they had come.

"Conference room!" he shouted as he stomped away from the elevator and down the long corridor that led to the area known as the "C" Wing.

***

The room had a funny smell, one Tony couldn't quite identify, but one that seemed vaguely familiar. The lights in the room were very dim and what little he could see was fuzzy. As his senses started to come back to him, he realized that he was lying on his back and that his entire body ached. He did a quick mental inventory and discovered he couldn't locate a single spot that didn't hurt. But the most annoying thing was the tickle of something under—almost in—his nose. He wiggled his nose several time, but the irritation wouldn't go away.

"Where am I?" he mumbled.

"Tony!" screamed a vaguely familiar female voice. "Thank God, Tony! You were in an accident and you're in the intensive care unit of the South Miami Hospital. Please don't move. I need to find the doctor and then I'll be right back!"

Tony sensed, more then saw, someone moving away from him. He was too weak to move anything except his eyelids, so he closed them and tried to make sense of what was happening around him.

"Mr. Nicoletti, are you still awake?" asked a male voice on his right side.

Tony carefully opened one eye at a time and mumbled, "I am now. And the name is Tony."

The male voice laughed.

"Alright, Tony it is. Tony, you gave us quite a scare. When you arrived here, about sixteen hours ago, you were in pretty bad shape. You came to us in a Coast Guard helicopter but the crew couldn't provide much background. Do you remember what happened?"

Tony searched his memory but everything was still foggy.

"Not yet. Why don't you help me out?"

"Okay, I'll tell you what I know. When you arrived here in our emergency room, you had two collapsed lungs, probably caused by your broken ribs, and you were unconscious. You were also bleeding from your right ear and a large amount of your body hair was singed or burned off completely. Does any of that help refresh your memory?"

"The explosion on the boat..." replied Tony, weakly.

"There was an explosion on a boat?" asked the doctor, jotting down notes on Tony's chart. "Is that right? Were you involved in a boating accident?"

"I was on a boat that I blew up, but it wasn't any accident. I set the charges and I pressed the detonator. It went just the way I had planned it." Tony paused and then finished with, "Well, almost the way I planned it."

"Well, that certainly explains the burns and even your lung issues. You suffered a rare dual pneumothorax—both of your lungs collapsed at the same time—but we were able to get your left lung re-expanded and partially working. With time, it should return to full capacity. However, I'm afraid your right lung is not responding to treatment and it may have to be surgically removed. We'll know more about that in a few days. And you've lost the hearing in your right ear, I'm afraid.

The broken ribs will mend in time and now that you're conscious, we'll want to run some brain scans to make sure there wasn't any damage from the concussion you sustained. You're going to be spending some time with us, I'm afraid, but we'll take good care of you and get you back on your feet as soon as possible. By the way, my name is Dr. Adams. Do you have any questions for me before I let you get some rest?"

"Why can't I see you?" asked Tony, looking to the direction of the man's voice. "Everything is dim and fuzzy."

Tony sensed a light shining in his eyes, one at a time, before the doctor replied.

"Your eyes don't appear to be injured, Tony, but we'll get a specialist in to see you as soon as possible. It could be that the intense light or the intense heat—or both—caused some damage I can't see but it's also possible that you're still suffering the effects of the concussion. I'll stop back a little later but, for now I recommend that you get some rest and let our staff take care of you. You're a lucky man to have a friend on the ICU nursing staff, Tony."

"A what?" asked Tony. But he could hear the doctor some distance away giving instructions and he didn't have the strength to talk any louder.

"A friend," said that familiar female voice that had spoken to him earlier. "How are you Tony? Long time no see."

Tony searched his memory again and then it came to him.

"Jill? Is that you?"

"Yes, it's me. I see you're still up to your same old stunts. Leave it to Tony to blow up his own boat!"

"Jill! Where have you been? I looked all over St John for you but they said you'd gone back to Las Vegas and I couldn't find any trace of you there, either."

The nurse pulled up a chair and sat down.

"Tony, I was on St. John for two years after I last saw or heard from you. You couldn't have been looking very hard. Not a call, not a word, nothing! One day we're at Linda's wedding and the next day you're gone. I really thought we had something, you and me, but you just walked out of my life with no explanation! How could you do that?"

"Jill, listen, I was locked up in an underground complex in Cancun for more than five years! I finally escaped about three months ago and I was on St. John looking for you less than three weeks ago."

"Tony, you've told some tall tales in the past but this…"

"It's true, Jill, I swear! Ask any of the crew. Well, actually they don't know the whole story, but they were with me on the trip from Belize to the British Virgin Islands and they watched me dive into Leinster Bay, make my way to shore, sneak up the hill and into your old back yard on St. John!"

Jill was silent for a long time.

"Tony, is this true? Because if I find out it's not, I swear I'll rip out your one good lung and feed it to you."

"It's all true, Jill! Do you remember a guy named Buzz Edwards from our Las Vegas days?"

"I think so. Wasn't he buddies with that nice man from the Department of Energy who convinced me to leave the country for a while? Gene Carlson, right?"

"Yes, that's right! Well, a lot has happened in the past five years, but in a nutshell, Carlson is dead and Edwards is— and was when we knew him—the leader of a secret international terrorist group called the Six. And Edwards is the one who, five years ago, locked me up in a highly classified underground facility underneath the Cancun airport. The day after Linda's wedding I dropped you at the airport for your flight back to St. John and then I called Edwards. Since I had recently liquidated the NWIDI holdings, I wanted him to understand that we were officially out of business. Instead, he grilled me about Frank's disappearance and the next thing I knew I was being transported back to the airport. Five years later, I managed to slip away, hitch hike to Belize and hide out in an attic above a waterfront tavern. It was there that I met

Rob Jefferies, bought the Dolphin Diver and organized the expedition to the Virgin Islands. Then we…"

"Whoa! Back up the bus a minute. You bought a Dolphin Diver? What's a Dolphin Diver?"

"It's an eighty foot research vessel and live-aboard dive ship. But that's not…"

"Is that the boat you blew up?"

"What? No, of course not! I blew up the Black Jack III, but that's not important right now. What's important is that you believe me. I did look for you Jill, just as soon as I could. I even risked my own safety to go ashore on St. John and search for you!"

"Well for somebody who's only been on the loose for three months, you've certainly done a lot of traveling and I can't begin to keep up with it all. But you're going to have plenty of time to explain it all to me, very slowly, while you recover. I'm not in charge, like I was back at the University Center in Las Vegas, but as soon as I knew it was you they had brought in I pulled some strings and I'm now your full-time care-giver. I'll be here for two shifts a day and I'll sleep when you sleep. I'm not letting you out of my sight again until I've heard your entire story. And when you leave the ICU I'm taking a leave of absence and going with you!"

"Nothing would make me happier, Jill, but I wish I could have found you before I got all busted up. I can't even see you right now."

"Busted up is better than nothing," replied Jill with a smile that Tony couldn't appreciate. "And you always did pretty well in the dark before—I'm sure we'll figure something out."

***

Jim was already seated on the far side of the table by the time Linda, Javier and Mariana entered the room.

"Please close the door," he said to Javier as the other man brought up the rear. "Does anybody have any ideas?"

Javier nodded towards the communications device in the center of the large table.

"Does that thing still work?"

"I think so," replied Jim. "But it's undoubtedly bugged. For that matter, this room probably is, too. I tried to tell Fitz to keep a low profile, but he wouldn't listen to me. What did you have in mind, Javier?"

Fitz grabbed a pen and one of the yellow pads from the table and wrote something. Before sliding the pad across to Jim, he folded the bottom of the sheet up to cover his note.

Jim read the message, jotted down a reply, refolded the sheet and slid the pad back to Javier.

Javier had asked, "Is there anyone on the outside that you still trust that we can call?"

Jim had replied, "Not against the U.S. Govt."

Linda pulled the pad to herself and folded down the flap. After reading the comments, she added her own thought, refolded the page and passed the pad back to Javier who read it, nodded and slid the pad across to Jim.

Linda had written, "How about a note to *the Teachers*?"

Jim wrote "My room, ten minutes" and sent the pad back across the table.

Javier showed Jim's reply to Linda and then signaled for her to bring Mariana and follow him. Jim waited alone for five minutes before picking up the pad making and his way to his own room.

When he heard the light tap on his door, Jim opened quickly and waved Linda and Javier, who was carrying Mariana, into the room. He pressed his index finger against his lips to indicate no talking, but then pointed to Mariana and gave the thumbs up sign.

"How's my favorite girl today? Did you have a good time at day care, Mariana?"

While the four-year-old was chattering away about a new trick that Sandstrom had learned, Jim scribbled a new note on the pad he had brought from the conference room.

"What's our message to them?"

While Jim picked up the conversation with Mariana, Linda and Javier whispered and then Linda wrote.

"Can they get us out of here if necessary and how can we signal them to do so?"

Jim nodded, composed the message on a fresh sheet of paper and laid it under his door as they had done the previous day. He then returned to the pad they were sharing and expressed a concern.

"If they're watching us, someone might spot that and grab it!"

"It's a chance we have to take," wrote Javier. Linda nodded her agreement, so Jim shrugged and turned to check the status of his note to *the Teachers*. Realizing that the sheet had already been moved, he waved to the others and ran to the door. He unfolded the sheet and laid it on the small table by the front window where all three of them could read it at once.

"Yes, we can extract you at any time but all of you who wish to leave must be in the same location. Signal us by pressing star-four-three-five-seven on any cell phone. It is not necessary to press the call button and it doesn't matter whether or not the unit has service. We will immediately remove anyone in the vicinity of the cellphone from their present location and bring them here until they decide where they actually want to go."

Jim looked to the other two for confirmation before folding the paper and stuffing it in his pocket. Just as the adults returned their attention to Mariana, there was a loud wrap at the door.

"Dr. Barnes, it's security. Please open the door immediately!"

Chapter 20

The Monday morning meeting of the Six's sequestered Committee had been brief and consisted mainly of routine reports presented by each of the twelve attending leaders. Only Aleksey Mednikov, the representative from Russia, had deviated from the typical sales and inventory statistics.

"Mr. Edwards, I would very much like to return to Moscow, where I can keep a closer eye on my operation. My people there tell me that there are no unusual police activities and I don't see any reason to hide out here in Cuba any longer. In fact, I'm not sure this was *ever* necessary. When will we be going back to our homes and families?"

Mednikov had become increasingly bold in recent days and had openly challenged Edwards on several occasions. Unfortunately, the Russian was next in line to assume Chairmanship of the Six, when Edwards' term was up, and several of the permanent members were already hedging their bets and favoring Mednikov over the lame duck, Edwards.

"As Chairman and ranking member of this Committee," replied Edwards sternly, "it is my opinion that the future of our organization depends on the safety of this group. And regardless of what your operatives back home are telling you, my intelligence suggests that there is a concerted effort by several countries to locate and destroy us—and by us, I mean the people right here in this room. Only when things return to normal on the outside will we leave the security of this facility, Mr. Mednikov. That's all for today."

And with that, Edwards turned his back on the group to discourage any further discussion.

In the hallway outside, Gomez, from Mexico, and Chen, from China, flanked a fuming Mednikov.

"It sounds like we're stuck here for the long haul," commented Gomez to break the uneasy silence. "At least for as long as Edwards has his way."

"As far as I can tell, the only place where there's any interest in the Six is in the United States," added Chen. "My intelligence hasn't picked up any international chatter about us or our organizations. The trouble all started in the U.S. as a result of that group Edwards has mentioned—the NWIDI, or something like that—and the search for us seems to be confined there. We're here because Edwards is afraid for his *own* safety, not ours!"

"And speaking of that group, I just heard that Edwards botched a hit job on one of its members. Apparently I lost a boat and captain in the Bahamas last night."

"Are you sure?" asked Chen. "I haven't heard anything about this and Edwards didn't mention it in the meeting this morning."

"He may not know yet," replied Mednikov, smiling for the first time since leaving the conference room. "I've had a number of assets in the Caribbean for some time now and one of them is—or was—a fifty-two foot sport fishing boat that we often use for surveillance. Unwittingly, one of Edwards' operatives chartered it to destroy a research vessel allegedly carrying one of these NWIDI guys."

"So, what happened," demanded Gomez as the trio entered the cafeteria for some coffee.

"I don't have the details yet, because my fishing boat was destroyed in a huge explosion early last evening. The authorities are currently on the scene, so my people haven't been able to get close but my captain is missing and I presume Edwards' thugs also perished."

"What about the research vessel?"

"It's gone and may have sunk, too. My boat was carrying a couple of cases of PE4, which is the British equivalent of C-4 plastic explosives. If the two boats were in close proximity of each other and all that stuff detonated at once, it's possible both of them could be on the ocean floor by now."

"Is there any possibility the authorities will trace the fishing boat back to you?"

"I don't think so, but there's always a chance. And this incident occurred solely because Edwards is determined to eliminate that NWIDI group at any cost. It's time we put a stop to his unilateral activities."

Back in his private office, Edwards was just reading the preliminary report about the incident in the Bahamas. Tom Danielson had dispatched a "cleaner' crew to South Bimini but initial reports indicated that there were no survivors and that meant there was no one who could positively confirm the death of Tony Nicoletti!

"How could this happen?" yelled Edwards to himself.

The objective of the mission had been to execute Nicoletti and then sink the research vessel to make it look like all hands were lost in a freak explosion. Instead, the boat his team had chartered had been destroyed and the research vessel was missing. The debris field around the explosion was under the control of the U.S. Navy so Edwards had no way to verify whether or not it contained pieces of the larger, metal-hull ship. But even if it did, there was no way to confirm the hit on the elusive Nicoletti.

Edwards' thoughts were interrupted by the ring of his private telephone.

"I hope you have some good news for me," answered Edwards.

"I'm afraid not, Buzz. The Navy has recovered several bodies from the site. One has been positively identified as our team leader, Ellison, and another was the boat's captain. He's a Russian and he was pretty well known by the local authorities. Apparently he's been in trouble before."

"A Russian?" asked Edwards, his mind already processing the possible implications.

"That's right. He went by the name of Anton Gromyko but it's beginning to look like that was a professionally-created fake identity."

"An intelligence agent?"

"Possibly. We should know more in twenty-four hours but we have very little to go on. The only information we have is what we've been able to pick up from Navy ship-to-shore communications. I'll let you know if we learn the identities of any more victims."

Edwards replaced the handset and buried his forehead in his hands. This was all he needed, on top of Mednikov's challenge this morning! At least his plan to take over the narco-sub routes was progressing smoothly.

***

As soon as Tony had been air-lifted off the boat, the Navy had ordered the Dolphin Diver escorted to the AUTEC research facility on nearby Andros Island. Traveling at full speed, the small flotilla had reached the military docks under the cover of darkness and the base commander had ordered the deployment of a full camouflage cover. By the time dawn broke Monday morning, the Dolphin Diver had, essentially, disappeared off the face of the planet. Restricted to their boat, the crew wasted away the hours worrying about Tony's condition and wondering what would become of them. Finally, just after noon, an ensign came aboard to update them on Tony's condition.

"He's conscious and coherent but he has some pretty serious injuries," reported the young officer. "There are definite lung, ear and vision issues and the doctors are currently running some tests to see if he suffered any additional head injuries. That's about all I can tell you right now."

"Someone should be there with him," said Captain Braydon. "Can you arrange to get one of the boys over there?"

"Not without the base commander's authorization, I'm afraid, but my understanding is that an ER nurse from Mr. Nicoletti's past works at the hospital and she's taking care of him. It sounds like he's in good hands for the moment and I doubt if any of you could get into the Intensive Care Unit other than for a short visit."

"So what's this about the commander's authorization?" challenged the Captain. "Are we being detained?"

"Ah," stammered the ensign, "let's call it protective custody. From what your divemaster told us, it's pretty clear that someone intended to blow your vessel out of the water and until we determine who that is, it's better if you and your boat remain here, out of sight. You could come ashore if you like, but I've been on this base for eleven months and, frankly, I'd prefer your boat to the base. If you will prepare a list of provisions you need, we'll make the necessary arrangements but I'm afraid you're stuck here with us for a while."

"Great!" exclaimed Cesar. "Do you have any idea who else was on that boat with Tony?"

"Not yet, but we have every available resource working on it," replied the ensign. "And that includes the U.S. intelligence community. We'll get this resolved and get you on your way just as soon as possible, gentlemen. If there's nothing else, I'll be on my way. Hail the port captain on channel twenty-two when you have that list ready and someone will come down and fetch it."

The ensign turned to leave but Cesar stopped him.

"I do have one more question. How deep is that long channel you brought us in through?"

"I don't know the answer to that, and of course it depends on the tide. However, I know it's deep enough for a two hundred foot Navy PC-class vessel, and they need a minimum of fifteen feet of water. Why do you ask?"

"Just curious if it's deep enough for dolphins to make the journey in from the open sea. We're into dolphin research, you know, and I was just wondering if…"

"Dolphins do come into our protected harbor from time to time," interrupted the ensign, "but I certainly wouldn't recommend diving here. There's too much marine traffic in this small space."

"Okay, I'll keep that in mind," replied Cesar, only half listening.

The minute the ensign was out of site, Cesar disappeared down the ladder that connected the aft deck with the lower dive platform. He had no intention of diving, but he hoped that he could use the translator and talk a dolphin into providing a little more information than the Navy was willing to share.

***

In his small apartment/office space, Gomez flopped into an over-stuffed chair and sighed. He hated this place and, like Mednikov, he wanted to be home but Edwards was still calling the shots. Of the six permanent seats on the Committee, only he, Mednikov and Chen had expressed the desire to see Edwards go. Daniel Manchester, from the U.K., and Peter Fleck, of South Africa, seemed solidly behind Edwards and the removal of a sitting Chairman required the unanimous vote of the other five permanent members. Most of the seven junior members also supported Edwards openly, but their loyalties tended to be with whoever was in power at the time.

Gomez moved to his computer to check on things back home and was surprised to see an email from an old friend in Columbia. Gomez and Luis Arenas had done business together back in the mid-eighties, when Columbia was first beginning to replace Bolivia and Peru as the cartel's primary source of cocaine. Arenas had spent several years in the jungles of Columbia with the FARC insurgents before he eventually tired of the paramilitary life style and moved to Panama to restart his life. He and Gomez had recently reconnected when Arenas returned to Columbia to live in semi-retirement.

"Greetings, old friend," began the message. "I understand that you and I are business partners again, after all these years! Apparently, one of your representatives just leased what's left of an old banana plantation I own in the northern part of the country and I understand that you're moving your boat factory there from its current location near Juardó. While I'm happy to have you as a tenant, I'm also curious about what prompted the move from the Pacific to the Caribbean."

Gomez reread the email message twice to make sure he hadn't misunderstood it. Why would Arenas think the narco-sub assembly plant was being moved to the opposite coast of northern Columbia? Although it was, technically, a FARC operation, any operational decision like this would have involved Gomez and he would never have approved such a change. He pulled up a map of the Caribbean on his laptop and studied it for several minutes. He spit out a single word before reaching for his phone—"Edwards!"

"I'm sorry, my friend, but I was told you were onboard with this move."

The voice on the other end of the line was Gomez' single point of contact with the now-diminished Revolutionary Armed Forces of Columbia—the FARC.

"Ortiz, why would I ever agree to such a plan?" yelled Gomez. "Have you ever looked at a map of your own country? Subs departing from the northeast would have to unload somewhere off the heavily populated and heavily patrolled coast of the Yucatan Peninsula. Why would I want to do that?"

"All I was told is that there's a security problem in the Pacific and that the plant was being moved to rectify that situation. A lot of money is being dumped into the move, so I assumed your organization was funding the project. There's even a Cuban on site personally managing the process."

"Ortiz, I assure you that I have nothing to do with this and until I find out what's going on, I want the move shut down, do you understand? And I mean immediately! If necessary, leak word of the project to the Federal Police and get them to disrupt things."

"I'll do what I can, but if you're not behind this move, then you have a very powerful—and wealthy—enemy, my friend. Watch your back!"

Gomez replaced the telephone handset and contemplated his next move. Clearly, Edwards had ulterior motives for holding captive the leaders of the world's most powerful cartels. Either Mednikov or Chen had expressed that very concern during one of their clandestine meetings, but now Gomez had the proof. And if Edwards was moving in on the Mexican cartels, he was probably making similar plans elsewhere. Gomez called his two friends and asked them to join him as soon as possible.

So that's why he's been pressuring you about the sub losses," frowned Mednikov after Gomez had explained his recent discovery. "He's building a case to take the drug routes away from you."

"Exactly!" exclaimed Gomez. "But he's not waiting for Committee approval to do it. He's even sent a project manager down there! My guess is that he plans to push the change through the Committee, but even if they don't agree, he's going to do it anyway!"

"I wonder how long he thought he could keep this from you?" asked Chen. "The man must be totally insane to try something like this."

"Well, I bought some time, I think, but we have to stop this lunatic permanently."

"The only way we're going to get the votes we need is if we can show the others that Edwards is also interfering with their operations," suggested Chen. "And we don't have any such proof, that I know of."

"Let me see what I can do about that," replied Mednikov. "Gomez, don't say anything to anyone about this Columbia deal until tomorrow morning's meeting. But come prepared with all your facts so you can present a solid case against Edwards. Spend the rest of the day doing whatever homework you need to do but make sure there are no cracks in your case. In the meantime, I'll see what kind of trouble I can stir up in England and South Africa."

***

The Tuesday morning meeting began just as every previous one had. First the junior members made their verbal reports, followed by the senior members, in increasing order of seniority. The first senior member to speak was Peter Fleck, from South Africa, and he had been clearly upset since entering the room thirty minutes earlier.

"Before I present my regular data I would like to lodge a complaint, Mr. Edwards. I learned early this morning that someone purporting to be from your American organization has been trying to cut a private deal with one of my Afghani suppliers. I thought we had an agreement, Mr. Edwards."

Edwards was caught completely off guard by the accusation and he was speechless for an awkwardly long time.

"I have no idea what you're talking about, Mr. Fleck, but I will certainly look into it if you will provide me all of the details after we finish here."

"Well, while you're at it, how about looking into a similar situation that's just turned up in Europe," added the U.K.'s Daniel Manchester. "Yesterday, London time, one of our major German suppliers of designer drugs was assassinated on the Victoria line of the London Underground. Several witnesses have reported overhearing one of the alleged shooters speak with a distinctly American accent. I don't have any proof, yet, but…"

"Well I do have proof," shouted Gomez, rising to his feet and slamming a file folder down on the table for effect. "I have verifiable evidence that Mr. Edwards, or someone directly connected to him, is attempting to disrupt the operations of the Mexican cartels."

Before Edwards could respond, Mednikov stood and addressed the group.

"Gentlemen, these are serious charges and I suggest that we all keep our heads here. Mr. Gomez, you claim you have proof. Are you prepared to present this evidence now?"

Mednikov knew, of course, that Gomez had spent most of the night preparing his documents, but as the second most senior member in the room, the Russian needed to appear to be above the battle that was unfolding.

"Sit down, both of you!" shouted Edwards, now also taking to his feet. "This has gone far enough! I'm still in charge here and I already said I would look into these allegations but at the moment I have no idea what any of you are talking about. Now come to order and carry on with your report, Mr. Fleck."

Mednikov made direct eye contact with Edwards and spoke in a very controlled and steady voice.

"I don't think so, Mr. Edwards. There have been concerns among several of our members about the real reason we were all brought here, so far away from our homes, our families and our organizations. And this morning there are three suggestions that you or someone from your organization might be attempting to interfere with sister groups. So I suggest that *you* sit down because the rest of us are going to hear Mr. Gomez' evidence whether you care to listen or not. Mr. Gomez, please continue."

Mednikov returned to his seat and glared at Edwards, who slowly followed suit.

"Mr. Gomez?" prompted Mednikov.

Gomez was well prepared, with copies of his evidence for each member. He outlined the plan, as best he knew it, to move the narco-sub facilities from Columbia's west coast to the east coast and he even included a map that showed the probable routes the subs would be taking if they launched from the new facility. Edwards tried to interrupt and deny the accusations several times, but Mednikov silenced him and apologized to the group at each attempt.

Gomez had saved the best for last, pointing out a sheet containing the photograph and brief biography of a Cuban national named Oscar Valdes.

Tapping on his copy on the table, Gomez concluded his presentation.

"This man was sent to Columbia on the direct orders of Mr. Edwards to secure a site and supervise the move of the existing sub facility. Unfortunately for him—and for Mr. Edwards—he leased a piece of land from an old friend of mine, who called me yesterday to say 'Hello' and fill me in."

"I've never seen that man before," shouted Edwards from the far end of the table.

With rage in his eyes, Gomez snapped his head towards Edwards and replied.

"We have him in custody, Edwards, and he has signed a statement detailing what I just said. According to him, he was working directly for you—not your organization, but for you, personally! Would you like to watch the video of his interrogation for yourself?"

The room was absolutely silent but Edwards chose not to respond.

Mednikov slowly rose to his feet again and scanned the faces of the group.

"I'm afraid I have to ask the non-permanent members to excuse us for a few minutes. Please wait in the hall and we'll let you know when we're ready for you to return."

Mednikov waited for the junior members to exit and then he asked Chen to lock the door.

"Gentlemen, it is with great sadness that I make a motion to remove Mr. Edwards from his position as Chairman of our group. I further move that we impeach him from the Committee and request that our U.S. division select a new individual to represent their interests at our meetings."

"You can't do this!" screamed Edwards, his face red.

"Oh, but we can, Mr. Edwards, and, in my opinion, we must. Gentlemen, please consider your responses carefully. All in favor, please say 'Aye.'"

There was a chorus of positive responses.

"All those opposed please say 'No.'"

"No!" yelled Edwards.

"Mr. Edwards, as the subject of this proceeding, you are not permitted to vote. The ayes have it and the motion is carried. Let the record show that at 9:42 a.m. on May 27, 2008, the Select Committee of the Six voted to revoke all rights and privileges of Michael Edwards, and to remove him from this facility immediately."

Mednikov paused to allow the proceeding to sink in and then he walked to the credenza behind Edwards and picked up the telephone handset.

"Security, this is Aleksey Mednikov, the new acting Director of the Committee. I'm in the executive conference room and I need you to send two guards down here immediately."

Mednikov remained behind Edwards until the guards arrived in case the ex-chairman were to try something, but Edwards just sagged in his chair, defeated and furious.

Mednikov gave the guards very specific instructions before they secured Edwards' hands with a plastic tie and escorted him from the room.

"Ask the others to come back in," said the Russian as he took his seat.

When the junior members were seated, he once again scanned the faces in the room before speaking.

"As you no doubt just saw, Mr. Edwards has been removed from his position as Chairman of this Committee. He has also been stripped of his rights as a member of our organization and he will soon be escorted from this facility. What his comrades back in the United States do with him is up to them, but he is no longer a member of this group. Since I am the next senior member in line, I will ask for a nomination to confirm me as the new Chairman. Just a reminder that only senior members may vote but I wanted you all to witness this process in case the Americans give us any grief later."

"I move that, according to the agreements that bind us together, we confirm Aleksey Mednikov as the new Chairman of this Committee," offered China's Chen.

"I second that motion," added Mexico's Raul Gomez.

"All in favor?" asked Mednikov.

It was clear that the vote was unanimous, but he had to ask the second question anyway.

"All opposed?"

The room was silent.

"Then let the record show that at 9:47 a.m. on May 27, 2008, the Select Committee of the Six voted to confirm me, Aleksey Mednikov, as the new Chairman of this Committee for a period of six years, beginning immediately."

There was an awkward silence in the room, and the junior members seemed particularly uneasy so Mednikov brought them back to the business of the day.

"Alright, I believe Mr. Fleck was about to read us his report. Mr. Fleck, the floor is yours."

After the reports were read, Mednikov nodded.

"Thank you all for the information you provided but I think we can dispense with that exercise from now on. We're all leaders of powerful and sophisticated organizations and I've never understood this school-boy treatment of us. From this day forward, we will meet if—and only if—there is something to discuss. Otherwise, I would much rather see you all taking care of business back home. And speaking of home, my top priority is to get you back there as soon as possible. I've always believed that Edwards was paranoid about his own safety, rather than that of our group, but I need to confirm that before we go dashing up the ladder to the surface. Unless someone else has something to add, that will be all for today."

While the room was emptying, the telephone on the credenza rang.

"This is Chairman Mednikov."

"Sir, there's been an incident in the holding area. Mr. Edwards somehow managed to break the restraint holding his hands and he attacked one of the guards. During the struggle, Mr. Edwards was able to free the guard's handgun from its holster and a single shot was fired."

"Did he hit the guard?"

"No sir, he shot himself and he's dead."

Chapter 21

Jim motioned for Linda, Javier and Mariana to hide in the bathroom and when they were out of sight, he opened his apartment door to face two uniformed members of the private security force contracted by the Meriwether facility.

"Dr. Barnes, please come with us," stated one of the guards in a manner that left no room for discussion.

Jim stepped into the hallway and closed his door.

"Am I under arrest?"

Confused, the guard shook his head.

"Arrest? Ah, no sir. The President is on the telephone in your conference room and he asked us to find you. Why would you think you're under arrest?"

Breathing a huge sigh of relief, Jim faked a laugh and replied, "Just kidding!"

When the trio reached the conference room, one of the guards opened the door for Jim and waved him on ahead.

"The President is already on the line—just press the green button."

The guard closed the door from the outside, leaving Jim alone in the room.

"Good afternoon, Mr. President!" greeted Jim, wondering why he, alone, had been summoned.

"Good afternoon, Dr. Barnes. I understand that you've been involved in all of the negotiation meetings thus far and I just wanted to get your opinion of the progress before tomorrow's meeting. I've just been briefed by my people, and they don't sound too optimistic. Is that also your sense of the situation?"

Jim had expected the call to be about the situation with Fitz and Susan so he was caught off guard by the question.

"Ah, yes, sir, I would have to agree with that. I haven't actually taken part in the discussions, of course, but I have been a silent observer and my impression is that things seemed to take a turn for the worse when your team started to make certain demands of *the Teachers*."

"You mean their jump technology, correct?"

"Yes, sir."

"But I'm sure you understand how much a technology like that would mean in our struggles with global terrorism in general and with the Six, in particular. It could change the course of world events."

"Maybe that's what they're concerned about, sir," replied Jim. "Maybe they have a policy, a 'prime directive' if you will, that prohibits them from interfering. Maybe they realize that providing such a huge advantage to you, or to any government, would change the balance of power too much, too quickly."

"It sounds like you've given this a lot of thought, Dr. Barnes."

Jim stammered.

"Yes, I guess I have, sir. I've spent a lot of time listening to the back-and-forth between your team and *the Teachers* and I understand the concerns. On the other hand, I also realize what an advantage that technology would be in the effort to eliminate the Six."

"So where, exactly, do you stand, Dr. Barnes? You've used their technology—or at least it's been used *on* you. Are there any conditions in which you could support our position?"

Jim was silent for several long seconds. When he finally replied, he spoke softly.

"Mr. President, with all due respect, I don't think I could ever support the transfer of this technology to the United States, or to any other government, for that matter because the abuse of this technology would be more dangerous than the current situation. If history teaches us anything, it teaches us that absolute power corrupts absolutely."

"So that's it, then? We just continue on, watching tens of thousands of our citizens die needlessly each year from drug additions and street violence?"

"Mr. President, there may be another way to take advantage of *the Teachers'* technology and defeat the Six but you would have to be willing to accept them as partners, rather than aliens."

There was a brief period of silence before the president spoke.

"Dr. Barnes, I have just cleared my office. It's just you and me now. Please continue."

"Sir, I recently learned that they have recruited, if that's the right word, a number of humans who have been trained in many aspects of *the Teachers'* technologies. Not just the jump trick, but other things as well. If you would be willing to accept help from some of these individuals, you could have temporary use of these powerful tools but the ultimate control of them would remain with *the Teachers*. Once the Six is destroyed, these individuals would return to wherever they hang out and take their technologies with them."

There was another period of silence, this time longer.

"Dr. Barnes, how could we be sure that these individuals wouldn't misuse their power and assume control of our own government? You're asking me to put a lot of trust in these *Teachers* and, frankly, I'm not sure I want these specially trained individuals walking among us."

"Mr. President, they already are, and have been for a long time. If they wanted to misuse their powers, they could have done it thousands of years ago!"

Silence again.

"Dr. Barnes, what you propose has serious and far-reaching implications that I'm going to have to consider very carefully. But how sure are you that *the Teachers* would even provide this help?"

"It was actually their idea, sir. The subject of technology exchange came up in one of our initial visits to the

Other Side and they mentioned the possibility of indirect assistance using this group of trained individuals. I'm not sure why they haven't mentioned it during the negotiations, but perhaps they were waiting to see how things turn out."

"I see," replied the President. "Thank you for the information, Dr. Barnes. I assume the rest of your team is aware of these human hybrids, but please do not mention our conversation to anyone. And speaking of the rest of your team, we've been chatting with your flight crew for the past few hours. It seems that they have some trust issues but I'll release them immediately and ask you to keep an eye on them. And I'll contact you soon about your suggestion. Good day, Dr. Barnes."

When the line went dead, Jim pressed the Cancel button and slumped in his chair. Things were a tangled mess and he suddenly felt as though he'd betrayed everybody—his team, *the Teachers* and even his own government.

"Hey, old buddy, how are you doing!" said a vaguely familiar voice behind him.

Jim spun in his chair and found himself face to face with Frank Morton, founder and former leader of the original NWIDI team.

"Frank? Is that really you? What...? How did you get here?"

"The same way you've been coming and going from this room lately, my friend. Only I can do it more or less at will. You see, I'm one of those 'human hybrids' the President just referred to."

Jim was stunned and jubilant at the same time.

"Frank, I am so glad to see you! Linda never gave up hope, but frankly, most of us thought you were..."

"Yes, I know, and I'm sorry about that, but it wasn't possible for me to contact any of you until just recently. Tony was helping me with a little situation in the Bahamas, but that's finally resolved. Do you know that Tony was injured in an explosion?"

"Yes, someone sent word back here while I was at a meeting with *the Teachers* but we didn't get many details. How is he?"

"Well, he'll recover, but I'm afraid his diving days are over. He's getting the best possible medical care and Jill—you remember Jill from Las Vegas—she's with him right now. I just came from there and he wanted to make sure you all knew that he was thinking of you. Speaking of you all, where's the rest of the crew?"

"Linda, Javier and Mariana are hiding in my bathroom and Fitz and Susan are, or at least were, in a holding cell being interrogated by government agents."

Frank laughed and replied, "There never was a dull moment with you guys around! Let's go round them all up and get some food. I'm starved."

At dinner, Frank was naturally the center of attention and the recipient of endless questions but it wasn't until after the dishes had been cleared away that the conversation finally got around to Frank's "training" and his current status.

"I don't understand it completely myself," he explained, "but I feel pretty much the same as I always did. I haven't had a headache in five years and my chronic sinus condition has long since disappeared, but otherwise I'm pretty much the same old me. I still get hungry and I still need to sleep. In fact, the hunger thing often limits my time on the Other Side because there's nothing suitable for humans to eat over there."

Lifting a back pack from the floor beside his chair, he continued.

"That's why I always carry this. Any time I'm over here I load it up with bottles of water and non-perishable supplies in case my work over there runs long."

"So how long can you stay with us?" asked Linda. "I hope you don't have to leave right away."

Linda had been ecstatic since she first laid eyes on Frank and she hadn't let him out of her sight.

"Just a short while, I'm afraid. I'm currently working on several important assignments and I have to be off shortly but Tony insisted that I make a stop here to bring you up to speed with his situation. He says, and I quote, 'Rumors of my death are greatly exaggerated.'"

Linda laughed, but a tear slid down her cheek.

"That sounds like our Tony! Can you take us to see him, Frank? I mean with your jump trick?"

"No, I'm afraid I can barely manage my own transportation. I don't know if I'll ever be able to control the transport of others because that's something currently reserved for *the Teachers*. However, I'll put in a good word for you and see what I can arrange. But why are you here in the first place? What have you guys done to get locked up down here?"

Jim and the others spent the next thirty minutes trying to explain how they individually and collectively ended up in the underground facilities known as Meriwether Mountain. Along the way, they also brought Frank up to date on what they had each been doing for the five-plus years since Frank had mysteriously "disappeared." Frank listened intently, trying to absorb everything that was being thrown at him. When the topic of Mariana came up, he smiled broadly at the little girl and congratulated Linda and Javier.

"Wow," he said, sitting back in his chair as Jim finished the story of how they were all finally rounded up by the government and asked by the President of the United States to broker a deal with *the Teachers*.

"It sounds like this group called the Six is really bad news and I had no idea Edwards was involved in anything like that. But now, as I think back over the time that I knew him, there were some pretty odd situations—like the time he showed up in the middle of the Yucatan and surprised Jim and me."

"Yes, I remember that," nodded Jim. "He must have had us followed, because neither one of us knew that we'd be at Uxmal on that particular day."

"And now I wonder about that whole deal with the Learjet," continued Frank. "He told me this complicated story about how it had belonged to a South American drug lord but maybe none of that was true. Especially since they had no problem finding it when they wanted to kidnap Fitz."

"Well, if it was bugged, they must have removed the device—or devices—when they had me in Cuba," replied Fitz. "When I landed at the Naval Air Station in Florida the government's finest techs went through the plane with a fine toothed comb and I don't think they found anything. At least not that I've heard about."

"Is the plane still in Florida?" asked Frank.

"As far as I know. Susan and I were airlifted to Washington D.C. to hook up with Jim, so unless someone else has moved it, it's still in a hangar in Key West."

"We should see about getting it back for you, don't you think?" smiled Frank. "I'll work on that after I leave here. And what was the name of that place where they took you?"

"It was a place called Varadero, about sixty miles east of Havana, Cuba. I had never heard of it before but apparently it serves an exclusive resort area visited by a lot of European tourists. But I never saw the resort. As I said, I was hustled off to a small fishing village not far from the airport."

"Interesting," replied Frank. "Well, hey, I hate to eat and run, but I have some things I need to attend to. Do you suppose I could beg a few bottles of water from your kitchen staff?"

Linda accepted the backpack and smiled. "I'll take care of that!"

Jim stepped closer to Frank and spoke with his back to the group.

"Frank, before you bail on us, there's something I need to ask you. A few days ago *the Teachers* told us about a group of civilians—humans—that had joined their cause and were trained in some of their technologies. Does that group include you?"

Frank smiled. "Yes, I guess it does, Jim. You see, Miles and I became aware of the true nature of *the Teachers'* mission during that dive so long ago. Miles threatened to take the information to the authorities and the only way I had to stop him was to push him into an underwater intake that sucked him into a facility operated by *the Teachers*. In a split second I decided to join him and see what was going on. Once I knew the truth, I felt compelled to stay and help and, by then, I was committed and I wasn't able to communicate my decision to anyone. I'm sorry, but if I had it to do over again, I think I'd react exactly the same way."

"No apologies necessary," replied Jim quietly. "And thanks for the info. Will we see you again?"

"I'll make it a point to check in with you whenever I can, Jim, but I can't promise any specific schedule. They're keeping me very busy right now."

Linda returned with the backpack and Frank grunted when she handed it to him.

Smiling, Linda explained.

"I remembered a few of your favorite things and piled in as much as I could—compliments of the U.S. Government! Frank, it was so good to see you again and learn that you're still alive. Just for the record, I never gave up hope, but you've had me worried these last few years!"

Linda hugged Frank tightly and then returned to her seat between Javier and Mariana.

"Well, I'm off," Frank announced to the group. "Good luck with your mission here and try to stay out of trouble!"

Two seconds later, Frank was gone.

"*Mami*, where did the nice man go?" asked Mariana.

The room erupted with several conversations: Linda was trying to explain Frank's sudden disappearance to her daughter while Jim and Javier wanted to know what had been happening with the Fitzgeralds, who had spent most of the day in a holding cell in another part of the facility.

The chatter was interrupted by a loud "Excuse me!" from a guard who was standing in the doorway of the dining room. When the noise subsided, he continued.

"Dr. Barnes, there is a phone call for you in the conference room."

Jim mouthed the words, "The President" to the group and then followed the guard outside.

"I'm here, Mr. President."

"Sorry to disrupt your dinner, but I have a full evening and this was my only opportunity to talk privately with you. Dr. Barnes, when we last spoke you mentioned a group of humans that have been specially trained by *the Teachers* and you suggested that they might be able to help us control—and possibly eradicate—this group known as the Six."

"Yes, sir, I did."

"Do you think *the Teachers* might actually help us? Could you talk them into it?"

Jim hesitated before answering.

"Yes, sir, I think I could. However, I believe that any help offered would have to be on their terms. Their people would have to call the shots—no pun intended—and any support personnel you provided would have to be willing to take orders."

"I see. Dr. Barnes, there's another negotiation meeting scheduled for 0930 hours tomorrow morning and I'd like you to attend. In fact, you will be the sole attendee from our side and your objective will be to convince *the Teachers* that we are willing to accept help on their terms. Although my generals disagree with me, I'm firmly convinced that we'll never defeat this group until we eliminate its leadership, and we're no closer to that than we were two weeks ago. We need their help, Dr. Barnes."

"I will certainly do what I can, sir, and I believe this is the correct approach. However, I do have one personal request."

"A request?"

"Yes. Just in the last hour I learned that Frank Morton, the founder and leader of our NWIDI team, is alive and—more to the point—that he's one of these specially trained humans now working with *the Teachers*. I would like to formally request that he be involved in any effort to control or eliminate the Six."

There was a long pause before the President spoke.

"Really! I'm familiar with Mr. Morton through his extensive dossier and I was under the impression he was lost in a diving accident several years ago."

"He was—or at least that's what we all thought, too. But he paid us a visit this evening to update us on another team member's health status and I assure you he's very much alive."

"I see. I have no objection to your request but I don't want it to be a make-or-break condition. If they won't provide Morton, we will take whomever they can give us, as long as that person can get the job done. Do I make myself clear?"

"Yes, sir, I understand. And about our flight crew…"

"They are not as dedicated to the cause as the rest of your team members, Dr. Barnes, but we knew we were taking some risks when we threw this group together so quickly. We're satisfied that there aren't any loyalty issues—only a very strong concern for their own safety. You keep an eye on them, we'll keep an eye on them and let's all hope that this ordeal is over soon so we can all return to our normal lives. They were released, were they not?"

"Yes, sir, thank you. I will contact you tomorrow morning as soon as I return from the meeting."

"Good luck, Dr. Barnes. We are *all* counting on you."

The line went dead and Jim suddenly felt the full weight of the task he had just undertaken. He was relatively confident that he could get *the Teachers* to provide help as long as they could do it on their own terms. He was much less confident that his own government would stick to the agreement once a plan of action was implemented. He just couldn't see the U.S. Military taking orders from one or more civilians, especially from ones they might view as "aliens."

***

At exactly 0930 hours the following morning, Jim vanished from the conference room. On the Other Side, *the Teachers* expressed their surprise.

"Where are the others? Has your government decided to break off talks with us?"

"No, in my opinion, they've finally gotten serious about this process. I'm here this morning speaking on behalf of the President of the United States. He now believes that the only way to defeat the group known as the Six is to solicit your help and he's willing to do that under whatever terms you feel necessary. I have relayed to him your comments about your human volunteers and I am here to persuade you to get directly involved through these individuals."

There was an unusually long silence.

"This is certainly an interesting change in attitude on the part of your government. Are you sure this is a genuine offer?"

"I believe it is, yes. But I'm only the messenger here, as I've said in the past. If you agree to help, you should do so with caution, but I support the President's plan and I personally ask that you consider it. I know our species isn't perfect, but the disruption caused by the Six and their subordinate groups adds challenges that makes it difficult to focus on the important things. They corrupt governments, they destroy lives and they currently have the upper hand. Without your help, this trend will spiral out of control and our civilization will most certainly fail. Your thirty-seventh effort will self-destruct and you will depart, leaving behind a doomed species."

"You should know that we have already resumed our preparations to leave based on a review of current events and the prospects for success. Unfortunately, those humans we have trained will not be joining us and must remain behind so

your proposition still has merit. If it makes even a small difference in the longevity of your species, it is worth the effort.

"However, our help must be accompanied by conditions. There will be no exchange of technology. You have already elaborated on why this is not acceptable and we agree with your reasoning. Only our trained volunteers will have access to these special tools and only they will decide when and where to use them. Is your President willing to accept these terms?"

"He is. I've already explained that to him—in my own words, of course—when he asked me to bring his request to you. But again, I must caution that there may be a difference between accepting your terms and abiding by them. Unlike you, my government is a complicated organization that often speaks with many voices. Your representatives must be aware of this and must be on guard at all times. Still, I think this is the only viable solution to the problem facing our world."

"We understand and we will take the necessary precautions. How do we proceed?"

Even though Jim now had some experience with *the Teachers* and their collective consciousness, he was caught off guard by the fact that a decision had been made so quickly.

"Are you agreeing to provide the help the President is asking for?"

"Yes."

"Ah, well, in that case I have a request—a personal request—that I would like you to consider," he stammered as he regained his composure. I am obligated to say that the President's position in no way changes regardless of whether or not you grant this request."

"Last night I learned that a friend whom I believed to be dead is, in fact, one of your trained volunteers. His name is Frank Morton and I would like to request that he be placed in charge of the team you send to help my government."

There was another long pause.

"He has only recently completed his training and he is currently working on several important projects for us. We have others who would be of more service to you."

"Perhaps, but I'll bet you don't have any others who have first-hand experiences with the man named Edwards who currently leads the Six. That type of inside information could be very important."

Another pause.

"We think the success of this task would be better served by someone else. The list of individuals who support us would surprise you and your choice isn't logical."

"I'm not asking based on logic!" shouted Jim, raising his voice to *the Teachers* for the first time ever. "I'm asking because Frank is a friend of mine and because I know he would personally like to see the Six destroyed. This is a personal request, but one that comes from the person who provided you with the triangles that now allow you to leave this place and return to your origin!"

Yet another pause.

"Your request has been considered and granted. Mr. Morton will join you shortly and arrange the details of the operation."

Before Jim could process *the Teachers'* statement, he shivered and found himself standing alone in the Meriwether conference room.

Chapter 22

The news that Edwards had died from a self-inflicted gunshot wound had been met with mixed reactions at the emergency Committee meeting Aleksey Mednikov had called the previous afternoon. Gomez and Chen had openly expressed their pleasure that Edwards was gone for good but the U.K.'s Manchester and South Africa's Fleck, the other two senior members of the group, regarded the event as an unnecessary disruption of the status quo. Their concerns had been reinforced when Mednikov announced that "a lot of things were going to change" regarding the organization and operation of the group known as the Six.

"As soon as we're done here, I'm going to do an extensive inventory of his office," Mednikov had told the group. "I would like the other senior members of the Committee to meet me there at 0830 hours tomorrow morning to review the results of that survey, which we will present to the entire group at 0900 hours."

At precisely 8:30 a.m. the next morning, Mednikov unlocked the door to the office formerly occupied by Michael "Buzz" Edwards and waved the other senior members of the Committee through the threshold. It was obvious that he hadn't slept much the previous night.

"Come in, gentlemen, and please be seated. We have a lot to go over and only thirty minutes to do it in."

When the others had found seats and quieted down, Mednikov pointed to five stacks of files he had arranged on a credenza behind Edwards' desk.

"I'm going to have to ask for your help processing all of this material, so I've arranged it in individual stacks. When you go through your documents, you'll see why I separated them. It seems that Edwards had gathered very complete—and very personal—dossiers on each of us. You may do whatever you want with the material, but I suspect you'll want to shred most of it. However, please take the time to glance at every page because it's important that you fully understand what Edwards was up to regarding your own specific operations. This information will not be shared with the junior members, so please conduct your reviews in the privacy of your own quarters.

"While I consider most of that information private and sensitive, let me give you an example of how much overlap there really is. Since the subject has already come up in a group meeting, I'm sure Mr. Gomez won't mind if I use his situation as an example. Documents I have provided to him show—beyond any shadow of doubt—that Edwards had implemented a plan to usurp control of all Columbian cocaine production. Not just the transportation, as we've already discussed, but *all production*. If this plan had been implemented it would have had a direct and significant impact on Mr. Gomez, of course, but it would also have invalidated any agreements you currently have with our friends in Mexico. Each of you would have been forced to renegotiate your product purchases and I'm sure Edwards' terms would have been much less generous."

A buzz went around the room as the representatives grasped the significance of what Mednikov was saying.

"That's not the only example I discovered, but I'll leave it to your own discretion to share—or not share—the other plans our former Chairman had in the works."

"Incredible!" replied Chen. "This is what happens when we let a single person have access to our combined knowledge—he uses it against us!"

"I agree, Mr. Chen, and that's only the tip of the iceberg, as they say. Please allow me to show you something you probably weren't aware of."

Mednikov made his way to the door that led to a small, adjoining conference room and turned the knob.

"This way, gentlemen."

Gomez had already seen the room, so he let the others crowd in ahead of him and he smiled at their reaction to the racks of electronic equipment and the vast array of blinking lights.

"Now you might think that this is part of this facility's elaborate security system, but you would be wrong. I checked with our security staff last evening and they had no idea this room full of equipment even existed."

"What is it, then?" asked Fleck, as he approached one of the flat-screen monitors. "Because it sure looks like security equipment to me."

"It is, Mr. Fleck. It was Edwards' private security system that he used to spy on each of us. There were tiny cameras hidden in every part of this facility—and I mean *every* room and *every* hallway! He even monitored our own security personnel. I left everything active so you could see the complete system, up and running."

"This is outrageous!" shouted Fleck. "And I assume he was recording everything on those servers over there?"

"I believe so. Since you seem to be somewhat familiar with what all this is, I would like to suggest that you be the one to 'pull the plug' on this system, on behalf of your fellow Committee members."

With the approval of the others, Fleck began systematically switching off the power to everything in the room. When all the blinking lights were out, he stepped back and admired his work.

"What's to stop Mr. Mednikov or someone else from sneaking in here in the middle of the night and firing it all back up?" asked a suspicious Daniel Manchester.

"Nothing," replied Fleck, "but I'm quite sure Edwards would have protected all of the CPUs with complex passwords and without that information none of the systems would reboot. I think we're quite safe for the time being."

"If you'll join me back out in the other room, I have one more discovery to share with you and then it will be time to meet with the others in the conference room."

In a final act of defiance, Fleck switched off the overhead lights and closed the door as he exited the smaller room and returned to Edwards' old office.

Mednikov held up a large image, obviously taken with a digital camera.

"Last night I took the liberty of searching Edwards' quarters and, although I didn't find much else of interest, I did run across this."

"It looks like a button of some sort," observed Gomez.

"That's exactly what it is. This button was installed on the side of the nightstand next to Edwards' bed. With the help of our technology gurus, I was able to determine that this button activated an automated system designed to cause this entire facility to self-destruct."

There was a collective gasp and Mednikov waited for the room to quiet.

"I assure you this button has been safely disabled, gentlemen, but this is what awaited us had Edwards been able to return to his room yesterday. In the end, he was only able to kill himself, but I have no doubt he would have taken us all with him if he'd had the chance!"

"I want out of here," demanded Manchester. "I don't want to spend one more night in this place. If this lunatic had one self-destruct plan, who's to say that he didn't have more?"

"I couldn't agree more," replied Mednikov, "but I'm going to have to ask you to indulge me just a bit longer. I have an exit strategy, gentlemen, but I need you to be patient for a few more hours."

At the 9:00 a.m. combined meeting, Mednikov summarized what he had found in Edwards' office and living quarters. During his presentation, he frequently looked to other senior members for confirmation. By the time he got around to the picture of the button, the junior members had already become very uneasy.

"Please pass this around and then I'll explain what this is."

While the photo went around the table, Mednikov turned on the projector built into the ceiling and focused a diagram of the CV-13 facility on a large screen that had lowered itself down the wall at the head of the table.

"I had our maintenance folks dig this out of the main computer. As you can probably tell, it's a floor plan of this facility. The red dots you see were placed on the diagram this morning by Travis Jensen, our head of security. They mark the spots where explosive charges have been removed from the facility's ventilation system. Does anybody recognize any of those locations?"

"I do!" shouted Ramelan Purnama, the junior representative from Indonesia. "There's one right over my bed!"

"Yes, mine, too," added the representatives from Libya and North Korea.

"That's correct. And after a little study I believe you'll find that there were explosive charges in every Committee member's bedroom. There were also charges in other places, such as the cafeteria, the gymnasium and this room. Security is still looking, but so far they have recovered and disabled more than twenty devices."

Accepting the picture from Gomez, who sat to his immediate right, Mednikov held it high.

"And they were all attached to this button, gentlemen—this button that I found next to Edwards' bed."

Mednikov waited for the uproar to die down before continuing.

"As your associate from the United Kingdom has already astutely pointed out, if Edwards felt it necessary to install a system like this, he may have taken other measures as well. Therefore, earlier this morning, the senior Committee voted unanimously to vacate this facility as soon as possible. I'm requesting that you all return to your own organizations immediately, taking whatever extra precautions you deem necessary. I'm in the process of arranging ground transportation to a nearby international airport where some of our people will be waiting to help you arrange flights to wherever you wish to go. Junior members will depart this facility in two hours, senior members will leave this afternoon. Once everyone is home safe and sound, I'll be in contact with each of you to discuss how we can continue to work together and yet remain apart."

While the room buzzed with conversation, Mednikov flicked off the projector, retracted the screen and put the picture of the button in his brief case. He had many things to do before his own departure and he was eager to get started.

"May I have your attention, please?"

The room instantly quieted.

"Thank you. There's one last point of business before we disburse. This morning I notified the U.S. delegation in Washington, D.C. about the unfortunate events of yesterday and I asked them to appoint a replacement for the late Mr. Edwards. While I fully expect that person to be Tom Danielson, Edwards' second in command, we will have to wait and see what the Americans decide. Thank you for your patience and understanding. I look forward to talking to you all soon. If there's nothing else, I suggest you begin preparing to travel!"

As previously arranged, the senior members remained in their seats as the junior members fled the conference room to begin packing.

"That was an interesting story, Aleksey," smiled Fleck once the room was secure. "When did you find time to mark up that diagram?"

"While your sleepy head was still on its pillow, I suspect," smiled Mednikov. "I hope you noticed that not a single one of them wanted to stay around an extra night!"

"So how many explosive charges have been found?" asked Chen.

"Almost twenty," replied Mednikov, "but they aren't actually in the bedrooms—they are all at critical structural points throughout the facility. And when they go off, this place is going to collapse into a giant sink hole."

"When? I thought you said the charges had been removed."

"I told *them* that, Mr. Chen. What I told you earlier was that the button had been disabled, and it has. What I didn't mention earlier was that it has been replaced by a device that can be triggered remotely once we are out of this place. We can't take the chance that anyone will find this facility or the assets it contains. When we leave, this place will cease to exist."

"What about the…" Manchester's voice trailed off as he answered his own question.

"It's unfortunate," frowned Mednikov, "but we can't take a chance on anyone talking. I wouldn't have let the seven of them go if we didn't need them back in their own organizations to maintain some short-term continuity. But you should all know that I've never supported the aggressive growth model conceived by our former Chairman and I don't plan to pursue that path. When you get home, I strongly urge you all to focus on making your own operations stronger and more self-sufficient. We should still work together, but we also need to be able to work independently if we wish to avoid another abuse of power like the one perpetrated by Mr. Edwards.

"And now I suggest we adjourn and prepare for our own departure. The others will be using various commercial flights to get home but I've arranged private transportation for the five of us and we can talk more once we're on the plane."

"The plane? Asked Gomez. "Are we all taking the same flight?"

"Yes, Mr. Gomez. I've arranged for a private aircraft large enough to cross the Atlantic and it will drop each of you off on a long flight that will terminate with my arrival in Russia. I believe in building trust the old fashioned way, Mr. Gomez, and the best way for you to learn to trust me is to keep your eyes on me until you are safely on the ground at your final destination. Besides, the flight will give most of you plenty of time to review the files I gave you in Edwards' office."

"I've been meaning to ask you about that," said Manchester. "What happened to the files on the junior members?"

"There weren't any specific files on the junior members and the few documents I did find I've distributed among us, depending on who they most impact. Anything else, gentlemen?"

When no one spoke up, Mednikov stood.

"Please call housekeeping and have your baggage collected no later than 1400 hours. I will meet you all in front of the main elevator at 1430 hours and our aircraft will depart promptly at 1500 hours. This Executive session is hereby adjourned."

***

After two long days of sitting around, the crew of the Dolphin Diver anxiously awaited the arrival of the AUTEC base commander. Captain Braydon had received a call an hour earlier informing him that the base commander wished to speak to the entire crew at 0900 hours but the caller had not offered any further details.

"Permission to come aboard!" boomed a deep voice from the starboard salon doorway.

"Permission granted!" returned Captain Braydon. "And welcome to the research vessel Dolphin Diver, sir!"

After introductions and pleasantries, the AUTEC chief, who introduced himself as Captain Gregory, pulled up a chair and faced the crew seated on the long bench seat that stretched across the back of the salon.

"First of all, I'd like to express the appreciation of the U.S. Navy for the help you provided in the waters south of Bimini. I was saddened to learn that one of your own was badly injured during that operation, but I want to assure you that he is receiving the best possible care and the Navy is taking care of all the medical expenses. As it turns out, I met

Mr. Nicoletti and several of his associates a few years ago and when I learned he was in the area I personally asked for the assistance of your vessel. I'm sincerely sorry that my request led to his injuries."

The Naval officer stopped, to punctuate his apology.

"And speaking of this vessel, I'm sure you're all wondering when you can get under way and return to your home port—Belize City, I believe?"

The Captain's statement brought smiles to the faces of the crew, who had speculated earlier just what this meeting might be about.

"Well, I have some good news and some bad news," continued the Captain. "The good news is that you are free to depart as soon as you wish. We have limited supplies here at AUTEC, but I will arrange to have a Navy resupply ship meet you east of Miami and offload whatever provisions and fuel you need for your long trip home. It's the least we can do to repay you for your service."

There was an awkward pause before Rigo finally asked the question that was hanging on everyone's lips.

"So what's the bad news?"

"Oh, yes!" laughed the Captain. "Well, it's not really bad news, in the strict sense, but I'm afraid I have to ask you all to sign binding non-disclosure agreements regarding everything that's happened since your arrival in the area. It now appears that the men who attempted to kidnap Mr. Nicoletti may be agents of a foreign government or organization and everything about their activities here is now classified. Since none of you are American Citizens, I can't legally force you to sign the agreement, but I do have the power to detain you indefinitely and I don't want to do that."

Rigo was the first one on his feet.

"Where do I sign?" he exclaimed. "I'm ready to get back to sea. This is the most boring place I've ever been!"

The Naval officer laughed at Rigo's comment, breaking the formal tone of the meeting, and produced a folder of official-looking papers from an aluminum briefcase his assistant had been holding. When the documents were all signed and returned to Captain Gregory, he bid farewell and left the Dolphin Diver, his assistant tagging along behind with the briefcase.

"Let's make ready to depart!" barked Captain Braydon. "Mr. Mejia please prepare a list of supplies you require in the engine room. Mr. Hedges, please do the same for the galley. Mr. Acosta, since I don't anticipate any diving activities on our trip home, you are hereby promoted to ship's quartermaster. Please itemize any other things we may need on our journey home and consolidate your list with the other two so I can transmit our needs to the Navy as soon as possible. Mr. Banks, you're with me on the bridge. Look sharp, boys—I want to cast off lines in one hour!"

While the crew of the Dolphin Diver busied themselves with their tasks, a scuba diver silently attached a Frisbee-shaped device to the hull of the vessel and swam away. A single pair of eyes watched the diver through the murky water of the artificial harbor before moving out through the channel and into the Atlantic.

***

Standing alone in the conference room, Jim reflected on what *the Teachers* had just told him.

"Your request has been considered and granted. Mr. Morton will join you shortly and arrange the details of the operation," they had said.

Jim smiled briefly. In a strange and bizarre twist, he had actually accomplished the mission the President had tasked him with—a mission that only hours earlier he had been sure would end in failure. It also appeared that with Frank on the scene, the government would have no choice but to allow his teammates to return to their normal lives and he knew that would make them all happy.

As for himself, Jim really had nothing to go back to. He had long ago resigned his teaching position at the University of Washington and everything he had been involved in since was now ultra-classified. He couldn't even go back to his work in the lab at AUTEC because the triangle-shaped artifacts that had been the focus of his life for the past five years were now in the possession of *the Teachers*. In a matter of seconds, Jim's mood had swung from one of accomplishment to one of darkness. Slowly, he made his way out of the conference room and towards his small room with his head hung.

As he turned the corner and started down the narrow hallway that led to his room, Jim crashed into Javier, who was going in the opposite direction.

"Oh, good, you're back!" he exclaimed. "Have you seen Fitz or Susan lately?"

"Not since breakfast," replied Jim, lost in his own thoughts. "Maybe they went topside for some fresh air."

"That's exactly what I'm afraid of! Look at this!" replied Javier, handing Jim a folded note.

Jim read the note aloud.

"We refuse to be treated like criminals by our own government. Please ask Mariana to take good care of Sandstrom."

The note was signed "Fitz & Susan" but it had clearly been penned by Fitz. The President had suggested that the flight crew didn't pose any risk to the operation, but obviously the temporary lock-up and interrogation had pushed Fitz over the edge.

"Where's Linda?" asked Jim, glancing over his shoulder

"Our room with Mariana and the dog. Shouldn't we go up after the Fitzgeralds?"

Jim thought for a minute before whispering a reply.

"No, the last thing we want to do is tip off the security people up there. My guess is that Fitz and Susan will be caught in no time, but I don't want to contribute to that outcome. Let's go back to your room and discuss this with Linda."

***

Just as Mednikov had ordered, the wheels of the Gulfstream G450 business-class jet left the runway of the Varadero International Airport at precisely 3:00 p.m., local time. Configured to provide generous space for twelve passengers, the five members of the Committee spread out and enjoyed the luxurious surroundings while the aircraft banked hard to the left and climbed to its assigned cruising altitude of thirty-five thousand feet. At five thousand feet the jet broke through a layer of low clouds and Mednikov glanced at his watch. No one aboard saw the small flash on the horizon as the facility once known as CV-13 disappeared in a blast that would be felt all across the entire northern part of Cuba. Mednikov smiled thinly, knowing that the massive explosion would close the airport for months and that the whole incident would be blamed on the "imperialist Americans" as part of their long-standing blockade.

The Gulfstream's flight plan would take it west to Mexico City, then southeast to the tip of the African continent. From there it would fly northeast to Beijing, then back west to London and finally east to Russia. In all, the flight would cover nearly 25,000 miles and it would be more than forty-eight hours before Mednikov would set foot on Russian soil but the men in the plane with him were vitally important to his future and this was the only way he could guarantee their safety. With all that he had learned about these four men while searching Edwards' office, he couldn't afford to lose any of them just yet. If one of them were to go down now, it would take Mednikov months to build a comparable file on the replacement.

As the Gulfstream leveled off, Mednikov reached into his leather satchel and pulled out the first of the seven files that he had secretly kept for himself. While he despised Edwards in general, he had to admire the man's obsessive need to document everything—including each of the existing junior members.

Chapter 23

Jim, Linda and Javier had spent the previous afternoon debating recent events. They desperately wanted to know what had become of the Fitzgeralds, but they didn't dare ask anyone associated with the Meriwether facility on the off chance that Fitz' escape plan had actually succeeded. On the other hand, if Fitz and Susan had been caught, Jim felt compelled to try to intervene on their behalf.

Another major topic of discussion throughout the afternoon and lasting long into the evening was what their own fates might be. If *the Teachers* actually intended to help the U.S. Government, by way of Frank Morton and others like him, what would become of the remaining members of the NWIDI team? They would no longer be needed as liaisons since Frank would probably take over that role. Tony's recent experience in the Bahamas clearly demonstrated that everyone associated with NWIDI was still in danger but living out their lives in the underground complex at Meriwether Mountain was definitely *not* an acceptable option for Jim, Linda or Javier and it probably wasn't the government's first choice either. But what other options remained? At the end of the day, the three team members had to acknowledge that they had no choice but to wait and see how things played out.

Jim had eventually drifted off to a restless sleep sometime after midnight and he didn't hear the first two or three series of knocks on his door the next morning. Finally rolling over, he called out to the unwelcome guest.

"Just a minute! I'm coming!"

Jim opened his door to find a smiling Frank Morton standing in the hallway.

"Jim! Rise and shine, buddy! It's way past 6:00 a.m. and the day's a wasting!"

Jim blinked in the bright fluorescent light of the hallway and stepped aside to allow Frank to pass.

"Did you say 6:00 a.m.? That's the middle of the night, man. Check in with me about noon, okay?"

Frank laughed, assuming Jim was joking, but one look around the room told him the other man really had been asleep.

"Uh, sorry, Jim. I was told to report first thing this morning and I assumed …"

Jim rubbed the sleep out of his eyes and reached for his glasses.

"When you live underground and have nothing to do all day, there's really no hurry to get an early start," mumbled Jim. "Besides, we were up late last night trying to figure out what's going to become of us."

"I don't follow," replied Frank, pulling the chair out from under Jim's small writing desk. "You have done a great service for your country and you should all be treated as heroes. After all, if it hadn't been for your involvement, *the Teachers* would never have agreed to intervene in this struggle with the Six."

"Well, the way we see it, we know way too much to be set free and we don't want to live like this for the rest of our lives. Fitz and Susan apparently pulled off an escape from this facility yesterday, but I don't really expect them to get very far. Linda and Javier have their daughter's safety to think about and I—well, I'm just too tired to fight anymore. This whole thing has left me very disillusioned with the government—and with governments in general."

"I can understand that, but you need to hang in there just a little longer. If we can make some progress on this Six thing, maybe we can improve your hero status even more and I'll use our continued support as a bargaining chip, if you really think you need that."

"When you say 'we' who are you referring to? Are you talking about us—the old NWIDI team—or are you now part of *the Teachers'* collective consciousness?"

Jim's statement gave Frank reason for pause.

R.J. Archer

"I guess it's a little of both," he finally replied. "Just so you know, I'm not hooked directly into their neural network. I have to communicate more or less the same way you do, one on one. I have been taught how to 'speak' without words, the way they do, but it only works with them. I can't communicate that way with you or any of my fellow volunteers. But when I used the word 'we' just now I meant myself and a small number of other volunteers that will be assisting me in tracking down and controlling the Six. But, initially, I'm going to need your help, too. So why don't you buy me breakfast and let me get some information from you before you and the others get whisked off to your ticker tape parade down Fifth Avenue! I'll go take care of a few things elsewhere and be back here in fifteen minutes."

Jim showered, shaved and got dressed while Frank was "away." He was just stuffing his wallet into his pocket when Frank knocked on the door again.

In the dining hall, the two men ordered breakfast and then Frank produced a small pad and a pen.

"One of these days, these things will be obsolete and we'll do it all electronically, he smiled. "The other day you mentioned a place in Cuba where Fitz was taken. Can you give me that name again?"

"Varadero International Airport," replied Jim. "I think Fitz said it was east of Havana about sixty miles or so. Is that where you plan to start?"

"Maybe. You said your folks in D.C. think they went into hiding and we know they were using a site under the Cancun airport because that's where we met with Edwards several years ago. It's reasonable to think they might have another such site, and the politics in Cuba are such that its government might even allow a place like that to exist. At least it's a good place to start. Do you still have that report you said you got from the German professor?

Jim nodded.

"It's in my room. It has three basic sections. The first section is titled *Those Who Know*, which is a one-page list of twenty-three names. The second section, called *The Six*, is another one-pager that lists six countries. The third and final section is called *The Teachers* and it's just some rambling notes about your new employers made by Professor Schmidt."

"Do you happen to remember the countries listed in the second section?"

"Of course. They are the United States, Russia, China, Mexico, the U.K. and South Africa."

"Germany wasn't on the list?"

"No, and I've wondered about that, too, because the bunch that attacked me—and almost killed my security detail at the time—confessed to working for the Munich regional director of the German BKA. As I told you a couple of nights ago, I came in contact with that file while I was in Germany, so it certainly seems to be a focal point. It's strange that it wasn't included on the list."

"So Munich would be another logical place to look for answers," replied Frank as he furiously jotted down notes. "Those six countries in the report are pretty broad targets, but we'll check them out as well. Is there anything else you can think of that might help us locate these guys?"

"For a brief time—just before being moved here—I was in charge of a small team located at the Naval Research Laboratory in Washington, D.C. One of my team members was an intelligence agent named Bill Blass. He was on a first name basis with the President and he dug up most of what we know about the Six, including the possible identities of the major players. You may want to talk to him at some point."

"Good, good. I assume Edwards was on this guy's short list, right?"

"Absolutely! And since Edwards and the other five all went off the grid at the same time, the assumption is that they are in lockdown somewhere."

"It sounds like I'll be visiting sunny Cuba very soon!" laughed Frank. "In the meantime, here's a cell phone number where you can reach me when I'm on this side. It's probably best to send me a text and don't worry if I don't respond right away. If I'm on the Other Side, I'll get the message the next time I come back across. What time does Linda usually have breakfast? I'd like to say 'Hello!' before I take off."

Jim glanced at his watch.

"Not for another hour or so. Our usual routine has been to meet here at 8:00 a.m. for breakfast because our meetings with *the Teachers* were usually at 9:00 a.m. I don't suppose we'll be doing that anymore, though."

"No, probably not, but I'm not privy to what *the Teachers* may—or may not—be thinking. I don't make the plans, I just execute them."

"Well, you're welcome to wait here and surprise her when she pops through the door but, like I said, it will likely be an hour or more before she gets here with Javier and their daughter. We adults are in limbo until we receive further instructions, but they try to keep Mariana on a regular schedule if they can."

"No, I don't think I'll wait, but let her know I asked about her and her family. I'm going to take off and start checking some things out but I'll try to get back here later today. What time do you normally have your evening meal?"

"Usually about 6:00 p.m.," replied Jim, "but if you're planning to join us we can make it any time that works for you."

"Let's stick with 6:00 p.m. I'll try to have some news for you all by then. Say, do you think you could arrange a room for me here? We sort of blew up my old hangout and, like I said, I still have to sleep."

"I'll make sure you have a place to stay," smiled Jim.

Frank nodded and disappeared from the dining hall.

***

The Dolphin Diver made a slow right turn as it passed out of the AUTEC harbor and into the Atlantic Ocean.

"Engine room, all ahead full," barked Captain Braydon into the ship's intercom. "Gentlemen, look alive—we are once again at sea!"

Their eight hundred mile journey would take them past Miami, where they would rendezvous with a Navy supply ship, then around the tip of Florida, past the northwestern tip of Cuba, and then southwest past Cancun to Belize City. Once they fueled up, courtesy of the Navy vessel, they would travel non-stop to their home port and spirits were high in anticipation of their arrival in Belize. Even the ship's new cook, Terry Hedges, was eager to make port, even though he wasn't added to the crew until they were in the British Virgin Islands when Carley made her sudden departure.

As the Dolphin Diver gradually picked up speed, a pod of Atlantic Bottlenose dolphins began leaping out of the water near the back of the boat. Cesar was at work on the dive platform securing gear that wouldn't be needed for the duration and he paused to admire the animals and ponder how much they had changed his life already. As he watched, he realized that these dolphins weren't actually playing; they were trying to get his attention. He raced to the bridge and asked the Captain to bring the boat to a stop. Borrowing the help of First Mate Banks, he quickly returned to the dive platform and unpacked the modified translator. Although Tony had always handled the equipment in the past, Cesar had watched several times and managed to get the unit deployed and activated.

Slipping the headset on, he spoke slowly into the attached microphone.

"This is the Dolphin Diver, do you read me?"

There was a pause and then the reply.

"Dolphin Diver, you should be aware that a device was attached to your hull while you were in port."

"Understood," replied Cesar. "Do you know what it is? I mean, do you recognize it?"

"No, none of us have ever seen anything like it before."

"Please stand by," replied Cesar.

After conferring with Captain Braydon, it was decided that Cesar should dive down to see if he could determine the nature of the device and where it had come from. Fifteen minutes later, Cesar was geared up and ready to dive. As he slipped off the dive platform, five dolphins greeted him and guided him to the device.

Cesar examined the disk-like object, being very careful not to touch it. There were no visible markings but he took a dozen photos with his underwater camera before returning to the Dolphin Diver.

When the Captain saw the images in Cesar's camera, he immediately contacted the AUTEC harbormaster on the marine radio and asked to speak personally to the base commander. It took some convincing, but Captain Braydon finally heard the voice of U.S. Navy Captain Gregory on the radio.

"I understand there's some sort of emergency?" asked an irritated Gregory.

"Yes, sir, there certainly is. While our vessel was in your harbor someone attached a disk-like object to our hull and I want to know if you had anything to do with this action."

There was a long pause before the naval officer replied.

"Captain Braydon, I assure you that I don't know anything about any device being attached to your vessel! Perhaps it was already attached when you entered our harbor, because it most certainly wasn't done by any of my personnel."

"Captain Gregory, I have it on good authority that a scuba diver attached the device sometime after your last visit to our boat and before we cast off from your pier. If it wasn't one of your divers, then perhaps you can explain who else is swimming around in your harbor."

Again, another long pause.

"Captain Braydon, I have just double-checked with my staff here at AUTEC and we have not had any divers in the water in the past twenty-four hours. There has to be another explanation. However, let's deal with this object first and then figure out where it came from. Can you give me a detailed description of it?"

"I can do better than that!" shouted Captain Braydon. "I can send you pictures of it!"

Minutes later Cesar's images had been transmitted to the base headquarters and reviewed by Navy ordinance specialists.

"Captain Braydon, this is Captain Gregory again. My men tell me that the device attached to your vessel appears to be a Russian MK-1 Limpet mine. If it is, and if it detonates, your vessel and anyone on board will be lost. Therefore, I am ordering you to abandon ship immediately and to move as far away from the scene as possible. I have already dispatched a SEAL team to investigate, but these mines can be very dangerous because they come in several varieties. Some are detonated by timer devices while others measure boat movement and detonate when you are a certain distance from the initial attachment point. But one thing they all have in common is that they are all fitted with anti-tamper circuitry which makes removing them almost impossible. Please initiate your abandon ship procedures immediately."

Captain Braydon lifted the microphone for the ship's intercom system and stated slowly and clearly, "All hands abandon ship. This is not a drill. All hands abandon ship immediately."

"I need to go make sure everyone understands the seriousness of the situation, but I assume you realize that I will not be leaving my ship. I will be here to assist your divers when they arrive. Over and out."

Without waiting for a reply, Captain Braydon laid the microphone down and quickly made his way back to the salon. The crew was gathered on the dive platform and Cesar had the Zodiac in the water, but no one had actually left the ship yet.

"Off you go mates," yelled Captain Braydon. "The Navy thinks that device might be a Russian mine and they have ordered us to declare a maritime emergency and abandon ship. As ranking ship's officer, First Mate Banks will be in charge. Now get in and move as far away as you can, lads."

"What about you?" shouted Nickolas Banks. "Aren't you coming?"

"You know the answer to that," replied Braydon. "My place is here. Now go—that's an order!"

Reluctantly, the members of the crew piled into the Zodiac, with Cesar at the controls and Banks in the bow. Just before he pushed away from the Dolphin Diver, Cesar grabbed the translator unit off the dive platform and tossed it into the bottom of the Zodiac. Then, with a thumbs-up to the Captain, he gunned the outboard motor and steered the Zodiac rapidly away from the Dolphin Diver at right angles to her starboard side.

***

When Frank made the jump to the Varadero airport he didn't know what to expect, but he certainly didn't expect to find the terminal empty and two dozen emergency vehicles swarming the far end of the main runway. Frank had jumped to a remote corner of the parking lot, hoping to avoid being spotted, but he could just as well have appeared in the middle of the empty terminal. A crowd of onlookers were pressed against a tall chain link fence in the opposite corner of the parking lot, so Frank made his way there to find out what was going on.

By eavesdropping on several conversations he gathered that there had been a huge explosion the prior afternoon, but his Spanish wasn't good enough to pick up many details so he hovered on the fringe of the crowd until he heard someone speaking English.

"Excuse me," he interrupted. "I've just arrived from the eastern part of the island to catch a flight. Do you know what happened here?"

"Sorry, mate," replied the older man in a British accent. "All flights from here have been canceled indefinitely until they investigate and make repairs to the runway. We've all been told to make our own way to Havana and try to book something from there."

"So, what happened, do they know?" pressed Frank.

"Apparently there was some sort of facility built under the runway down at the far end. Some are saying it might have been an air traffic control center but I have my doubts. Anyway, yesterday afternoon the whole place exploded and caved in, taking the end of the runway with it. The state media isn't saying anything but rumor has it that they've removed several dozen bodies already."

"Wow," exclaimed Frank. "What a shame. Well, I guess I'd better think about getting to Havana. With this airport closed, flights are probably going to be very full in Havana."

"You can say that again! We're tentatively booked on a flight back to London the day after tomorrow, but we're not counting on anything at this point. This is certainly a terrible way to end a vacation!"

"Good luck and thanks for the information," replied Frank as he moved off.

He was tempted to try a jump directly down to the accident scene but he didn't want to take a chance on being seen popping into view. Scanning the area, he spotted a large dump truck just passing through a security checkpoint next to the main terminal. As the driver worked his way up through the gears, Frank jumped and reappeared in the back of the truck, landing quietly in some sand that covered the large bed of the rig. He ducked under a tarp that was obviously used to cover loose loads and waited until the truck came to a stop at the explosion site.

When he heard the driver slam his door and call to someone in the distance, Frank poked his head out to take stock of his situation. The truck was parked near the edge of a large hole in what had been the end of the concrete runway. Hearing the sound of heavy machinery approaching, Frank looked up just in time to see a large front loader tilting its bucket towards the truck. He slipped out the opposite side of the bed and onto the ground just in time to miss being buried alive by dirt and broken chunks of concrete.

Frank maneuvered his way to a position behind some twisted steel and peered into the deep hole. Whatever had been here was now covered with broken pieces of large concrete slabs. Along the near edge, Frank could make out pieces of massive steel I-beams that had once held up the roof and he quickly realized that this site was probably identical to the one where he, Tony and Linda had first been introduced to Javier several years earlier. That site, known as MX-2, had been part of a global network of top secret facilities intended to provide protection to traveling world leaders in case the worst should occur while they are out of their own countries. However, Cuba would certainly not have been a part of the coalition that shared the network, so this site had probably remained unknown to the free world until yesterday's blast.

Surveying the damage, Frank surmised that Edwards and his associates had felt it necessary, for whatever reason, to abandon the site and then they had destroyed it to eliminate whatever they had left behind. If Frank had arrived a day earlier, he might have been able to jump inside the facility and have a look around, but he might also have been blown to pieces by the explosion.

"Timing is everything," he said to himself grimly.

If, indeed, Edwards and friends had fled, they would probably have used this very runway to make their escape! Their final act would have been to destroy the runway and create a diversion that would occupy authorities for weeks.

Frank jumped back to his "base" on the Other Side and immediately jumped to the administrative wing of the now abandoned terminal. All the outside doors were locked and military guards were posted at each entrance, so no one would be looking for anyone inside.

Frank searched the immediate area until he found a door marked *Aviación General*. Slipping inside, he searched the room until he found the hand-written log of private aircraft arrivals and departures. Happy that technology had not yet reached Cuba's aviation industry, he turned to the last page, he slid his finger down to the very last entry: a Gulfstream G450 private jet with a flight plan to Mexico City. Frank noted the tail number and then started searching backwards until he located the entry for the plane's arrival. It had come in on May thirteenth, more than two weeks ago, and the log indicated that its origin had been Moscow, Russia!

Thinking back on his conversation with Jim, Frank recalled that Mexico and Russia were both countries on Professor Schmidt's list titled "The Six." He snatched a pen off a nearby desk and jotted down the tail number. If the leaders of the Six had fled to Mexico City, they were going to be hard to find among the twenty million other people who lived there but at least it provided a place to start.

Frank jumped out of the Varadero terminal building and reappeared, seconds later, in the conference room of the Meriwether Mountain complex. Making his way to Jim's room, he knocked.

Jim opened the door, surprised to see Frank again so soon.

"You told me earlier that you had access to an intelligence operative. See what you can find out about the aircraft carrying this tail number. It's a Gulfstream G450 and it might be registered in Russia. We need to know where it is right now."

"I'll get right on it," replied Jim. "What's the connection?"

Frank gave Jim an update on what he had found in Cuba.

"And I have reason to believe that the leaders of the Six all left together on this plane! If we can track down its current location, I think we'll have a fix on our bad guys. If we can take them all together, this adventure will be over before it even gets started!"

Chapter 24

After briefing Jim, Frank 'jumped' to Toluca International Airport, about forty miles west of Mexico City. This was the destination he had found in the flight plan logbook in Cuba and it was the best information he had on the whereabouts of the Gulfstream business jet that had departed Varadero International Airport just minutes before the huge explosion that had closed the runway and apparently killed a number of people. Frank wasn't sure what he would find because the log entry could have been intentionally falsified, but he had to start somewhere.

It took Frank some time to find the general aviation offices and then it took him additional time to find a private pilot who spoke both English and Spanish well enough to convey his inquiry. Through his new friend, Frank passed along a story about how he was supposed to meet some friends who were on a charter flight inbound from Cuba. Frank told the office manager that he had been delayed but that he hoped they were still waiting for him.

The pilot translated Frank's story and then Frank handed the Mexican official a slip of paper with the tail number of the Gulfstream printed on it. A few taps on the computer keyboard and the man had the answer.

"Brasilia," he said, followed by something more that Frank didn't follow.

The pilot nodded and turned to Frank.

"I'm afraid you missed them," he said sympathetically. "One passenger, a Mexican national, deplaned here. They topped off their fuel tanks and then departed about 5:45 p.m. last night. He says they were headed for Brasilia, the capital of Brazil, with an estimated arrival time of 1:30 a.m. this morning."

Frank thanked both men and walked away trying to look disappointed. Brazil didn't seem like a logical destination for the leaders of the Six, but Frank really needed to study a map of the world before letting himself become too concerned. He turned into the first restroom he came to, walked to the nearest open stall and jumped to the Brasilia International Airport.

In Brasilia, he ran the same scam: he found a private pilot in the general aviation area that spoke both English and Portuguese, told him basically the same story he had used in Mexico, and talked the pilot into serving as his translator.

This time, the answers made more sense. The Gulfstream had landed right on schedule at 1:30 a.m., taken on a full load of fuel and had been airborne again just after 2:30 a.m. The only person to leave the plane was the pilot, who filed a flight plan to Cape Town, South Africa, and then returned to the aircraft. They were scheduled to land in Africa at 10:00 a.m., Washington D.C. time.

Frank glanced at his watch, hastily thanked the pilot and the lady who had provided the information and raced off down the hallway. He had just a little more than an hour before the Gulfstream was scheduled to touch down in South Africa and he planned to be there, waiting, when that plane rolled to a stop!

***

Cesar and the crew of the Dolphin Diver, minus Captain Braydon, who had refused to leave his ship, took refuge behind a small cay about a thousand yards from the now anchored research vessel. When the Zodiac was more or less stationary, Cesar lowered the hydrophone portion of the translator over the side and slipped the headphones on. Resting the main unit on his lap, he turned it on and listened for a minute. When he heard nothing of interest, he spoke.

"This is the crew of the Dolphin Diver. Do you read?"

"We hear you, but not clearly. Are you still aboard your ship?"

"No. We were ordered to abandon ship and, except for our captain, we are all west of the vessel taking cover. The Navy claims that the device you warned us about is probably an explosive charge and there's a danger that it might detonate at any time. If you or others are still in the vicinity of the ship, please move away quickly! The Navy is sending a scuba team out to evaluate the situation."

"Understood, and thank you for the warning, but what about your captain? If there is an explosion, he will be seriously injured or killed."

"That's true, but it's customary for a captain to remain with his ship, no matter what. It's a strange tradition that dates back to the beginning of our days on the water."

"Just one of many strange traditions that you humans seem to have!" came the reply. "Perhaps we can help. One among us has received extensive demolitions training from your Navy. Please stand by."

"Don't take any chances!" yelled Cesar, but there was no reply.

***

While Frank waited inside the general aviation terminal at the beautiful Cape Town International Airport, he pondered the stops the Gulfstream had made thus far. From Cuba it had flown to a major airport near Mexico City where, Frank guessed, the leaders of the Six had deposited their Mexican member. The next stop was Brazil, which was probably just a refueling stop, before making the long flight that was about to end here in Cape Town. If the plane had originally arrived in Cuba from Russia, it was safe to assume that's where it would eventually end up but it seemed to be on a long journey that would probably take it from Cape Town to China, England and, finally, Russia. What puzzled Frank was why there hadn't been a stop in the United States before the long flight across the Atlantic. It was possible that Edwards had found his own way back to the Washington, D.C. area, but by now his name would be on every "no-fly" list in the world. He certainly couldn't take a commercial flight into the nation's capital so why not take advantage of the Gulfstream? Frank worked through a dozen different scenarios but there was only one that made sense—maybe Edwards wasn't going back to Washington! Maybe Jim's team had made things so hot that Edwards didn't feel it was safe to return to the United States!

Frank smiled. Since only one person, a Mexican, had deplaned in Toluca and no one had stayed behind in Brazil that meant Edwards must still be onboard. Perhaps there would be one more stop scheduled than Frank had projected. But it didn't matter, because this freedom flight was going to come to an end as soon as the plane landed here in Cape Town.

Frank glanced at his watch. It was 10:15 a.m. and the Gulfstream was now fifteen minutes overdue but that wasn't too unusual, given the length of the flight. Unexpected headwinds on a four thousand mile flight could easily account for thirty minutes or more.

At 10:30 a.m. Frank began to pace the small waiting room used for private flights in and out of the Cape Town airport. Finally, at 10:45 a.m., Frank sought out the office and inquired about the inbound flight.

"Oh, I'm sorry, sir," replied the woman behind the metal, government-issue desk. "This aircraft called in about two hours ago and amended its flight plan for Eros Airport. Apparently there was a fuel concern, so they diverted there rather than trying to make it here."

"Where exactly is this place?" asked an exasperated Frank.

"It's in Windhoek, Namibia, sir, about eight hundred miles north of here. By diverting, they saved about an hour of flight time and however much fuel that represents. Let me check something for you."

The clerk banged away on the computer keyboard for a minute and then jotted some notes on a pad.

"Here's the information I have in the system, sir. It looks like they touched down about an hour ago, refueled and took off just minutes ago."

Frank accepted the note and frowned.

"Does it say where they are headed?"

"Ah, no, it doesn't. That's most unusual, but maybe the flight plan just hasn't been keyed in yet."

"Did anyone stay behind when they took off?"

"Oh, I wouldn't have access to that information, sir. If Eros were in South Africa, I could have probably told you, but we don't have access to that information for flights that land across the border in Namibia. I'm terribly sorry, sir."

Frank thanked the young woman and returned to the waiting area to figure out his next move. With the plane now airborne for an unknown destination, he didn't have many options except to return to Jim's underground fortress and wait for information from the intelligence agent Jim had mentioned.

"So close!" thought Frank as he jumped across the Atlantic to Meriwether Mountain in rural Virginia.

***

"You may return to your vessel. The device has been removed," said a synthetic voice in the headphones of the translator.

"Are you sure?" replied a startled Cesar. "Are all of you okay?"

"We are all well and your ship is safe to occupy."

"Yes, thank you, but what of the device? You say it has been removed, but has it been disarmed? If not, some of you might still be in grave danger!"

"Thank you for your concern, but our specialist was able to determine that the device did not contain any explosives. Perhaps it was a listening device or a tracking device of some kind, but it definitely was not an explosive device."

"What has become of it?" asked Cesar, knowing that Navy divers were already on their way to the Dolphin Diver.

"It was allowed to drop to the sea floor. When your inspection team arrives, they won't find anything attached to the hull but they should spot it in the relatively shallow water.

Perhaps they can determine who and why it was attached to your hull in the first place."

"Well, thank you, again, for your help. If there's anything we can do to…"

"There is much you can do, and it is our hope that the translators you now possess will allow both our species to cooperate and prosper. We wish you a safe journey and if you need our help along the way, use the translator. We are everywhere and your call will be answered."

Cesar switched off the translator and radioed Captain Braydon with the news.

"Okay, I'll find some way to convince the Navy to look around and find it, but you mates need to stay where you are until they give the official 'all clear' so we don't tip them off about our dolphin friends. I see lights headed this way, so it shouldn't be too long."

"Roger that," replied Cesar.

A few minutes later the radio crackled and then Captain Braydon spoke.

"They've come and gone," he reported. "They were a bit put out when they couldn't find anything on our hull, but I just shrugged and suggested that maybe it had fallen off. They got a big laugh out of that, but I had the last laugh when one of their divers surfaced with the device in his hand. They jumped back into their boat and high-tailed it out of here like their butts were on fire. Come on back, mates, we've been cleared to get underway again!"

***

At the evening meal Frank brought Jim, Linda and Javier up to date on the results of his rather frustrating day.

"Wow!" remarked Linda. "You almost had them all—well, except for the Mexican. But we know their names, right? And now you have a pretty good idea of where two of them hang out, so hunting them down should be pretty easy."

"I don't know about that!" laughed Frank. "The Mexico City metropolitan area includes a lot of people and there are plenty of places for someone to hide, especially if they know they are being hunted. But some of my associates are already at work, both in Mexico and South Africa. And, yes, we do have their names, thanks to Jim's guy in D.C."

"Frank, I've been meaning to ask you about these associates you talk about," said Javier. "Are they just regular people who have received the same training as you?"

"Yes, basically," replied Frank, pouring himself another cup of coffee. "We refer to ourselves as Volunteers because that's what *the Teachers* call us, but they also refer to us as trainees. I've never met a human called anything else, so I don't know if anyone has ever graduated, so to speak."

"And how long were you in this training?" followed up Javier.

"I was away for the better part of the last five years. I came back to eat, of course, and I was here on extended stays a few times for one reason or another, but basically I was on the Other Side from shortly after I 'disappeared' in the diving incident until about two weeks ago."

"Didn't you go crazy?" asked Linda. "We've all been there for short periods of time and I can't imagine what you would do for five years!"

I know what you mean," agreed Frank, "but you only saw artificial environments they created for you. With some training, I was able to create my own environments depending on my need. And of course there were many hours of training each day—learning how to jump and how to communicate directly with their collective consciousness."

"What kind of environments did you create for yourself?" asked Jim, intrigued.

"As you all know, I've always been interested in ancient civilizations, archeological mysteries and stuff like that so my most common environment was a library. *The Teachers* have been here a very, very long time and they have collected and catalogued an incredible amount of knowledge. I created a virtual library, if you will, that allowed me to tap into that knowledge in a structured kind of way that my brain could deal with. *The Teachers* can somehow hold, process and recall all that information at will but human brains aren't capable of that. We have to put things together in small, logically ordered packets and that's what I spent a lot of my time doing. Of course I made some remarkable discoveries along the way and got a lot of lifelong questions answered, so the five years went by pretty quickly for me."

"And what happens to all that work if *the Teachers* pull out, as they have threatened to do?"

Frank frowned.

"That's a very good question, Jim, and I have no idea what the answer is. Obviously their collective consciousness that I was able to tap into will disappear when they do. I don't know if there's any way for me to preserve what I've sorted out or not, but I doubt it. At least I've never seen a USB port anywhere on the Other Side!"

"Maybe they'll change their minds—or is that *mind*?— and stick around," speculated Linda.

"Sadly, that's not the word I'm hearing," replied Frank. "The triangles we found near Cuba—the ones Jim traded back to them for your location—seems to have rekindled something inside of them that was almost dead and their desire to return 'home' seems to be growing exponentially with every passing day. I can sense the increased energy when I communicate with them."

"What will become of you and those like you after they leave?" asked Linda as tactfully as she could. "Who is in charge? Who decides on priorities and projects?"

"Another good question!" replied Frank. "I have to believe they have a plan, because they have a plan for everything, but they certainly haven't shared it with me yet and I don't believe any of the others like me have a clue, either."

"That brings up another interesting question," said Jim, who seemed to be getting more depressed by the minute. "Will you still be able to jump once they are gone?"

"That's actually a question I think I *can* answer!" smiled Frank. "The technique that we call jumping is actually pretty simple if you ignore the "how" part. A jump from Point A on this side to Point B on this side actually involves a third point, let's call it Point C, located on the Other Side. You've seen this work yourselves when you were transported from this facility to the Other Side. The only difference is that you have always been returned to your original starting place instead of another location. When I traveled from here to Cuba this morning, I jumped from here to a special place on the Other Side, and from there I immediately jumped to Varadero. When *the Teachers* leave, the alternate universe we call the Other Side will remain as it is. That universe, the one of *the Teachers*, has been around as long as our universe has and there's no reason to believe it will ever go anywhere. *The Teachers* may move around in their own universe, just as we do, but the universe itself will remain unchanged. What I was taught, over the course of the last five years, was how to move between these two universes and how to control that movement—how to navigate, if you will."

"But you're not immortal, right? I think I remember you saying that the other day."

"That's correct, Jim. I'm probably tuned up a little better than most men my age but I'm not immortal and eventually I will wear out, just like every other human being. And if you're wondering what happens to my abilities, I'm afraid that's another question that I can't answer. I can't teach you to jump because your brain has to be prepared—conditioned, as the teachers call it—in order to initiate a jump. Even if I could tell you what to do, you couldn't mentally do it. So unless we figure that out on our own, the jump technology dies with me and those like me."

"Not a very promising outlook for the world, is it?" scowled Jim. "Even if we destroy the Six, another group equally evil will eventually come along and when we lose our platoon of super heroes, we'll have no one to protect us."

"Wow, this conversation has certainly taken on a dark tone," laughed Frank, trying to lift everyone out of the doom and gloom. "Let's move on to something else until we know what *the Teachers'* intentions really are, shall we? Has there been any word about Fitz and Susan?"

"Not yet," replied Jim. "The longer they're gone the more positive I feel about it, but they could already be sitting in a detention facility somewhere. I have no way of knowing where they are."

"I'll tell you what," smiled Frank. "While we wait for information on that Gulfstream, I'll slip out and see what I can find out. I'll be back as soon as I can."

None of the others saw Frank again that evening and he wasn't in his room the next morning when Jim stopped by to see if he was ready for breakfast.

On his way back to his room, Jim stopped off at the conference room and checked in with Bill Blass, who was still working out of the office Jim had hastily staffed at the Naval Research Laboratory in Washington, D.C. Bill had put every resource on tracking down the Gulfstream that Frank had been tailing and he had some good news for Jim.

"It left Windhoek without filing a flight plan, but we were able to pick it up again when it landed in a place called Socotra, Yemen. From there it flew to Beijing, China, arriving about 1:45 a.m. this morning, where it took on a full load of fuel and was back in the air by 3:00 a.m. bound—we think—for Moscow. If that's actually its destination, it should be on the ground in about an hour."

"Thanks, Bill! Frank isn't here right now but I'll try to reach him and pass along your intel. Please stick with that plane until it stops moving."

Okay, we will. Hey, there's something else you should know. There's word out of Cuba that the emergency workers at the Varadero bomb site have found at least one person alive. I'm trying to contact an agent we have down there to see if she can confirm this and possibly even find a way to speak to the survivor. I should know more this afternoon."

"Excellent! I'll call you back around dinner time so the rest of the gang can hear your report."

Jim snatched his cell phone out of his pocket and speed dialed the number Frank had given him. When the call went to voice mail, Jim remembered Frank's instructions and sent a text message instead of leaving a voice mail message.

As he walked back to his quarters, Jim considered Bill's information. The plane had stopped in Yemen, probably just for fuel, but the city would have to be added to the watch list in case Edwards got off there. The same was true of the previous day's stops in Brasilia and Windhoek. Although the diversion from Cape Town to Windhoek was probably due to a legitimate fuel issue, it could also have been a ruse to get Edwards off the plane without being documented.

If the next stop was, indeed, Moscow that should leave only the United Kingdom representative—and possibly Edwards—still onboard. It would be very interesting to see where the plane landed.

Jim paced his room for an hour waiting for a response from Frank but his phone remained silent. After ninety minutes, Jim realized that if an opportunity to apprehend one or more of the Six' leaders had existed, it was now gone as the Gulfstream was probably back in the air again.

Lunch time came and went with no word from Frank so Jim, Linda and Javier were surprised to see him tilted back in a chair with his feet up on a corner of the table when they entered the dining room for supper.

"Frank!" exclaimed Jim. "Did you get my text message in time to intercept the plane in Moscow?"

"No, I'm sorry but I was on the Other Side until about noon and this afternoon I was busy tracking down Fitz and Susan. They send their regards, by the way."

"You found them?" shouted Jim. "Where are they?"

"Yes, I found them and they're fine but Fitz believes— and I have to agree—that it's probably better that you don't know where they are. You can't be forced to reveal something you don't know, and all of that. However, they asked if you would take care of Sandstrom for them and they wanted you all to know that they are safe."

"Well, that's certainly a relief," smiled Jim. "Will they ever get to see the Learjet again?"

"I'm working on that, but certainly not for a while. Now what about our other plane—the Gulfstream. I received your text message but do we know for sure if the destination was Moscow? Is there any recent news?"

"I told Bill Blass that I'd call him right after dinner, but if you want we can go do that first and then eat," replied Jim.

"Yes!" said Linda, casting her own vote.

The others agreed, so the group moved temporarily to the conference room and gathered around the communications device.

"Bill, this is Jim and I have Linda, Javier and Frank Morton here with me. Do you have any updated information on the plane?"

"Yes, as a matter of fact I do. It would appear that the Gulfstream's long journey is finally over. I just received confirmation that the plane is parked in a private hanger at a regional airport just outside St. Petersburg, Russia. It did make a stop in Moscow after leaving Beijing, but then it flew on to an airport near London before returning to its current location. It would appear that it stopped in—or at least very close to—every country represented on your list of the Six' member countries."

"Except the United States!" interrupted Frank. "Do we have any idea where Edwards might have ended up?"

"Ah, yes, I forgot the most important part! There are now two survivors of that blast in Cuba and they both confirm that they saw Edwards' dead body inside the facility before it was destroyed. It would appear that the Six has a new leader and my guess is that he's currently enjoying a vodka somewhere in western Russia. It also appears that he barred no expense to see that his remaining comrades arrived home safely, since he personally delivered each and every one."

"Well, they couldn't fly commercial airlines, so he really had no other option," commented Frank. "Thanks for your help, Bill. If you don't mind, I'd like to stop by and see you sometime soon."

"It would be my pleasure," replied Blass.

When the conversation terminated, Jim slumped into his chair.

"So now what?" he asked no one in particular.

"Well, for me the job is suddenly a lot more difficult," replied Frank. "Now my associates and I will have to track these guys down the hard way, one at a time. The objective is still the same—to cut off the head of the beast by eliminating its leadership. But it would have been a lot easier if I could have caught up with that plane while they were all still aboard. Let's go get some supper and then I think I'd better take off. Jim, I'll need a copy of the complete Schmidt file. And I think you can cancel my accommodations here—I have at least six countries to search and the sooner I get started, the better."

Chapter 25
(June 7, 2008 – One Week Later)

The Dolphin Diver eased up against the commercial dock in Belize City where it was met by a small crowd of onlookers. Among those in the crowd were Rob and Anne Jefferies and several staff members from the Turneffe Wild Dolphin Foundation. The trip from the Bahamas, which should have taken four days, had been delayed by a longer-than-expected rendezvous with the Navy supply ship and a two-day lay-over in Cancun to repair an intermittent power generator that had left the ship's interior in total darkness for the better part of one night.

Rob greeted the crew members as they made their way down the gang plank and he thanked each one, individually, for their perseverance during their long layover in the Bahamas. When Captain Braydon finally reached the pier, Rob shook his hand warmly.

"Captain, before you disappear into the city on a well-deserved shore leave, could I have a word with you?"

"Of course," replied the Captain, "Is something wrong?"

"It's about Tony."

The two men stepped away from the crowd and Rob explained.

"I talk almost daily with the doctors and they're concerned about his recovery progress because he's so depressed. I want him to come out here and join the team when he's well enough to travel but all he talks about is what he can't do anymore. I was hoping you could talk to him."

"Of course," nodded the Captain. "How can I reach him?"

Rob took his cell phone out, pressed a button and handed it to Captain Braydon.

"The next voice you hear will be Tony's," he said before rejoining Anne and the crew.

The Captain found Rob a few minutes later and handed him back his cell phone.

"How did it go?"

"He'll be here as soon as the doctors release him from the hospital," replied the Captain. "However, there are a couple of conditions. He wants you to find him a place to live out on the island where you are and he wants to bring a friend along. Someone named Jill, I think."

"Agreed, agreed!" smiled Rob. "What did you do to get him to consent?"

In an unusual display of emotion, the Captain lowered his head and said, "I told him my life story and it cheered him right up."

Before Rob could ask for details, the Captain continued.

"Listen, I need to get to immigration before our new cook runs off without a visa. You have my cell phone number and I'll probably stay aboard the Dolphin Diver most nights but right now I need to take care of our vessel and her crew."

And with that, Captain Braydon disappeared down the pier towards shore. Curious, Rob redialed Tony's hospital room number and waited for the other man to pick up.

"This is Tony Nicoletti."

"Tony, Rob here! I understand you've agreed to join us and before I go out and spend all your money on real estate, I thought I should get some idea of what you're looking for."

"Something similar to what you and Anne have would be perfect," replied Tony. "If I'm going to be working at the research institute, I need to be out on the island where it is. I don't know how long it will be before I'm able to walk very far, so I need to be close by."

"Understood," replied Rob. "But you should know that only the actual dolphin research will be remaining out on the island. We've decided to move the growing administrative functions into a commercial office here in the city because we just don't have enough space out there."

"Well, why don't you see if you can find me a home on the island and maybe a small apartment in the city? I'm sure Jill and I will spend enough time on the mainland to justify a place there, too."

"Consider it done, my friend. And what about your friend?"

"Jill Harris, a U.S. citizen and skilled intensive care nurse. Maybe we can put her to work in the local clinic once I don't need round-the-clock care."

"I'm sure we can work something out," laughed Rob. "Tony, it's good to hear you talking and thinking about the future again! Let me know when you're ready for transportation back here and I'll take care of everything. But you have to promise to tell me the Captain's story one of these days."

"I don't think he'd appreciate that very much but if everything he told me is true, it's one heck of a story. It made me realize just how lucky I was—and still am! I think I hear my lunch cart rolling this way, so I'll talk to you later."

***

In the week since the destruction of the underground facility in Cuba and the reported death of Buzz Edwards, a lot had happened. Frank had met on several occasions with both Bill Blass and the President. The intelligence portion of Jim's old team at the Naval Research Laboratory had been reactivated, minus Jim, of course, and a worldwide manhunt was on for the disbursed leaders of the Six. Frank had even stopped in from time to time to chat with his old comrades at Meriwether Mountain.

On this particular morning, however, he was waiting in the dining room when the team arrived for breakfast.

"Any progress?" asked Jim once they all had their food.

"Actually, we may be getting close to one of them," nodded Frank between bites. "The Mexican, a guy named Raul Gomez, seems to be losing control of the cartels under him and we think he's about to go on an extended fence-mending expedition. When he comes out into the open, we'll be ready to nab him."

"But he's just one cog in the wheel down there, right? If you take him into custody, someone else will come along and fill his shoes."

"Not necessarily. Our intelligence guys, including your own Bill Blass, are convinced that if we can capture Gomez alive the cartel turf wars will break out again. Only this time, we'll be ready for the chaos. Our President and the president of Mexico have had some interesting chats this past week and the U.S. military is standing by to provide whatever assistance is necessary. We hope to downgrade the situation from a super cartel that controls all of Latin America to a bunch of loosely organized street gangs with no real power."

"But there will still be drugs trafficking and all that implies," objected Linda.

"Certainly! As long as the United States continues to be the largest consumer of illegal drugs in the world, there will always be drugs and drug dealers. But the more we confuse and intimidate them, the harder it will be for them to make a profit. It's not a great plan, but it's better than the situation that exists now, where one of the richest men in the world is nothing more than a very successful drug dealer with no concern for the consequences of his actions. Trust me, when this operation is over, they will all be spending a lot of their time looking over their shoulders."

"And what about the bigger picture?" asked Jim. "Are *the Teachers* still planning to bail on us?"

"During one of my first encounters with them I was given a brief synopsis of their time here and what they had attempted to accomplish. They refer to our current civilization as 'Initiative 37' because there have been thirty-six civilizations before us that all failed for one reason or another. With *the Teachers* about to depart, it will be up to us to save ourselves or perish. But this will be the first time volunteers like me have been allowed to offer hands-on assistance. Let's hope that provides humanity with enough of an advantage this time."

"So what about us personally?" asked Javier, as he helped Mariana with her food. "How much longer are we going to be stuck down here?"

"Well, that's actually why I'm here," smiled Frank. "Blass and his friends are now convinced that the threat to NWIDI and its members was purely an Edwards obsession. With him gone, the President is willing to allow you all to leave this facility, but he has asked *the Teachers* to assist with your 'transportation' so you aren't unnecessarily exposed. The problem is that with *the Teachers* about to leave us, you don't have much time to decide where you want to go."

"I don't think there's any question about where we want to go," stated Linda emphatically. "We want to go home! But, just out of curiosity, how much time do we have?"

Frank glanced at his watch.

"About an hour."

A few minutes later, Linda, Javier, Mariana and Sandstrom, the Fitzgeralds' dog, were all transported out of the Meriwether conference room while Jim and Frank looked on.

"Will they be safe?" asked a sad and concerned Jim.

"As safe as we can make them," replied Frank. "When they arrive back at their house in Mexico's Baja, they will find two volunteers—a new maid and gardener—waiting to greet them. One of those two people will be near them at all times until it is determined that there is no longer any danger."

Jim smiled and nodded.

"They will soon grow tired of the constant surveillance, but they deserve the best protection possible for as long as necessary."

"Agreed. And now what about you, Jim? What are your plans?"

"I still haven't decided, but I definitely don't want to be shadowed every minute of the day. I'd like to help with the dismantling of the Six, but I know my own limitations and I'd just be in the way. I don't have any ongoing research, since the triangles are gone—or soon will be—so I just don't know, Frank."

"You have to decide soon, Jim, or I'm afraid *the Teachers* will decide for you. You're now the only thing standing between them and their long-overdue trip home."

"Then so be it!" replied a dejected and defiant Jim. "It's their call. Tell them to make the decision with that big, virtual brain of theirs and just get it over with!

"Jim, I'm serious about this. They…"

"I don't care! I've had it with *the Teachers*, I've had it with the Six and I've had it with my own government! Just do it!"

As Frank stood in the large room all alone, he smiled to himself. He had correctly predicted Jim's reaction and he had pre-selected a location in case Jim couldn't or wouldn't pick one for himself. Frank smiled because he knew that once the initial shock wore off, Jim would be very happy among the many Mayan mysteries of Guatemala!

Frank sensed a change and he intuitively knew that *the Teachers* were gone. He stepped to the table and punched a button on the communications device. After a series of clicks and tones, there was silence.

"They're all gone, Mr. President, and now I must be off as well. I'll provide regular updates using the protocols we agreed on but this won't be an easy or a quick task."

"Mr. Morton, we're all counting on you and those like you. God speed."

The line went dead and Frank punched the End button on the device just before he vanished.

And this, too, was recorded by the tiny camera hidden in the clock on the wall.

THE END

Read the entire Parallel Ops series:

The Scientists (ISBN 978-0977910946)
From their secret laboratory, scientists work to protect alien artifacts from powerful international terrorists.

The Informants (ISBN 978-0977910960)
While on the run from international terrorists, a young couple stumbles upon a dark secret in the mountains of Mexico's Baja.

The Guardians (ISBN 978-0977910984)
From their floating base in the Caribbean, a multi-national team struggles to protect a secret hidden deep beneath the sea.

The first three novels in this series take place at exactly the same time and may be read in parallel—a chapter from each book before moving on to the next chapter. They may also be read in series, the normal way. 'The Teachers' follows the first three books and reunites Tony, Linda and Jim in a mission to save the world from self-destruction. Will mankind learn before time runs out…again?

The Teachers (ISBN 978-0988423626)
Sequestered in an underground bunker for their own protection, the NWIDI team's four amateur investigators—joined by a husband-and-wife flight crew, a four-year-old child and a dog—are tasked by the President to serve as the first U.S. emissaries to make contact with an alien intelligence.

What Fans Say About the Series

"After 'Seeds of Civilization' and the first three books of 'Parallel Ops,' hang on for the exciting conclusion with 'The Teachers' ...R. J. Archer has done it once again! You will not want to put the book down until you have read the final sentence. So get comfortable, kick back and enjoy the ride."
   – Tommy Vawter

"Parallel Ops is a series that weaves different story lines together into one cohesive plot. If the first three in the series are any indication, the last one will be great."
   – Jon Hudson

For more information about this series, visit
www.ParallelOps.com
and for a complete list of all books by R.J. Archer, visit
www.RJArcherBooks.com.

www.ingramcontent.com/pod-product-compliance
Lightning Source LLC
Chambersburg PA
CBHW070548260626
47161CB00002B/545